The Healing Place

Prequel to *Murder at Whalehead*

The Healing Place

Prequel to *Murder at Whalehead*

Joe C. Ellis

Upper Ohio Valley Books
Martins Ferry, Ohio

The Healing Place
Prequel to *Murder at Whalehead*
Second Edition

Upper Ohio Valley Books
Owner: Joe C. Ellis
71299 Skyview Drive
Martins Ferry, Ohio 43935
Phone: 1-740-633-0423
Email: joecellis@comcast.net

ISBN: 978-0-9796655-1-6

PUBLISHER'S NOTE

Although this novel, *The Healing Place—Prequel to Murder at Whalehead*, is set in an actual place, Martins Ferry, Ohio, it is a work of fiction. The characters, names, and plot are the products of the author's imagination. Any resemblance of these characters to real people is entirely coincidental. Many of the places mentioned in the novel—Scotch Ridge Presbyterian Church and Cemetery, the Martins Ferry City Park, the Martins Ferry McDonalds, the Belmont County Jail and Courthouse, are wonderful places to visit in eastern Ohio, however their involvement in the plot of the story is purely fictional. The monument known as "The Chair" is a real monument in the Scotch Ridge Presbyterian Church Cemetery. If you would like to attend a service at the Scotch Ridge Presbyterian Church and see "The Chair" in person, drop me an email. I've been the pastor at Scotch Ridge for more than 15 years.

Joe C. Ellis

CATALOGING INFORMATION
Ellis, Joe C., 1956-
The Healing Place—Prequel to Murder at Whalehead
ISBN 978-0-979-6655-1-6
1. Martins Ferry, Ohio—Fiction 2. Mystery—Fiction
2. Suspense—Fiction 4. Inspirational—Fiction
5. Ohio Valley—Fiction

Acknowledgements

The author would like to thank the following people for their help:

Thanks to Donna Swanson, a great writer and nationally award-winning poet, for her first draft critiques and numerous suggestions for alterations on subsequent rewrites. I tip my hat again to Gretchen Snodgrass, a great English teacher at Martins Ferry High School, and my daughter, Rebekah Shirley, for their excellent line edits of the novel. I offer kudos to everyone at Novel Alchemy, an online critique group, who read over the first six chapters and offered their insightful suggestions. To all the readers who helped sell out the first edition of the book, thanks for giving a first-time novelist the opportunity to entertain you. Your encouragement and support inspired me to write *Murder at Whalehead* and prompted me to put out a "new and improved" edition of *The Healing Place*. My wife, Judy, should be enshrined in the Writers' Spouses Hall of Fame for putting up with me and the endless hours I spend doing all the things I do. I can't forget to mention Joseph and Sarah, my other two kids, who seem to be a lot like me.

A Note to Readers

The Healing Place is based on my experiences as a lay preacher for the Scotch Ridge Presbyterian Church in Martins Ferry, Ohio. Yes, this church does exist. It is a humble structure nearly 150 years old set atop one of the highest hills in Belmont County. Yes, there is a monument in the church graveyard known as the Chair. Is the monument cursed? Has everyone who sat on it at midnight died? Is there a Healing Place near the church? I invite you to come and see for yourself (although I don't recommend sitting on The Chair at midnight). Our worship service starts at 9:30 a.m. every Sunday morning. If you like *The Healing Place*, you should check out the second book in the series, *Murder at Whalehead*. Also, keep your eye out for the third book in the series, *The First Shall Be Last*, scheduled for publication in May of 2008.

Chapter One

Joshua Thompson and his buddy, Billy McGlumphy crouched at the edge of the woods and watched Elijah Mulligan walk along the path through the meadow and up the hill. White butterflies danced and flickered just above the tall yellow grass. They could hear him singing in a deep voice the song about the old rugged cross. He sang loudly like he did in church on Sunday mornings. Because the man was so huge and always wore bib overalls, Joshua thought he looked like Hillbilly Bubba, the professional wrestler. Billy had told Joshua that Mulligan had killed a man with his bare hands, claiming his father told him so. Joshua wondered if it was true. Billy made things up sometimes. When Mr. Mulligan reached the top of the hill, he pushed aside leafy branches and stepped between two tall trees, disappearing into the shadows of the woods.

"What's up there, Doc?" Billy asked.

"That must be the place he walks to every morning. We gotta check it out. I bet he's hiding something up there," Joshua said.

"How do you know?"

"I'm smarter than the average bear. Come on, Boo Boo." Joshua stood and bounded into the sunlight.

"Wait," Billy said. "What if he sees us in the open field?" But Joshua had already picked up his pace, trotting up the path toward the top of the hill. Billy jumped to his feet and ran to catch up. When they reached the top they dropped to their hands and knees and crawled through the grass to the edge of the woods. Joshua could hear Elijah talking to someone. To the left Joshua saw a patch of thick blackberry bushes. He nudged Billy's shoulder and motioned for him to follow. Like an army ranger, Joshua scooted silently across the ground on his belly until he entered the thick growth.

To see into the woods, Joshua reached up and pulled the branch away in front of him. His eyes widened and heart pounded when he saw Mr. Mulligan aglow in the rays. He stood in the middle of a circular opening, hands clasped just below his chin. Sunlight sifted down through the branches, a thousand beams splashing over the man like a rock star on stage. The light spots dotted his shoulders, chest, curly brown beard and long hair that rimmed the bald top. A sudden breeze blew, trembling the bushes around Joshua and scattering leaves across the clearing. He heard Billy's teeth chattering so he raised his finger to his lips, and Billy clamped his mouth shut. The wind calmed, and with the stillness came silence. A chipmunk near the bottom of a big tree froze, clutching an acorn.

"Now it's time to bring up that old subject again, Lord," Elijah Mulligan said. His eyes closed, and his head swiveled back and forth as he spoke. "Some days I hate to think about it, but I know there's something you want me to do. It's just . . . Oh, hell's fire. It's just that the man scares me a little. There. I admit it. That feller gives me the creeps. Forgive me for judging a man before I truly know him, but I just don't trust the rascal." His head lifted, but his eyes remained shut. The beams from the tops of the trees lit his face. "I need some guts, Lord. I know you want me to stop by his house and talk to him—invite him to church. I've put it off long enough. Since Easter." He lifted his arms, positioning his hands in front of his face, and the rays filtered though his fingers. "Years ago I did plenty of bad things. He can't be much worse than I was. I know you washed the black stain of sin away, but the scars are still there. They remind me of the second chance you gave me. That's why I gotta talk to that strange feller. Perhaps you want to give him another chance."

He lowered his hands and head. "Go before me, Lord, and open the door." Clenching his fists, he said, "Give me the courage to approach the gates of Hell and snatch a soul from Lucifer himself. In the good Lord's name I pray. Amen."

The breeze picked up, swirling the leaves around the big man. The quick burst of wind stabbed at the two boys, and they shivered behind the bushes. As Elijah pivoted, leaves tumbled off his shoulders. His large body cast a shadow across the forest floor. Joshua thought Elijah spotted him, but then the giant lifted his hands to the sky and yelled, "Thank you, God Almighty! Thank you for the wonder of this new day!" With a low voice he sang, "There is pow'r, pow'r, wonder-working pow'r in the blood of the Lamb. There is pow'r, pow'r wonder-working power in the precious blood of the Lamb . . ." Taking a deep breath, he repeated the chorus, crossed the circle and pushed through the limbs. Sunlight poured over him as he descended the path that cut through the meadow and wound its way down the hill to the woods. Scurrying around the oak, the chipmunk disappeared into the hollow of a log. The wind calmed again, and the clearing quieted.

The boys kept silent and still, giving the man time to advance far from where they hid. Finally, Joshua spoke. "Shewweee, Boo Boo, I thought we were goners. He looked right at us. I told you he walks into the woods every morning. Now we know where he goes." His brown eyes widened, reflecting his friend's amazement. Joshua's smile revealed a chipped front tooth.

"Why does he come here, Doc?" Billy asked.

"To pray, I guess. It's kinda like an outdoor church."

"Did you see the leaves blow around him? Was that the Holy Ghost?" Billy asked. He had red hair, parted in the middle, and densely freckled cheeks.

"Nah. That was just the wind. But it sure freaked me out."

Joshua stood, angled through the bushes, and crossed the clearing to where the beams of light brightened the ground. Looking down, he saw a circular stone embedded in the soil, large enough to stand on.

Billy stepped onto the stone, raised his arms, mimicking Elijah Mulligan. "Thank you, God Almighty! Thank you for the wonder of this new day!" he bellowed in his deepest voice.

Joshua danced around Billy and tossed leaves over his head. His dark brown, bowl-cut hair bounced with every spring of his wiry legs.

"Hallelujah, Billy Boy! Hallelujah, Billy Boy!" he shouted.

"No," Billy said. "Call me Brother 'Lijah Mulligan."

"Hallelujah, Brother Mulligan! Hallelujah, Brother Mulligan!"

A gray cloud moved across the sun, blotting out the beams that had dabbed the boys. Its shadow darkened the clearing like a theater when the lights go out at the start of a movie. A cool breeze blew through the trees, scattering leaves. Joshua tilted his head upward, eyes narrowing. He gazed through the crisscrossing branches at the thick cloud.

"We better go now," Billy said.

"Shewweee, Boo Boo. That was weird."

"This place is freaky."

"Get off of that," Joshua said.

"Off of what, Doc?"

"That stone."

Billy stepped off, and they crouched to inspect. Joshua brushed away dirt and a few dead leaves. The word "ROBIN" was carved into the surface, and below the word someone had chiseled a cross. Light spots joined and separated over it like small ghosts.

"I knew something was buried here," Joshua said.

"Something or someone, Doc?"

"It says 'ROBIN'."

The boys raised their heads and stared at each other, eyes big as moons.

Billy gulped. "I told you what my father said."

Joshua nodded slowly and pointed at the rock. "Swear to God on that cross."

Billy reached and touched the etched cross. "I swear my daddy told me Elijah Mulligan killed a man."

Joshua pounded on the ground. "We've got to see what's buried here."

"Why?"

"Don't you wanna know?"

Billy shook his head sideways. "What if . . . what if it's a body? What if Elijah Mulligan murdered someone and hid the body here?"

"Then we'll tell the cops. But I doubt if it's a body. Why would he mark the grave? Besides, a murderer wouldn't come here to pray. "

Billy shrugged. "Some killers are crazy."

"Come on, Boo Boo. Let's find a couple sticks and get to work," Joshua said in his best Yogi Bear voice.

On the outskirts of the clearing they found a couple of medium sized branches and broke off all the twigs to create good digging sticks. Together they pried under the stone and lifted, flipping it over. Underneath a night crawler squirmed and a couple of centipedes scurried across the crater. After several minutes of loosening dirt with the sticks and scooping it out with their hands, they hit something solid about a foot down.

Joshua held his hand up to Billy. "Hold on there a second, Boo Boo. Let me check." He cleared the dirt from around the hard object and discovered it was flat and circular. Carefully he edged his stick around its perimeter and cleared the soil out with his fingers. "It feels like . . . It feels like glass. I think it's a jar."

"Maybe there's money in it," Billy said.

Joshua clamped his fingers around the lid, wiggled the object loose and eased it out of the hole.

"That looks like the kind of jar Grammy uses to can green beans from Grampa's garden," Billy said. "Let me see it."

"Shewwweeee, Boo Boo, hold your horses." Joshua spit on the glass and cleaned it with his t-shirt. The sun broke through the clouds and rays shot through the branches above, spilling over them. Joshua raised the jar into the beams.

Billy's mouth dropped open. "Bones!" he gasped.

"Yeah, but what kind of bones?"

Billy drew closer and pointed. "Look there, Doc. I see a beak and feathers in the bottom of the jar. Those are bird bones."

"Bird bones?" Joshua frowned. "What are we gonna do with a jar of bird bones?"

"We better put it back. We don't want Elijah Mulligan to know someone was messing with his dead bird."

"Good idea." Joshua carefully slipped the jar back into the hole. They covered it with the dirt and slid the stone back into place. To hide any evidence of digging, Joshua stomped on the loose soil, flattening it into the ground. "Scatter some leaves and twigs over top," he ordered.

After covering up all signs of their grave digging, Joshua gazed at the canopy of branches, squinting into the bright flecks of sun peeking through. "This sure is a strange place, ain't it, Boo Boo?"

"Yeah. It's like that old TV show, *The Outer Limits*," Billy said.

"Shhhhhhhhhhhhh. Did you hear that?"

"H-h-hear what, Doc?" Billy asked.

"I thought I heard a voice," Joshua whispered. "Maybe it was just the wind."

Billy's knees wobbled. "Let's get the heck out of here!"

The twelve-year olds tore towards the meadow and exploded through the branches and vines. They jumped and rolled down the hillside, tumbling through the tall weeds.

Chapter Two

Nathan Kyler turned and dropped the newspaper on the threadbare recliner. Glancing around the room, he listened. The house was silent. He inhaled deeply and exhaled to relieve tightness in his chest. A loud *CLAP* snapped the stillness. Nathan froze but then peered into the darkest corner of the room. He walked into the shadows, knelt, and lifted the mousetrap. *Another one bites the dust.* Delicately he carried the trap between thumb and forefinger, the mouse dangling from the snapper, and set it on the stand next to the lamp. When he noticed the mouse twitching, he smiled.

He picked up the newspaper, slid into the recliner and tilted the lampshade. The light shifted across the sports page. The color photograph displayed a tall girl with a wide smile holding a running trophy. *What have we here? The beauty from down the road? Miss Butler. So you've become the neighborhood celebrity. The track star. You are a sweet young thing.* He raised the newspaper and rubbed the image against the three-day stubble on his cheek.

His dark eyes narrowed as he lowered the picture and refocused. His voice trembled: "How would you like to take a walk in the woods with me? I could have lots of fun with a gal like *you.* What? Your parents would never allow it? They're probably afraid you'd lose your head over me. I'm the bad-boy of the neighborhood. Your mama told you to stay away from guys like me." Nathan reached into his jeans pocket, extracted a penknife, and flipped open the blade. He tilted it until he could see his reflection. As he glared at himself, his eyes widened and his nostrils flared. Slowly, he angled the blade down to reveal his grin. His laughter rumbled deep in his chest. It grated into his throat, making him cough. His hacking swirled dust motes through the path of light.

He stabbed the knife into the arm of the chair, stood, dropped the newspaper behind him and picked up the mousetrap. Nathan crossed the room and kicked open the screen door. As he stepped onto the porch the floorboards creaked, and two wasps darted toward his head. Squinting into the morning sunlight, he swatted at the angry insects, stumbled to the banister and spat across the yard. A crow swooped and landed on the rusted hood of an old red Pinto mounted on concrete blocks just beyond the rutted driveway.

"Good morning, Mr. Crow," he said.

The bird cawed.

"Look what I caught just for you." He lifted the spring and the mouse dropped onto the wide banister. He picked the mouse up by the tail and tossed it into the yard. The crow turned, sprung and fluttered to the ground to peck at the rodent.

"You're welcome," Nathan called.

He peered up Raven's Run and spotted the carcass of a raccoon in the middle of the road. It was huge. *Damn coon almost broke my axle. Got 'im though. Almost wrecked my car, but I flattened 'im.*

As he turned back to the house, he looked down the hill to where the road disappeared. Emerging from the steep-banked turn, a tall girl trotted up Nixon's Run. She ascended with strong, flowing strides, her blonde hair bouncing with each step. The heat rising from the asphalt produced a shimmering vision, and Nathan squinted. Her short trunks and ankle socks exposed long legs highlighted by the sun's rays slanting through the tops of the trees. He looked at his watch. "Like clockwork, Blondy." he said. "Same time every morning." As she neared, he leaned on the banister and leered at her. Wearing headphones, she passed, as if in a trance, not even noticing him. His eyebrows tensed. He wanted to go after her. In his mind he replayed a fantasy of chasing her through the woods and overpowering her. Something twisted within him as he watched the girl diminish and then disappear around a turn.

Ignored me again, bitch.

He pivoted and staggered into the house. The shadow of the knife stretched over the seat of the chair and across the newspaper, shading the girl's face. Nathan reached into the pale glow and jerked the knife free. He could see her image now. Lifting the paper from the chair, he held it near his nostrils and drew in a long breath as if enjoying the aroma of freshly cut flowers. "Come with me, my young champion," he whispered.

Nathan walked into the kitchen and placed the paper and knife on the table. He stepped back and leaned against an old Frigidare. From a rust-stained sink came the steady drip-drip-drip of the faucet. The water droplets ticked like a clock and jarred his nerves. His heart thudded against his ribcage and his breathing quickened. *I need a cigarette. Where the hell are my matches?* He stepped toward the stove and flipped on the knob. The blue flame flared across the bottom of an iron skillet. He slid the pan off the burner, shoving the handle away from the flame. When Nathan withdrew his hand, he noticed a grease smudge across his fingers. He wiped it on his t-shirt before pulling a cigarette from the pack in his front pocket. With the cigarette dangling from his lips, he bowed to the flame, lit the tip, and drew the smoke deeply into his lungs.

He flipped off the burner and exhaled. When the smoke cleared, he stared at the newspaper. He picked up the knife and placed the tip on the corner of the photo and drew it down and across with surgical precision, then up and over. The sharpness of the blade required little pressure to slice the paper cleanly. Delicately he pinched the corner and peeled the picture from the newsprint frame.

Nathan laid the picture on the table and said, "The day will come when we'll take that walk through the woods. Until then I'll keep you next to my heart," Gently, he slid the knife across the throat of the girl in the photo. "Did you feel that, my long-legged Bambi? You can't ignore me forever. You may lose your head over me yet." He folded the picture and slid it into his t-shirt pocket.

When he entered the front room, his grandmother's picture caught his eye. It hung on the wall above the stereo, reflecting the sun's rays streaming in the front door. In the photo a gray-haired woman, smiling and wrinkled, hugged a nine-year-old boy, his eyes downcast. They stood in front of a redbrick church beneath the dappled shade of a walnut tree. Her voice echoed through the hollowness within him: *Nathan! Nathan! Come here and give Grandma a hug. Pastor Caldwell wants to take our picture.* He drew closer and looked at the woman's eyes. *You were the only one who ever hugged me, Grandma.* A knot formed in his throat as he reached out and brushed the image with his fingertips. Feeling ashamed, he looked away.

Chapter Three

The sweat burned Christine Butler's eyes. She blinked and tried to squeegee them with her fingers, but it only made it worse. Squinting through the discomfort, she focused on the top of the hill. *Almost there. Not far now. Lift those knees. Pump those arms.* Chrissy had been running uphill for more than a mile. With the Backstreet Boys crooning from her Walkman, she maintained the rhythm of her stride until she crested the top. To release the tension in her body, she dangled her arms and relaxed her leg muscles as she crossed the crown. A white horse in the field to her right snorted and whinnied. "Hey Avalanche!" she managed to yell between huffs. The horse swished its tail and shook its mane. Chrissy waved.

Ahead she saw the Scotch Ridge Church sign with its arrow pointing to the left. She turned down Treadway Road, a dirt lane that crossed the ridge of a series of Appalachian foothills. The descent lasted only about forty yards. She had two hundred yards to go to the church, the steepest stage of the run. Passing through the shadows of a stand of oaks offered momentary relief, but then she turned right and headed up the challenging church driveway. Because of the severity of the climb, she wanted to drop into a jog, but she saw Joshua and Billy standing by The Chair. *Gutcheck time.* She lowered her head, lifted her knees and pumped her arms. Halfway up the driveway her stomach twisted. She blocked out the agony. *Fifty yards to go.*

Beyond the chorus of the Backstreet Boys' "Shape of my Heart" she heard Joshua and Billy yelling, "Run, Penelope. Run! Run, Penelope. Run!" She hated that nickname—Penelope Pitstop. Joshua and Billy could be so immature. They spent too much time watching classic cartoons on Nickelodeon. She refused to call them Doc and Boo Boo. They thought it was funny, but she thought it was childish. She slowed to a stop in front of the church, a humble redbrick structure with a sandstone foundation. After catching her breath, she trudged through the grass to where they stood. At five feet nine inches, Chrissy towered over the two boys. Feeling light-headed, she plopped down in front of the Chair, the most elaborate monument in the church cemetery. Sweat poured down her face.

"Did you run clear from home?" asked Billy.

"Had to," Chrissy said.

Joshua knelt beside her. "Why?"

"Dad made me."

"That's not fair." Billy dropped onto his hands and knees next to her and then sat back on his haunches. "He got here ten minutes ago in the van. Why didn't he run with you?"

Chrissy swiped sweat from her forehead and flung it towards Billy. "'Cause he's the preacher, you goober. He can't teach communicant's class smelling like a locker room. Besides, I don't mind. I'm in training."

"But that's more than a mile uphill, Penelope," Joshua said.

"Don't call me Penelope, you Looney Tune dropout. I know how far it is from the parsonage to the top of this hill. And I know something else—you two could never do it."

"So what," Billy said. "We don't want to."

"Wimps," Chrissy said.

"Oh yeah," Joshua said. "There's something I'll do that you'd never do."

Chrissy sat up straight. "Name it."

Joshua thumbed over his shoulder. "I'll sit in the Chair."

Chrissy twirled her finger. "Big whup. I'll do it right now."

"Not now," Joshua said. "At five minutes till midnight."

"What?"

"You heard me."

Billy scrunched his forehead. "You know the curse: from eleven fifty-five until midnight—*the dying minutes of the day*—that's the only time it works."

Chrissy twisted her torso and stared at the monument. The intricately carved stone loomed above them. Slowly she rose and circled it. The base was carved to look like a tree trunk, its four corners thick roots. A five-leaf fern adorned the back of the base. The trunk broke into five cut-off branches with intricately carved ivy climbing from the bottom and intertwining around each branch. Chrissy paused at the front and stepped back. The seat was a huge scroll, each rolled end forming armrests. A rectangular slab, supported by the other three branches, composed the Chair's back. Weatherworn, yet still beautiful, ivy vines and leaves bordered the slab. The words, *Theodore MacPherson --Born 1865--Died 1889—Meet me in heaven,* had been cut deeply into the slab.

The inscription on the scroll seat was harder to make out because its flat surface was directly exposed to the weather. Chrissy tried to read it. "'Thou shalt' . . .I can't quite see the next two words. Then it says, 'because th . . .' can't read that either." She pointed to the line below. "'seat will . . .' This is really hard to see. The last line says, '1ˢᵗ Sam . . .' something. And then the number 'twenty' and then 'eighteen.'"

Billy bumped into her. "Step aside, Chrissy. I'll tell you what it says."

She glared at him like a cat that didn't want to be petted.

Billy ran his finger along the words. "'Thou shalt die, fool, because this seat will destroy your life.'"

"No way," Chrissy said.

Joshua squeezed between them. "Yes way. My grandpa told me all about Theodore MacPhearson and why the Chair was cursed. Gramps lived on Scotch Ridge all his life. He knows the history of these parts."

Chrissy put her hands on her hips. "Let's hear it."

Joshua cleared his throat and motioned to the date carved into the slab. "Back in 1889 Theodore MacPhearson attended church here. He was only twenty-four years old, but you never know when the Reaper's comin' for ya. One Sunday morning, right in the middle of a hellfire and damnation sermon, he tumbled over. Doc Green, another church member, examined him. Couldn't find a pulse. Held a mirror up to his mouth and didn't see any fog from his breath. Best he could tell, the poor sucker bought the farm—that's how Gramps put it—bought the farm. He died."

"I know what 'bought the farm' means," Chrissy said. "Tell the story."

"Some people said Theodore must have committed a terrible sin to keel over in the middle of a sermon. Maybe even witchcraft—spells and curses and stuff like that. The next day the congregation buried him right here where we stand. They didn't embalm people back then like they do now. They had to bury the body before it started to stink. After they said their prayers and shoveled the dirt into the hole, they heard faraway screaming. At first they thought it came from inside the church. After a couple of minutes they looked at the ground. Theodore MacPhearson was still alive. He kept yelling, 'Get me out of here! Help me! Can't breathe! Curses on you! Curses on you!" By the time they dug up the coffin, it was too late. His hands were a bloody mess from scratchin' at the lid, and his face looked like some ghost just spooked him to death. They found out later he had some kind of condition that made him look dead. I think it's called narcoholism. The congregation felt so guilty they all pitched in to buy this monument. Not more than a month later some teenager sat in the Chair at midnight and drowned in the Ohio River the next day. That's when word got round that Theodore MacPhearson had cursed the Chair."

"You're like that old outhouse out back," Chrissy said.

"Whadaya mean?" Joshua asked.

A toothy grin widened Chrissy's face. "Full of crap."

"You don't have to believe the curse, but we know it's true," Billy said. "My mom has a scrapbook with a newspaper article in it. During her senior year five boys from her high school sat in it. She knew all of them. On the way home they slid around a turn, went off the road and hit a big tree head on." Billy frowned and slid his finger across his throat.

Chrissy's eyes narrowed. "Did they all die?"

"Yep! All of them. Don't believe me? I'll prove it to you. I'll get the scrapbook."

Joshua's voice trembled, "It was the Chaaiirrrrrr."

"Shut up!" snapped Chrissy, her short blonde locks swinging forward and then recoiling.

"He's not kidding, " Billy said. "The curse on this chair has killed lots of people. Theodore MacPhearson was twenty-four years old when he died. That's the key number. After you sit in it you've got twenty-four hours, twenty-four days, or if you're lucky, twenty-four weeks—like that guy that crashed into the Limestone Road water tower."

"Yeah. His name was Chance Black," Joshua said. "He sat in the Chair at midnight and then broke into the church. After upsetting pews and knocking over the pulpit, he took hymnals and threw them through the stained-glass windows. Exactly twenty-four weeks later he crashed his car into the water tower. He didn't have a chance. Theodore MacPhearson made sure of that."

Chrissy had heard her father tell that story several times. She believed it was true because her dad knew the guy. "Just because one person who sat in the Chair died, doesn't prove the curse," she said, but doubt tugged at her like a puppy yanking on a shoestring.

"Oh yeah," Joshua said. "Will you sit on it at midnight?"

"I'm not afraid of this stupid gravestone." She reached out with both hands and smacked Joshua and Billy on their heads. "You guys are the chickens."

"If you sit on it, I will too," Joshua said. "I'll swear to God."

They looked at Billy.

"What about you, Boo Boo?" Joshua asked.

He shrugged. "I guess I will too, then."

"All right," Chrissy said. "We'll meet at the bottom of the hill at quarter till midnight on Saturday. Can you guys get out of your houses without getting caught?"

"No problem," said Billy. "I can pretend to fall asleep on the couch. My parents always go to bed at 11:00. I'll sneak out the back door once things get quiet."

"My mom makes me go to bed at 10:30, even on Saturday," Joshua said. "Good thing my bedroom's on the first floor. I'll fix up some pillows under my blankets to look like I'm asleep just in case they check on me. Then I'll crawl out my window into the side yard."

"My bedroom's on the second floor," Chrissy said. "I'll have to climb onto the porch roof and shimmy down the drain pipe."

"Do you think you can do it?" Joshua asked.

"I can do anything I put my mind to," Chrissy said. "The question is, will you goobers have the guts to sit on the Chair?"

"If you do it first," Billy said.

"Do you promise?"

"We promise," both boys said at once.

"Then it's a pact," Chrissy said as she extended her hand palm-up above the seat. The boys placed their hands on top of hers. "We meet at the bottom of the hill at quarter till twelve Saturday night."

"Kids, it's time to get started." The tall man blared from the church door. "Everyone's in here except for you three." He peered through wire-rimmed glasses, and although his face appeared youthful, his hair was white-silver, wavy, and slicked back. His silver mustache was neatly trimmed above the lip.

"We'll be right in, Dad," Chrissy said. "Come on, ya wimps, we can't hold up communicant's class."

"Wait a minute, Chrissy," Billy said, then turned to Joshua. "Whadaya think, Doc? Should we tell her?"

"Tell me what?"

His eyes widened. "Oh yeah. I know what you're talkin' about." Joshua met Chrissy's gaze. "Do ya promise to keep it locked in the chest?"

Chrissy zipped her lips, held up an imaginary key, pulled out the collar of her t-shirt and dropped the invisible key inside.

Joshua motioned her to step closer and spoke quietly, "We followed Elijah Mulligan into the woods this morning."

Chrissy's face puckered like she just took a big bite out of a sour gumball. "You morons. Leave Mr. Mulligan alone. He's a good friend of my father."

"But he goes to this weird place," Billy said.

"Weird place?"

"Yeah, about a mile from here out in the middle of nowhere," Joshua said. "And that's not all. We found something buried there."

"What?"

Joshua stepped back and said, "Maybe we better not tell her."

Chrissy snatched Billy's ear and twisted it.

"Owww. Owww. Quit it. Let go, Chrissy!" Billy screeched.

"Kids! Get in here right now!" the preacher yelled from the door.

Chapter Four

The image of the girl lingered in Nathan Kyler's mind. When he recalled how she gazed straight ahead, ignoring him as she passed his house, he jammed his knife into the arm of the recliner. *Why didn't she look at me? She's stuck up. That's why. Doesn't know anything about me. Good. It's better she doesn't know what I have in mind.* He reached and pulled a *Penthouse* magazine from a stack on the floor beside the chair. As he thumbed through the pages, he tapped his foot to the heavy beat of AC/DC's "Highway to Hell" blaring from the stereo. *Damn bitch. Thinks she's so high and mighty. No one ignores me. No one.* For thirty minutes he smoked cigarettes and flipped through the pages of skin magazines, picturing her face on the models. Finally, he took one last, long drag on the cigarette, setting its tip aglow, and extinguished it across the neck of a blonde in a centerfold. He blew a shaft of smoke against the page, and it swirled and drifted to the ceiling like a departing spirit. Coughing, he stood and tromped to the kitchen to get something to eat.

When he looked out the back window, a stroke of orange caught his attention. He squinted to focus on an old, crooked-eared cat hunched in the foot tall grass on the slope below the tree line. The animal inched forward, stalking an invisible prey. With his eyes fixed on the cat, he reached across the table and grasped the feathered end of a steel-pointed arrow. A nervous fluttering entered his chest like a bird caught in a small room. *A chance to kill.* He envisioned the shot—the arrow piercing the target, pinning it to the hillside. The bow stood against the wall below the window with five more arrows scattered on the floor. He stepped slowly, placing his feet between empty beer cans, and advanced to the window. After unhitching the hook on the screen and swinging it open, he lifted the bow and slid the nylon string into the slotted end of the arrow.

"Cats," he hissed. "I hate cats." He raised the bow. "I have a place for you kitty. . . not far from where you are. You won't be lonely there." He half laughed and half coughed, but then re-steadied. "Stay . . . stay." The cat waited, watching its prey.

"Marilyn," a voice from his past called. Nathan's eyes widened. His focus upon the cat clouded and faded, but beyond the animal and the hillside he envisioned a large, pock-marked-faced man in a black leather jacket. "Nathan! Nathan! I heard your mother screaming," the man said.

"What're ya talking 'bout, Pa?"

"Outside my window. I heard Marilyn screaming. She's back."

"You're crazy, Old Man. That was just a cat."

"Dammit! I tell you I heard her. She's out there."

"Go back to bed. It's only a cat."

"Are you calling me a liar, boy?"

"Ma left three years ago. She's gone."

"I'll beat your smart mouth to a bloody pulp. I'm telling you she's out there."

"Listen, Pa, listen. Can't you hear? That's a cat screaming. It just sounds like a woman."

The eyes of the man became vacant. "You're right, boy. That is a cat. Your mother's gone. No good slut. She got religion and left us to fend for ourselves—gave her soul to God and told us to go to hell. Get rid of that cat." He covered his ears with his hands. "Now! Now! Get rid of it. I can't stand the screams. No more screams!"

My pleasure, Pa. My pleasure.

As the vision faded into the hillside, Nathan blinked and zeroed in on his target. "Stay right there," he whispered. The cat took one step and then resumed its concentration on its prey. Nathan pulled the feathered end of the arrow back until the steel tip slid to meet his fingers. His eyes narrowed, and he let go. The arrow zipped as the cat pounced. It punctured the animal's left hind thigh. Twisting and contorting, the cat bit at the stick. Nathan watched the orange blur as it rolled and screeched on the hillside. The arrow whipped back and forth with every writhing movement.

He scooped up another arrow and slid it into position. The cat stopped biting at the stick and clambered up the hillside with the arrow flapping behind. Nathan followed his target and steadied for the fatal shot. BAM! BAM! BAM! A loud thudding broke his concentration. The cat crawled into the shadowed safety of the high weeds as the arrow flip-flopped and disappeared.

Nathan cursed. Turning, he saw a hulking silhouette in the front doorway. He placed the bow on the kitchen table, feeling like a child caught in the act of playing with a forbidden object.

"Mr. Kyler! Are you in there?" The voice was deep and forceful. Nathan was puzzled. His mind raced through all the possibilities. Had someone seen him siphoning gas from that old couple's RV on Friday night? Then he remembered he had shoplifted some wine last week at the Kroger store in town. Maybe they had caught him on tape. A knot formed in his throat and his fingers tingled. He cautiously approached the door. Through the screen, the outline of the man contrasted and blurred with the glow of the morning sun.

"Nathan Kyler! Are you in there?" The voice rumbled.

"I'm here," Nathan said. He decided he'd lie like a used car salesman if the joker on the other side of the screen tried to blame him for anything. As he passed the table, he picked up the newspaper and dropped it into the trashcan. He crossed the front room, reached for the handle, and flung back the screen. The light poured in from behind a large, bearded man wearing bib overalls.

* * *

Elijah Mulligan had never set foot on Nathan Kyler's property. Few people did. He lived in a small house. Half a house really. Maybe three rooms and a bath. The guy was a loner, an odd feller. Elijah lived a couple hundred yards up the run on the same side of the creek but had spoken to Kyler only a few times.

About four months ago, he saw Kyler standing along the road hitchhiking. Elijah picked him up and drove him across the river to Wheeling Island where Kyler worked as a dog walker at the Wheeling Downs Racetrack. When Elijah asked him why he was thumbing, Kyler mumbled something about his car needing a new starter. Elijah went the extra mile that day, hoping to establish neighborly ties. When they arrived at the track, Kyler opened the door, slammed it, and walked away without looking back or saying a word.

Another time last March on a walk through the woods, Elijah crested a hill, glanced up and saw the young man aiming a bow and arrow directly at him. "Hey, neighbor. I'm no grizzly bear. It's me, Elijah Mulligan. What're you hunting?" With eyes like burning coals, Kyler said, "Anything that moves." Elijah stood still, frozen, eyeing Kyler until he lowered the bow. "Better watch yourself sneaking up on me like that," Kyler said. "Meant no harm," Elijah replied. Kyler descended a ravine beyond a layer of brush and branches. Elijah took a deep breath, exhaled slowly, turned, and went in the opposite direction toward home.

The third time, unexpectedly, was at church. Kyler slipped into the last pew during the past year's Easter sunrise service. Elijah, sitting in the next row, turned, extended his hand, and said, "Welcome to Scotch Ridge Church, Mr. Kyler." Hesitantly, Kyler shook his hand and mumbled, "My Grandma used to bring me here on Easter when I was a boy." Elijah nodded and said, "There's no better place to be on Easter morning." After the service Kyler took off like a spooked rabbit and hadn't returned since.

When Elijah saw the NO TRESPASSING sign lying on the ground in front of the porch steps, he considered retreat. *It must have fallen off the post.* He took a deep breath and scanned the cluttered yard. *What a mess.* The grass needed cut. An old push mower rusted near the front of the property by the bridge that lacked railings. Engine and body parts from a disabled Pinto littered the ground—an old tire, a fender and several hubcaps. Against the flood of anxiety rising in his chest, he mounted the steps. They groaned under the mass of his 240 pounds.

He rapped on the door and yelled. The darkness of the interior made it hard to distinguish any forms, but he thought he saw movement in the kitchen. He knocked and yelled again: "Nathan Kyler. Are you in there?" As he waited, he noticed a wasp tucking its head in one of a hundred holes of a nest suspended about a foot above his head. The sudden whoosh of the screen door startled Elijah. The young man glared at him, and the uneasiness quivering in his stomach intensified. Kyler's black hair framed his pale complexion with a jagged fringe, and his deep-set coal eyes narrowed, darkening.

Elijah composed himself and spoke first. "Hate to bother you, Mr. Kyler, but I've been meaning to invite you back to church. Ever since you came on Easter morn', I thought there might be a chance you'd come again. I know it's been a few months. Danged if I ain't a procasternator, but this morning I felt downright moved by the Spirit to stop and offer an invite."

Kyler glared at Elijah, but the big man smiled back. Seconds passed. Elijah felt the muscles sustaining his smile tighten with exertion as the warmth drained from his face.

"You're trespassing," Kyler finally said.

"Just trying to be friendly."

"Be friendly somewhere else."

"All right, Mr. Kyler. Sorry to bother you. Didn't mean to overstep my boundaries." Elijah turned and walked to the steps.

"Old man, wait a minute."

Elijah hesitated and pivoted.

"Did you come here to save my soul?"

"I can't save your soul, Mr. Kyler."

"Am I too far gone?"

"No one's too far gone. What I meant to say is I'm just flesh and blood like you. Only God can save a man."

Kyler laughed, coughed, and spit a wad of phlegm past Elijah over the banister. He straightened. "You think God can save me?"

"All things are possible with God."

"That's nice. Real nice," Kyler chuckled. "But what I really need is a woman."

"Can't help you there, Mr. Kyler."

"I saw a long-legged beauty pass by here 'bout half an hour ago. Runs by here all the time. Would she happen to go to your church?"

"That would be the preacher's daughter, Chrissy Butler."

"I wouldn't mind meeting her. A trip to church would be worth that."

"She's only twelve years old. Don't get any ideas about her."

"Why'll be a sonovagun! I'll be damned if she don't look eighteen. You sure she's only twelve?"

"Positive."

"Jail bait. Who'd a believed it." Kyler shook his head and rubbed the black stubble on his chin. "She sure is puuurrty though, ain't she, Mr. Mulligan?"

Elijah glanced down and shifted his weight from one leg to the other. "She's a nice young gal."

Kyler smiled. "Does she have an older brother?"

"No," Elijah said, refocusing on Kyler. "Two younger ones."

"Well then, maybe I could be like an older brother to her."

Elijah studied the man's devilish eyes and half-cocked smile. A cold chill rushed up his back, prickling his shoulders and neck with goose bumps. "I think I made a mistake stopping here today. Forget the invitation. I won't bother you again. Goodbye, Mr. Kyler."

Kyler stepped back, his jaw angling oddly. "That's not very friendly of you—inviting me to church and then jerking the welcome rug out from under me." He raised his hand. "Don't be so sure, Mr. Mulligan. Maybe God did send you here. Maybe it wasn't a mistake."

"I guess it depends doesn't it, Mr. Kyler?"

"On what?"

"On what's going through your mind. Are you seeking the truth or looking for trouble?"

"Good question. I admit I've been in trouble before." Kyler nodded and stared at the ground. When their eyes met again, he said, "You might not believe this, Mr. Mulligan, but lately I've become a religious man."

Elijah tried to look through the veneer of Kyler's pasted on expression, his half-crazed eyes and sickening smile. "What do ya mean, you've become a religious man?"

"Trust me. I've studied life and death. I know all about offerings and sacrifices."

"I don't know what religion you're talking about, but I doubt if it's similar to the walk of faith we preach at Scotch Ridge Church."

"Don't be so sure, Mulligan. All religions are about the same. Anyway, I'll see you on Sunday morning."

"Please don't come if you have bad intentions."

"I think I'll be there whether you like it or not."

Elijah knotted his brow. "Mr. Kyler, I've made it clear that the girl's only twelve. Stay away from Chrissy Butler." He about-faced, stomped down the steps and through the yard.

"Mr. Mulligan," Kyler called triumphantly. "You shouldn't have told me not to come. No one tells me *not* to do something." He laughed as if he just got the punch line to a stupid joke.

As Elijah crossed the bridge spanning the creek, Kyler's laugh intensified. Elijah turned up the run but suddenly stopped, startled by what lay a few feet ahead of him. A large crow, balancing atop a dead raccoon, cawed in rhythm to Kyler's cackling.

"Get!" Elijah yelled. The crow sprung skyward in a flurry of wing beats. As Elijah ascended the hill, he shook off the revulsion that had gripped him. He refused to allow the darkness of one man's soul to peck away at his own. *Hope I haven't made a big mistake. The last thing I wanted to do was let a demon out of its cage.*

He intended to walk over the hill and into the next valley to visit his friend, Peter Nower, but as he approached the bridge that crossed to his house, he heard a high-pitched, wailing cry. He looked across the creek, and there, crawling out of the woods by the garden, was his crooked-eared cat, Juniper. As he squinted, he noticed something stick-like dragging behind her.

Chapter Five

Below the flapping sheet, Elijah saw Annie Ferrier's ankles, and above, her fingers clipped a clothespin to the corner. The breeze pressed the white cloth against her face and form presenting a fleeting image as if an angel had been caught between this world and heaven. Elijah glimpsed the vision in that moment before the wind whipped away the bonds of earth and the angel escaped into thin air. Her feet sidestepped, and the shadow of a basket slid along the ground. Elijah took a quick breath, feeling his heart thumping. Finally she appeared from behind the sheet in a yellow sleeveless blouse and white shorts.

"Elijah!" Annie gasped. "You 'bout gave me heart failure. I didn't know you were standing there."

"Sorry," he said. "Didn't mean to scare ya, but . . .uh . . . I need your . . . medical . . . uh

. . . expertise." Elijah's tongue fumbled the words as he gazed at Annie. To Elijah, this middle-aged widow glowed with an outer beauty that rivaled what was inside of her. At about five-feet-seven-inches tall, she was lean but shapely, with long brunette hair, usually gathered into a ponytail. For a forty-six year old, her skin radiated a youthful glow with few subtle wrinkles.

"What ya got there?"

"Juniper. She's been shot with an arrow."

"Lord have mercy." She reached out and gently cradled the cat as Elijah extended his hands in support underneath. For a brief moment their fingers linked under the animal. "Who would do such a thing?"

"Don't know, but I've got the arrow at home, and I'm gonna do some investigating."

Annie snuggled the cat close to her face and tenderly rubbed its cheek with her thumb. The bleeding had stopped where Elijah had pulled out the arrow. A folded paper towel with a red spot in the middle adhered to the drying wound on the upper hind leg. The cat seemed passive, possibly feverish, not wanting to encounter the pain caused by any movements.

"Let's take her inside and see what we can do," Annie said.

Annie turned toward the two-story white farmhouse. The path from the side yard, where the sheets and towels gently fluttered in the breeze, to the back porch was patched with dirt, dandelions, and grass, tended by tiny white butterflies and an occasional yellow jacket. It wound its way around two large pine hedges to the back steps, which were laden with flower boxes overflowing with violets, touch-me-nots, and Sweet Williams. The fragrance of the flowers lifted Elijah's head as he trailed Annie up the steps and onto the porch. He breathed the scent deeply into his lungs and exhaled slowly as if to saturate his being with the sweetness that surrounded him.

"Let me get that for you," Elijah offered as he reached around her, slightly brushing against her shoulder as he pulled open the screen door.

"You're a gentleman and a saint," she said.

"Two for the price of one," he chuckled. "But I must admit, not many ever accuse me of being a gentleman."

The kitchen was bright and countrified. A knotty-pine table with four red plaid place mats stood in the middle of a gray and red squared linoleum floor. The counters were crowded with colorful ceramic containers and knickknacks—wooden cutout pigs and cows with smiling and winking cartooned faces. Fresh flowers in jars half-full of water sat here and there ushering the fragrance of the back porch into the kitchen. On the wall above the table hung a framed black and white photograph of a black woman who gazed at Elijah with warm, compassionate eyes; and a little, pony-tailed girl, a younger version of Annie, stood next to her.

"Get a towel out of that closet for me, would ya please, Elijah?"

Elijah pulled out a fresh white towel and placed it on the kitchen table. She carefully placed the cat onto the towel, and Elijah stroked his pet's ears and whiskers. "I've got to get me medicine," she said with a sassy Scottish flare.

After she exited the room, Elijah's mind drifted and settled into his thoughts. He was confused about his yearning for this woman. She was seven years younger than he, but the age difference didn't bother him as much as the feelings she stirred within him. After his wife and daughter had died ten years ago, Elijah centered his life on God. This higher focus had delivered him from depression and the empty aching of devastating loss. With the passing of time he grew to enjoy the bachelor life and compared himself to a monk—no longer interested in the ways of a romance-obsessed world. Assuming he'd never marry again, he committed himself to his duties as an elder at the Scotch Ridge Church.

Then Annie Ferrier had joined the church after her husband died in a farming accident. Being a nurse at the East Ohio Regional Hospital and a farmer's wife, she had only occasionally attended Scotch Ridge's services before his death. Afterwards, the widow had leased her land to other farmers but kept the house. She'd concentrated on her nursing career and sought comfort among the Scotch Ridge parishioners, the rustic beauty of the sanctuary, and simplicity of their worship.

For several years Elijah had kept his distance from Annie, briefly greeting her after the services or engaging her in light-hearted conversation whenever they would cross paths. But for the past year they had spent more time together, opening the guarded places of their souls to one another.

Whenever he prayed about the possibility of a closer relationship with her, he sensed the Lord saying, *Seek first my kingdom and my righteousness, and all these things will be added unto you.* Then he would try to block out all thoughts about her and center on the Lord's work. Sometimes the harder he tried not to, the more he thought about her.

"Elijah. Elijah!" Annie called, startling him out of his trance. "What could you be thinking about that would put such a look on your face?"

"Oh, you'd be surprised," replied Elijah as he felt his cheeks flush. Then he turned and focused on the task at hand—comforting and securing Juniper while Annie operated.

"You think I'd be surprised?" she asked while applying a cloth soaked in cleansing solution to the wound.

"Mebbe," he said as he steadied the cat.

"I'm just a woman. I wouldn't understand a man's thoughts. Right?" As she talked she wiped and nursed the wound.

"Mebbe. Mebbe not."

"*You'd* be surprised. A gal like me can read a man's mind. See right into his soul."

Elijah gulped. "You can read my thoughts, huh? Okay. I'll bite. What was I thinking?"

Annie glanced up and smiled. "You've got to hold her tight now, Elijah."

"What? Hold who tight?"

Annie laughed. "You silly hillbilly. The cat. You've got to hold the cat tight. This is gonna hurt." Annie poured a potent-smelling astringent onto a clean cloth and dabbed it onto the wound. The cat stiffened and screamed under Elijah's grasp.

"Do you think she's gonna be all right?" he asked as he gently rubbed the top of the cat's head.

"The wound is deep, but clean. The arrow missed the bone. If we can keep it from getting infected, I think she'll be fine. Such a beautiful cat." Annie lowered her head and spoke softly to the animal: "Juniper, we'll do everything we can to get you back on all fours."

The cat mewed.

"Did you hear that, Juniper?" Elijah smiled. "You're gonna be good as new. Annie'll fix you right up. You got to get better. It'd be too lonely at my house without you."

"Your house doesn't have to be so lonely."

Elijah slowly raised his head and met Annie's gaze.

She smiled and shook her head. The glow of her complexion and the beauty of her blue-green eyes sent a wave of desire through him. Quickly he shifted his eyes to the cat and stroked its back.

"Elijah, what *were* you thinking a few moments ago?"

"Didn't you just say you could read my mind?"

"I can. I'm just double checking."

"Well," Elijah chuckled, "something very mysterious and profound."

"Really?" Annie said.

"Fer sure."

"Well then, thank you very much."

"Why are you thanking me?"

She picked up some gauze strips, medical tape, and scissors. "Because you were thinking about me." She shrugged. "So, I must be mysterious and, what'd you say? Profound?"

"I . . . uh . . . well . . . I was thinking . . . uh . . ." Elijah's tongue stalled as Annie's gaze lanced deeply into that secret place in his heart. After blinking several times, he regained his composure. "Why, Annie Ferrier, you think I was thinking about you, huh?"

Annie concentrated on the cat and the scissoring of the strips for what seemed like minutes. Finally she looked up, eyes narrow, and nodded. "That's right."

"Okay. I was thinking about you. But I try to keep my thoughts on a spiritual level, of course."

Annie raised her eyebrows. "Of course."

Elijah wanted to caress her cheek or stoke her hair, but his arm felt heavy, as if something was weighing it down. "Do you . . . do you ever think of me?"

"Sometimes," she said.

Elijah nodded slowly. "Do you think of me like a brother?"

"A brother?"

"Yeah. You know, like a brother in the faith."

Annie shrugged "I guess so. Is that how you feel about me—like a sister?"

Elijah took a deep breath and blew it out. He didn't want to lie. "Sometimes I get confused about you."

"What do you mean?"

"After my wife died I didn't want to get involved with someone again. Get hurt again. Do you know what I mean?"

Annie smiled. "Sure. I felt the same way when Homer passed. But time eases the pain. Life begins again."

Elijah took a few seconds to choose the right words. "You know I'm a good bit older than you and set in my ways too. Been a bachelor for a long time."

"I can do the math. You're seven years older than me, Elijah Mulligan. That's not so much. And I'm set in my ways too. But that doesn't mean we can't change."

With Annie's words, Elijah's confidence grew. She must be feeling those same yearnings. "You're good at math. You've got the healing touch with people and animals. You've got a green thumb. You're a good cook. You might be the perfect woman."

"If that's what you're looking for, I can tell ya right now the perfect woman doesn't exist."

"Neither does the perfect man."

"That's a well-known fact."

Elijah stepped back and put his hands on his waist. "You even have a good sense of humor."

"Elijah, how long have we known each other?"

"Five or six years, I guess."

"By now you should know what kind of woman I am, and I should know what kind of man you are."

"I reckon so."

"Is that all you have to say?"

Sensing a serious tone in her voice, he met her stare. "No." He smiled. "I've got more to say. Just not sure when the right time will come to say it."

"Time slips on by, ya know."

"I know. But I'm a man that needs time to sort things out."

"Uh huh," Annie said as she bandaged the cat. "You know what I need besides a good sense of humor?"

"What's that?"

"Patience."

The room quieted. Annie shook her head as she unraveled another gauze strip. Elijah gradually allowed his thoughts to fade as he watched Annie work. He was amazed at the skill and dexterity with which she bandaged the animal. Her fingers shifted, adjusted, extended, and directed the gauze and tape with precision.

Finally, he spoke, trying to clarify his feelings. "Seriously, Annie, I think about you all the time. I've been praying about us."

"Well, Mr. Mulligan, I've been praying about us too."

"Has the Lord given you any answers?"

"Yes indeed."

"What did God reveal to you?"

"The Lord told me with a man like you I'm gonna need the patience of Job."

Elijah laughed—a loud, joyous explosion of laughter. "I could have told you that much."

Annie shook her head. "Hold her mouth open."

"Yes ma'am." Elijah wedged his thumb and index finger, one on each side of the Juniper's mouth.

She held the eyedropper above the cat's mouth and squeezed in three drops. "Make sure you give her three drops of this a day for the next four days. It will help stop infection," Annie said as she extended the bottle.

He cupped his large hands around hers with the bottle still in her grasp. "You know I appreciate all you do. You've got the gift of healing. And you're a good friend." Keeping hold with his right hand, he put his left hand under the bottle as she dropped it into his grasp, and then put the bottle into his pants pocket.

"Elijah."

"Yes, ma'am."

"Why are still holding my hand?"

"I want us to pray for my cat."

She gripped his hands firmly and looked up, exposing a beautiful smile. "You pray first," she said. "I'll close."

Elijah bowed his head and felt her strong grip. He saw her eyes were closed and noticed her skin looked soft and smooth. The morning sun shining through the kitchen window lit her countenance with a tender glow. He wanted to wrap his arms around her and passionately kiss her. Fighting off the urge, he blanked his mind and searched for words to pray: "Thank you, Lord, for this dear woman and the gift of healing you have given her. Thank you for her friendship. Help us to keep our eyes focused on you. May the work she has done be touched by your power to bring about healing in this creature. Juniper has been a comfort to me through many difficult days. May I enjoy the blessing of this cat's company for many more years."

After a momentary silence, Annie began, "Precious Lord and Master, we pray for the one who shot the arrow that injured this creature of yours. Speak to his heart about who you are. Break through the hard shell of his conscience and reveal to him the depths of your love. Prevent him from harming any living creature, dear Lord. We pray for his soul. You have the power to save those who are lost in darkness. Shine your light upon him. Continue to shine your light upon Elijah and me. Guide us along the path of your will. In the Lord's name we pray. Amen."

"Give me a hug, sister," Elijah said. The two embraced, Annie placing her head against Elijah's chest. He lowered his nose into the sumptuous softness of her hair. Smelling the lilac fragrance, he longed to draw her closer and feel the softness of her body, but instead he dropped his arms and inched backwards. She held him a second longer and then let go. Elijah picked up his cat, smiled, and ambled out the door.

Chapter Six

During the half-mile walk across the ridge to Nixon's Run, Elijah's thoughts tumbled and spun like a rickety carnival ride. *Annie Ferrier, you are so beautiful . . . so tempting . . . but I'm like the Apostle Paul—single . . . single and committed to God alone . . . Poor Juniper . . . Lord heal this cat and make her whole again.* As he gazed at the bandages, his chest tightened and arm muscles tensed. *Whoever did this is gonna face consequences. He's gonna pay. I'll ring his neck.* He shook his head. *What a low-life scoundrel. How could anyone hurt a defenseless creature?* He pictured himself punching a faceless man over and over. His heart raced, and he blinked his eyes. *Stop it. Stop it. No more violence. No more hurting people. I'm gonna find out who did this, Juniper. Somehow I'll make sure it doesn't happen again.* Annie's face appeared in his mind. *Annie did such a good job on you. Annie, Annie, Annie—Oh how that woman gets to me . . . stirs me up inside. Makes me weak.*

When he reached the bridge, he looked down Nixon's Run and snapped out of his reverie. Remembering the encounter with Kyler, he said, "Juniper, I wonder if that strange feller had something to do with this. Hope this day doesn't go from bad to worse."

Elijah's house reflected the bachelor's life—unkempt and undecorated. He wasn't lazy but rather believed excessive housework was a waste of time. Still cradling the cat in his left arm, he opened the refrigerator door and noticed his fingers stuck to the handle. Suddenly the crumbs, spilled juice, spoiled leftovers, several unidentifiable perishables, and a puddle of sludge confronted him.

"Great Caesar's Palace. What a mess!" He reached for the half-gallon jug of milk. *I need to clean this refrigerator sometime today.* He stepped around the oak table and knelt to pour the milk into Juniper's bowl. Carefully he lowered the cat and coaxed it to drink. Juniper trembled on three legs, looking at Elijah with an injured animal's wordless pain.

The cat was ten years old and a comforting presence to Elijah—a gift of sympathy given to him by a local farmer. At the time he had been staggering through the valley of the shadow of death. The pet helped to fill that hollow place left behind by the tragic loss of loved ones. He gently picked Juniper up and placed her in the cardboard box lined with a yellow beach towel. "You sleep now. Later you'll want to drink."

Elijah stood, looked around, and remembered where he had left the arrow. He walked into the living room and extracted it from the black vase beside the front door. Holding it by the ends, he positioned it at arm's length to adjust to his far-sightedness. "The Grim Reapers," he read aloud. "The Grim Reapers . . . hmmph. I guess the Grim Reaper tried to get you, Juniper. Tried to take you away from me, but he left his calling card." Below the larger script, he detected more writing, but it was too small to make out. He looked around the darkly paneled room for his reading glasses. A well-worn crimson Bible sat on a rectangular table stained by the bottoms of coffee cups, the circles biting into the varnish and randomly overlapping. He picked up the Bible and inspected the floor at the base of the table but couldn't see the glasses. The top of the television, an early 80's RCA cabinet model, was empty except for a layer of dust. He checked the plaid couch and his new recliner, a top-of-the-line Broyhill covered in beige corduroy. Between the cushion and the arm of the recliner, he saw the tip of the spectacle's wire frame. *Must've fell asleep in my chair and sat on 'em.* After retrieving the glasses and twisting the bent arm back to its normal angle, he positioned them on the end of his nose and read the smaller print on the arrow: *Live Free, Ride Hard, Die Young.* "What's that all about?" He shook his head and raked his beard.

Peter Nower will know something about this; he knows a little bit about everything. He stepped into the kitchen to see if Juniper had fallen asleep. She lay quietly, her breathing barely noticeable. He pivoted and marched out the front door and into the sunlight toward the top of the hill.

* * *

Peter Nower lived at the bottom of the other side of the hill where the road made a one-hundred-and-eighty degree turn at a steep angle, flattened out, and wound its way through the valley to Mount Pleasant. He had inherited his father's farm property and hired a skilled contractor to build the extravagant house. It contrasted with the smaller, older homes scattered on the sides of the hills and nestled in the valleys and along the creeks. Peter's home was an all-brick, two-story structure with three gabled sections of various sizes facing the front. Expensive bushes and red-and-white-stained decorative stones lined the walkway. The house, too big for a retired bachelor, looked out of place in this poor, rural community as if it had been plucked out of a new subdivision in St. Clairsville and plopped down by a tornado on this spot. After striding up the driveway and onto the front porch, without hesitation Elijah threw open the door and walked into the entry hall.

"Nower! You home?" he shouted.

"Is that you, Mulligan?" his friend answered from upstairs.

"Yeah, it's me. Who'd you think it was, the county assessor come to raise your taxes again?"

"What?" the voice echoed in the upstairs hallway.

"Never mind. I need to talk to you. Hurry up and get down here."

"I'm in the bathroom. Pour yourself a cup of coffee. I'll be down in a couple of minutes."

Elijah shuffled into the kitchen to the cupboard and pulled out his favorite mug, an over-sized white cup with the words *Purple Rider Football* stamped in violet. He poured out the remainder of the coffee and flipped off the switch. "I got something I want to show you," he yelled. "Get a move on!"

"When I'm shaving, I take my time," Peter called down.

"Sorry," laughed Elijah. "I wouldn't want you to nick that ugly mug of yours. You should give up shaving. Grow a beard, like me."

"No thank you," Peter yelled. "The women prefer my baby face."

"Your face looks like an old leather boot," Elijah hollered back.

He tapped the tip of the arrow on the dining table and glanced at the artificial silk flower arrangement in the middle. Turning, he inspected the shelves of books on the wall opposite the bay window—mostly science textbooks and reference books, but a few books on world religions, humanism, atheism and philosophy. On the top shelf near the end with a very worn cover, he noticed Darwin's *Origin of the Species*. Elijah shook his head and smiled. *How many times have we debated that issue?* On the wall next to the doorway that led back into the kitchen hung a framed golf scorecard under glass with the words: *Muirfield Village Golf Club – The Memorial Tournament*. He walked over to inspect it. *What in the world? Haven't seen this before.* Leaning closer he noticed the signature. "Jack Nicholas," he read aloud.

"What do you think about that?" Peter said from behind him.

"Very impressive," Elijah said. "You met the Golden Bear?"

"Shook his hand and told him how much I idolized him."

"I'm surprised you didn't bow down and kiss his golf spikes."

"I almost did. He is the god of golf, you know. And now I have his autograph."

"Big deal. He's only a man, just like you and me." Elijah pointed at the card and shrugged. "It's a few letters scribbled onto a piece of paper."

"You're jealous because you don't have one and I do."

"I bet you don't have one of these." Elijah turned and extended the arrow like a fencer ready to score a fatal stab.

"Whoa," Peter said. His wiry arm reached out to take the arrow. Peter Nower was five feet, ten-inches tall, lean and muscular from years of playing thirty-six holes a day—even in the winter when the weather permitted. A large swath of brown and gray hair crossed his forehead and framed a suntanned, hollow-cheeked face that usually sported a sarcastic smile. He wore a tan coaching shirt and light blue shorts that hung on him like the clothes of a scarecrow. He was fifty-eight, but only his face reflected his age. To Elijah, he seemed to have more energy than a teenager.

"Where did you procure that projectile, ol' buddy?" he said with his sour smile.

Elijah winced. "I guess you could say the cat drug it in. Unfortunately it was embedded in her thigh."

"You're kidding."

"I wouldn't kid about something like that."

"Your orange cat, what's her name . . . Jupiter?"

"Juniper."

"Is she dead?"

"No. Annie operated on her. I think she'll be all right."

"Annie Ferrier?"

"What other Annie do I know?"

"The Widow Ferrier, huh?" Peter's voice lilted and his eyes shone with an ornery glint.

"She's a natural healer. She's got a gift."

"She's a natural all right," he said, raising his eyebrows. "When are you going to follow your natural instincts and ask her for a date?"

"I didn't come here to talk about my love life. I was hoping you might help me identify the owner of this arrow."

"Let me take a closer look." Peter read the inscription. "It looks like it belongs to the Grim Reapers."

"Yeah, but who are the Grim Reapers?"

"In literature the Grim Reaper is Mr. Death. He wanders around in a black-hooded cape and carries a scythe. It's not good to answer the door when Mr. Grim Reaper comes to call."

"I don't need a literature lesson. What I want to know is who shot this arrow."

"Do you remember the motorcycle gang that used to hang out at the Rainbow Inn in Martins Ferry in the mid-sixties?"

"Oh yeah," Elijah said. "That crew of lost sheep and rebels would hang out in front of the joint with their Harleys scattered across the parking lot. That was a long time ago."

"The name of their gang was The Grim Reapers."

"That's right! But they must all be in their sixties by now."

"I doubt if many of them are still living. Their motto was, *Live Free, Ride Hard, Die Young.* It's inscribed here on the arrow. The ones who survived the crazy years are probably suffering from heart disease and cirrhosis of the liver."

"What makes you think this arrow belongs to an old Grim Reaper?"

Peter shook his head. "This is just a hunch, but I'd say it's been passed down to the next generation."

"Next generation? Whadaya mean?"

"Have a seat, ol' buddy. I've got an interesting story to tell."

"Oh boy. This ought to be good." Elijah pulled one of the mahogany chairs out from the dark table. "I might as well make myself comfortable, knowing how long your stories can be." He leaned back, his hands cupping behind his head.

"About seven years ago I had a student in biology class—a troubled lad. Came to class every day wearing black t-shirts and a cold, hard look on his face. Always seemed on the verge of violence, like he wanted to hurt someone. Usually he was unsocial, but when he interacted with other students, he tried to prove he was one bad dude—willing to do dirty deeds. Even the jocks avoided him. He had the ability to make you feel uncomfortable.

"Occasionally he wore a jacket—a beat-up leather jacket that belonged to his father—with the words *The Grim Reapers* sewed on the back. Below the words was a caped skeleton with a scythe. His dad had been a leader in the gang. After the glory days faded and most of them were either dead or reformed, the Grim Reapers disbanded. Guess the boy eventually found the jacket, or maybe his old man gave it to him. The coat added to his dangerous image. Wore it everywhere he went.

"I rarely spoke to him. He got average grades, but I could tell he was intelligent. He never studied for a test; just showed up for class most of the time and got C's without much effort. One day he arrived with a horrible black eye and bruised cheek. No one asked him what happened. I'm sure everyone wanted to know, but nobody bothered him. He sat at his desk with his head lowered, staring at the floor. Curiosity got the better of me. I called him up front to check his notebook and asked him where he got the shiner. He gave me one of the strangest answers. He said, 'There was a cat fight outside my old man's window last night and I ended up getting the worst of it.' Then he stared at me with those dark eyes. I couldn't think of anything to say.

"I knew his father had beaten him. Guess I should have reported it but figured he was eighteen and could take off if he wanted. Besides, he'd survived living with the ogre for years. His mother left when he was a boy. Rumor had it she was a prostitute. The father made her turn tricks for drug money. She eventually disappeared. No one knew where she went. It's hard to say. My guess is she took off with another man. The father must have taken it out on the boy. Made his wife sacrifice herself for his drug addiction, and then he hated her for what she'd become. She wanted out, so she left them both. The boy was caught in the middle."

Peter's story kept bringing a certain face to Elijah's mind—one he'd just confronted that morning. "What was the kid's name?"

"That's another funny thing. You probably know him. He inherited the house right down the road from you a year or so ago."

"Nathan Kyler?"

"That's him. His grandmother used to live there. Her name was Ida Mae Chesney. She used to attend your church 'bout twelve or thirteen years ago."

"I've noticed a few Chesneys buried up in that cemetery."

"The house sat empty for ten years after she'd been placed in the McGraw Nursing Home. When she died last year, he moved in."

"I was there today."

"Where?"

"In that house. I went to invite Nathan Kyler to our church service and covered-dish dinner this Sunday."

Peter grinned and shook his head. "Not too friendly, is he?"

Elijah sat forward and placed his hands flat on the table. "He came to our Easter Sunrise service last April. I had a funny feeling about him then. Two times since I've tired to talk to him. Both times were odd encounters. Like you said, he gives a person a cold chill. But I finally got the nerve up to invite him to church."

"He probably attended on Easter out of respect for his grandmother—living in that house where she lived. He must have felt compelled to return for some reason."

"That's what he told me. His grandma took him to church every Easter. Anyway, I had a confrontation with him today."

Nower's facial muscles tightened, forming deep wrinkles on his forehead and along the sides of his cheeks. "What do you mean a confrontation?"

"He turned down my invitation, but then changed his mind. Said he was looking for an opportunity to meet a particular girl—the preacher's daughter, Chrissy Butler. I told him she was only twelve years old. I didn't want him coming to church with the wrong intentions."

"Sounds like he was yanking your chain."

"I know. I shouldn't let a guy like that get to me. For some reason, he wanted to make me mad. Well, he succeeded. I left his place in a fury. He thought it was funny. I pray he doesn't show up Sunday morning. Now I'm worried. You never know what a feller like that might do."

Peter shook his head. "I wouldn't worry. He was just playing mind games with you. You came onto his property uninvited, and he got even by rattling your cage."

"He definitely poked this old lion in the wrong places."

Peter slid his chair back and stood up, picked up the arrow and walked around the table tapping the pointed end in his hand. "Well, at least you have a possible suspect—*The Scotch Ridge Grim Reaper.*"

"Ever since my wife and daughter died, that cat has been a comfort to me."

"I know."

"Old Tom Patterson brought her over from his farm after my daughter's funeral. Said he had too many kittens runnin' around the barn."

"I'm sure the cat will recover."

Elijah crossed his arms, then raised his hand to his chin and looked up at the crystal chandelier above him. "Now what am I gonna do?"

"You don't know for sure that Kyler shot that arrow, Elijah."

"That's right, but I'm gonna find out."

"Just remember what you said a second ago."

Elijah turned and gazed at his friend. "What's that?"

Peter leaned forward with one arm on the table. With the other he extended the arrow and poked Elijah in the center of his chest. "He knows how to rile up old lions. Don't let Kyler get to you. Don't do something you may regret. Remember what the Good Book says: *Revenge is mine, sayeth the Lord.*"

"For an agnostic you sure know your scriptures."

"For your benefit I quote scripture, ol' buddy. I know you'll listen to reason if it's grounded in religion." Peter grinned—that familiar sarcastic grin.

"Truth is truth. Even if it comes from the mouth of an unbeliever."

"What is truth?" Peter asked, still smiling.

"There you go, quoting scripture again."

"John 18 isn't it?"

"That's right. It's one of the last things Pilate asked Jesus before he sent him away to be executed."

"You better watch your step if you go back to Kyler's house—just in case the boy gets overprotective of his property. Maybe he's a Grim Reaper wannabe."

"I'm not scared. I've never been one to run away from a fight. If that boy injured my cat, I'll let him know that I don't like it in no uncertain terms."

Peter put is hand of Elijah's shoulder. "I just have one question before you leave."

"What's that?"

"If the Grim Reaper swings his scythe in your direction, so to speak, could I have your new recliner that you've been bragging about?"

"No. I'm leaving that to my cat. You can have the old couch, though."

"Thanks a lot, ol' buddy," Peter said.

The men rose from their seats and headed to the front door. "I'm gonna put the fear of the Lord in that boy if he's the one who shot my cat."

Peter stuck out his right hand. "Let me shake your hand in case this is the last time I see you alive." Elijah's huge hand engulfed Peter's as they both squeezed hard. "Ouch! Ouch! You win," Peter said.

"I'll stop by tomorrow and tell you what happened." Elijah turned and went out the door. "Hope you make a fresh pot of coffee by then."

"Don't count on it." After Elijah crossed the porch and descended the steps, Peter yelled. "Hey! Hey, Mulligan!"

Elijah, now standing in the full light of the noon sun, shielded his eyes as he turned back to look at Peter. "What do you want?"

"I'm starting to get this strange compulsion to wash my hands."

"Mathew 27:24. Right?" Elijah asked.

Peter smiled and nodded.

Chapter Seven

With every step Elijah Mulligan took, the foul smell of death increased. Four crows hopped and flitted around the coon's carcass fifty yards ahead of him. Their black silhouettes combined and contorted in the mid-afternoon heat rising from the asphalt as if a pit had opened from the depths of hell and a demon writhed and struggled to escape. The arrow dangled from his fingers. The demonic shape raged—jagged and changing, the four crows pecking, ripping, and swallowing.

Elijah focused on the vision before him. *What am I doing? This is a mistake. I should turn around and walk home. Who knows what a man like Kyler might do? He's crazy enough to try to kill me.* An intense sensation of evil flowed over him. *I can feel it crawling on my skin.* Elijah closed his eyes, and suddenly the arrow slipped from his fingers and rattled on the asphalt.

He opened and closed his hand, extending and contracting the muscles to increase the circulation. With the light buzz of blood flow through his fingers, words came into his mind like a beam of light cutting through a moonless night: *Though I walk through the valley of the shadow of death, I fear no evil, for thou art with me.* A sudden fluttering erupted. Elijah opened his eyes to see the crows scattering. Bending over, he picked up the arrow.

He walked, slowly at first, and then with more courage toward the raccoon and Kyler's house. He limited his breathing as much as possible until he neared the dead animal. By then the oxygen demand forced him to suck in air, and the stench sickened him. The mass of fur and guts could no longer be identified as a raccoon except for the tail with its distinguishing gray and white markings rippling in the breeze. The head was missing. *That's odd. How could crows decapitate a raccoon and carry off its head? Haven't seen that before.* He turned, half nauseated from the road kill, and gazed at Kyler's shack.

A white Ford Escort, dented and dirty, was parked at the side of the house. *He must be home; his car's here.* Elijah navigated through the obstacles in the yard: the push mower, various engine parts, the red Pinto on concrete blocks, and several tires. When he reached the ramshackle steps, he looked up at the screen door. The house was quiet except for the buzzing of wasps hovering below the growing nest that hung from the porch ceiling. He climbed the steps tapping, the arrow on the tread in front of him. The buzzing volume increased. The wasps, agitated by the Elijah's presence, darted toward him and then shot upwards to the nest, warning him to back away. Elijah banged on the door. Two wasps charged again glancing off the side of his face and then hovered above his head in the final hostile threat before an all-out attack.

Elijah opened the screen and ducked inside just as the wasps began to swarm furiously below the nest. His eyes blinked adjusting to the darkness. He glanced nervously around the sparsely furnished room. The only light spilled in from the front door next to him and the kitchen door in the back.

"Kyler!" he shouted. "Where are you? Kyler! Are you here?" He stood in the rectangle of light just beyond the door. Motes of dust swirled in the glow. Through the passageway between the front room and the kitchen, Elijah saw the corner of the kitchen table with objects scattered across it. He edged forward stepping on something that crunched under his foot. *That's either a cockroach or a pretzel.* Elijah squeezed the arrow again and rubbed his thumb across the etched words—*The Grim Reapers.*

As he entered the kitchen, his foot bumped an empty beer can. It rolled across the floor and clinked against a cabinet. On the table lay a bow and an arrow that teetered on the edge, defying the laws of physics. When Elijah reached for it, the powers that held it released, and it slid forward into a dive, but he caught the feathered end in his free hand. He knew immediately the arrows were identical.

Now what? What do I do? Maybe the worst thing would be to confront him. Kyler seems to get a kick out of making people angry. He wants me to lose control. Maybe I ought to just call the sheriff and tell him what happened. If I weren't a man of God, I'd put this bozo through a wall. Suddenly the presence of death crept into the room—the odor of rotting raccoon wafted into the kitchen making Elijah breathe through his mouth instead of his nostrils. He could feel needles rushing up and down his back and a rubbery trembling in his legs. He listened but heard nothing. He knew he was not alone. Slowly he turned around.

"That's right. Face me, you big sonovabitch. You're a squeeze away from hell. Make the wrong move and die." The voice was metallic as if it issued from the muzzle of the double-barreled shotgun that protruded from the black shape standing starkly against the doorway's light.

Holding an arrow in each hand, Elijah squinted at the ominous outline. He realized the arrows were useless in defending himself, so he stood facing Kyler like an overgrown drummer boy on the battle line.

"You got a lot of nerve, staking out my house this morning so you could rob me this afternoon."

"Put the gun down, Kyler. I didn't come here to steal these two worthless arrows from you," Elijah said as calmly as possible. He inched into the front room.

"We'll let the sheriff decide that, old man. Anyone who enters my house without my permission, in my opinion, is guilty of breaking and entering and attempted robbery."

"You know I didn't come to rob you. I just came to find a match."

"Find what?"

"Does this arrow belong to you?"

Kyler's nostrils flared, and his focus shifted rapidly around the room as if the answer eluded him like a fly escaping the swatter. "I don't know what you're talking about."

"This arrow here." Elijah held it out. "Is it yours? Are you the *Grim Reaper?*"

Kyler stood motionless against the lighted doorway.

Elijah walked toward him. "Here let me give you a closer look."

The explosion from the weapon flashed in the darkened room, throwing ghastly light and shadows in all directions. Elijah felt the whoosh of air pass his ear and the blast throughout his entire being. Glass shattered behind him.

For a moment he could not hear. He blinked several times and swallowed.

Kyler's voice reverberated from a distant tunnel. "You better believe I'm the Grim Reaper." He stepped forward and thrust the barrel into Elijah's chest jolting him backwards. "Are you ready to die, old man?"

The barrel burned through his shirt against his skin. Beneath, his heart raged, violently pumping blood that electrified every nerve in his body.

"I pull this trigger and your heart get splattered against that wall behind you."

Elijah noticed a strange expression pass over Kyler's face—an ecstasy of power, the arrogance of one who has gained total control. Kyler's eyes became vacant as if his violent act had triggered some inner fantasy—perhaps imagining what it would be like to take another man's life. As Elijah focused on Kyler's eyes, he sensed the young man had drifted momentarily into dreamland

Elijah's left forearm knocked the barrel upward, jolting Kyler out of his daze. The arrows rattled on the floor as Elijah grabbed and yanked the hard steel forward with such velocity that the butt and trigger instantly ripped out of Kyler's hands. Elijah spun and whirled the weapon twirling through the kitchen doorway. It crashed against the table and discharged upward with a loud BOOM, blowing a hole into the ceiling. White chunks showered down in a flurry of smoke and dust. Before the debris settled, Elijah pivoted and locked his hands onto the shoulders of the surprised man. Grabbing skin and fabric with a vice-like grip, he thrust the lean body backwards into the wall. He charged forward and lifted Kyler several inches off the ground and almost embeddeded him into the plaster. Elijah leaned within an inch of the shocked face and growled, "I'm not afraid of you, Mr. Reaper! I'm not afraid to die. You're the one who needs to fear death. I could twist your scrawny neck right now like a chicken and drop you onto this floor dead before you even knew you landed."

Kyler began to tremble as he glared with wide-defiant eyes.

"You're shaking like a leaf, Mr. Reaper. I didn't realize Grim Reapers were such cowards."

"Let me go, old man," he hissed.

"I'll let you go when I want to let you go. Cowards like you don't tell me what to do."

"I'm gonna to kill you."

Elijah stepped back, pulled Kyler forward and shoved him hard. Kyler thudded against the wall and slunk to the floor. He glared up at Elijah.

"I'm waiting," Elijah said. "You couldn't kill my cat, but maybe you can kill me. Go ahead."

Kyler sat like a de-stringed marionette in the shadow cast by the open door against the wall. He remained motionless in the darkness. Elijah stepped into the doorway's light.

"Get out of my house," Kyler barked.

"Not before I say what I came to say." Elijah lowered his head to make eye contact. In the shadow Kyler's face appeared distorted, features rigid with rage. His irises were black circles against bulging white orbs set into deep sockets. "I am the avenging angel, Mr. Kyler. You hurt something or someone, and I'll make sure you pay. You harm an innocent creature, and I'll be at your door. Death doesn't scare me. Go ahead and try to kill me. I know where I'm spending eternity. Just remember, we all die sooner or later. There's a heaven and a hell beyond this life. You can count on it."

"Get out!"

"I'm not sure what kind of twisted thoughts go through your mind, but I'm warning you: Stay away from our church. If you harm one hair on the head of Chrissy Butler, the Lord's vengeance will come down upon you . . . and I'm willing to be the avenging angel. Don't darken the doorway of that church unless you come willing and ready to repent."

"Get out!" Kyler screamed.

"I'm leaving, Mr. Kyler, but only because I want to. Not because you ordered me." Elijah headed toward the screen door.

Kyler struggled to his feet and grabbed the doorknob. "Get out!" he screamed again, but Elijah was already halfway out the door.

On the second step across the porch Elijah felt the rushing air of the slamming door and the loud crash behind him. He also sensed something touch the middle of his back, and then heard a furious buzzing. A burning explosion of pain pierced his neck, cheek and right hand simultaneously. He shook his hand and reached to his neck as another shot of hot pain seared the other side. His hand clasped against a vibrating, angry fury. Its body crackled but not before injecting another fiery dart into Elijah's palm. He whipped away the crushed body of the wasp and twirled around swatting and waving at the flying squadron. Looking down, he saw the fallen nest with three stunned wasps fidgeting around it.

He stumbled backwards and his foot slipped off the edge of the porch. Falling forward, he caught himself, his face inches from the gray honeycombed nest. He scooted backwards down the steps and rolled onto the grass in hopes of avoiding more stings. Stumbling to his feet, he sprinted toward the bridge, hurdling the rusted lawnmower. He stomped across the bridge as the foursome of crows shrieked in unison with diabolical cackling. Elijah faced them, incredulous. The crow's hideous squawks combined with insane high-pitched laughter from Kyler's front window. Six throbbing welts pulsated on his neck, arm, hand, and cheek.

He looked at the window where a shape behind the screen shook with delirium. *This must be what hell is like.* He turned and faced the birds.

The four crows guarded the foul carcass. A strange urge invaded Elijah's brain. Slowly at first, he neared the crows. His steps quickened, and they scattered with caws and wild flapping. Elijah planted his left foot in perfect rhythm to the side of the headless coon and thrust his right foot straight through the body. It shot off the road ten feet into the air and landed in the deep weeds. He looked at his feet. A wet spot remained on the road where the coon had lain, and he noticed a large red smudge on his boot. The scene became strangely quiet. The crows were gone and the laughter had stopped. In the silence an intense shame washed over him.

Chapter Eight

The barking awakened Joshua. When he looked out of the triangular opening of the tent into the brightness of the Saturday dawn, he saw Elijah Mulligan walking up the road carrying a picnic basket. "Boo Boo. Hey, Billy, wake up," he whispered.

Billy stirred in his sleeping bag and peered up with puffy eyes.

Joshua opened the tent flap wider. "There he goes," Joshua said. "There goes 'Lijah Mulligan." At the edge of the property, Joshua's beagle yelped and howled, prancing back and forth along this side of the creek. Mulligan ignored the dog.

Billy rolled over and peered through the bright triangle. "He's carrying something."

"It looks like a picnic basket. I bet he's heading back up to that place in the woods."

"Why would he take a picnic basket up there, Doc?"

"Maybe he's gonna have lunch with the squirrels and possums," Joshua said.

Billy giggled. "That'd be something to see. He kinda looks like Grizzly Adams."

"Or else he's got something in there he doesn't want anyone to know about."

"Like what?"

"Old coins maybe."

"Shewwweee, Doc. You really think so?"

"Or gold or precious jewels."

"Maybe he's gonna bury it somewhere in the woods," Billy said.

"Why are we still sittin' here?"

"We ain't gettin' no place fast!"

"Then let's get goin'!" Joshua said.

The boys laughed. Each raised his right hand and slapped them together at the peak of the tent.

The beagle barked even louder.

"Be quiet, Buster," Joshua commanded. The dog trotted across the yard and poked its head into the opening.

"We better tie Buster up or he'll follow us," Billy said.

"I'll tie him to your back porch. Come here, boy." Joshua gave the dog a big hug as Buster licked his face. "Come on. You gotta get tied up."

He crawled out of the tent, reached back and grabbed the dog by the collar. The beagle stubbornly resisted as Joshua tugged it to the front porch, connected the chain to its collar, and tied the end of the chain around the base of the porch rail support. The dog yelped and yanked on the chain.

"You stay here," Joshua said. "We'll be back in a little while." He patted the dog's head, and it whined with high-pitched sighs.

"Let's peel outta here!" Billy said. "He's already a couple hundred yards up the road."

Buster's tugging rattled the entire porch rail as the boys scurried across the front yard and turned up the hill.

* * *

The path through the woods to the natural sanctuary was well worn in most places, but tricky to find as it passed over sections of rocky ground and gullies. About halfway there, at the top of a shady knoll, Elijah stopped and set down the picnic basket at the base of a thick, tall elm. He bent over, lifted the lid, and peeked inside. "Everything'll be all right, Juniper." He looked up at his favorite spot on the tree. Reaching out with his index finger, he gently traced the letters: *Emily—1949.* "A long time ago she stood right where you are, my friend," he said. "Her daddy brought her here. She loved to go for long walks with him. In 1949 he carved her name right there.

"She was the one who showed me the Healing Place. I remember it well. She was seventeen, and I was nineteen. We'd only been dating for two months, but I knew I loved her. I told her so right here. I said, 'I love you, Emily,' and she started to cry. I don't know why. She just began to bawl. She put her head on my chest, and I held her tight. When she finally stopped she looked up with those big green eyes full of tears and said, 'I love you too, Elijah.' We didn't get married for another two years because of my prison sentence . . . Well . . . never mind that. I don't want to talk about those shameful days. Anyway, whenever we'd come back home to visit her parents, we'd go and pray at the Healing Place."

He paused and touched the name carved below the first name. "*Amy—1970*. I carved that one, and my daughter sat on that rock and watched me. She asked, 'Will my name stay there forever, Daddy?' I said, 'It'll be here long after you and I are gone, honey.' We'd come back every Thanksgiving to visit Emily's parents; me and Amy would walk out to this tree after the Thanksgiving dinner and look at her name. Then we'd walk back and gobble down more of Grandma Murray's homemade pumpkin pie. I miss those days, Juniper." Elijah brushed the corner of his eye. "But you have kept me company since those hurtful times. The Lord giveth and the Lord taketh away."

He reached down, closed the lid, and picked up the basket. "Come on now. Let's go. The Lord's waiting for us at the Healing Place."

* * *

"It looks like he's talking to that tree," Billy whispered.

"And he keeps looking into the basket," Joshua said. "Do you think he's crazy?"

"I don't know too many people who talk to trees."

The boys had worked their way to within fifty feet of Mulligan and were crouching behind a fallen maple tree as they spied up the knoll to where the man stood. Suddenly, Mulligan turned in their direction.

"He's looking at us," whispered Joshua. "Stay completely still."

The boys froze behind the log. Mulligan's gaze fell on them like a paralyzing beam. Joshua felt an electrifying sensation across the surface of his skin and couldn't keep his knees from shaking.

When the leaves crackled five feet below them, their eyes met. The sound seemed amplified in the quiet woods. The boys turned at the same time to see a shiny, black-scaled tube slither through the leaves toward them. Two feet from Joshua's hi-top basketball shoes a black snake lifted its head and eyed them like the periscope of a submarine. Joshua's mouth dropped open in a silent scream as his eyes grew wide. The thick, long serpent had them pinned against the log. Trembling, Joshua stared at the snake. Its eyes looked like black beads, and its red tongue poked the air. Its head waved back and forth as if it wanted to hypnotize them.

"Stay perfectly still," Joshua whispered. "It won't bite you if you don't move."

Billy's teeth rattled when he tried to speak. "I . . .I . . .I c-c-can't k-k-keep still. I'm sh-sh-shakin' all o-over."

The shuffling and movements of the big man as he walked farther into the woods broke the snake's spell. Realizing Mulligan had moved on, Joshua sprung straight into the air, rolled over the log and spilled onto the other side. Billy followed. After regaining their nerve, they peeked above the log, but the snake had disappeared. They turned but saw no sign of Mulligan.

"I thought we were goners," Billy gasped.

"Where'd the snake go?"

"I don't know. Do you think it was poisonous?"

"Nah. It was just a black snake," Joshua said. "But they still bite."

"Shewwweee, Doc. I've never been so scared in my life."

Joshua stood and brushed dead leaves off his jean shorts. "I thought that snake was going to start talking to us—the way it raised its head up and stared at us."

"That was cool!" Billy exclaimed.

"It was like that snake was sent here to test our courage."

Billy stood and stepped on top of the fallen tree. "Do you think we passed the test?"

Joshua jumped up next to him. "Well, we didn't scream, did we?"

"No."

"We didn't run like a couple of girls, did we?"

"No."

"Mulligan never saw us, did he?"

"Don't think so."

"Well, then I reckon you could say we passed the snake test." Joshua crossed his arms and smiled.

"We're the Snake Boys," Billy declared.

"The Black Snake Patrol."

"That's it. We're the Black Snake Patrol." Billy began an odd dance on top of the log, his arms weaving up and down, his rear end shimmying. "We can slide and wiggle and sneak in and out and never get caught."

"We're cool." Joshua raised his hand high in the air, and Billy slapped it.

"Hey, Doc!" Billy said. "We ain't gettin' no place fast."

"You said it, Boo Boo. It's time for the Black Snake Boys to get a move on." Joshua clasped his hands together and pointed them toward the path. Rhythmically he wove them back and forth in the direction of the tree at the top of the knoll. Billy imitated the movement as they mounted the incline, winding their clasped hands in a snake-like motion to the top of the hill and down the other side.

* * *

Elijah knelt in the center of the circular clearing as the beams of the August sun penetrated the canopy of oak and maple leaves above him. The rays danced over and around him with the gentle shifting of the boughs in the light easterly breeze. With the lid of the picnic basket propped open, his head bobbed with the murmuring of intense prayer. Quietly, in whispers, the words poured forth in a steady stream. For moments his eyes would close, then open again as he peered into the basket. The splotches of light shifted and shimmered in the shadowy clearing as if keeping time to the flowing words of supplication. The sounds meshed with the rustling leaves, the chirping robins and wrens, and the creaking branches.

"Dear Lord, I don't deserve all the blessings you've given me. I'd be a no-good bum sittin' in some prison cell if it weren't for you. I know I'm far from perfect, but every day I come here to give another whack at it. I haven't quit yet. You've led my through some dark valleys. Without you I 'd be lost. But I still fall flat on my face. Why do I fail you so often? I try to do what's right, but before I realize it, I do the wrong thing."

He shook his head and raked his beard. "I'm in need of your mercy. I lost control of my temper when I confronted Nathan Kyler yesterday. Forgive me for the hatred and violence that exploded within me. Thank you for rescuing me from death. I felt the stings of evil upon me. You disciplined me but delivered me from destruction. Shower me with the cleansing water of forgiveness, O Lord. I lift up that young man's soul to you. Is it possible to reach him?

"Then there's Annie. What am I gonna do about that woman, Lord? I confess I have allowed my fleshly longings to control my thoughts. Her beauty distracts me from your will. The Apostle Paul said that single people should devote all their energies to serving the Lord. But sometimes I can't get her out of my mind. What am I gonna do about this, God?"

He took a deep breath and relaxed all his muscles. "I know. I know. The same thing you always tell me: Patience, patience, patience. The answers will come according to your time table, not mine."

He paused and opened his eyes. Reaching into the basket, he carefully lifted the cat, cradling it to his chest, and slowly stood. The sun's rays spilled onto him like a waterfall dabbing the man and animal with splashes of light and color. He lifted the cat high above his head and blocked the beams from his face.

"Heal this animal, O Lord. Heal this creature. Send the power of your Spirit through its body. Touch every fiber with the flow of your healing presence."

Elijah stretched his arms higher and lowered his head. Closing his eyes, he stood in the stillness, envisioning the invisible. He felt energized points of sensation throughout his entire body and trembled ever so slightly at first but then noticeably. He opened his eyes. The shimmering rays lighted upon him like luminescent butterflies. "Thank you Lord. Thank you for your healing touch. Bless you, Lord. Bless you for the power of your Spirit that flows through this creature and me. Your healing touch is upon us. By faith I know you are here. You are making whole what once was broken. Praise you, my Lord."

Elijah lowered the animal to his chest and cradled it, gently rocking back and forth as one would tenderly hold an infant. Looking up into his face, the cat mewed. With thumb and finger Elijah rubbed its cheeks and ears.

"You're feeling better now, aren't you?" he said. "Do you want to walk a little bit?" To lower the cat, Elijah squatted and gently eased it down between his knees until he could feel it stand on its own power. It meowed again and walked with a slight limp back and forth against his leg and passed under his outstretched hands.

Then the cat paused, distracted by something on the outer edge of the clearing. It riveted its eyes on a clump of thick bushes and crept slowly towards them.

"What do you see over there, girl? A bird? A chipmunk? You must be feeling better. What's over there?" The cat moved forward limping and creeping awkwardly on its bandaged leg. Squinting into the tangled greenery, Elijah observed Juniper's investigation.

When the cat disappeared into the shadows beneath the patch of growth, Elijah detected something of substantial size shifting through the foliage. The cat meowed from its camouflaged position. It was a familiar meow, one with friendly overtones— the same meow that greeted Elijah whenever he returned home from an outing. The cat mewed again. *What's over there?* He took a step toward the bushes, then another. The shapes behind the greenery shifted again. Panicky whispers escaped through the maze of leaves. Elijah advanced.

A jostling of branches and vines erupted on the other side of the bush. Elijah's heart jumped in his chest. The brush shook and shifted as shapes scurried through the undergrowth. He waggled his head peering through the spaces and crevices of leaves and branches but only detected glimpses of quick flashing shapes and color. "Who's there?" he shouted. "Come back here!" Elijah charged forward three more steps. He leaned, his hands upon his knees, and peered into the woods. The rustling faded as the blurry shapes wove in and out of the tangled growth and disappeared.

Juniper mewed.

Elijah looked down. The cat had reappeared below him. "Great Caesar's Palace. Look what the leprechauns left behind," he chuckled. Elijah reached down and lifted the cat to his chest and snuggled it into his beard. "My little pot of gold. This must be my lucky day." Elijah turned and walked back to the center of the clearing. He looked to the east into the waving boughs and squinted into the beams. "Thank you for this blessed day. Be with me now as I try to do your will. Whoever was watching me, O Lord, may the wonder and power of your presence in this place affect their lives. May they know that you are God Almighty. Amen." Elijah reached down, lifted the lid, and lowered the cat into the basket. "You rest now, girl. We got a long walk home," he whispered.

When he looked up, the long black snake startled him. A thick-curving 'S', the serpent stretched out before him guarding the exit to the natural sanctuary. It lifted its head and flittered its tongue.

How dare you enter this sanctuary. This is sacred ground. You have no right to cross into this holy place. The irrationality of his thoughts flustered him. *It's only a snake. A dumb reptile. It doesn't know this is the Healing Place.*

Refocusing on the snake's eyes, he thought he heard someone whisper: *I am everywhere— in the Garden of Paradise and in these sacred woods. You cannot escape me.*

Elijah blinked his eyes. The snake lay motionless. *Lord, am I going crazy? I'm starting to hear voices.*

The snake raised its head higher. *Why do you resist me? Why do you fight the anger and lust within you? Just give in to them.*

A scripture flashed across Elijah's mind—*Away from me Satan! For it is written: 'Worship the Lord your God and serve him only.'* Elijah's eyes widened as he spoke aloud: "Leave this place or I will crush your head with my heel!"

He took one step toward the black snake. Immediately it turned and wove its way through leaves and dirt to the outskirts of the clearing and disappeared into the cover of the weeds. "It was only a snake. Get a hold of yourself, man," Elijah uttered as the tension in his body began to subside and his heart slowed. *What an imagination I have.*

Chapter Nine

Billy struggled to breathe: "Hhhhhhhhh. Awrrrrrrrrrrrrrrrrrgh."

"Are you all right?"

"Hhhhhhhhhhh. Awrrrrrrrrrrgh, Its my as....HhhhAwwrrrgh . . . Its my asthma . . .," the redheaded boy gasped.

"Your face is all red," Joshua said.

"Hhhhhh. Awrrrrrrgh, cough, cough . . . I'll be okay . . . Hhhhhhhhh."

"Do you think he saw us?"

"I don't Hhhhhhhhh know . . . Awrrrrrrrrrrgh."

"We must have run a mile."

"It seemed like . . . Hhhhhhhh..two miles . . . Awrrrrrrrr."

"Do you think you can walk? The road's not too far from here."

"I'll be okay Hhhhhhh . . . If we don't have to run anymore Awrrrrrrrrgh."

"Look. I'm bleeding. A thorn bush must have got me." Joshua pulled his right elbow back to reveal a line of fresh blood that had dripped along his thin biceps. "I didn't watch where I was going. Just ran as fast as I could."

"That cat knew we were there. Hhhhhhhhh," gasped Billy. "He came right over to us." The boys walked towards the road through the last few hundred yards of woods. "Why was he holding that cat up in the air like that?"

"He was praying for it," Joshua said.

"Did you see the bandage on its leg?"

"Yeah. Something happened to it, but when he put it on the ground, it seemed all right."

The boys came to a thorny thicket blocking their progress. "Watch it. If I let this branch go it could cut you." Joshua carefully peeled back the thorny strand and allowed Billy to follow through. "It's like the cat got instantly healed. That place must be magic."

"Shewwweee, Doc," Billy said. "It was freaky."

"Then it came straight over to us and showed Mulligan where we were hiding like it knew we were there all the time."

"Do you think God healed it?" Billy asked.

"It sure seemed like it, didn't it?"

By now the boys had wandered in and out of the trees and underbrush to where the woods ended, and the view opened before them.

"Where are we?" Billy asked.

Joshua pointed. "Look. There's a house. The road's on the other side."

"That house looks familiar."

"You're used to seeing it from the front. It's that shack no one lived in for years. Now that Kyler guy owns it."

"Oh, yeah. He always sits on his front porch reading magazines," Billy said.

"I betcha they're dirty magazines."

"How do you know?"

"I was in town a couple weeks ago. My mom dropped me off at the Martins Ferry Pool. I went to the convenient store after I got done swimming to buy some candy. He was in front of me in line and asked for this month's *Playboy* and *Penthouse*."

Billy raised his eyebrows. "I wonder if he ever throws the old magazines away?"

"Are you thinkin' what I'm thinkin'?"

Billy slapped his hands on his thighs. "What are we waitin' for?"

Joshua raised his hand. "Shhhhhhh. What if Kyler's home?"

"Look and see if his little white car is parked by the side of the house. It's always sitting there when he's on the front porch," Billy said.

The boys crept down the steep embankment and peeked around the corner of the house. "No car in sight. He's not here," Joshua said.

"Where we gonna look?"

Joshua studied the rundown property. "I betcha there might be some on the back porch. I can see some papers stacked up over there. Come on."

"What if he comes back while we're checking through his trash?"

"If we hear anything, we'll run up and hide behind that old green shed on the side of the hill. He'll never know we were here."

The back of the house butted up against the embankment, which began as a slight grade and quickly became steeper as it advanced to the tree line. The boys walked through the foot tall grass to the rotting wooden steps.

"Shewwweee, Doc," Billy said. "I've got a funny feeling inside."

The steps rose before them to the paint-peeled porch. A stack of old magazines tied with a cord and surrounded by crumpled papers and discarded boxes cluttered the opening between the posts beyond the last step.

"Look. There's some magazines." Joshua stared at the potential X-rated jackpot. "Are we men or mices?"

"We're the Black Snake Patrol," Billy grinned.

"That's right. The snake would want us to climb the steps and take the treasure."

Halfway up the steps the old wood creaked and squealed like a hag. The boys stopped momentarily, tensing their shoulders, wide eyes meeting. They climbed more slowly. Small pieces of glass were scattered across the porch. Like an angry mouth, the back window threatened with fangs of jagged shards protruding from the frame. Against the house leaned a fluorescent-orange-handled shovel with PROPERTY OF WHEELING DOWNS printed on the bright paint in black marker. A brownish-red coated the sharpened flat end of the shovel's blade. The boys crouched in the midst of the crumpled papers with the stack of magazines between them. Joshua grabbed the twine and pulled toward the corner of the stack.

"Pull the top one out, Boo Boo," he ordered.

Billy scrunched the magazine so that it would slide between the two retracted cords.

"What is it?" whispered Joshua.

"*Field and Stream*," sighed Billy.

"Are they all *Field and Stream*s?"

"I don't know. Let me pull a few more out."

The boys fumbled and yanked until the twine loosened and the magazines spilled out and slid slanting to the porch in several directions.

"Jackpot!" Billy shouted.

"Shhhhhhhhh!"

"Look. Here's a *Playboy* . . ." Billy paused as the sound of a car rumbled over the wooden bridge at the front of the house.

"Kyler's back." Joshua dropped two magazines onto the pile. The car's engine coughed, sputtered, and stopped as a door cranked open.

"We're outta here," Billy said.

The boys jumped to their feet and headed for the steps, but Billy's back foot planted on a dirty magazine and slid backwards tumbling him into Joshua. The steps squealed with glee as the boys tumbled down and rolled off into a tangled ball of arms and legs. Springing to their feet, without time to rub bruised shins and forearms, they sprinted to the shed. The grass slowed their progress like a slow-motion nightmare. Although the pine-planked shed was only twenty-five yards away, each stride across the open yard seemed to take forever.

The boys rounded the corner and pressed their stomachs and cheeks against the back wall of the shed. Joshua heard Kyler kick open the screen door and step onto the back porch.

Struggling to control his breathing, Joshua suddenly became aware of a horrible smell filling his nostrils. He peeked around the edge of the shed and saw Kyler with his bow and arrow peering into the woods. Then Kyler looked down at the scattered magazines. *Oh no, he knows we're here.* Kyler raised the arrow to the bow and positioned it for release.

The awful stink made Joshua feel sick. He wanted to escape the odor, but he knew Kyler would shoot that arrow at whatever moved. He elbowed Billy's ribs and motioned him to turn around. Maybe they could cut back into the woods. Together they pivoted to face the hillside. When they did, a bunch of glaring and terror-filled eyes stared at them from a tortured oak tree that shuddered in the morning breeze. Sticking out from the bark up and down the trunk were the round tops of big nails that pierced through cut-off animal heads—squirrel heads, deer heads, possum heads, groundhog heads, cat heads, dog heads, rabbit heads, fish heads, and at the top—a large raccoon head. The spike entered between its eyes, which glared at them with a frozen snarl. The old oak groaned and swayed as if in agony.

The image imprinted itself deeply into the tender plate of Joshua's mind. Fear and shock etched the eyes of the creatures permanently onto his memory. Each head pleaded with the deep sadness of a captured soul. Dried skin clung to the skulls. Blank eyes, fur, noses, fangs, fin, and scale produced a variety of tortured faces. Joshua trembled, unable to understand the horror before him.

In his mind the animal heads came to life. Screams, groans, and howls of suffering echoed along the confused pathways of his imagination. Emotions tumbled with the images in a swirling storm of voices and shrieks. The squirrel's head screeched, *Leave here!* A collie howled. A large-mouth bass gurgled. A cat's head screamed in terror. A possum cried, *Go away.* The raccoon head pinned to the top of the body of heads, cried out, *Run from here! Escape from this place of torture and death!*

"Who's there!" Kyler screamed. "Come out from behind there! I said come out from behind there now! I'll put an arrow through your heart if you don't show your face!"

Joshua snapped back into conscious-clear thought and looked at Billy.

"I'm not kidding. I'll kill you!" Kyler shouted.

Joshua and Billy bolted around the animal-head tree and into the thick bushes behind the shed. They rushed up the hillside, rustling the branches, and stomping over bushes. With legs and arms churning, the boys crawled, clawed, and scrabbled through thorny patches and weeds, past tree trunks, fallen branches, and rotting logs.

Their progress came to a sudden stop when down through the branches, an arrow whistled and thudded into a wide white sycamore tree five feet in front of them. Huffing and gasping, they looked at each other, made a ninety-degree turn, and took off along a deer path that traveled along the side of the hill.

They plowed forward energized by fear—a fear inspired by the tormented faces of half-decomposed animals; a fear that bubbled up from deep within the their hearts; the natural fear to flee evil as if a monster chased them, on their heels, its claws reaching to clutch at their backs. They ran slapdashedly through vines and thorns in an all-out effort to distance themselves from that place of horror.

* * *

The woods behind the gray house quieted. Nathan turned back to the house and lifted the orange-handled shovel. He studied the dried blood on the blade and rubbed his hand across it. Flecks of dark red cracked off and fell to the porch. *Trespass on my property, and this is what you'll get. Sonsabitches. Damn thing needs sharpened.* From the window ledge he picked up a sharpening stone. Back and forth he slid the stone against the metal edge of the shovelhead. The rhythm lulled him into a familiar fantasy—the one where he stalked the preacher's daughter through the woods.

Chapter Ten

Fear drove the boys through the woods, across the creek, and finally to the road near Joshua's house, but a stronger emotion jolted them to a stop. By the side of the road, whimpering in pain, lay Joshua's beagle, Buster. Joshua dropped to his knees and embraced his dog. "Buster, are you hurt?"

The dog yelped at the touch of the boy's hand upon his backside.

Billy hovered over Joshua and the dog. "A car hit him. He's bleeding."

"I don't understand," Joshua said, sniffling. "I tied him up. Besides, Buster always gets off to the side when cars come along."

"Maybe . . ." Billy swallowed. "Maybe the driver ran him over on purpose."

Joshua glanced up. "You think someone swerved off the road and him hit him?"

Billy nodded. "Someone like Nathan Kyler. Not too many cars come up this road. Remember, Kyler just got home."

Joshua could only shake his head and squeeze his eyes shut as the tears trickled down.

"What are ya gonna do?" Billy asked. "He's really hurt bad."

"Go get my dad, Billy. Tell him Buster's been hit. I'll stay here with him."

Joshua's house was only fifty yards down Nixon's Run. Billy entered the yard at full speed, passed the swing set, and jumped over a sandbox and tricycle. He sprang up the steps and banged on the door. "Anybody home!" he yelled.

"Billy, be quiet," chastened a woman's voice. "Mr. Thompson's sleeping. He worked midnight last night at the mill." A pretty blonde in her mid-thirties appeared in the doorway in old jeans and a *Willie Nelson* t-shirt. She carried a curly-haired child who sucked her thumb.

Billy pressed his face into the screen. "Mrs. Thompson, Buster's been hit by a car. Right up the road. Josh is with him. He's hurt real bad."

"Oh my heavens," gasped the blue-eyed woman. "I'll get John." She lowered the toddler to the floor and disappeared into the shadows of the house. The little girl looked at Billy and pounded the screen.

Two minutes later, the man, tall with broad shoulders and black hair, appeared at the door tying up the strings of his gray sweat pants, shirtless and wearing black slippers. "Where is he?" Mr. Thompson asked gruffly. "I knew that dog was gonna get hit. Josh never ties him up." The screen door flew open, and Billy dodged to the side.

"This way. Right up the road," called Billy from behind. Then, legs churning, he skirted around the man, padded down the steps, and trotted across the yard. Joshua's father, square jawed and unshaven, dark-eyed from lack of sleep, had to jog to keep up with the boy. When he reached the road, he could see the huddled figure of his son over the dog. He picked up his pace and covered the distance quickly, running with the strides of an ex-wide receiver.

With pleading eyes and tear-lined cheeks, Joshua looked up at his father. "He's dying, Dad. Look how much he's bleeding." Raising his red-smeared hand, the boy revealed the deep gash on the dog's hind thigh.

"I told you to tie him up whenever you left the house. Now look what happened," Thompson said gruffly.

"But, Dad, I did tie him up at Billy's house. Honest."

"Well, you must have done a sloppy job of it," the man said with strained control. "The dog is suffering."

"Can we take him to the vets in town? Please?"

"Are you crazy, boy? You know how much that'll cost us? We go from pay to pay as it is. You want me to spend a couple hundred dollars on a dying dog? Look how bad he's hurt, Joshua. He's not gonna make it."

"I'll pay for it, Dad. I'll work. I'll make money cutting grass. Please, Dad. I promise."

The man's eyes began to soften, and he crouched to get a closer look at the animal. "Son, he's in bad shape. He's lost a lot of blood already. I can tell he's gonna die."

Joshua placed his hand more firmly over the dog's wound. "No he's not, Dad. He's gonna be all right."

"Can't you see he's sufferin', boy? Can't you see he's in misery? You'd be wasting time and money taking him to the vets. Listen to me, Joshua. I know what I'm talkin' about."

Joshua embraced the dog's neck with his left arm while keeping the wound covered with his right hand. His tears began to flow again.

"I'll be back," the man said solemnly. He stood, pivoted, and walked down the road.

"What's he gonna do?" Billy asked. "Is he gonna take you to the vets?"

"I don't think so. He thinks Buster's gonna die. He said the dog's in misery."

"Does your Dad gotta gun?"

"Yeah. Why?"

"He might be thinkin' it best to put the dog out of its misery."

"No way," Joshua said. He sat up, and the dog raised its head. "Come on. We're gettin' outta here." Joshua carefully scooped up the beagle and struggled to his feet.

"Where're we going?"

"To see Elijah Mulligan. He's the only one I know who can help us."

* * *

The boys progressed slowly up the road. A golden Lexus swerved into the other lane, picked up speed, and disappeared as it flew around the next turn. After walking a couple hundred yards, they realized they had entered the territory of that morning's horrific encounter—Kyler's property. Joshua remembered the back porch with the scattered glass, the red-stained shovel blade, the magazines, the animal-head tree, and the arrow. Looking to his right across the wooden bridge, he saw the small gray house and white Escort. He wondered if his dog's blood was on the tires.

"Listen," Joshua said. "Do you hear that?" As they walked, the faint, steady sound of metal against stone echoed off the hill behind the house. Fear raised goose bumps on Joshua's skin and quickened his heartbeat. He could sense evil in the air, a terrible feeling pressing upon him with each echo of metal upon stone. Their feet shuffled to the rhythm as if marching to a funeral song. As they moved up the hill away from the un-railed bridge and the drab house, the metallic beat died away; Joshua's aching arms grew heavy. Elijah Mulligan's house was still a couple hundred yards ahead.

"That Kyler is scary," panted Billy. "I guess we shouldn't a been on his property. Do you think he recognized us when we took off through the woods?"

"I don't think so," Joshua huffed. "Just be glad that arrow didn't stick in one of our backs. Then your head or my head would be nailed at the top of that tree."

"Are you afraid to die, Josh?"

"I guess so. That's the closest I ever came. I guess if I wasn't afraid to die, I wouldn't a run so hard to get away," Joshua stopped to re-adjust his grip on the beagle. "This dog is getting heavy."

"Do you want me to carry him?"

"Nah. I can make it. We're almost there." Sweat dripped from his forehead, and the dog whined with each step. "Not far now, Buster. I can see the house just ahead."

As they crossed Mulligan's bridge, they could hear someone talking inside the house.

* * *

Elijah slid his finger across the page of the Bible as he read:
"When I am afraid, I will put my trust in Thee.
In God, whose word I praise, In God I have put my trust;
I shall not be afraid. What can mere man do to me?
Thou hast taken account of my wanderings; put my tears in Thy bottle;
Are they not in Thy book?
Then my enemies will turn back in the day when I call;
This I know, that God is for me. In God whose word I praise,
In the Lord whose word I praise,
In God I have put my trust, I shall not be afraid.
What can man do to me?
Thy vows are binding upon me, O God; I will render thank offerings to Thee.
For Thou hast delivered my soul from death . . ."

The loud knocking interrupted his reading, and looking up, he saw the silhouettes of two skinny kids—one slumped slightly by the weight of a large burden. As he leaned forward to rise from his chair, he could still feel the throbbing pain from the back of his neck, cheek, and hand. *What now?* He folded the crimson Bible and placed it on the coffee table.

"What can I do for you boys?" Elijah said as he pushed open the screen.

"Mr. Mulligan, you gotta help us," the Thompson boy said.

"What happened?" He knelt before them. His heart stirred as he viewed the bloody dog and the red-smeared t-shirt. The boy, half bent over, tightly gripped the hound.

"He was hit by a car right down the road from here," the redheaded boy said.

"God Almighty have mercy," whispered Elijah. "Let me help you set him on the floor."

"My dad said he should be put out of his misery, but I don't want Buster to die."

"What do you want me to do, son?" Elijah looked into the boy's tear-filled eyes.

"You can ask God to heal him. I know you can," the Thompson boy said with confidence.

"What gave you that idea?"

"We saw you . . . and the cat at that place . . . I mean . . . we heard about you . . . I

mean . . ." the Thompson boy placed his hand over his mouth, and his face reddened.

"I see," Elijah said. "So you two are the leprechauns who got away from me today."

"We saw the cat," the redheaded boy said. "It was real sick, but then it got healed. When you held it up, God healed it."

"It walked right over to us like it knew we were there," the Thompson boy said.

"That was only about twenty minutes ago. I just got home," Elijah said.

"We know," the Thompson boy said. "We found Buster about five minutes ago. Can't you help him? Can't you pray for him? I don't want him to die."

"Let me get a blanket and a box. I'll be right back." Elijah headed toward the kitchen.

* * *

The orange cat, hobbling on a bandaged leg, entered the same doorway through which Mulligan passed. It mewed loudly at the boys and plodded toward them. The cat inched up to the beagle's nose and sniffed. Lifting its head, the dog cried with wheezing sighs and then licked the cat's face. The cat mewed again and rubbed its cheek against the dog's nose.

They're talking animal language," Joshua said.

"How do you know?" Billy asked.

"I can tell. Animals can read each other's minds."

"I wonder what they're saying?"

"The cat's telling Buster that he's gonna be all right. God's gonna to heal him. It said, 'God healed me, so God can heal you too,'"

Carrying a cardboard box with *Nickles Bakery* imprinted on the front, Elijah entered the room, bowed, and placed the box in front of them. A red-plaid blanket lined the inside of the box. "Let's put him in here," said Mulligan. "I know a lady who can help us, Annie Ferrier up on Treadway Road. You know Annie, don't you?"

"Yeah. I see her at church all the time," Joshua said.

"I knew I've seen you fellows in church quite a bit. Your moms are regulars, aren't they?"

"Right," Joshua said "We're in the communicant's class."

"You're the Thompson boy. I know your dad. His name's John, isn't it?"

"Yes sir. I'm Josh."

"And what's your name, son?" Mulligan asked, looking at the redheaded boy.

"Billy McGlumphy. I live right up the road near the top of the hill."

"Of course. I know your folks too." Mulligan paused as he reached over the box and under the dog to find a secure grasp. Joshua helped from the other side, and both lifted and lowered the animal onto the blanket. "Well, Josh and Billy, we'd better get this poor animal to Annie fast. If there's any hope of saving your dog, she's the one who can do it. God has blessed her with the healing touch. Her house is about a half mile up the ridge. We can take my car. It's around back." Mulligan squatted and lifted the box like an experienced weight lifter. Turning, he marched toward the kitchen, his huge frame filling the doorway as Joshua and Billy followed.

* * *

The morning shadows of pines and locusts drifted across the gravel road that rolled up and down the ridge where Scottish farmers had plowed, planted, and harvested for the last two hundred years. The few clouds above floated eastward unnoticed, patches of white fluff against a blue expanse. Over the stones and gravel rumbled Elijah's '90 Suburban, whipping up dust and scattering pebbles behind it. The thick brown clouds barely settled along the road before the white and blue vehicle slid to a stop in the driveway of the Widow Ferrier's house. Three car doors popped open at once. Elijah and the two skinny kids emerged. Elijah yanked open the back door, lifted the box, and marched toward the worn path where the smell of summer flowers met him and quickened his pulse. The boys followed.

"Annie! You home?" Elijah called. The back screen door swung open. Stepping onto the porch wearing blue sweat pants and a white blouse, the pony-tailed woman glowed before Elijah. Varicolored flowers on each side of the steps and flowing green plants surrounded her. He gazed at her, holding the box, not speaking. The two boys stepped out from behind him to see the smiling lady.

"It looks like you've found some new friends, Elijah." Her voice broke his momentary trance.

"We need help," he said. "This boy's dog just got hit by a car. Don't know if there's anything you can do or not, but I told them you'd be the one to help if there's any hope."

"Lord have mercy," she said looking into the box. "Bring that poor creature up here. Come on inside. I'll get my fixin' tools and medicines."

Elijah and the boys entered the gleam of Annie's kitchen and stood quietly. Josh and Billy glanced around the room at the many knickknacks that lined the shelves and counters. Buster lay in silence, not moving. Annie entered and went to work immediately. She carefully examined all parts of the injured dog. Her touch brought whimpers from the suffering animal, but her voice, gentle and steady, seemed to soothe the beagle and ease the pain. In minutes she was applying disinfectant and ointment to the open wound and preparing to set a broken bone in the leg. She worked quickly and efficiently.

"You're good at what you do," Elijah said.

"I can't tell how badly this animal has been damaged internally. God only knows. All we can do is hope and pray," she said.

Elijah nodded. "The Lord has the power to heal and restore if it be God's will. If not, and the animal dies, we'll just have to accept it."

Joshua shook his head. "He won't die. God'll heal him if we believe."

"Is that right?" Elijah asked, smiling. "I didn't know you were a young man of such great faith."

"Don't you believe that, Mr. Mulligan? Your cat was healed, right?" Joshua asked.

"Well, I've seen God do many powerful things, boy. I've seen the Lord move in circumstances when no one had much hope. Faith is a powerful force, but you also have to pray for God's will."

"I know God don't want Buster to die. How do you get faith, Mr. Mulligan?"

Elijah glanced at Annie. She looked up from the splint she had been securing and smiled. A flood of warmth entered his barrel chest. "Help me out, Annie. How does a feller get faith?"

"Do you believe God can heal Buster, Josh?" Annie asked.

"Yes . . . Yes . . . but . . ."

"But what, son?" Elijah asked.

"But I wish I could . . . I wish we could . . ."

"Spit it out, boy. Say what you're thinking," Elijah insisted.

"I wish we could take Buster to your praying place." After finishing the sentence he looked down at his feet.

"These two leprechauns spied on me this morning when I walked to the Healing Place," Elijah said, stifling a smile.

"We didn't mean any harm. We just wanted to see where you were going with that picnic basket," Billy said.

Annie put her hands on her hips. "Now you see, to me that's faith."

"Whadaya mean?" Elijah asked.

"To me, faith is believing and then acting. Josh here believes God can heal his dog. Not only does he believe it, he wants us to take a journey of faith with him. To me, that's what it's all about."

Elijah raised his eyebrows and blew out a big puff of air. "Well then. I'm ready to go too. We can all go up to the Healing Place and pray for Buster."

"Why do you call it the Healing Place?" Billy asked.

Elijah twisted a handful of his beard. "Because I believe healing takes place there—heart, mind, spirit, and body."

Joshua's eyes narrowed. "We saw a stone in the middle of the Healing Place. It had a cross and a name carved on it."

Elijah nodded. "That's right. I call it the Robin Stone."

Joshua shrugged and looked at Billy.

"I'm almost finished here," Annie said. "Hand me the gauze, and I'll patch up this gash on the thigh. Give me the tape too." Elijah fumbled for the tape and gauze that was nestled between some dark colored bottles and cotton balls on the table. When he extended the tape to her, their hands clasped momentarily. He felt her touch upon his fingers and dropped the tape into her palm. She quickly went to work securing the gauze over the area she had shaved, and wrapped bandages around the thigh several times to hold the gauze in place working with a surgeon's precision. She peeled the tape with quick, efficient maneuvers and applied it to the bandages, securing her work well.

"Okay, I'm finished. Now we need to put this animal into God's hands."

Elijah cradled the dog and gently positioned it back in the box. "Let's go," he said as he turned and headed for the back door. "We can drive to the path, but we'll have to walk about a mile to get to the Healing Place."

"No problem," Billy said as he and Joshua scampered around the big man, trotted out onto the porch, and skipped down the steps.

Elijah turned and eyed Annie. "I hope this dog is gonna to be all right," he said with a note of caution in his voice.

She smiled as she stepped in front of him, heading out the back door. "Where's your faith, Mr. Mulligan?"

As Elijah watched Annie cross the porch, her ponytail bobbing and hips swaying, desire surged through him. He lowered his eyes and stared at the injured dog. *Good question. Where is my faith? Got to keep my eyes on the Lord.*

The boys were already in the back seat before the adults descended the steps. "I'll hold the dog." Annie said. "You can drive."

"Yes ma'am," Elijah said.

* * *

As the four approached Elijah's natural sanctuary, his large arms ached from carrying the box over the hilly terrain, and his back hurt. He had refused to let anyone else carry the dog and kept saying, "I'm all right. It won't be long and we'll be there."

At mid morning, the full beauty of the Appalachian foothills flourished in the warmth of the August sun. The four figures moved through the light and shadows under oaks, maples, birches, chestnuts, and an occasional blue spruce or white pine. When they reached the outdoor cathedral and moved to the center, the sun's rays through the canopy of branches fell on them. Robins, sparrows, and jays chirruped near and far, orchestrating a heavenly chorus that floated down from the treetops.

Elijah lowered the box onto the Robin Stone. The four circled the box, one on each side and viewed the motionless beagle. Its eyes were half-open. The bandaged thigh and broken leg, carefully set into place with wooden slats and medical tape, shimmered in the glow of the sunbeams.

Elijah glanced from face to face. Their heads lifted to meet his eyes. "This place is very special to me. I come here every morning to meet the Lord. My faith has grown here. I believe God has blessed this place as holy ground." He paused and panned the circumference of the wooded edges. "God's Spirit overflows here. Can you feel it?"

All nodded, and the boys eyes grew wide.

"There's no doubt in my mind that if we focus upon God right now, his Spirit will fill us and overflow onto this animal. That's the way God works—through people who believe. If it be God's will to heal this dog, the Lord will do it. All we can do is open our hearts and let God's power flow."

The boys' brows tensed in sincerity at Elijah's every word.

Annie smiled.

Elijah held his hands just above the dog. "Everybody, very gently, put your hands on Buster. Annie, would you lead us in prayer?"

"I'd love to," she said.

Elijah placed his hands on the dog, and Annie, kneeling opposite him, placed hers next to his, their fingers overlapping. The boys lowered their hands and joined the two adults as Buster lifted his head slightly and opened his eyes. The light spots wavered over them as a slight wind rustled boughs of leaves above them.

Then Annie prayed, "Lord God Almighty, we bow before you in this holy place. We sense your presence in the gentle touch of the morning breeze, in the beams of light that fall upon us, in the warmth of your Spirit dwelling in us and flowing through us. Pour out your healing touch, O Lord. Take bone, muscle, fiber, and tissue and saturate all in your healing light. Bring the warmth of your presence into this animal right now." She paused.

Elijah opened his eyes slightly and noticed Annie's face lifted upward in the glow of the beams. In the strange light she seemed otherworldly, like an angel. Odd sensations of energy charged through his shoulders and arms. Her hands began to quiver

"Yes, Lord," she continued. "Move now through all of us. Flow through our souls and into this suffering animal and heal the torn flesh and broken bone."

Elijah, feeling moved by the Spirit said, "Yes, Lord! Yes, Lord! We believe you can."

Annie said, "Give this poor dog more time to share in the lives of these boys. Bless them with the joy of seeing your healing power. Give all of us faith, Lord, for we entrust Buster into your hands. We pray all these things in the good Lord's name. Amen."

The dog's head rested on the blanket, its eyes closed, its rib cage slowly rising and falling in the rhythm of peaceful sleep. Together they stood.

Annie put her arm around Joshua's shoulder. "All we can do now is trust God. Whatever happens, God knows best."

Elijah squatted and grasped the box. "We better get back." He rose with the burden securely held against his wide girth. "Your father may be angry with you. He's probably looking for you."

"I don't care," Joshua said. "I wasn't gonna let him kill my dog. He won't be mad when he sees Buster still alive and patched up. I'll tell him about God and how he's healing Buster. Maybe Dad will even come to church then."

Elijah laughed--a deep, hearty laugh that made the others smile. "Wouldn't that be something? You never know. The Lord works in wondrous ways. Your dad may just start coming to church because of a dog. Stranger things have happened."

Stepping out of the shadows of the woods onto the hillside meadow, the four figures walked into the brilliance of the late-morning sunshine along the path back to Elijah's car. Re-entering woods, crossing over gullies, up the knoll past the Emily tree and along a deer path, over some bare stony ground and back onto a trail through heavier green growth, they finally arrived at the road.

They piled into the Suburban, and Elijah drove the boys to Joshua's house.

"We can carry the dog from here," Joshua said.

"Are you sure? I can carry it up to the porch if you want," Elijah said with a twinge of discomfort in his voice.

"We might be skinny, Mr. Mulligan, but we're strong. We can do it," Billy said. The boys reached up and braced the bottom of the box, one on each side, and Elijah gradually released the full weight of it into their hands.

"Take good care of that dog now," Annie said. "And if anything happens, come and get me."

"We will," Joshua said. "Thanks for everything." Walking sideways, the boys progressed through the yard, zigzagging, reorienting their course with every few steps.

"Would you like to come over for a cup of freshly brewed iced tea, good Doctor?"

Annie leaned back and smiled. "Don't mind if I do," she answered in a sprite Scottish accent. "And, Mr. Mulligan, I must say I'm a little bit befuddled. You've never invited me into your home before."

"Well, my good lady, I have ulterior motives. I need you to lay hands on my back and pray. Whewwee it sure aches from carrying that dog for two miles."

The two climbed into the car and drove the few hundred yards up the hill to Elijah's house. As Elijah and Annie walked to the front steps, Annie placed her hand on the middle of his back and rubbed with a circular motion. "Oh, I think your back is going to be fine, you big, strong hillbilly," she said.

"You forgot 'old,'" Elijah said placing his right arm around her soft shoulders. "Big, strong and old hillbilly."

"You're only as old as you feel."

"Right now I feel about eighty."

"Well, I feel young enough for the both of us."

"Ya do, do ya?" he said as he pulled her closer to his side, hugging her tightly.

Ascending the steps, Elijah delighted in the warmth of her body against him. He couldn't keep from glancing at her profile, the slight curve of her nose and healthy complexion.

At the door Annie said, "Would you like me to carry you over the threshold?"

Elijah winked. "Carry me? You must be Supergirl or Wonder Woman."

Annie flexed her biceps. "You'd be surprised how strong I am."

Elijah laughed--that deep hearty laugh--then halted abruptly, arching backwards. "Maybe one day I'll carry you over the threshold." He pulled open the screen, thinking he shouldn't have made that last statement.

Annie blushed. "I'll believe that when I see it."

At the kitchen table, with tall glasses of homemade iced tea, the balding yet handsome man and the soft featured woman laughed and talked and teased each other for several minutes with the playful attitude of teenagers. Finally Elijah asked, "How do you like my house?"

"Well . . ." she paused thoughtfully. "You've got a very clean refrigerator."

"Why thank you. I just cleaned it last night."

"And you did a good job, but . . ."

"But what?" prodded Elijah.

"But the rest of your house needs a woman's touch."

Chapter Eleven

Byron Butler wiped the sweat from his forehead with a white handkerchief as he ascended Nixon's Run to Elijah Mulligan's house. The sun plodded across the sky, occasionally slipping behind a lonely patch of cloud, casting filtered tones across the hills and road before him. It hadn't rained for ten days. The Ohio River Valley typically experienced uncomfortable humidity in July and August, saturating the air with moisture, and then the sky would break forth with cataclysmic thunderstorms and cloud bursts. *There's a big rain coming soon. Next couple of days we're in for a whopper.* He tucked the handkerchief into the back pocket of his knee-length shorts. Crossing the wooden bridge, he looked at the small brown cottage, a one story, two-bedroom frame house similar to many of the homes in the community—humble but inviting.

Elijah was Reverend Byron Butler's sounding board for yet-to-be-preached sermons. Elijah had been chairman of the pulpit committee two years before when the Scotch Ridge Church sought a new pastor. From the first time he debuted in their pulpit, Butler had become a favorite of the congregation and especially of Elijah Mulligan. Butler, thirty-eight years old at the time, had just finished a twelve-year stretch as an associate pastor for a church in downtown Pittsburgh. After Scotch Ridge called him, he had uprooted his young family (his wife, Lila, daughter, Chrissy, and twin boys, Matthew and Mark) and headed back to the Ohio Valley convinced of the Divine calling upon his life to pastor a rural church near his hometown, Martins Ferry, Ohio.

The six foot, two inch preacher led the services with great sincerity and down-home informality. Beginning slowly and quietly, with a well-crafted introductory sentence, he would build his sermons one spiritual truth upon another knitting them together with wonderful images and illustrations. His goal was to etch the truths of God's word into the hearts of the listeners with incisive teaching and effective illustrations, ending his sermons with both an intelligent conclusion and an emotional appeal to the soul. Although he considered himself middle-of-road theologically, he preached with the fervor of a Southern Baptist.

Butler took the call to present the gospel seriously. He felt drawn to Elijah, not because the man had great theological knowledge, but rather Elijah had an uncommon love for God. The preacher didn't agree wholeheartedly with his friend's fundamentalist outlook but admired his unwavering faith. In Pittsburgh he had ministered to liberals. Atop this Appalachian hill in eastern Ohio, he preached to conservatives. Butler prided himself in his flexibility to meet the needs of a wide variety of people. To Byron, finding the spiritual truth below the surface of the text was the key to presenting the principles of faith. He had to admit it, though; visiting Elijah on Saturday afternoons to review his sermon ideas sharpened his efforts. Because of Elijah's input, the impact of the preacher's messages on the lives of the parishioners had increased.

"Brother Elijah!" Byron hollered through the screen door as he peered into the darkened front room.

"Preacherman! Come on in. I'm in the kitchen," bellowed Elijah from the back of the house. Stepping into the paneled front room, Byron glanced at the three large fish suspended on the wall. *I'll never understand what motivates a man to keep dead things hanging around. Guess I'm just not the outdoorsman type.* He could hear the sink's water splashing and Elijah washing something in the stream. The kitchen smelled of fresh vegetables; dozens of onions and tomatoes lay on the table.

"I got here just in time, didn't I?" Byron asked with his hands on his hips.

"You always show up when I'm just about done with the hard work."

"It's all about timing, my good man," he said with a big grin. "How about if I help you wash all these onions and tomatoes left here on the table, put them in that grocery bag on the counter and take them home with me to get them out of your way."

"That would be so kind of you, Byron, to help lessen the load of all these vegetables from crowding my refrigerator."

"You know what the Good Book says—we're to bear one another's burdens. And from the Old Testament: God's anointed prophet is worth his weight in home-grown vegetables."

Elijah laughed. "You better give me the scripture reference for that last one so I can look it up."

"Habakkuk 3:23."

"There you go, making up Bible verses again. The Lord probably turned your hair pre-maturely gray for misquoting scriptures so often."

"No. A strong-willed daughter and twin boys made my hair go gray years ago. Back in my twenties. But at least I got hair." Byron winked.

"Please. No bald jokes." Elijah turned off the water and grabbed a towel. He spun around and looked at the preacher. "Boy, I hope you've been working hard on tomorrow's sermon, because if I give you all those onions and tomatoes, I expect you to knock my socks off with your message. And none of that liberal garbage either. I want to hear good, solid preaching."

"That's why I'm here. I was hoping you'd write the sermon for me today."

"Write your sermon? I've been praying for you every morning. What more do you want? Should I get up and preach it for you on Sunday too?"

"Would you?" Byron smiled, but then the smile faded and his eyes filled with concern. "I appreciate your prayers, Elijah. I haven't been at peace lately. Don't know why, but I can't seem to get rolling on this one. There's something strange going on inside of me—a spiritual struggle every time I sit down to write."

"Writing a good sermon demands a spiritual struggle. Maybe the Lord has a new revelation for you."

"If he does, I can't seem to tune in on it. I've been reading, praying and meditating, but I don't have any sense of direction yet."

"Have a seat, Byron," Elijah said, walking over to the cupboard. As Byron took his usual seat, Elijah pulled down two mugs and filled them with steaming coffee.

"I could use a cup of java. Maybe the caffeine will jolt my brain cells."

He delivered the coffee to the table, wheeled and cupped his large hand over the sugar bowl on the counter and slid it across the table to within Byron's reach. Elijah seated himself and gripped the handle of his mug. "Now, where were we?"

"I'm lost on this one. The devil must be having a high ol'time. I think he put the writing whammy on me."

"I thought you didn't believe in a devil with horns and a pitchfork. Didn't you tell me that . . . how'd you put it . . . Satan was the embodiment of evil?"

"I just said you can't turn evil into a cartoon character. It's real. It gets into the fiber of our souls. There's an uneasiness in my soul, Elijah.

Maybe it's everything that's happening in the world—so much darkness. When I sit down to write, I feel like I'm preparing for a battle, but I don't know where to start."

"You're right, Byron. Spiritual warfare is occurring all around us. Every time you turn on the television or read the newspaper, you find out about the latest drive-by shooting in Steubenville or a beating or robbery in Wheeling. People everywhere are afraid to come out of their houses. The Bible says that in the last days people's hearts will grow cold because of fear and violence."

Byron nodded and gazed out the window. "Our small towns aren't excluded. Last spring a high school girl was murdered just a few miles from here. Beaten to death by a doped-up ex-boyfriend because she broke up with him. A life snuffed out for no good reason—just senseless violence."

"She was a granddaughter of a friend of mine. It was a terrible crime. Such a loss." Elijah shook his head. "I'm worried about what's happening in our communities. Even out here on Scotch Ridge we *are* vulnerable."

"You're right."

"You could never imagine the ugliness of the world touching our little community on top of these hills, but we'd be naive to think it couldn't happen here."

Byron took a big sip of coffee and stared blankly at the tabletop for a few seconds. Then his eyes met Elijah's. "I know this sounds strange, but did you ever get the feeling that the shadow of evil is falling upon us?"

Elijah bobbed his head. "Lots of times. Like I said, we're in a battle with forces we can't see. What's the topic for tomorrow's sermon?"

"The power of God's love to reach into the deepest pits of this world--pits of sin, pits of darkness, pits of depression, pits of sorrow, pits of whatever—to reach in and lift a person up and out into the light of God's kingdom."

"What Scripture are you considering?"

"Psalm 40:1-3. I know it by heart. It's one of my favorite verses:
I waited patiently for the Lord;
And He inclined to me and heard my cry.
He brought me up out of the pit of destruction, out of the miry clay;
And He set my feet upon a rock making my footsteps firm.
And He put a new song in my mouth, a song of praise to our God;
Many will see and fear, and will trust in the Lord."

As the preacher finished the quote, Elijah continued:

"How blessed is the man who has made the Lord his trust,
And has not turned to the proud, nor to those who lapse into falsehood.
Many, O Lord my God, are the wonders which Thou has done,
And Thy thoughts toward us;
There is none to compare with Thee;
If I would declare and speak of them, they would be too numerous to count.

"I know that Psalm too. It's a part of me." Elijah's eyes became distant as if he was staring into another place and time.

"You must have experienced God's power of deliverance, Elijah. You quote those verses like you've been in the deep trenches of life."

"I have been in the pit," Elijah said, staring at a picture of his wife and daughter hanging on the wall across from Byron.

"Most of us have been there at one time or another."

Elijah slowly shook his head side to side. "Most people have never descended to the depths I've known."

Byron kept silent, waiting for him to continue. He sensed Elijah was ready to share experiences he rarely mentioned to anyone. As he waited, Byron studied the big man's round face and could see his eyes watering. Elijah took a deep breath and blew it out slowly, then clasped his hands around his coffee mug.

Elijah's eyes refocused on Byron. "I . . . I . . . was working at the mill in Steubenville about eleven years ago when my wife got word of the test results. We had moved back into this area the year before. Her father had died and left us the house and some money. Emily was so happy to be back in her hometown and away from the big city. We had started going to church regularly. Pastor Caldwell was here then, and I was growing in the Lord. I came home that night, and I knew something was wrong. Her eyes were red from crying all day. She tried to be brave, but I knew she had received the worst news possible.

"She started to cry. I held her for twenty minutes while she sobbed. I didn't ask about the results. I knew already—knew deep inside. When she settled down, we sat at the kitchen table and had a cup of coffee. I told her we would fight this thing together, this breast cancer. I knew there was great hope with the advances being made in cancer research. However, we didn't realize how far along the disease had progressed.

"I never went into work the next day. I knew she needed me. I wanted to be with her. Surgery was scheduled immediately—a complete mastectomy. I told my boss that I would need a month off and somehow he worked it out. I had transferred from the Pittsburgh mill to the Steubenville plant after my father-in-law died. I liked my job; I was a foreman at the sheeting plant, but there was no way I could return to work. She began chemo treatments soon after the surgery. The months went by quickly, filled with hospitals, doctors, and treatments. I called my boss up and said I needed another month off. He said he'd see what he could do. As time went by and the doctors gave us their honest prognosis, our hopes began to fade. My daughter, Amy, drove up from North Carolina to spend the summer with us. She'd just finished her first year of teaching at a high school near Kitty Hawk. She loved to be close to the ocean.

"That was the best and the worst summer of my life. I knew every moment was precious. We spent every day together, Emily, Amy, and me. Emily was getting weaker, but we drove down to the Outer Banks and spent two weeks, staying at Amy's apartment. I remember standing on the beach one morning with my wife, looking into the big blue sky, the waves crashing in front of us, seagulls suspended above us in the sea breeze. I bent down and cupped a handful of sand. It sifted through my fingers. I tried to grab it, but the harder I squeezed the faster it drained out. I turned to Emily and embraced her and began to cry. Sometimes I cry like a baby. There I stood on that beach—a 240-pound baby sobbing in that weak woman's arms. She was always stronger than me, emotionally and spiritually. 'Everything will be all right, Elijah. You wait and see,' she said. 'God will take care of me, and God will take care of you.'

"Amy was a great encouragement to both of us. She was only twenty-two then, but she had the wisdom of an old saint. Every morning she'd greet us with a big smile, a hug, and a kiss. She'd say, 'This day is a gift from God. Let's make the most of it.' We all knew by then that Emily's time on this earth was about up barring some miracle. Amy had the strength and sense to enjoy each precious moment. The love we had for each other seemed to multiply. We tried to get a lifetime of love and sharing in three short months. By mid-August Emily had to be hospitalized. I would not leave her side. I got word from the mill that my position was going to be terminated if I didn't return. I'd worked for that company for twenty-five years—the best years of my life, rarely missing a day. They told me if I didn't come back I'd have to take an early retirement. There was no way I was going to leave her side. So I retired.

"On August 28th she woke up and took my hand. She was very weak and thin. Her eyes were sunken, but I could still see the beauty of her face despite the suffering of cancer. She said, 'Elijah come closer. I must tell you something.' I hovered over her and pressed my ear to her mouth. 'I have a message for you. The angels will come for me soon. You must be strong, no matter how dark your days become.'

"She had such a hard time getting the words out, but somehow she focused all her energy and went on: 'The Lord calls you to move forward. God will lift you up and strengthen you. Remember the good times and blessings. Don't question or blame anyone for what happens. We'll all be together again some day.'

"I said to her, 'The Lord could still heal you. We've got to believe.'

"She gripped my arm and shook her head. 'God's calling me home,' she said. Then she told me to remember the Healing Place where she took me long ago. She said, 'Go there often and draw near to the Lord. The Spirit will meet you there and light your way.' Her eyes closed. I gently kissed her lips and said, 'I love you,' and she was gone."

Elijah swallowed, blinked, and inhaled deeply. "We scheduled the funeral for two days later. If it wasn't for Amy standing next to me, holding onto my arm and supporting me at the gravesite, I don't think I could've made it through. But Amy had to go back to Kitty Hawk. The school year had begun and she couldn't miss any more days. The morning she left, two days after the funeral, I was still numb—just staring off into space. She said, 'I love you, Daddy,' and climbed into her little blue Pontiac and started the engine. I stood there feeling sorry for myself. She slowly pulled away. Then a strange sensation came over me. I had to stop her. I ran across my bridge yelling at the top of my lungs: 'Amy! Amy!' She was thirty yards down Nixon's Run, but I began to chase the car with my hands in the air screaming her name. The brake lights flashed, and the car stopped. I stepped up to it, and the door flew open. 'Daddy, are you all right?' she asked. 'Hey, kiddo,' I said. 'I forgot to tell you I love you.' She got out of the car and we hugged each other. I didn't want to let her go. 'I know you love me, Daddy,' she said. She climbed back into the car and drove away.

"That night the phone rang. I didn't want to answer it. It rang and rang. But I knew I had to answer it. It was the North Carolina State Highway Patrol. A truck driver, one of those semi-tractor-trailer trucks, had fallen asleep at the wheel, crossed over the centerline and hit my daughter's little blue Pontiac head-on. Killed her instantly."

Byron blinked, feeling tears welling up. He didn't know what to say in the face of all that relived pain.

"Byron, in one week—seven short days, I lost my job—that which gives a man his identity, his sense of worth—and I lost the two people I love the most in this world." Elijah swallowed and blinked. "I was in the deepest, darkest pit of grief that a human could experience. But I'm here to tell you that God's love can reach deeper than the deepest pit. God's light can break through the thickest darkness. The Lord reached down into that lonely black hole and cradled me in the palm of his hand. He lifted me out of the pit and made me stand on solid ground.

"As I was drowning in sorrow and hurt, the words of my wife kept coming back to me: 'Remember the Healing Place where I took you long ago. Go there often and draw near to the Lord. The Spirit will meet you there and light your way.' It's about a mile from here to the Healing Place. For the last ten years, every morning, rain or shine, sleet or snow, I go there. Byron, if the Lord has the power to lift me out of that pit, raise me up, and make me stand strong again then anyone in any pit has hope."

The preacher slowly nodded as he absorbed the impact of the story. He drew Elijah's words within him and tried to crystallize the spiritual truth. "I know that wasn't easy to share."

"You are one of a few people I've told this story to. I only talk about these things when I feel strongly led by the Lord. I hope it helps you with your sermon."

"Thank you, Elijah. Remembering those times must cause you great pain."

Elijah nodded slowly.

"I think you've given me plenty of inspiration for tomorrow's sermon."

Elijah reached over and slapped the preacher on the back. "I'll pray for you, Preacherman." A smile returned to his face.

Byron slid his chair back, and with hands on the table, raised himself to his feet. "I've got to get back to my study. I'm ready to go to work. The devil be damned."

"The real devil be damned? Or just the embodiment of evil?"

"Both," Byron said.

"Seems to me you're moving a little more to the right, Preacherman."

Byron smiled and shook his head. "Let's just say I'm still growing."

Both men walked into the front room. The late afternoon rays slanting through the window gilded the coffee table and crimson Bible with golden strokes.

"By the way," Byron said. " Are there any blackberries left out in the woods this time of year? My wife wanted to make some blackberry jam. The jar you gave us last year was delicious."

"I was planning on picking a bucket full tomorrow after church sometime. Tell your wife I'll make her another jar."

"Sorry, my good man, but Lila insisted that I get her fresh blackberries. She wants to make about three or four jars herself."

"Well, I'll pick you a bucketful then. I know all the great places in the woods where no one goes. The bushes will be overflowing this time of year."

"I tell you what, Elijah," Butler said, putting his hand to his chin. "How about if my daughter, Chrissy, accompanies you on this berry-picking expedition. She can pick a bucket for my wife if you'd be her guide."

"My pleasure," Elijah said. "She's a cute kid. We'll have a good time and bring you the tastiest blackberries this side of Belmont County."

"What time do you want her to meet you?"

"I'll walk down to your house and pick her up about three."

Byron extended his hand. "Sounds good." The two shook hands firmly.

"Have a good afternoon, Preacherman," Elijah said.

"Aren't you forgetting something?"

"What's that?"

"My bag of onions and tomatoes."

"You preachers are always thinking about food."

"You know what the Bible says: 'Food is for the stomach and stomach for food'—I Corinthians 6:13. I'm just trying to follow God's word."

Elijah patted his wide belly. "I'll have to agree with you on that one. Back in a minute." He returned with a grocery bag filled with onions and tomatoes. "You're gonna have to clean 'em yourself," he said.

"My pleasure," replied the preacher as he took the bag from Elijah. He pushed open the screen door and crossed the porch with long strides. Bounding down the steps into the sunlight, he passed into the stretching shadows of pines and maples cast by the late-afternoon sun.

Elijah watched him amble down the road. *The preacher is feeling the same thing I'm feeling. The shadow of evil has fallen upon us.*

Chapter Twelve

On Saturday evening Elijah sat on the concrete steps leading to Peter Nower's porch and waited for his friend to return from his day of swatting a golf ball around the links at Becwood near the hamlet of Mount Pleasant. Through the trees Elijah spied the golden Lexus on its descent before the turn that leveled off then rose to Peter's driveway. As the car slowed to a stop, Elijah wondered how a man could spend a whole day chasing a little white ball around. *Time's too precious to do that. What good does it do?*

Wearing a red and white Ohio State ball cap, Peter stepped out of the car and said, "You still alive? Thought I might be picking out my best black suit to attend your wake."

"That's not funny. You don't know how close I came to shaking hands with the real Grim Reaper."

Peter popped opened the trunk and pulled out a large golf bag with Looney-Tune-character head covers—Bugs Bunny, Daffy Duck, Sylvester. "A close shave with Nathan Kyler, huh?"

Elijah held up his hand with his thumb and forefinger barely apart. "One of Kyler's shotgun shells came this close to my ear."

Peter slung the strap over his shoulder and walked to where Elijah sat. "You're kidding?"

"Not a bit," Elijah said.

"What happened?"

"He's the one who wounded my cat."

"How do you know for sure?"

"I found a matching arrow on his kitchen table."

Peter straightened. "You just barged into his house and started looking for arrows?"

Elijah tilted his head and squinted one eye. "Kinda."

"Kinda? Well no wonder he shot at you."

"No. He knew I was there. He shot at me for the thrill of shooting at me."

Peter shook his head and lowered his clubs to the ground. "What did you do then?"

"The screws came off the hinges and I went a little nuts."

"That doesn't surprise me. You've always had a hard time controlling your temper."

"I know." Elijah nodded. "I confess. Anger is a weakness. But when that gun exploded, I saw red."

"Why'd he shoot?"

"I stepped forward to show him the arrow. He pulled the trigger and blew a big hole through the kitchen window. His eyes went wild then."

"I'm afraid to ask this." Peter leaned the golf bag against the house. "What happened next?"

Elijah stood up and Peter took a step back. "With his eyes glazed over in that wild stare, I reached out and yanked the gun right out of his hands."

"Nooooo."

Elijah bobbed his head.

"Man, O man, you're lucky you're alive."

"I told you I almost shook hands with the real Grim Reaper."

"He could have blown your heart right out between your shoulder blades. What did you do with the gun?"

"I hurled it into the kitchen. It went off and shot a new skylight through the ceiling."

"My God, you're crazy. You're absolutely nuts."

Elijah inhaled deeply and blew out the air, his lips blubbering. "I know. I don't feel proud about the whole shebang. Especially what I did next."

"Don't tell me you hurt the guy. Please don't say that."

Elijah stared at his feet and then looked into Peter's stunned expression. "I man-handled the boy. 'Bout put him through the wall."

"Oh no. Is he all right?"

Elijah pictured Kyler crumpled in the shadow of door, eyes wide with rage. "I don't know. I think so."

The muscles in Peter's face tensed as the pace of his words accelerated. "Man you shouldn't have done that—especially in his own house. You could get into a lot of trouble. You know what happened in your younger years."

"Don't remind me of that incident. I paid my price to society for that mistake. There's nothing I can do to turn back time and undo what I did."

"I know that," Peter said with an uncharacteristic soberness. "I'm just saying you could end up in that kind of trouble again."

"God forgave me for what I did."

"God may have forgiven you, Elijah, but I'm sure God doesn't want it to happen again."

"Sometimes you talk about God as if you believed our Creator existed," Elijah said.

"I don't know for sure if God exits or not. But I do know this: the law exists, the Belmont County Sheriff exists. You better hope they don't come knocking on your door with a warrant for your arrest for breaking and entering and physically abusing a man in his own house."

"I appreciate your concern, Peter, but I don't think he'll go to the law. That boy has too much to hide. "

"Maybe so, but consider yourself lucky if you don't end up in court over this."

Elijah raked his fingers down his jaw line through his beard. "Maybe not so lucky."

"What do you mean?"

"I'm afraid Kyler will seek his own style of revenge. I have this hunch that he's disturbed—the kind of person who attacks the innocent. He inflicts pain and agony on animals or people who can't fight back—they become like sacrifices. They pay the price for wrongs he has suffered. He tried to kill my cat."

Peter's eyes narrowed as he glanced up at Elijah. "If you're right, then no one around here is safe."

"Exactly. Torturing and killing animals can only satisfy a sick mind for so long. Sooner or later he may do something more drastic."

"Kill a person? Who?"

"Anyone in the community is at risk. But I worry most about the kids around here, especially Chrissy Butler. He's got his eye on her. There's something else." Elijah spoke slowly: "I've got this strange uneasiness—a dark feeling is in the air—something terrible is about to happen."

"Now you're getting a little spooky, Elijah." Peter hummed the Twilight Zone theme.

"O ye of little faith," Elijah said. "There's a whole lot more to this life than what you and I can see with our physical eyes and hear with our physical ears."

"I'm going to stick with what I can see and hear. If Kyler's a nutcase, we'll have to keep our eye on him. But he's flesh and blood like you and me. No more, no less."

"You don't understand what I'm saying. We're not just physical beings, Peter. We're spiritual too, and we can be influenced by the spiritual realm—whether it be good or evil. Kyler may be controlled by something beyond him—something diabolical."

"No, Elijah. I can't accept that. I'm not sure about God, but I know there's no such thing as Satan. If Kyler chooses to do something evil it's because he has the freedom to make that decision. It's all on him."

Elijah reached down and grasped Peter's shoulder. "There's a battle that we can't see between good and evil for every man's soul."

Peter stood and stepped away from Elijah. "If that's the case, then let's give God a chance to convert me right now. If God would send a cardinal over here to land on this step, I'll show up in church on Sunday. . . guaranteed."

"Don't be ridiculous," Elijah said.

"I'm not kidding. If there is a God, I don't think that's asking too much. I will become his humble servant. All I ask is that a redbird land right here on this step. Surely God could do that much for me. If I'm willing to commit my whole life to the Lord, surely God could bring a bird to this step right now."

Peter's tone irked Elijah, but he stifled the temptation to get upset at his friend's irreverence. "God will never be your genie in a bottle. Faith in God isn't a wishing game. In fact, it's the exact opposite."

"What're you talking about?"

"Faith requires a person to humble himself and yield to God, not visa versa."

Peter shrugged and reached for the railing. "Enough religious debate. I need to get something to drink. I've got a fresh pitcher of iced tea waiting. We can talk while I'm downing a pint of my home brew." Peter grabbed the golf bag, climbed the few steps, and crossed the porch to the front door. Elijah followed.

In the kitchen the lean man wrangled a couple of tall glasses and jolted open the refrigerator, pulling out a pitcher of iced tea. "How's your cat doing?" he asked as he poured their drinks.

Elijah slid out a kitchen chair and sat. "Much better. I took her out to the Healing Place and prayed for her. I believe the Lord healed her."

"I'm glad Jupiter is feeling better, but that doesn't convince me a miracle occurred. If she recovers, then the timing was right. Your prayers for your cat coincided with the time its fever broke."

"My cat's name is Juniper, Einstein," Elijah corrected. "Anyway, that's not the end of the story."

"You called me Einstein. I'll take that as a compliment," Peter said as he fingered the droplets of condensed water on the surface of the glass.

"I should have called you Darwin."

"That would also be a compliment."

"Whatever." Elijah waved his hand in Peter's direction. "Anyway, later that morning two boys showed up at my door carrying a beagle that had just been run over by a car. That dog was about dead, bleeding like a stuck hog. It should have been put out of its misery."

"Who were the boys?"

"The Thompson boy. He lives along the run not too far from here. Just below my house. And a redheaded boy named Billy McGlumphy. He lives near the top of the hill."

"Oh yeah. I see those boys around here all the time. In fact, when I was coming home from town this morning they were marching up the road toward your house carrying that dog."

"That's right. We took the dog up to Annie's. She patched it up, and then all four of us went to the Healing Place and prayed for it."

"So the dog fully recovered?"

"I don't know. It still looked very weak. It lost a lot of blood."

"Then I'm not so sure your journey with the boys was that good of an idea."

"Why's that?"

"What if the dog dies? You'll do more harm to the boys' faith than good, won't you?"

Elijah paused, placing his thumb and forefinger just below his bottom lip. His eyelids lowered momentarily. After several seconds he glanced up. "Sometimes you do what you can do, and then leave it in the Lord's hands."

"Wait and see," Peter said.

"That's right. Wait and see. There are lessons to learn from life *and* death. It wouldn't surprise me, though, if that dog recovered. I could sense God's presence and power when we prayed."

Peter lifted the pitcher. "You want some more iced tea?"

"No. I need to get home. I've got some things to do around the house before dark." Elijah pressed his hands on the table and rose to his feet. "This has been some day."

Peter poured himself another glass. "You better be careful."

"You think so?"

"You never know what a guy like Kyler might do."

"I'm not worried about what he might do to me. I do worry about the young ones, though. That guy can't be trusted. I sometimes wonder if a person can get so lost, become so evil that he completely shuts out the light of God."

"I'm surprised to hear you say that."

"I mean is there a point when you become so cruel, so wicked and devlish that an outer shell forms so that the light of God just can't penetrate—a complete cutting off of the heart to the Spirit?"

Peter took another big gulp of tea then wiped his mouth with his hand. "Thought you told me God's love can transform even killers and rapists. Have you forgotten about your own religious conversion. If I recall correctly, you were reborn after you served time in prison."

"You're right. There's no limit to God's forgiveness and grace. The only thing that prevents God from entering in and saving a soul is the person himself. Even the most evil person has hope if something happens to soften a hardened heart."

"So there's hope for young Kyler," Peter said with arms crossed, smiling with a hint of sarcasm in his eyes.

"Yes, my friend. And there's still hope for you. A man doesn't have to be evil by the world's standards to shut out the light of God."

"Ouch," Peter said. "Point well taken. You never know, Elijah, there may come a day when I see the light."

"I hope I see that day."

"If it happens, I'll let you know, but don't hold your breath."

"How would you like to see the light of the Golden Arches tomorrow?"

"Our usual Sunday evening feast at McDonald's?"

"Yes, indeed." Elijah smiled. "Only first class cuisine for us."

"Six o'clock?"

"Yessir."

"It's a date. I'll meet you there. I have some things to take care of in town tomorrow afternoon."

"Sounds good. Well . . . I'm on my way," Elijah walked to the front door.

"Tomorrow. Six P.M., Mickey D's," Peter called out as Elijah crossed the porch and descended the steps.

The large man inhaled deeply as he advanced down the sidewalk lined with decorative stones, leafy plants, and flowers. Near the end of the driveway, he paused as a cardinal chirped and flashed its red wings directly in front of him. It fluttered for a couple of moments above him and then glided toward the porch, landing on the second step. Elijah turned and watched the bird pecking at an insect. *Where were you fifteen minutes ago?*

Chapter Thirteen

The moon glowed through a thin cloud, casting a blue-gray sheen onto the porch roof. Chrissy's foot extended through the open window and planted solidly, anchoring her long leg. She dipped her head under the frame as blonde hair swung forward. Shifting her weight, she thrust herself onto the porch roof and lifted the other leg. The pale light tinted her skin blue-gray. Like a statue, she stood motionless as her eyes adjusted to the night. *What am I doing out here? I must be crazy. It's a half-mile up to Josh's house—a whole half-mile walking by myself along that road. Oh, well. I said I'd do it.* She bent slightly and stepped on down the slope toward the edge. She reached out and grasped the downspout that connected to the gutter ten feet above her and then focused her eyes just beyond the porch roof.

Like Spiderman, she descended hand over hand, feet silently scooting downward step-by-step until she released and pushed off with her feet landing squarely on the grass. *Hope those boys didn't chicken out.* She brushed her hands together and turned toward the driveway. Looking into the shadows, she hesitated and realized the journey up the run to the churchyard would be darker still because the tall trees that lined the hills on each side of the road would block the moon's light. There were no streetlights this far out in the country, only a few porch lights if left on by the residents along Nixon's Run.

Up until now Chrissy had not been afraid, but as she progressed, a breath of terror passed over her. Dark shapes became creatures and the sounds of the night intensified in the solitude of the journey. She kept looking behind her, sensing a presence but seeing no one. *It's only my imagination. There's nothing to be scared of.*

She rounded the first turn. Looking several hundred yards ahead, she could barely detect a light from the small house on the right side of the road. *Just make it to that light.* The thought gave her a goal—motivation to advance more quickly. As she neared the house the light from the front window made it easier to see. She couldn't remember who lived there, but she could see the box-shape of a small car parked on the side. A television blared from the front screen door. She stopped to listen. Tortuous screams erupted. Violent sounds of hacking and thrashing were followed by more hideous screams and gurgling. The television's light through the window shifted and altered with the action on the screen as howls and thuds continued. Her eyes widened, and the noise electrified her body. The darkness of the road ahead seemed safer than the sparse light in which she stood as the terrible sounds continued. She turned and walked as fast as she could into the blackness, leaving behind the shrieks and thuds. *Whoever it is must be watching a slasher flick.*

The next three hundred yards were the darkest stretch of road. The few houses offered no light and the silence seemed to thicken. Even the owls and crickets grew quiet, making her ears super sensitive to the few perceptible sounds. Stopping again, she could not shake off a creepy feeling that someone was following her, watching her. Opening her eyes as wide as possible, she tried to detect some form in the shadows. Turning around slowly, she inspected every variation of black and violet hues. The moon, tucked behind a tall pine tree, flickered—two chips of light breaking through the branches like eyes gazing on her. Then she heard the words, spoken deeply with wavering tones: "Are you afraid, little girl?"

"Who's there?"

"I've been watching you."

Chrissy took a step back. "Who are you?"

"I'm the one who brings death to all who sit on the Chair."

"What? Who said that?"

"I'm the ghost of Theodore MacPherson," the voice bellowed, but the deep tones broke into crackling laughter, and another hyena joined in.

"Billy and Josh, I'm gonna kill you," Chrissy growled.

The laughter became uproarious as the two boys emerged from below the pine.

"I 'bout peed my pants," she protested, setting off another explosion of laughter.

"I'm the ghost of Theodore MacPherson," Joshua groaned as he walked toward her with hands outstretched, stiffly teetering like a ghoul from a zombie movie.

"This is the night of the living dead," Billy said, following him.

"Shut up before I whack you upside the head . . . and you *will* be the living dead." Chrissy demanded.

"I've never seen you soooooo scared," Joshua said.

"I should've known it was you two goobers." She finally smiled.

"You were shakin' like a wet puppy," Billy said.

"Oh yeah. We'll see who does the most shaking," she said, "when we get to the Chair. We'll see."

Joshua pressed the button on his watch, and the little light illuminated the digital numbers. "Let's get going," he said. "It's twenty till twelve."

The final two hundred yards to the bottom of the church driveway passed quickly as the three twelve year olds laughed, skipped, and joked their way through the shadows of the moonlit night. At the bottom of the driveway, they stopped and looked to the top of the hill. The small church, a black silhouette against a blue-gray cloud, stood starkly on the highest point in Belmont County with its large cross mounted at the pinnacle of the cupola.

Chrissy had heard the older church members often talk about their Scottish ancestors. Two hundred years ago, these pioneers would gather on that same spot to pray as they endured the difficult conditions of their new land. Most of the people now living on the ridge were descendants of these hardy farmers. The church had been built in the mid 1800's after one of the settlers, Eleanor Young, left enough money to build the church on that spot where many people spent time asking God to grant mercy, healing, and help as their families struggled to make it from one season to the next.

The churchyard was filled with the graves of those hardworking people who lived and died on these Appalachian foothills. In the moonlight the several hundred stones and markers, most simple and humble, a few large and elaborate, dabbed the hillside with ashen strokes—uneven, squared, cloistered, and scattered. But the dominant stone, the Chair, sat supremely at the top just to the left of the church.

"Look. There it is," Joshua said as he pointed. "Let's go. It's a quarter 'til midnight. The curse is against anyone who sits in the Chair five minutes before midnight . . .that is, Chrissy, if you still got the guts to do it."

Chrissy put her hands on her hips. "Listen to you." Her gray sweat pants and white t-shirt reflected the full glow of the moon. "I'm the one who's gonna sit in it first. You're the ones who will chicken out."

"No way," Joshua said.

"No way," Billy echoed.

Chrissy waved her hand. "Let's go."

The 150-yard march from the bottom of the driveway to the top of the hill ascended a severe slope over gravel and tire ruts. In the winter, if it snowed more than an inch, most people walked the incline unless they owned a four-wheel drive vehicle. Three inches of snowfall required the men and boys of the church to show up two hours early and shovel the drive; by the time the service started, they would be sprawled across the pews ready to fall asleep. If it snowed more than three inches, the service would be canceled. In the summer heat, the steep climb tested even the youngsters. By the time they crested the top, Joshua and Billy breathed heavily, but Chrissy quickly recovered, being a distance runner.

"Watch where you're stepping," Joshua said as he stood on the edge of the grass where the gravestones began. "Don't trip over one of the small ones. They're hard to see."

The Chair stood thirty feet beyond the driveway below the outstretched limbs of a dead walnut tree. Joshua led the way, and Chrissy placed her hand on his shoulder as he weaved through the gravestones.

"Ow!" Billy cried.

"What's the matter?" Chrissy called behind her.

"I banged my knee on the corner of a tombstone."

"I told you to be careful," Joshua said.

"I couldn't see it. It's a black one."

Joshua and Chrissy cautiously moved forward with mini-steps. Billy hobbled behind them. The wind rattled the dead tree's branches, causing spidery shadows to dance across the stone slabs.

"I feel cold," Chrissy said.

"Why? You're wearing sweat pants," Joshua said.

"It's windy up here. This t-shirt isn't warm enough."

"Do you want to go home?" Billy asked.

Chrissy turned and faced the redhead. "Do you?"

"If you do, I will. How about you, Josh?"

"If you two want to go home, I'll go too."

Now she had them where she wanted them. Although the three were the same age, Chrissy felt years older. Sensing fear in their voices, her courage multiplied. "Aren't we gonna sit in the Chair?"

The wind gusted again, and the three gazed upward into the rattling branches of the dead tree. A cracking noise erupted, and a limb tumbled through the maze of branches, landed on a grave marker, and fractured into innumerable pieces.

"This tree is starting to break apart," Billy said. "Maybe we better go. It's too windy."

"What do you think, Chrissy?" Joshua asked. "We can sit in the Chair some other night."

"I see," Chrissy said.

"You see what?" Joshua asked.

"I see a yellow streak"

"Where?" Billy said.

Chrissy pointed at his freckled forehead. "Going right across your face, around your neck and down your back

"Really?" Billy wiped his hand over his face.

"Boo Boo, you birdbrain," chided Joshua. "She's calling you a coward."

"Whadaya mean?" Billy said.

"There's no yellow streak on me," Joshua said. "I'm no coward."

"Are you sure?" Chrissy smiled.

"Go ahead. Sit on the Chair." Joshua said.

"What time is it?" she asked.

Joshua pushed the button on the watch. "It's seven minutes till midnight."

"We've got two more minutes to wait," Chrissy said.

"W-What if one of these b-branches falls on us?" Billy sputtered as the wind whipped through the tree again clicking and creaking the limbs. "Y-You could be sitting in The C-Chair and that big branch—that thick one r-right above us—could fall on top of you."

"That's right," Chrissy said. "If you're too scared, you better not sit in it."

"I'm not scared. It's just this d-doggone tree is d-dangerous," Billy pleaded. "It could fall at any minute."

Chrissy took a deep breath and tensed her brow. "You don't have to sit on it if you don't want to. I don't care. But I didn't crawl out on my porch roof, shimmy down the drain pipe, walk a mile up that dark road, and climb this steep hill for nothing."

The two boys stared at her, eyes wide, mouths open.

"You don't have to if you don't want to, but I came here to sit on the Chair. What time is it, Josh?"

Joshua glanced at his watch and pushed the small button. The back of his hand glowed dimly in the light. He spoke slowly. "It's five minutes 'til midnight."

"Stand back," Chrissy said. She spread her arms and placed her hands on the rolled end of each scroll—the arms of the Chair—and bent her legs slightly to prepare to jump. The boys stepped back. The wind picked up again swirling leaves and twigs around them. Chrissy focused like a gymnast ready to mount the balance beam. Then another branch cracked and tumbled through the brittle branches landing on a gravestone a few feet away.

Chrissy, as if the falling branch were a starting gun, sprung upwards, and with natural agility, spun in the air releasing her hands as her rear end made a perfect landing on the scroll seat. She threw up her hands like a football official signaling a touchdown. "Yes!" At once the wind died down, and the clattering branches quieted. "Okay, you Looney Tune rejects, your turn . . . that is if you got the nerve to go through with it." She scooted forward and pushed off the seat landing in front of the boys, whose knees were now visibly shaking.

Billy looked up into the tree's limbs and then at Joshua. "Y-Y-You first."

Looking beyond the Chair down the hill, Joshua slowly raised both hands and said, "Oh no."

"What's wrong?" Chrissy asked.

"Look." He pointed to the bottom of the driveway about 150 yards away. From a porch light across Treadway Road, they could make out the shape of a figure starting the steep climb up the gravel driveway to the church. "We've got company."

"W-What're we gonna do? W-Where are we gonna hide?" Billy blubbered.

"Follow me," Chrissy said. Turning, she scanned the top of the hill to find a particular monument. "There it is. This way." She quickly crossed the top, stepping between upright slabs, chunks of box-shaped granite and marble crosses. Joshua and Billy stumbled behind her.

"Ouch!" Billy cried.

"Quiet," Chrissy whispered harshly as she arrived at the large, white stone. It was about five feet high by five feet wide. "Quick. Get behind here." The three kids plopped down and pressed their backs against the slab, trying to slow and control their breathing. A silent minute passed. Chrissy felt her heart pounding in her chest. With the beat of her heart, almost imperceptibly at first, came the sound of footsteps planted on gravel, one after another, gradually growing louder and louder, closer and closer. The three kids sat frozen against the stone. The footsteps muffled into grass and stopped not far away. Chrissy leaned forward tucking her feet beneath her as she moved into a crouching position.

"W-What are you d-doing?" Billy whispered.

"I'm gonna take a peek." Slowly she rose and turned to face the Chair. At five feet, eight inches tall, she could easily see above the large gravestone. There, six yards in front and to the left, standing before the Chair, was the black form of a person about six feet tall. From his hand came a click and a spark. After another click, a small flame appeared, and the black shape's edge became clearer as the glow of the lighter contrasted and sharpened it.

Joshua slowly stood. "What do you see?" He whispered barely loud enough for Chrissy to hear.

"He's lighting something," Chrissy answered just as quietly.

Joshua leaned to his right placing his hands on the side of the stone and looked beyond the edge. The black figure extended the lighter to the wick of a candle. Billy sat between them, shaking. Chrissy watched as the arm of the man extended the candle over the middle of the seat and tilted it so that the flame heated and melted the wax, dripping it onto the center. He turned the candle upright and stuck it into the hot wax. Chrissy observed with fearful fascination as the silhouette reached into his front shirt pocket and pulled out a folded piece of paper. He unraveled what looked to be newspaper article. Holding the paper by the top corner with thumb and forefinger of each hand, he positioned it above the flame.

"It looks like some kind of photograph from the newspaper," Chrissy whispered as the flame revealed the surface.

The man spoke, his words oozing forth slowly, low and vicious:

There will be a sacrifice soon.
The time to kill is nigh.
There will be a sacrifice soon.
The Reaper will swing his scythe.
By the light of this flame,
Her life I will claim,
As the smoke ascends to the sky.

There will be a sacrifice soon,
On this altar my pledge I've made.
There will be a sacrifice soon,
And blood will flow from the blade.
By the light of this flame,
Her life I will claim,
And the innocent lamb will die.

He then lowered the photograph into the flame and held it steadily. When the fire leapt up at his hands, he released it, dropping it onto the seat. Lifting his hands, he cackled, a maniacal sound that shook the flame with every rush of air from his lungs until both the candle and burning paper was snuffed out. As the smoke rose from the ashes, the dark figure lowered his hands into the dissipating swirls. After several seconds, he turned slowly. Chrissy and Joshua ducked behind the monument. Chrissy's heart beat so hard she wondered if the man could hear it. Several seconds passed, and the palpitations coincided with the footsteps scuffing through grass and onto gravel as the figure descended the driveway. The pounding in her chest continued long after the footsteps faded.

"Get up, Billy. We're gettin' outta here," Joshua said.

"Is he gone?" Billy squeaked.

"Yes. He's gone," Chrissy said.

Chrissy and Joshua pulled Billy to his feet.

"Who was he?" Joshua asked.

"Who knows? We couldn't see his face." Chrissy said.

"Man that was freaky," Joshua said.

Billy held out his hands. "Shewwweee, Doc. Look at this. I can't hold my hands still. They're shakin' like leaves."

"I just want to go home and crawl back into my own bed," Chrissy said. Her voice trembled noticeably.

"Me too," Billy and Joshua said together.

The three cautiously descended the hill.

Chapter Fourteen

Elijah Mulligan usually walked to church on Sunday morning. He enjoyed walking. At six feet, two inches tall, and 240 pounds, the fifty-three year old could still walk five or six miles a day without undue physical strain. The final 150 yards up the steep grade, however, provided an excellent challenge to measure his fitness. Looking forward to that morning's service, he stopped on Treadway Road and stretched his hands to the sky. The sycamores, maples, and pines bestowed the sweet doxology of robins, jays, and cardinals, filling the air with trills and warbles. "Thank you Lord," he said aloud. "Thank you for this new day."

It was warm, but at 9:45 in the morning, not yet too warm. The sky, half-filled with puffy clouds, provided a white-patched ceiling, and the dirt road, a soft, crunchy floor as he neared the bottom of the church driveway.

Hearing a vehicle approaching from behind, Elijah moved to his right to allow room for it to pass, but the engine slowed, and the car pulled up beside him. A pretty blonde on the passenger's side said, "Good morning, Mr. Mulligan."

Elijah stopped, and the white Dodge Caravan stopped. "Good morning, Mrs. Thompson. It's good to see you." Peering into the van, Elijah couldn't believe his eyes. At the wheel sat John Thompson, the steel worker and former high school football star, who rarely came to church. Elijah stepped forward, placing his hand on the car's window frame. "John Thompson, is that you?"

"It's me," the man said, smiling. "Don't be shocked."

"Are you just chauffeuring today or are you actually going to enter the doors of the church?"

"I'm comin' in," he assured Elijah. "And guess who else we brought?"

"I can see Joshua sitting back there and the little one. What's her name?"

"Chelsea," Mrs. Thompson said.

"We also brought a surprise guest," John Thompson said.

"Who could that be?" Elijah asked.

"Look, Mr. Mulligan," Joshua called out from the back seat. On the floor of the van with its bandaged leg lay the beagle, Buster.

"Great Caesar's Palace!" shouted Elijah. "He's looking good."

"God healed him," Joshua said with great conviction. At those words the dog barked loudly.

"That means *Amen* in dog talk," Elijah said and chuckled.

"I couldn't believe it when Buster's barking woke me up yesterday evening," Thompson said. "That dog was about to die when I saw him lying on the road. If Joshua hadn't hauled him up to your house, I would've put the creature out of its misery. From what I can gather, the boys believed you could heal Buster."

"Not me, John. Only God can heal."

"That's true. What I mean to say is that God worked through you."

"I'm only a servant. Joshua had the faith to bring the dog to me."

"Guess that's why I'm here today," Thompson said. "I need to learn more about the Lord's ways."

"Sometimes it takes the faith of a child," Elijah said.

"When Joshua told me that Annie doctored the dog and you all prayed for it, I was doubtful at first. Last night Buster was hobbling around and even eating. I cooked him a big deer steak I had stored away in the freezer. Anyway, I knew it was time for me to get back to church. There comes a time when a man has to get his priorities straight."

"God's gonna bless you and your family for that decision. I guarantee it," Elijah said.

The soft-featured woman put her hand on top of Elijah's hand as it rested against the window frame. "Thank you, Mr. Mulligan, for taking care of our boy and our dog. God bless you."

"God bless you too, Mrs. Thompson. Maybe old Buster could stand up and give a testimony of God's healing power in church today."

They all laughed, and Buster barked.

"Well, if Buster don't, I will," said Thompson.

"That would be wonderful," Elijah replied.

"Could we give you a ride to the top of the hill?" Thompson offered.

"Oh no. It's my challenge every Sunday morning to walk to the top of that hill. It keeps me young." He pounded his chest. "I'll be up there in a few minutes. You good people go on ahead."

The car pulled away, the horn beeping twice. *This is gonna be a good day.* As Elijah resumed his pace with a spring in his step, he sang his favorite chorus:

God is so good,
God is so good,
God is so good,
He's so good to me.

He answers prayer,
He answers prayer,
He answers prayer,
He's so good to me.

I love him so,
I love him so,
I love him so,
He's so good to me.

By the time he finished the third verse he had arrived at the bottom of the driveway. Looking up, he noticed a crowd had gathered to the left of the church around the Chair. As he mounted the gravel grade, an ominous sensation swept over him. Halfway up the driveway, the sun disappeared behind a thick cloud and the colors of the exquisite morning faded.

The tall, silver-haired preacher stood in the midst of the crowd, dressed in a white shirt and black tie. An expression of disgust marred his face, and he shook his head as he examined the Chair. The people around him reflected his concern.

"I hope the vandalism doesn't start again," Harvey Hershaw said. He was sixty-five years old, thin, bald, and long-legged. A former mayor of Martins Ferry, Harvey served as the head of the trustees of the church. He eyed Elijah, who had reached the top of the hill. "Did you see this, Elijah?"

"What's going on?" Elijah said.

"We've got devil worshipers again. They left behind their candle and ashes. Next thing you know they'll be breaking the stain glass windows and knocking over the gravestones," Hershaw said.

Elijah nodded. "I'll never understand the twisted minds of some of these delinquents. Why do they want to desecrate something that was intended to honor the dead in Christ?"

"Remember the summer of 1982?" Grace MacIntosh asked as she turned away from the Chair to face Elijah. "Four windows were smashed. They broke into the sanctuary, tipped over the pulpit and ripped apart hymnals." Grace and her husband, Archie, were seventy-five years old and had seen the destruction the church suffered at the hands of occult worshipers and vandals. "It's been a while since we had any real problems, but it looks like bad things might start again."

"I hope not," Reverend Butler said. "There must be something we can do to protect this property."

Several people agreed and talked at once, voicing their opinions and ideas.

* * *

Away from the crowd, in front of the right entrance to the redbrick church, the three twelve-year olds talked quietly. Buster looked up at them as if listening to their conversation.

"Should we tell them?" Billy asked, his red tie disheveled and his right shirttail hanging out.

"No way," Joshua said. "Are you crazy? If my mom and dad found out I was up here last night I'd be grounded for a month."

"Besides," chimed in Chrissy, "we have no idea who that man was."

"I think I know," Billy said.

"Are you thinkin' the same thing I'm thinkin', Boo Boo?" Joshua asked.

In unison they repeated the name: "Nathan Kyler."

"Who's that?" Chrissy placed her hands on her hips. She wore a yellow blouse and a knee-length, green plaid skirt.

"He's that strange man who lives down the run halfway between here and your house," Joshua said. "You've seen him before. He's always sitting on his porch reading magazines."

Chrissy gazed into the sky, trying to picture the man's face. "Oh yeah. I jog by his house on my morning runs. He's a weirdo. Why would he come up here?"

"He sacrifices animals," Billy said.

"How do you know that?"

"It's true," Joshua said. "We saw proof."

"What'd you see?"

"Behind his house, in the back yard near an old green shed we saw proof," Joshua said.

Chrissy leaned forward. "What? Tell me what you saw."

"You wouldn't believe us if we told you," Billy said.

"Try me." She tapped her foot.

Joshua knotted his brow, eyes serious. "On a big old tree behind that shed, he nailed spikes into the heads of animals he'd sacrificed."

"You're lying."

"I told you she wouldn't believe us," Billy whined.

"It's true. I swear," Joshua said.

Suddenly, Buster burst forth with two loud barks, and the kids looked down at the dog.

"See, Buster knows. Don't you, boy?" Joshua knelt and patted the dog's head.

"I won't believe it 'til I see it," Chrissy said.

"I'm not going back there to show you," Billy said. "We almost got killed."

"Now I know you're lying," Chrissy said.

"He's not lying. Kyler tried to kill us with a bow and arrow. I'll swear on a Bible."

"If I go in this church and get a Bible, you'll swear that what you just said is true?"

"I'll swear," Joshua said.

"Me too," Billy echoed.

Chrissy stuck out her palm and tapped her pointer finger against it. "On the Bible?"

"On the Bible," both said.

"I'll be back." Chrissy whirled and bounded up the steps. Flinging open the wide gray door, she disappeared and reappeared in a matter of seconds with a black, dog-eared Bible in her right hand. She double-stepped down to the boys and extended the book. They could see the gold lettering, *Holy Bible,* in the middle of the cover and *King James Version* on the right bottom corner.

"Go ahead . . . swear," she said.

The boys placed their hands on the cover and looked at each other. "We swear," they said together.

"Go on . . ." she said, not satisfied with their brief pronouncement.

"I swear I saw a tree in Nathan Kyler's back yard with animal heads nailed into it," Joshua said looking unflinchingly into Chrissy's eyes.

"And he shot an arrow at us," Billy added.

Buster barked again.

"It's r-really true," stammered Chrissy lowering the Bible.

"Heck yeah," Joshua said. "He's a real sicko."

"Why were you on his property?"

The boys looked at each other, their faces turning red.

The shadow of the tall minister fell across the trio, and his low voice startled them. "What are the Three Stooges up to now?"

"We're just talking, Daddy," Chrissy responded quickly.

"Can you believe someone was up here last night fooling around?" he father asked.

"Who do you think it was?" Chrissy spouted before Billy had a chance to confess.

"That's what I was going to ask you."

"What did they do?"

"Some kind of occult ritual. Whoever it was left behind some ashes and a candle on the seat of the Chair. We hope they don't have more dastardly deeds in mind." Her father placed his hands on his hips. "Oh, well, I've got to get inside and prepare for the service. It just makes me sick that someone would do those kinds of things on church grounds. It was probably just some kids goofing around."

The trio stood speechless.

"What happened to your dog, Joshua?"

"He got hit by a car yesterday, but God healed him."

"Really," Reverend Butler said raising his eyebrows.

"Yessir. Miss Ferrier doctored him and Mr. Mulligan and us guys prayed for him. My dad thought Buster was gonna die, but God healed him. Right, Buster?" the boy said looking down at the beagle.

The animal barked twice.

"That's an amazing story," Chrissy's father said. "I saw your dad over there talking with some of the men of the church. This is the first time he's been here in quite a while, isn't it?"

"Yessir."

"I hope to talk to him before the service starts. We need young men like your dad to become more active." The tall minister turned toward the steps but stopped and looked at his daughter. "Where'd you get that Bible, Chrissy?"

"In the church, Daddy."

"Why do you have it out here?"

"We were using it."

"Using it for what?"

"Excuse me, Reverend Butler," an elderly lady said. Wrinkled and short, she wore a little red hat that looked like an upside-down french-fry box.

"Yes, Miss Stephens," he said redirecting his attention to the woman.

"I have some concerns I want to share with you this morning. Matilda Longfellow has pneumonia, and Effie Conroy just got word that her granddaughter has the mumps. Could we go inside and talk?"

"Yes, Miss Stephens. Come on in. I've got my prayer list right here." The minister patted his breast pocket and turned to usher her into the church.

Chrissy faced her friends and said, "I think my dad knows we've been up to something."

"How do you know?" Billy asked.

"I can tell by the sound of his voice."

"Do you think we should tell him who we saw up here last night?" Joshua asked.

"We still don't know for sure who it was," Chrissy insisted.

"Yeah, but we're almost sure," Billy added. "And remember what he said: 'There will be a sacrifice soon. There will be a sacrifice soon.' What if he's planning on killing somebody?"

"You guys told me he sacrifices animals, right?"

"Right," the boys answered.

"He's probably looking for a cat or a dog . . . ." At her words, all three children looked at Buster. The dog whined with a high-pitched cry.

Joshua snapped his fingers. "Maybe that's what he does."

"Whadaya mean?" Billy asked.

"He kills animals. Runs over them, or hunts them with his arrows . . .however he can kill them. The killing is the sacrificing. Then he cuts their heads off and nails them to that tree to keep a record of it."

Joshua's words brought a sickening sensation into the core of Chrissy's belly. "Even if it was him, we can't prove it. We didn't see his face. Everyone would think we were crazy. You can't accuse someone of something unless you know for sure. Besides, all three of us would get in a lot of trouble—and if it wasn't him, we'd even get into more trouble."

"Why looky there." The big man's booming voice interrupted the three kids.

"Hi, Mr. Mulligan," they said almost together.

"I'm glad to see everyone here today . . . and you too, Buster." Elijah glanced down at the dog.

"It's good to know that there're still some young people who have their priorities straight. Not like these hoodlums who came up to the cemetery last night to goof off and dabble in the occult." Elijah pointed to the Chair where a half dozen church members still lingered.

Billy gulped and then asked, "Do they know who did it?"

"No. Probably just some high school kids who are experimenting with witchcraft," Elijah said. "Hopefully they won't do anything worse than light candles and scatter ashes."

"Yeah. I hope that's all they do too," Joshua said.

Annie Ferrier came up behind Mulligan with her forefinger pressed to her lips to signal the children to keep quiet. She reached up and tapped his left shoulder then stepped to the right. He turned to his left, seeing no one; when he turned back, she stood before him smiling, a sparkle in her eyes.

"Why, Annie Ferrier, are you playing tricks on me?"

"That wasn't me. It was the ghost of Theodore MacPherson. Right kids?" Annie winked at them.

"That's right," Chrissy said. "He tapped you on the shoulder and ran around to the back of the church."

"Well, he's probably upset that someone was up here last night messing around on his gravestone," Elijah said.

Annie stooped to get a closer look at Buster, held the dog's face in her hands, and then inspected his eyes, nose, and mouth. She continued the examination by firmly pressing against parts of the dog's stomach and leg. Buster licked at her face. "I am amazed at God's power to heal. This dog is on its way to full recovery."

"Faith is the victory," Elijah said.

"It's like Miss Ferrier told us yesterday," Joshua added. "Faith means believing and doing. We believed, and we took Buster to the Healing Place."

Elijah bent forward, planting his hands on his knees. "Never forget that experience, kids. You learned there's a power far greater than any earthly power."

Elijah gazed at Annie as she examined the dog. She stood and the blue sun dress with tiny white and yellow flower designs accented her lean yet shapely body. As the sun peeked out from behind a cloud the fullness of its light fell upon her. Elijah marveled at the youthfulness of her face and figure. She looked much younger than her forty-seven years. As she smiled and talked to the children, he could not look away. He wanted to reach out and stroke her hair. Gazing upon her, he battled something inside—an urge to yield to passion, to Eros, to the kind of love that gratifies a basic need. *How can it be wrong, Lord? She's so beautiful. I want her . . . but you have called me to . . ."*

"Elijah . . . Elijah . . . Elijah Mulligan!" a man's voice called from beyond his thoughts.

Annie placed her hand on his forearm. "Elijah, Harvey wants you."

"Oh . . . oh," Elijah said. "I'm in a daze. Must have been thinking about something."

"He's over by the Chair," she informed him.

Mulligan shook off the strong emotions that had infiltrated his soul. He blinked his eyes as he walked away from the lady and three twelve year olds. Focusing on Harvey Hershaw who had a small piece of burnt paper in his hand, Elijah strode across the gravel driveway and over to the Chair.

"Look at this." Harvey held up the paper.

"What do you got there?" Elijah asked.

"It might be a clue. We found it on the ground. It was a piece that didn't completely burn. It looks like a newspaper photograph of someone," Harvey said. Christopher Ross and James O' Donnell stood on each side of him looking at the charred remains.

Elijah took the blackened paper and inspected it. He could see what looked to be the face of a person, possibly a girl, but he couldn't tell for sure. "Who could this be?" He extended the paper, and the men lowered their heads to examine it.

Chapter Fifteen

Reverend Byron Butler placed his hands on each side of the pulpit and leaned forward. "We had a visitor last night as most of you already know." The seventy or so people who filled the sanctuary scooted to the edge of their pews. Byron scanned their faces, noting the concerned look in their eyes and tenseness of their expressions.

He stood before a large mural he had painted on the wall behind the pulpit when he began his ministry at Scotch Ridge two years before. It was a one-point perspective design of a hallway—a stone corridor supported on each side by Ionic columns painted three-dimensionally, in gray tones. The lines of the passageway led to one point located at the center of a golden cross that stood in the middle of a bright-blue rectangular opening. From behind the cross, white and yellow beams of light penetrated and illuminated the gray passageway. The painting gave the illusion of great depth, and the beams contrasted against the dark tones, providing a fitting background to present God's word.

"I don't know why a person would delve into darkness when the Lord God offers an eternity of light and life." He swallowed and his voice steadied. "Maybe it's our fault. Maybe this person lives in our community, and we haven't offered him the right hand of fellowship. Perhaps if you or I would be more sensitive to God, we would have touched this person's life by now with the power of God's love. All we can do is pray and hope. We'll pray that this person turns from the occult and sees the truth of God's kingdom."

"Amen!" exclaimed Archie MacIntosh from the next to last row.

"And we must pray that the Lord protects this property from destruction. You've seen firsthand the kind of damage done by people with sick minds and violent hands."

"Pastor, can I say something?" Christopher Ross stood up. Tall and lean with an even distribution of thick black and gray slick-backed hair, Ross was fifty-five years old and the best handyman in the congregation.

"Yes, Chris."

"Everybody keep their eyes open, especially at night. If everyone does his part, we may be able to stop any trouble before it happens. There hasn't been any major vandalism up here for twelve years—mainly because we've been keeping a close eye on things."

Colin Dutton stood up wearing a red flannel shirt and jeans. He worked at Barkcamp State Park in the western part of Belmont County as a ranger. "I'll come up here on a regular basis at night with my rifle and check things out, Pastor," he said sternly. Colin was a tall, strong man in his mid-twenties with a full reddish beard and long brown hair. Being an avid hunter, he handled a gun with great skill.

"No." The preacher spoke with authority. "Don't bring any guns up here. Someone might accidentally get hurt."

"Or intentionally," Colin responded.

Ernest Miller, a short, heavy-set dairy farmer, spoke up. "Pastor Butler, sometimes you gotta cut the head off of the snake before it bites you."

"Just don't cut your own toe off first, Ernie, before you get to the snake," Byron said. The congregation laughed and turned to look at Mr. Miller whose big smile eased the tension in the sanctuary.

When the laughter quieted, the preacher opened his bulletin and said, "Let's come before the Lord and worship him. Our Call to Worship this morning is from the book of Romans, chapter eight, verse 39: *For I am convinced that neither death nor life, neither angels nor demons, neither the present nor the future, nor any power, neither height nor depth, nor anything else in all creation will be able to separate us from the love of God that is in Christ Jesus our Lord.*"

The pianist struck the introductory chords, and hymnals were pulled from their slots and pages shuffled to the selection, "The Solid Rock." The congregation sang loudly as if they wanted the song to sound forth from the top of that hill down through the valley and somehow reach the ears of the culprit who dared trespass on hallowed ground to perform such an unholy ritual.

* * *

Elijah sat in his usual spot on the right side of the church, fifth row back. Annie occupied her usual spot—left side, forth row. The big man tried to focus on the order of service: the Prayer of Confession, the Declaration of Pardon, the Apostle's Creed, the Responsive Reading, the Offering and Offertory Prayers, and the Doxology. But he could not erase the strong memories of the time spent with Annie that week from his mind—the words they shared at her house and his house, the teasing and flirting, the laughing, the prayers for the cat and the dog. He could remember every touch, every soft unintended brushing against her. Looking up, Elijah realized the window above Annie framed the image of the Good Shepherd, holding a lost sheep. The eyes of the Shepherd burned into him, and a flood of shame poured over him. He turned, lowering his head and closing his eyes. *Forgive me, Lord, for not focusing upon you.*

* * *

The three adolescents sat in the pew in front of Lila Butler, Chrissy in the middle, Billy hanging on to the pew's right armrest and Joshua on the left bent over, elbows on his knees, his hands cupped around his chin. The six-year-old twin boys, Matthew and Mark, both with short sandy hair brushed straight up like an athlete from the 50's, sat on each side of Mrs. Butler.

The pastor's wife, a tall, quiet woman with beautiful green eyes and thick, shoulder-length, auburn hair, liked to keep her children within arm's reach. She was a disciplinarian. Most people would think that the twin boys would be hard to handle, but her greatest challenge was raising Christine. From birth this child was strong willed. As she grew she exhibited exuberance and daring that at times frightened her mother. "That girl is going to get killed one of these days," she would tell her husband. "Falling out of trees, wrecking on the bike, jumping off porches with open umbrellas—either she's going get killed, or I'm going to end up in the nut house."

But the anxiety the girl caused was balanced by the great pride she inspired in her mother. Christine wanted to be the best—the best student, the best runner, the best singer, the best artist—best at whatever she attempted. She loved to compete. Academically and athletically she pushed herself to the limit. The star on the junior high track team, she had broken all of the distance records. In almost every race she ran last season, she had taken the lead early and had held it to the tape.

This morning, however, Lila Butler sensed something uncharacteristic in her daughter's behavior. By now she would have usually had to warn the Three Stooges at least two or three times to behave, but Chrissy, Joshua, and Billy sat soberly as if they were actually paying attention to the proceedings.

* * *

"We have a special time of sharing this morning," Reverend Butler announced. "Before we get to the scriptures and the sermon, I would like to give a man, whom most of you know, a chance to share with you how God has touched his life this week. Now his wife, Sherry, attends here regularly, and his son, Joshua, is a member of the communicant's class, but John Thompson rarely enters these doors. However, this morning he tells me that things are about to change. John, please stand up and share with us."

The tall, broad shouldered man arose. He was handsome and still maintained the physique of his high school glory days as an all-state wide receiver. Clearing his throat, he looked down and then up again. "I know most of you ain't used to seein' me here. I've always had the idea that church was for women and children. I've often told my wife that God was goin' to have to show me a miracle to get me to come to church regularly. Well, yesterday the Lord did just that. More importantly, God opened my eyes to the truth about my lack of responsibility at home and church."

He paused and looked around the congregation. All eyes were on him; even the toddlers sat quietly as the emotion of the man's voice permeated the air. "Yesterday, Josh's dog, Buster, got run over by a car. That dog should have died. Its back end was injured, and blood poured out of the wound. I went to get my gun to put the dog out of its misery. When I got back, the dog and the boys were gone. Course, I was madder than hell . . . oops. Sorry. That just slipped out." Thompson cringed momentarily but then continued: " I'd just worked all night long and wasn't in a good mood, so I stomped back into the house, yelled at my wife, slammed the bedroom door and crawled back into bed. Josh was sure gonna get a whuppin' when he got home. Late that afternoon, I guess it was almost six o'clock, barkin' woke me up. I walked out onto the back porch and this is what I saw—"

John Thompson stepped out from the pew and walked to the entrance door of the church. He opened the door and whistled. "Come here, Buster," he called. He disappeared momentarily and re-entered with the dog limping in front of him. The dog stopped halfway down the aisle, sat down, looked around and barked twice. The congregation broke into applause and laughter with scattered "Amen"s and "Praise the Lord"s.

"I couldn't believe my eyes," Thompson continued once the room hushed again. "This dog should have died. But he's alive. I want to thank Annie Ferrier and Elijah Mulligan for caring about a young boy and his dog. Annie doctored the dog and patched him up. Elijah carried Buster to a special place of prayer in the woods. These two grownups showed what faith was all about. They set an example for Joshua and Billy. And God Almighty. . . God looked down and saw their faith and touched the animal. When I walked out on that porch yesterday evening . . ." Thompson's words slowed, and his strong clear voice began to quaver slightly. "When I walked out on that back porch yesterday evening . . . and saw that dog alive and recovering . . .God touched my life too."

Around the sanctuary many women pulled tissues from their purses and wiped tears from their cheeks. Even several men reached and touched the corner of their eyes.

"God touched my life," Thompson said again, his voice reflecting the emotional swelling around him. "And I realized it was me who needed to experience the power of God. I needed to get my priorities straight. Because I'd been living a selfish life, I'd neglected what needed to be done. Bringin' home a paycheck wasn't enough. My wife held everything else together without much help from me. Well . . . I was wrong. I was a failure as a daddy, a husband, and as the spiritual leader of my family, but not any more. Things are gonna change. If the Lord can touch a dog with his power, God can touch me. Sometimes it takes the faith of a child for an adult to see the light. You're gonna see me in church on a regular basis. I guarantee it. I'm dedicating myself to be a better man—a better husband to my wife, a better father to my children, and I hope a better servant to the Lord."

The congregation applauded loudly. Reverend Butler shook his head affirmatively as the response continued from the pews. Thompson looked around at the faces in the congregation and said, "Thank you," several times although his words were hard to hear because of the applause. When the sanctuary quieted, Thompson said, "I thank you, and

Buster thanks you." He tugged on the dog's chain and walked it toward the door. "Come on Buster, back outside."

"Let the dog stay," the red-bearded Colin Dutton called out. Several others seconded the man's motion.

"Yes," Reverend Butler said. Everyone turned to look at the preacher. The beams of light from the mural behind him shone out in all directions, and the glowing cross in the wall painting seemed suspended above him. "John's testimony and this animal is an example for all of us. Let the dog stay with us as a reminder of God's power." Thompson sat down next to his wife, and Buster curled up in the middle of the aisle and placed his head on his paws.

"Brothers and Sisters, God is powerful!" Byron Butler spoke with great fervor. He sensed the congregation had been deeply moved by Thompson's testimony and drew energy from the charged atmosphere.

"Listen to God's word," he said as he flipped open his Bible to the book-marked page. "I am reading from Psalm 40.

I waited patiently for the Lord;
And He inclined to me and heard my cry.
He brought me up out of the pit of destruction, out of the miry clay;
And He set my feet upon a rock making my footsteps firm.
And He put a new song in my mouth, a song of praise to our God"

He pressed his hands flat onto the pages before him and looked up with great intensity. "God is powerful." He paused to allow the words to sink in. "The writer of this Psalm, David, knew what the pits of life were all about. David had been a hunted man. King Saul wanted him eliminated. David was a threat to the King's rule so Saul ordered David to be hunted down and executed. David knew what the pit of danger and fear was all about. For many months he looked over his shoulder, not knowing when an enemy would appear and attempt to murder him. There are pits of fear, anxiety, and danger.

"We know that David went on to become Judah's greatest king. But there were more pits in store for him. He was out on a balcony one day and looked down to see a beautiful woman, naked, bathing below him. Her name was Bathsheba. He could not control his passion and obsession for this woman. He turned away from God and traded the precious pearls of God's Kingdom for the temporary pleasures of the flesh. Before long he found himself in the deep pit of lust. He chose to please himself rather than the Spirit, and that choice led to adultery and eventually murder. Bathsheba's husband, Uriah, a faithful soldier, was ordered by David to go to the front lines where he was killed in battle. My friends, there are deep, deep, pits of lust and immorality.

"David had a son by the name of Absalom. He loved this son, but through a series of circumstances, Absalom rebelled against David and formed an army that opposed his own father's kingdom. You think you may have a rebellious child, but you still love that child. David's son, Absalom, was in total rebellion, but David still loved him. His heart ached because of Absalom's insurrection. In a great battle one of David's commanders killed Absalom. Upon hearing about his son's death, David fell into a deep pit of sorrow, loss, and depression. 'O Absalom, Absalom, Absalom,' he said. 'If only it was me who died instead of my son Absalom.' My Brothers and Sisters, there are deep pits of sorrow, loss, regret, and depression.

"What is a pit? My dictionary says, 'an abyss so deep that one cannot return from it, as the grave, or hell.'" Reverend Butler leaned forward, conscious of his increasing volume. "There are pits that you and I can fall into that are so deep, so dark, that we can't by our own power escape! The walls are too steep! The hole is too deep! The darkness is too thick!" He paused to allow the drama of the words to sink in. "But friends, I am here to tell you this morning these three words: GOD IS POWERFUL!" His voice exploded and resounded off of the back wall.

"You heard John Thompson's testimony a few minutes ago. All that John said could be summed up in three words: GOD IS POWERFUL!" his voice thundered again. "You heard me read Psalm 40—David's own words. David found himself throughout his life in deep, dark pits. What did he say? He said this: *I waited patiently for the Lord; He turned to me and heard my cry. He lifted me out of the slimy pit, out of the mud and mire.* I am here to proclaim to you this morning that God is all-powerful. There is no pit too deep. There is no fear too strong. There is no sorrow too dispiriting. There is no loss too devastating. There is no evil too overwhelming that God cannot . . ." He extended his hand over the pulpit and with a scooping gesture continued ". . . reach down into that pit and by his power lift you up out of the muck and the mire, and set your feet on solid ground.

"You may be in the grips of tremendous worry and anxiety. You may be continually looking over your shoulder thinking calamity is about to strike. You may wake up in the morning not even wanting to face the day with its stress and confusion and trials. I'm telling you right now that God can lift you out of that pit and put you on solid ground.

"You may have suffered great loss. You may have lost your job . . . a loved one . . .a friend. You may have suffered some kind of personal illness or injury that has taken away some capacity that you once had. You may go through your day in a deep pit of sorrow or depression. I'm here to tell you this morning that God can lift you out of that pit and place you on solid ground.

"I don't care if you have fallen into the deepest pit of sin, or if you have turned away from God to serve the devil himself. We've seen the kind of handiwork of someone who is in the deep pit of the occult out there on that stone chair in the churchyard. Is there a sinner too vile that God cannot save? Is there a person too wicked and immoral that God cannot reach? Is there a man who has gone so deeply into darkness that God's hands are tied?"

No one in the church at that moment expected an interruption as Reverend Butler built to the climax of his message, but in the short pause after the preacher's question, the entrance door of the church opened, and the shape of a man stood against the oblique rectangle of light that could not penetrate his form. All heads turned away from Butler to look at the lean figure. He stood in the uncomfortable silence. With each passing moment the atmosphere thickened with uncertainty. An eerie uneasiness rippled through the congregation. Buster growled. Looking at the man with teeth bared, the dog stumbled to his feet and barked.

"Lay down," John Thompson scolded. "Lay down and be quiet." The dog sat back down but remained vigilant.

"Welcome," Reverend Butler said. "Please come in and sit down." As the preacher smiled and extended the church's hospitality from the pulpit, the iciness that had chilled the congregation dissipated, and many of the back-lookers smiled and nodded at the man as he side-stepped into the last pew, an empty pew on the left side of the church, and sat down.

"Glad you could join us this morning," Butler said as he fumbled with the few notes in front of him trying to re-gather his thoughts and finish his sermon.

* * *

"That's him," whispered Joshua sliding down in his pew. "That's Kyler."

"Do you think he saw us?" Billy asked.

"Be quiet, you three," chastised Lila Butler from behind. "Or I'll knock your heads together."

* * *

Elijah could not believe his eyes. He stared angrily at the man in the back left corner of the church. When Kyler noticed Elijah's glare, he smiled menacingly and nodded his head at the big man. Elijah turned and faced the front. *He's up to something. I don't like this at all.*

Clearing his throat, Reverend Butler began again. "Are you in a pit of deep darkness right now? I've got good news for you this morning. GOD IS POWERFUL!!! There is no pit too deep that God cannot reach you. There is no pit too dark that God cannot shine his light. Look up! God is there. Look down! God is there. Look all around you. GOD IS HERE." The preacher spread his arms. "Trust the Lord today. He will deliver you from that pit. Amen."

Chapter Sixteen

The covered dish dinner preparations began immediately after the benediction. Lila Butler led a procession of ladies toward the front of the church and then turned left through the doorway that led to the fellowship room. The women would arrange the food on a long white-paper-covered table within ten minutes. The men and children hung out in the sanctuary until Lila Butler gave the okay.

As the tall preacher meandered up the aisle shaking hands and greeting the men and children left behind by the cover-dish exodus, Elijah turned to see if Kyler still skulked in the back of the church. He hoped the odd man might be the first one out the door like on Easter morning. To his dismay, Kyler stood, arms crossed in the last pew on the left glaring at everyone in front of him.

"Brother Elijah!"

The greeting startled the big man, and he turned to see Byron's hand extended before him. He reached out and grasped it firmly saying, "Good job today, Preacherman."

"Thank you," Byron said. "I could sense the presence of the Spirit this morning. The people's hearts were ready to hear the word." Seeing his daughter on the far right side of the sanctuary, Byron called out, "Chrissy! Hey, Stilts! Come over here!"

The tall blonde pivoted away from the two boys with whom she was chatting and gazed at her father.

"Come over here," he repeated as he motioned to her.

She said something to Joshua and Billy and then walked down the aisle. As she passed by the stained-glass window, colored light rays fell on her, creating a translucent vision as if the girl momentarily became a spiritual being. Elijah glanced back at Kyler. His dark eyes followed

Chrissy as she walked to the front of the church. Elijah's heart quickened. Kyler would not look away. Struggling to control his agitation, Elijah turned back to Byron as Chrissy stepped up to them with a glowing smile.

"Hi, Mr. Mulligan."

"Good morning, young lady. And if you want to make me feel younger, call me Elijah. How are ya doing today?"

"Just fine, Elijah." Chrissy winked. "How 'bout you?"

" If you're fine, then I'm dandy."

"Fine and Dandy. That's a good combination," Byron chuckled.

"Your daddy informed me that your momma wants some blackberries."

"Oh yeah. She wants me to pick a big bucket full today. Are you gonna take me berry picking?"

"Sure am." Elijah nodded. "We'll get plenty of ripe ones today."

"Elijah knows where all the good blackberry patches are. Now you might have to walk a couple miles," Byron said.

"That's no problem. I could walk ten miles and not even get tired."

"I don't think you'll have to walk that far, will she, Elijah? . . . Elijah?"

Elijah's attention had shifted to the back of the church. With arms crossed, Kyler stood by himself, eyes fixed on Chrissy. Upon hearing his name, Elijah snapped back into the conversation. "I'm sorry. Yes. That's right. Only a couple of miles. Four at the most."

"She says she can go ten if she has to."

Chrissy put her hands on her hips and stuck out her chest. "I'm in good shape 'cause I run every morning rain or shine. Last Wednesday I won the Betty Zane Days 5K road race in Martins Ferry."

Elijah nodded but couldn't keep from glancing at Kyler again. The dark-haired man seemed plastered to that back wall. *Why won't he leave?* Kyler stared in their direction, arms crossed. When Elijah turned back to Byron and Chrissy, he noticed they were eying Kyler too.

"I forgot about the young man who came in late," Byron said. "Excuse me a minute. I need to go back and extend the right hand of fellowship to him."

As the preacher navigated his way through the few people who stood talking in the aisle, Elijah kept shooting watchful glances in Kyler's direction. *Kyler's going to lay it on thick now. Make the preacher think he's actually here to seek enlightenment.*

"I'm looking forward to picking berries today," Chrissy said.

Her voice snapped Elijah back to their conversation. With a quick shake of his head he tried to vanquish Kyler from his mind so he could focus on Chrissy. "We'll have a good time this afternoon. Do you like to take hikes into the woods?"

"Oh yeah," she said, smiling. "I love to explore the outdoors."

"We'll definitely wander through God's creation. I'll show you where to find the best blackberry bushes in the county."

"Great."

Her eyes gleamed, and for a moment she reminded him of his daughter, Amy. A quick surge of warmth went through him followed by the aching of loss. *Kyler better not touch a hair on this gal's head.* He quickly glanced to see the preacher shaking Kyler's hand. Kyler's expression transformed—the features softened and a smile appeared. The preacher's words were barely audible: "Welcome to our church, I'm Byron Butler."

* * *

Kyler's handshake felt cold, but he spoke very pleasantly, "I'm sorry I interrupted your sermon. I'd forgotten your service started so early."

"Now you're Mr. Kyler, right?" Byron asked.

"Right. Nathan Kyler."

Byron studied his face. He looked young, probably mid-twenties, but there was a hardness about his features. "You live down Nixon's Run not far—about halfway between here and my house."

"Right. My grandmother used to attend here years ago, before she became sick. I live in her old house. She died 'bout a year ago."

"I didn't know your grandmother. I started preaching here two years ago. When she died, no one requested a funeral service."

Kyler shrugged. "She was in a nursing home for many years with Alzheimer's disease. Most people forgot about her. She's buried on the south side of the graveyard."

"I'm sorry I never got to know her."

"She used to bring me here when I was a kid. Every Easter sunrise service she'd make sure I was in church with her."

Even though he sensed a strangeness about the man, Byron didn't want to allow that impression to quench the Spirit. Perhaps Nathan Kyler had come to a crossroads in life. "Didn't you attend our sunrise service this past year?"

"Yeah," Kyler said shifting his gaze to his feet.

"Now I remember." Byron rested his hand thoughtfully on his chin. "I wasn't quite sure who you were. I wanted to meet you, but you went out the door so quickly, I didn't get a chance."

"Guess I don't feel comfortable around people I don't know yet. I enjoyed the service. Just felt kinda out of place," Kyler said.

"I'm curious. What made you decide to come today?"

Kyler stood straight and nodded toward the front of the church. "One of your members visited me Friday morning and invited me."

"Who was that?"

"Elijah Mulligan." Kyler pointed in the direction of the big man and Chrissy.

"Oh . . . you know Elijah then. Well great. Let's go over and talk to them. I'll introduce you to my daughter, Chrissy," Byron took Kyler by the elbow and ushered him down the aisle.

* * *

Chrissy enjoyed talking to Elijah, especially after discovering his love for athletics. "What was your event in track?"

"I threw the shot and discus," Elijah said. "Set the school record in the shot back in . . ."

From the corner of her eye, Chrissy noticed two figures approaching—one of them her father and the other that Kyler guy. She noticed Elijah immediately clammed up when he saw the young man. Her father smiled with his hand on the Kyler's arm. She met Kyler's gaze, and it sent a shiver through her.

"Chrissy," her father announced. "I want you to meet Nathan Kyler. He's a neighbor of ours. Lives about a quarter mile up the road from us."

Chrissy made a quick study of the man's face, his eyes, dark and intent upon her, his mouth half-grinning. She said, "Hi," and lowered her head.

"Hello there, young lady." Kyler's voiced oozed out coolly. "You sure have a pretty daughter, Reverend."

"Why thank you, Nathan," her father said. "We are very proud of her."

"You'll have to stop by and visit me sometime." He uttered the words slowly, his voice metallic.

Chrissy looked up into the dark eyes again. They appeared as black pools; she stepped back, sensing a danger in being too close as if it were possible to slip and slide helplessly into the bleakness of his gaze.

"We'll have to stop up and visit you in the near future," assured her father. "We appreciate the invitation." Her father patted him on the shoulder, and Kyler's grin widened. "Elijah, Nathan tells me you've already made a visit to his house and invited him to come to church today."

Elijah cleared his throat, his broad face wrinkling around the eyes and mouth with an uncharacteristic tightness. "I made two visits to Mr. Kyler's house on Friday. I'm very surprised to see him here today."

"Oh, you convinced me to come." Kyler said, and his smirk turned into a rigid line.

"If I remember correctly, I told you not to come for the wrong reasons," Elijah said, meeting the young man's icy stare.

Chrissy sensed Elijah's anger toward the guy and wanted to step out of the cold chill between them.

Her father said, "Two visits in one day. You're becoming quite the evangelist, Elijah."

Elijah's eyes seemed to fill with fire. "So, Mr. Kyler, I take it your attendance today means you're here for all the right reasons."

"Let me put it this way," Kyler said. "I think I'm ready to take a big step in my life." Kyler's creepy grin returned. His gaze shifted from Elijah's glower to Chrissy. She redirected her eyes to the floor, not wanting to look into the black pools.

"That's wonderful," her father said. "The Lord loves you, Nathan. Don't be afraid to take that step."

Kyler faced the preacher. "Why thank you for the encouragement, Reverend. I'm not quite ready yet, but hopefully in the near future I will be."

"We'll pray for you," her father said. "It's not an easy decision for a person to make, but believe me, it's the most important decision of your life."

"I know what you mean, Reverend. It's not easy. Sometimes important things involve sacrifice, don't they?"

"That's right," her father said with surprise. "There's a great sacrifice involved. You are beginning to understand."

"Well, Reverend, I know I didn't get to hear all of your sermon, but what I did hear made a lot of sense."

Elijah took a deep breath, bit his lip, and blew air out of the side of his mouth. His face reddened. "You say you're almost ready to take the big step. Let me assure you, Mr. Kyler, I will be near. When you get ready to take that step, I will be right there. You can count on me. I will keep my eye on you."

"We're always here to help you, Nathan," her father chipped in. "If the Lord is knocking at your heart's door, don't turn God away."

"Okay, everybody. We're ready to eat!" Her mother's voice rang out through the sanctuary as she stood in the doorway leading to the fellowship room. The hungry men and children headed toward the front of the church filtering through the pews and lodging at the doorway.

"You must join us for lunch, Nathan." Byron warmly gestured toward the fellowship room.

"I would, but . . . I left my oven on at home. I'm cooking a rabbit I killed yesterday. I've got to get back before it's overdone. 'Preciate the offer, though."

"I'll stop by your house and visit you sometime this week," Byron said as the young man turned to go.

Kyler stopped momentarily. "That would be fine. Bring your daughter with you if . . . if she can come." He grinned, and to Chrissy it seemed that his eyes widened to swallow her. She stepped closer to Elijah. When she looked up again, Kyler's dark form swept toward the exit.

"You never told me you stopped by Nathan's house," her father said, eying Elijah.

Elijah watched Kyler go out the door, then shifted his eyes to her father. "I tried to put that visit out of my mind, Byron. It wasn't very pleasant. I was surprised . . . almost shocked to see him here today."

"Well, you must have had some kind of impact on him. He came didn't he?"

"That's what I'm afraid of."

"I'm not sure I understand."

"He was here this morning because of me."

Her father put his hands on his waist. "You're not making sense."

"Byron! Byron!" her mother called to her father. "We need you in here to say the blessing."

"I'll talk to you later about this," her father said. "Maybe I'll stop up tomorrow and see you." He headed toward the fellowship room and squeezed through the crowd in the doorway.

Elijah glanced down at Chrissy. Reaching out and putting his large hand on her shoulder, he said, "We better get in line and get something to eat. We're gonna need our energy for all the walkin' and pickin' we're gonna do today."

Chrissy smiled at the bearded man. "Don't worry about me, Elijah. I'll eat plenty." She led the way to the end of the line, but halfway there she stopped and looked up at him. "You know that Kyler guy?"

"What about him?"

"He gives me the creeps."

Elijah nodded. "Me too."

Chapter Seventeen

By 3:00 P.M. the day had become gray. The sun hid behind ashen masses of clouds, and the few blue spaces shrank in the atmospheric blur. The walk to the Butlers' home was about a half mile. When Elijah passed Kyler's house, he saw the white Escort, but the dark-eyed man was not in sight. *I'm glad he's not on the porch. That smart-aleck smile sickens me.* Elijah concentrated on the road ahead. *At least I don't have to step over that headless raccoon.* He picked up his pace to escape that section of the road.

Clusters of multi-colored flowers bordered the front of the preacher's yard. To Elijah they presented a welcoming entrance to the home, even though the thickening clouds had dulled their brilliance. Last spring Lila Butler had planted geraniums, pansies, daisies, marigolds, sword lilies, and dahlias. Now their full bloom splashed the yard with the textures of a Van Gogh landscape. Elijah breathed deeply as if the intake of the scented air could renew within him a joy for life that had faded with the sun's disappearance.

He stood at the large paneled door of the brick home, built in the 1860's by the forefathers who had founded the Scotch Ridge Church. When the door opened, the tall girl's face and form flashed in his memory an image from years ago of his own daughter. *Amy?* The name echoed in his mind. He stepped back and blinked his eyes.

"I'm ready, Mr. Mulligan," Chrissy said as she stepped into the filtered afternoon light.

"Remember, I want you to call me Elijah."

Chrissy slapped her forehead. "Right. I forgot. Calling you Elijah makes you feel younger. Right?"

"That's right. Anything that makes me feel younger helps—especially on long walks like this."

"Come on now, Elijah. Four miles isn't that far." She held a yellow plastic pail that had once contained a large amount of peanut butter. Her yellow t-shirt and bib overall shorts gave her a countrified appearance, but her long legs and Nike running shoes revealed her athletic prowess. The glow of Chrissy's face and natural enthusiasm stirred an energy reserve within Elijah. He thought of the walks he had taken with his daughter to the elm tree at Thanksgiving, of the spunk and contagious laughter of the child he so loved and missed. Suddenly he looked forward to the afternoon's hike.

"Well then," he said with newfound optimism, "What're we waiting for?" Elijah and Chrissy headed out the driveway into the aroma of the flowers and then turned up the road to walk the half-mile to the top of the hill where the path started.

"My bucket's bigger than your bucket," Elijah said. "Bet I get more blackberries than you."

"No way," Chrissy said. "I plan on eatin' half the ones I pick. I looooove blackberries."

"You're gonna eat a half gallon of blackberries?"

"That's right."

"I might have to carry you home."

"You'd be surprised how much I can eat."

"No, I wouldn't. I've seen you in action. How many times did you go back for dessert today at church?"

Chrissy laughed. "I lost count."

"And you probably never gain any weight."

"Nope. I run it off. The more I run, the more I eat."

"Where I'm taking you, there'll be more ripe blackberries than you could ever eat. It's the best patch in eastern Ohio, and nobody knows about it but me."

Elijah had worried that he might have difficulty keeping up a conversation with a junior high kid for more than a couple of minutes. It had been so long since he had spent time with someone Chrissy's age, but as they advanced up the road, he sensed a kindred spirit with the girl. Words flowed back and forth easily, forming a connection between the two. Despite their age difference, he enjoyed the interaction. But their words staggered and halted when Elijah noticed a dark figure on the steps of Kyler's porch.

As they approached the house in silence, a shadow of a crow glided across their path. The bird cawed and alighted in the yard near an old tire. Smoking a cigarette and holding a magazine in his lap, Kyler sat on the top step. He wore a camouflage t-shirt and dark green pants. Next to him, a red-handled knife had been jammed into the step. When the crow shrieked again, Kyler looked up from his magazine, picked up a dead mouse by the tail, and tossed it to the bird.

Elijah tried to keep pace with Chrissy in order to block Kyler's view of the girl. He glared at the young man. Kyler met his gaze, smiled that sickening smile, and nodded. Gritting his teeth, Elijah shifted his eyes to the road ahead. *Keep your mouth shut. Don't say anything. Just keep walking. Maybe he'll ignore us.*

"Hey, Chrissy," Kyler called. The crow sprung into the air, violently flapping. Elijah ducked when the bird darted over their heads with the mouse in its beak. "Chrissy," came the man's voice again followed by a vicious laugh. Chrissy quickened her already fast pace and Elijah kept stride. "Remember me, Chrissy! We met at church today," Kyler yelled, but the girl ignored him. Elijah noticed an odd look on her face—anxiety bordering on panic.

* * *

Chrissy now realized Kyler's house was the same one she had passed the night before. Remembering the eerie glow of the television screen through the front window and the tortuous sounds that blared from the screen door, she sensed needles of fear prickling her back and neck. Once she and Elijah had advanced beyond where they could no longer hear him, their pace slowed and the tension eased. But an uneasy quiver still remained in the pit of her stomach.

"He's weird," she said.

"I know what you mean," Elijah agreed.

"Billy and Josh think he's the one who left the candle and ashes on the Chair last night."

"Could be," Elijah said. "What makes them think so?"

"They told me he sacrifices animals. I don't know if *that's* true, but that's what they told me."

"I wouldn't put it past him."

"Do you think the Chair really has a curse on it?" She looked into Elijah's wide, bearded face.

"No. That's foolishness. There's no curse."

"Then why do people come there to light candles and do other weird stuff?"

"People sometimes create their own darkness, kiddo."

"Create their own darkness?"

"Yep. They create their own darkness, and then become blind to truth. They even begin to believe their own lies. They end up diggin' a hole deeper and deeper for themselves—kinda like a false world. In the world they create, they believe they have some kind of power."

"That person who put the candle on the Chair last night and burned up the picture, do you think he wants some kind of power?"

Elijah nodded. "No doubt in my mind. That person must believe in the darkness he has created around himself. You see, from believing comes the power to act. That's what scares me." They approached the top of the hill. "Here's our path right up ahead. The good berry bushes are about a mile from here."

As they started onto the path, Chrissy said, "You said something scares you. I'm not sure what you mean."

Elijah led the way on the narrow trail and had to turn back to talk. "From belief comes the power to do. Do you believe you can break all of your junior high track records again this year?"

"You bet."

"Do you believe enough to train hard even in the off season?"

"Of course. I'll train harder than anyone."

"In other words, your belief is strong enough to make you act."

"I see," she said as she caught up to him where the path widened. "Because I believe, I have the power to do."

"That's exactly right," Elijah said. "That's a positive belief. But that same power to act can be used by someone with bad intentions. That's what scares me."

"Whoever lit that candle might believe enough to do something that's evil?"

"Exactly," Elijah said. "Their belief might push them over the edge—make them crazy enough to do something very bad."

"What happens then?"

"Grave stones get knocked over, stained-glass windows get broken, property gets destroyed. But that's not what scares me."

She glanced up at Elijah. "What scares you?"

"I've seen it over and over again—in the newspapers, on television, all over this country, sometimes even in this Ohio Valley. This kind of darkness doesn't stop at damaging property. It's not even satisfied with killing animals. Obsession with evil can eat a person up. Eventually someone gets hurt. Either the person hurts himself, or someone else—suicide or murder."

Chrissy shuddered. "That *is* scary."

"I don't mean to frighten you, but you do need to be careful around here. Don't go anywhere by yourself."

"I'm not afraid. I can handle myself."

Elijah chuckled. "I'm sure you can, but keep your eyes open."

"I can out run anyone that would come after me."

"That's if you see them coming, kiddo." Elijah patted the top of her head. "This way," he said as the path broadened into a clearing of dirt and stone with very little vegetation. He skidded down a slope and stepped halfway across a trickling watercourse that flowed along a gully toward the bottom of the hill. With his foot on a rock he said, "Give me your hand. I'll help you across."

"I can jump." With ease Chrissy leapt the three-foot span onto the other side. At the top of the ravine the path reappeared, and she resumed her questioning. "How do you know what's true and what's not true? How do you know what you should believe, Elijah?"

"Lies will lead to destruction . . . sooner or later. Truth will lead to understanding. Truth makes you stronger inside and keeps you steady. Truth never changes. When you discover real truth, hold onto it." Elijah stopped at the bottom of a knoll and looked up at the big elm tree at the top. "We're about half way there."

The memory of sitting on the Chair at midnight kept nagging her like a burr that gets caught in a sock, pricking her with a little fear and guilt. "Elijah, I've got an important question." Elijah slowed his pace and met her gaze. "How about those kids who come up to the Chair and sit in it on a dare. If they believe strongly enough in the curse, could they die?"

"All of us are going to die some day but not because of any curse we may believe in. Believing gives power to a person, but it doesn't make a lie true. Someone may sit in that chair, believe he is gonna to die, and with his mind occupied with fear, step out in front of a truck, and get run over. His belief didn't make the curse true, but it increased his chances of getting killed."

Chrissy nodded. "That makes sense." She determined she wasn't going to allow fear of that old monument's curse trip her up. No way.

Chrissy glanced up the hill and saw a tall tree. She led the way, her long legs quickly propelling her to the top. When she crested the hill, she eyed the upper branches of the tall tree and then drew near it. *That's really cool. People carved their names here.* She reached and touched the words.

* * *

When Elijah made it to the top, the vision of the tall girl before the tree tracing the carved name *Amy* with her forefinger stunned him, transporting him twenty years into the past. In a hazy memory he saw his daughter on that same spot tracing those same letters.

"Hey, kiddo," he said to the memory.

"What?" The girl turned, and her features did not quite coincide with that of his daughter. Elijah's eyes adjusted from the inner vision to the outer vision and snapped back into the present.

"You've found my tree," he said.

"Do you know who these people are?"

"Yes. I know them very well." Staring at the names, he approached the tree and stood beside her. "Emily was my wife, and Amy was my daughter."

"Oh," Chrissy said. She stood still, her large green eyes fixed on him.

Elijah smiled, trying to assure her he didn't mind talking about his loved ones. "Amy was a lot like you. She was tall, blonde, and full of spirit. She thought she could take the world by the tail."

Chrissy's voice became very soft. "Sometimes I walk around the Scotch Ridge graveyard looking at the names on the monuments. I remember seeing her name on one of the newer stones. And there was another one next to hers with "Mulligan" on it.

"That's right," Elijah said. "Her mother, Emily, is buried next to her."

"I'm sorry that . . . that you lost them."

"Ten years ago they passed. Sounds like a long time to a young person but seems like yesterday to me."

"Did your daughter ever go berry picking with you?"

"Oh yeah. We'd go in the summer when we'd come down from Pittsburgh for a visit. Emily's parents lived where I'm living now. All three of us would walk out past here to the berry bushes. Amy and I would pick berries, and my wife would go to the Healing Place to pray. Amy would fill a bucket to the top with blackberries for Grandma Murray."

Elijah's stared into the blurring overlap of trees through the woods but he saw memories of times he treasured. "Grandma Murray could make the best blackberry jam; she gave me her secret recipe. I still make it just the way she told me."

"My mom's gonna to make a couple jars of jam from the berries I pick."

"Well, then, kiddo," Elijah said, refocusing on Chrissy, "we better get going 'cause your bucket's empty." The young girl grinned as Elijah placed his hand on her shoulder and directed her back to the path. Walking away from the tree, he felt twenty years younger, almost as if he had stepped into a world gone by.

"My Grandma gave me something to remember her by," Chrissy said.

"Is that right?" Elijah turned down an incline where the path divided into two distinct trails—the one to the right, a deer track, led east toward the river; the one to the left led to the Healing Place and berry bushes. "This way." He turned left at the bottom of the incline.

"Grandma called it her Watchover Ring,." She held her right hand up.

Elijah paused to inspect the bright golden band that sparkled even in the overcast light of the gray day. On the third finger of her right hand the large ring with inter-connecting hearts inscribed around it, glowed before his eyes. "Wow. That's a big ring."

"My grandma gave it to me before she died. She said she was going to heaven to be with God. We stayed with her a lot when Daddy ministered in Pittsburgh and Mom had to work. She took care of us, my brothers and me. Grandma said this ring would remind me that she loves me and would be in heaven praying for me."

"She must have loved you very much," Elijah said.

"I know."

"One day, kiddo, we'll all see our loved ones again—in the presence of God. Our time on this earth will be over, and we'll be ushered into eternity, and all those people who are dear to us will be there to greet us."

"That's what the hearts mean." Chrissy held the ring up to his face. "See. They connect and go all the way around the ring. My grandma told me they represent the people in my life who love me. 'Love lasts forever,' Grandma would say. Sometimes I take the ring off at night and put it in the kitchen window. When the sun comes up in the morning, it makes the ring glow and get warm. When I put it back on my finger I can still feel her love inside me."

"She's kinda like your guardian angel," Elijah said, smiling.

"Kinda like that. I don't know if she has wings or anything."

"You've got a lot of people in your life who love you. Don't you?"

Chrissy bobbed her head. "That's true. I guess you could say I'm blessed."

"That's the best kind of blessing," He pointed to an opening in the heavy mass of greenery that entangled the hill to their left. "We've got to go up this steep path."

"Are we near the berry patch?"

"Not far now." Elijah climbed up to the opening that tunneled through a thick cluster of vines and creepers. "The meadow is on the other side of the hollow just ahead of us."

"Are we gonna be near that place where you took Buster?"

"The Healing Place?"

"Yes."

"It's not far from the berry patch. Did the boys tell you about taking the dog there?" he asked as he ducked under a low hanging branch.

"Yes. They said it was a magical place."

Elijah chuckled. "I don't believe in magic."

"They said it seemed like God was really there."

"God is everywhere."

"I know that. But they said that you said it was a special place. Didn't you say your wife would pray there when you and your daughter would pick berries?"

"That's right. Emily would do the prayin', and we'd do the pickin'. She'd bring her prayer list with her. There's a round, flat sandstone in the middle I call the Robin Stone. She buried a robin under it years ago when she was a little girl. One of the neighborhood cats got a hold of the bird. Her daddy walked her out here to bury it. On their way home he carved her name in that elm tree you saw a half-mile back. As she got older she kept coming out here to pray. She would stand on that stone with her list in her hand, look up into the branches as the sun's rays shone down upon her."

"What was on the list?"

"Mostly sick people. She'd write down the names mentioned when the minister asked for prayer requests during the worship service. Regularly, she would come to the Healing Place and pray for everyone on the list. Most of them got healed. She always told me it was a special place of prayer."

"So it is special place."

"It's special, but not because there's some kind of magical glow. To me it's special because I go there to focus on God. The beauty of the setting—the tall trees and beams of light that come down through the branches, the songs of the birds—all these things inspire me to focus on the Lord. It's easy for me to get into the Spirit there."

"So it's really not a magical place, but a spiritual place," Chrissy said.

"Emily thought it was a place of resurrection. Whenever she'd pray there, a robin would land in the tree above and look down on her. 'That's my resurrected robin,' she'd say. 'He's carryin' my prayers to the Lord. People are gonna be healed.' "

Just then the woods ended and the path cut across a large meadow of tall yellow grass and climbed a long hill, about two hundred yards up to the next section of woods. Elijah and Chrissy broke from the green shadows into the faded ochre meadow as gusts of wind blew the gray clouds eastward and pressed the grass in front of them.

Elijah waited for Chrissy to draw even with him before speaking. "It is a spiritual place. Any place where people stop and put their minds on the Lord can be a spiritual place. It's not magic. It's simply a place to come face to face with God."

"Do you think that because you pray there a lot, God's presence can be felt there more easily?"

"Yes. I know I sense God's presence there more easily. But it's not so important where you go to meet the Lord. What's important is that you do it."

"Could you show me where the Healing Place is?"

"Sure." Elijah stopped. He pointed to the top of the hill where the path disappeared into the woods again. "It's right there," he said. "The berry patch is fifty yards across the top and to the right."

* * *

Chrissy saw the tall oaks and maples near the top of the hill on the edge of the meadow. Remembering the story Joshua and Billy had told her about the miracle of Buster's healing, she wanted to see the Healing Place with her own eyes.

"Can I run to the top and go in and look?"

"Sure," Elijah said, surprised at her eagerness. She broke into a gallop, her excitement energizing her muscles. She felt like she could fly, quickly climbing the remaining 150 yards to the top. At the end of the path where the meadow bordered the woods she slipped into the leafy entrance.

The cathedral ceiling vaulted by branches of oaks and maples instantly mesmerized Chrissy. The light of the gray day filtered through, giving the place a mysterious glow. It reminded her of an empty church with the lights out and the setting sun slanting its rays through the windows. Reverently, she stepped to the center of the circle looking upward, and then she slowly rotated to see the thick tree trunks and tangled greenery around the outskirts. Beyond each tree the forms of more trees repeated into the blurring browns, blue-greens, and grays of the deeper woods.

Looking down she saw the sandstone embedded in the ground. *The Robin Stone. I wonder if the resurrected robin is here?* She raised her head again, squinted into the branches, and saw several birds. She stooped, put her pail down, fidgeted and pulled the heart-encircled ring until it slid off. Standing up, she closed her right eye, extended the ring before her left eye, and scanned the ceiling until she focused upon a bird straight above her. "That's a robin. I think." She maintained her aim on the creature like a photographer until it flew toward the meadow and escaped through a white-gray opening. Stooping again, she extended the ring and placed it on the center of the stone between the word ROBIN and the etched cross. The golden band sat alone on the flat rock as if on display as the centerpiece in a dimly lit museum. *I wonder if my ring could absorb some of the power of this place?* She picked up her pail, stood, and pivoted toward the meadow. In awe, glancing around and above her, she exited, pushing through the branches of the entrance just as Elijah arrived at the top of the hill.

"Well, how'd you like it?" he asked.

"It's beautiful. I felt like I was in church."

Elijah pointed across the top of the hill. "The berry bushes are right over there. This meadow used to be an old farm back in the 1940's. The farmer planted all kinds of blackberry bushes along the edge of the woods. They've been growing ever since."

"How come no one farms the land anymore?"

"The farmer's son got killed in World War Two. He was a real hero, a Marine infantryman. On the Island of Peleliu in the Pacific, a grenade landed near a bunch of soldiers. He jumped on it to save his buddies. They gave him the Iron Cross for bravery. Course a medal can't come close to replacing a son. No one was left to work the land. The farmer and his wife lived there until they died in the late fifties. Some relatives inherited the property, but they only use it for hunting. The land hasn't been farmed since."

"That's sad."

"The old farm house is over the next hill. You can't see it from here. No one even knows it's out here. There used to be a dirt road about a quarter mile up from where you live that led out to it. It's overgrown now. You can hardly tell where the road used to be. I doubt if anyone has been inside that house for over thirty years."

"Can we go see it?"

"No. I don't have time today."

"I'd love to explore an old house. Betcha people leave neat stuff behind in old houses."

"Maybe someday soon we'll come back."

Chrissy stopped in front of a berry-laden bush. She picked a plump, ripe one and popped it into her mouth. "I'm glad I took my ring off," she said.

"Why'd you do that?" Elijah plucked berries off the bush ten feet beyond her.

"I didn't want to get black berry stains on it. And I thought . . . maybe . . . maybe God will bless it."

"Oh," he replied, shaking his head and smiling. "Where'd you put it?"

"On the Robin Stone," she responded. "Don't let me forget it."

For the next hour they picked and talked. Elijah, with his large bucket, kept a steady pace; Chrissy, with the smaller pail, ate more than she collected, but slowly filled her container. Chrissy enjoyed the older man's old-time stories of life in bygone days. She encouraged him to share oft-repeated tales of long walks to school, Elvis and the beginning of rock and roll, high school football in the early sixties ("Martins Ferry was a state powerhouse then," he boasted), and life without computers and cable television. She asked a hundred questions, but Elijah didn't seem to mind. She enjoyed this new friendship with this old guy. Elijah was becoming a good buddy.

* * *

As the minutes flowed quickly by, Elijah figured he'd answered about a hundred questions, but he loved it. This young gal rekindled the best memories of his life—especially of his daughter, Amy. Lost in the joy of words and laughter that rambled effortlessly between them, he forgot the passing of time until the overflowing berries reminded Elijah of his regular Sunday supper meeting at McDonalds with Peter Nower.

"Great Caesar's Palace. It's 4:40 already. I've got to get back," he said. "There's a Big Mac and super-sized fries calling me." He laughed a deep, roaring laugh that caused Chrissy to smile and shake her head. "I'm meeting a friend at McDonalds for dinner," he explained.

"I'm ready to go. My pail's full." She rubbed her belly. "I don't think I could eat another berry."

"Let's get going. We've got a long walk back to your house."

"If you're late, you don't have to walk me clear down to my house."

"Well, I'll at least walk you halfway down."

"I can walk fast if you want."

"I'll try to set a good pace," Elijah said. "By the time I get home, I bet I'll have walked six miles today."

She reached out and patted his wide stomach. "If you're gonna be eating Big Macs and fries, you need to walk six miles."

"That's all muscle." He pulled in his belly and stuck out his chest. His laughter bellowed again, and Chrissy joined in.

The sky gradually darkened as they made their way along the path, up and down hills, through thick patches of green growth, and sparsely vegetated bare sections of ground, across small trickling streams and up the sides of steep ravines. Along the way their lively banter continued unhampered by the darkening day. When they reached the end of the path and stepped onto Nixon's Run, Chrissy set a brisk pace passing Treadway Road near the top of the hill. One hundred yards went by, and Elijah's house appeared on the left side of the creek across the wooden bridge. "Elijah, I can walk home from here myself. I know you're late for your dinner appointment at McDonalds."

"No, no. I'll at least walk you halfway down. Let me set my bucket on the bridge, then we'll go a few more hundred yards together."

"You don't have to worry 'bout me. I'll be fine."

"Now don't be stubborn, kiddo. I'll walk you halfway down," he insisted. As he set his bucket of berries on the bridge, he could feel the dull aching in his back. *I must be getting old. My back is hurting and my legs are tired. But there's no way I'm gonna let her walk by Kyler's house alone.*

One hundred yards farther they saw Joshua's house on the right side; there were no signs of anyone home.

Elijah struggled to keep up with the long-legged girl. He wondered if Kyler would still be there. As they rounded the turn, he could see Kyler sitting in the same spot. Elijah decided he would walk Chrissy down to Kyler's house. From there he would watch her cover the two hundred yards around the next two bends. She would only have another two hundred yards to go once she disappeared from sight. Besides that, he wanted to make sure Kyler knew he was on his gurard. Standing in front of Kyler's house and keeping his eye on her would make that point clear.

As they approached the house, Elijah said, "I had a wonderful afternoon, Chrissy. I'm glad we got a chance to know each other better. I'm gonna stop right down here and watch you walk the rest of the way."

"You don't have to watch me. I'll be fine. You can walk on home."

Kyler, seeing them approach, placed his magazine down on the top step and stared at them.

"Go ahead. I don't mind. It won't take you long."

"I'll walk fast," she said.

"We'll have to go for a walk again sometime soon. I had fun."

"Maybe we could go look at that old farmhouse. I'd really like to go there."

As he stopped just below the unrailed bridge, he could sense Kyler's gaze upon them. To Elijah's surprise, Chrissy placed her pail on the ground, turned toward him, spread her arms without hesitation and hugged him—a full affectionate hug, and he patted her on the back until she let go.

"Thanks, Elijah. I had fun too." She stepped back and smiled. "See ya later." She stooped, picked up her pail of berries, and walked away. Elijah kept his eye on her as she neared the first turn.

Kyler's voice oozed from across the creek: "Must be nice spending the afternoon with a purty young thing." Elijah ignored him and kept focus on Chrissy's diminishing figure. "Quite a looker for a twelve year old," Kyler continued. "I bet you enjoyed it when she put her arms around you, huh Mulligan?" Elijah could feel blood rising to the surface of his face. "An old man like you doesn't get to hug a young purty thing like that too often." He laughed grotesquely. "Maybe her daddy would let me take her for a walk next time."

One hundred yards away the tall girl rounded a turn and disappeared. Elijah looked across the bridge to the grinning man. "You didn't learn much from today's sermon did you, Kyler?"

"You'd be surprised, Mulligan. I learned more than you could ever imagine."

"Did you hear the part about God's power to deliver a sinner from the pits of hell?"

Kyler sat silently with his half grin for several moments, then answered: "I don't remember that part too well, but I do remember the preacher said a sacrifice must be made."

He ignored Kyler's twisted words, not wanting to lose his temper again. Looking back down the road, he saw Chrissy reappear about 150 yards away. "Just remember. I got my eyes on you."

Elijah saw Chrissy approach the next turn. She was only about two hundred yards from home, and he knew he could no longer see her once she rounded the bend. By now she was a safe distance away from Kyler. The big man turned and headed up the road to his house. He wanted to escape the creepy smile of the dark-eyed man, get away from the vileness in the atmosphere surrounding that gray shack. Elijah felt the spiritual residue of evil adhering to his skin like invisible dust. Although he was exhausted, he walked fast.

Almost out of earshot, Elijah heard Kyler holler: "You can't always keep your eyes on me, old man."

Chapter Eighteen

Chrissy was halfway up her driveway when she remembered. She stopped suddenly, and stomped her foot. "Oh no. My Watchover Ring. I left it on the Robin Stone."

She pivoted and walked back to the road. *I've got to go back and get it.* When she started to jog, she realized she was still carrying the pail of blackberries. The jarring of her stride bounced several berries out of the pail and into her path. She stopped and held the pail in front of her looking for a place to put them. The edge of the front yard bordering Nixon's Run was lined with flowers. The overflowing marigolds made a perfect hiding place. Chrissy walked to the edge, separated the dense yellow and bronze blooms, and nestled the pail securely on the soil. When she pulled her hands away, the flowers sprang back over the opening completely covering the pail. *No one will find them there. It won't take me long to run back to the Healing Place and get my ring.*

She sprang to her feet and sprinted the first hundred yards up the road. Realizing she had almost a half mile to run to the path and another mile to the Healing Place, she slowed her pace as her breathing rate increased. After about two hundred yards she eased into a jog thinking that she could maintain that pace all the way to the path. When the dingy house with the Escort parked on the side came into view, a queasiness developed in the pit of her stomach. She didn't want to slow to a walk, especially in front of Kyler's house, but the nausea intensified, and she knew she had eaten too many berries. Walking eased the pressure that pressed high into her stomach and belched up bitterly into her throat.

He's not on the porch. I'm glad. He gives me the creeps. Keeping a steady pace, she looked into the darkened window, the same window that emitted the eerie and shifting television light the night before. The screaming and violent thuds echoed in her memory, aggravating the instability of her belly. She thought she saw the form of a man through the reflection of gray sky that glinted on the window but couldn't tell for sure. When she tried to jog again, bile climbed up her throat, making her gag at the taste of half-digested berries. Swallowing the vile fluid, she walked as fast as she could without increasing the level of nausea. Then she thought she heard her name. "Chrissy," someone said, or she thought someone said. It was more like a hissing noise, yet it sounded like her name, but when she turned around and looked at the house, no one was there. *I'm imagining things. Come on now. Don't go loony, girl.* She tried to remain calm by relaxing her muscles just like her father always told her to do before a race.

Gazing up the road, she picked up her pace. Something rustled in the woods to her right. She stopped. Peering at the hillside, she listened, but the sounds had ceased. Her throat tightened and she tried to swallow. Ignoring the burning in her stomach, she resumed the steady climb. From somewhere in the not-too-distant woods, the noises started again, hardly detectable. *Maybe it's my stomach gurgling. Yes. It must be. It's burning so much. I feel like I'm gonna puke.* She stopped again and leaned forward on her knees. The shuffling sound continued for a second or two.

"That wasn't my stomach," she said aloud. She examined the hillside. Loud scattering sounds erupted twenty feet above as she barely caught a glimpse of a swiftly moving squirrel that had leapt off a walnut tree, landed on some dry leaves, and scurried down to the rocks by the creek. It stopped and glanced up the bank at her, hesitated, then bolted back up the hillside scrambling up the same tree. *It's just a squirrel. Only a squirrel.* The tension eased. Her stomach settled.

As she neared the top of the hill, she looked for the path. The day had become leaden; a raindrop struck her forehead. In the dull light of the late afternoon, she found it hard to recall exactly where the path began. *I think it's farther up.* She jogged a few paces. *There. There it is. Now the hard part. I've got to remember what twists and turns to make to get to the clearing.*

The first four hundred yards of the path were easy to follow. The vegetation was thick on both sides, but the trail was well worn. Not until she reached a section of rocky, sparsely weeded ground did she sense some confusion. She stopped in the middle of the gravelly section where no sign of the path existed. She inspected the woods around her, looking for an opening, a possible reappearance of the path. As she panned the tangled greenery, a bright orange flash flickered deep in the woods. "What was that?" she asked aloud. Squinting, she focused in the direction of the orange blip, but it was gone. Greens, browns, ochres, and tans filled her vision. "That was strange." She turned to her left and saw the familiar ravine. "There," she said. "It's that way."

She hurried down the bank and jumped across the three-foot stream of water. Quickly climbing the other side, she crested the top and found the path again. Feeling confident of her direction she picked up her pace and progressed rapidly for several hundred yards until she heard it again—those rustling noises. She stopped and the noises continued for several seconds. Looking in the direction of the scuffling, she listened to detect any advancing of the sound, any motion or movement. Fifty yards into the woods fluorescent orange flashed again and then disappeared. *Am I seeing things or what?* She stood a full minute staring into the woods. The flash of orange set to boiling a fear that had been simmering since she had passed Kyler's house. Although she could not understand what the bright orange flash could be, she knew it wasn't a part of the natural surroundings. With the passing of seconds, she gathered her courage. To turn back without the ring was not an option. She had to press on. *The open meadow can't be too much farther.*

Once she resumed the walk along the path, the anxiety eased again. The next several hundred yards went by quickly. When she reached the meadow, the world appeared like a black and white television show. The dark clouds cast gray shadows across the once-yellow field. The scene seemed unreal. A cold splash of water struck her cheek as she ran across the open meadow. She felt vulnerable, exposed, an easy target.

She remembered a dream: screaming, grotesque monsters—half human, half animal—chased her up a muddy hill. The ground below her feet spun like a conveyer belt, and she couldn't escape. Then claw-hands raked at her shoulders and dragged her to the ground.

Not caring how badly her stomach hurt, she charged up the hill, glancing behind her at thirty-yard intervals but seeing no one. As she pushed herself to the top, her breathing became labored, harsh. She stopped. With her hands on her knees sucking in air, she glared one last time down the hill and across the meadow. Another cold droplet splashed on her forehead. Her stomach gurgled and she swallowed down an up-surging rush of bile. She turned and stumbled through the leafy branches of an oak tree on the perimeter of the clearing.

Huffing and swallowing, she made her way to the center of the circular sanctuary. Her head spun and her vision blurred, but she could see the golden ring on the flat stone at her feet. She dropped to her hands and knees. Eight months before she had caught the 24-hour flu on

Christmas Day. By sheer will power she had stopped herself from heaving up her guts. She hated the taste, the spastic pain, the choking. *I won't throw up this time either. I won't. I won't. I don't care if I have to stay on my hands and knees for an hour.*

The ring was two feet in front of her face, but she didn't reach for it. Her stomach cramped again. *Stay perfectly still.* She steadied herself. *Relax. Don't move a muscle. The sickness will go away.* She belched twice. Two minutes went by, and the dizziness faded. The pressure on her stomach began to ease. Opening her eyes, she saw the ring glistening in front of her. She picked it up, sat back on her calves, and placed it on the third finger of her right hand. As her head cleared and the nausea decreased, she smiled, knowing her grandmother's Watchover Ring was where it belonged. A sense of security flowed over her. But then she heard the footsteps, and turning, she saw a flash of fluorescent orange from the handle of a shovel.

Chapter Nineteen

To Elijah, the water flowing from the showerhead felt refreshing, cleansing, renewing. He wanted to wash the presence of Kyler from the surface of his skin. He tried to scour away the menacing grin, the metallic voice, the grotesque laughter, but as he stepped onto the cold floor, the feeling of revulsion adhered to his soul, and the vigorous drying with the towel could not wipe it away.

He remembered how Kyler had leered at Chrissy when she passed through the light of the stained-glass window. As he entered his bedroom, a violent urge welled up in him. He envisioned grabbing Kyler by the shoulders and slamming him to the ground. Wanting to stomp on him, Elijah lifted his foot. Then he shook his head, took a deep breath, and looked down. Below his foot was a pile of dirty clothes. When he turned, leaned on the dresser, and faced himself in the mirror, he noticed his face had reddened and felt his heart pounding. He hung his head in disgust. *Why can't I escape these violent urges? At least I know she's safe. She has to be safe. I watched her walk most of the way down the road. There's no need to worry.*

He shuffled through the shirts in the second drawer of the mahogany dresser. Pulling out a light blue t-shirt, he funneled into it. As he glanced down, he noticed the shirt was too tight and had a small coffee stain just above his belly. *Too bad. I'm already late. I told Peter I'd meet him there at six o'clock and it's already ten till.* He stepped into his favorite well-worn jeans, the ones that had an extra inch or two in the waist, and slid into his loafers, bare feet squeezing into place.

To shake off the oppression that burdened his spirit, he began to think about food: a Big Mac, super-sized fries, and a large coffee. By the time he pulled out of the driveway, his mouth watered and his stomach growled. The growling twisted into a knot when he passed the gray house. A quick glance found no sign of Kyler.

He's not there . . . not on his front porch anyway. Where is he? Probably hunting down some helpless creature in the woods. Lord have mercy.

The car sped down the run, and his mind drifted to thoughts of Chrissy and Amy. The young girl was a breath of fresh air. Their berry-picking expedition made him feel like a thirty-four-year old father with his only daughter by his side—talking, laughing, and sharing life.

People are so important. Our relationships make up the very fibers of our lives. Maybe the Lord has sent Chrissy into my life to help me connect more with people again. Sometimes I fear growing too close. It hurts so much when you lose the ones you love.

Images filled his mind of his daughter at twelve years old. Although the windshield displayed the familiar way into town—the winding turns and few stops as one county road intersected another—instead, he saw a twelve-year-old blonde girl who looked slightly like him, shooting and dribbling a basketball, throwing a softball, jumping off a high dive, catching a fish, dancing with him around the kitchen as she stood on his feet, giving him a big hug and kiss and saying, *I love you, Daddy.*

"I love you too, kiddo," he said aloud.

These were the strands of memory that composed a part of his being. The wonderful afternoon reawakened that place in his mind where those memories waited to be lived again. As the images and words brightened his inner vision, he basked in the warmth of joy that good thoughts generate.

Before he knew it, he slowed to a stop at Route 7 and gathered all his faculties in an effort to merge into the traffic. Although cars flew by at 50 to 65 miles per hour, there were no on ramps along this section of the road. From a complete standstill a driver had to ease his way out, extend his neck to make sure no cars were coming, then floor it to pick up speed before a semi-truck came rumbling up his rear end. Within minutes he was at the Hanover Street intersection.

McDonalds sat like a castle on a hill with a huge block wall 30 feet high that supported its parking lot. Some people called it Fort McDonald. Elijah looked at the wall that loomed before him and the tops of the golden arches above it. Martins Ferry was a three restaurant town, McDonalds, the newest of the three. The other two were family-owned establishments—The Antler, located at the end of Broadway Street for as long as anyone could remember, and First Ward on 4th Street. Three restaurants, three banks, four car dealerships, two hardware stores, three grocery chains, four fire stations (totally organized and operated by dedicated volunteers), six gas stations, a nice library, a bowling alley, a pet store, a jewelry store, two newsstands, two Laundromats, and lots of churches.

Martins Ferry was a pleasant, working-class town sustained by one of a series of steel mills and a couple of many factories that lined the banks of the Ohio River from Pittsburgh to Marietta. At one time the town boasted 12,000 residents, but with the death of the industrial age, the population had slipped slowly to 8000 as coalmines shut down and the mills cut back production or completely folded. Most of the people had lived there for generations with deep blue-collar roots; they filled the high school football stadium on Friday nights; they faithfully passed school levies; they did their best to provide a good life for their families. When they sent their sons and daughters to college, they knew the brightest and best of their children would probably never return to the Ohio Valley. Like most rust-belt towns, it needed a boost from the coming technological age.

When Elijah pulled open the entrance door to the restaurant, five four-foot-tall Indians marched out wearing brown homemade costumes, war-painted faces, and feathers stuck in colorful bands, followed by two moms chatting about the upcoming school year. Betty Zane Days, Elijah concluded as he smiled and held the door open for the passing procession. Martins Ferry's claim to historical fame was the heroine, Betty Zane, who was buried in the Walnut Grove Cemetery at the end of 4th Street. Suspended in the act of carrying an apron full of gunpowder through a hail of gunfire and arrows, her granite statue stood proudly in front of the graveyard. In September of 1782, the sixteen-year old girl had raced to the blockhouse and back to Fort Henry to re-supply the soldiers with gunpowder as they held off a vicious Indian attack during the Frontier Border Wars.

Zane's daring charge to the powder house in the face of death provided the inspiration for The Betty Zane Days Festival. The celebration opened on Tuesday with a parade. A five-kilometer footrace through the town streets highlighted Wednesday's schedule (Elijah recalled his young buddy, Chrissy, had won the race earlier that week). A carnival, food stands, contests, and musical entertainment drew crowds to the park. The bright colors of the whirling rides and mingling people charged the scene with festive energy. Honky-tonk strains of country bands or the ethnic rhythms of polka music blared from the amplifiers stacked on the park stage. The climax of the celebration featured the dramatic re-enactment of Betty Zane's run to glory at the little league ball field on Sunday evening.

Peter Nower sat in their favorite booth by the rest room. "You're late," he said.

"Five minutes late. That's not bad."

"You owe me four bucks, ol' buddy," Peter said.

"You ordered for me?"

"Big Mac, super-sized fries, and a large coffee--two creams."

"Are the fries hot? If I'm paying that much for fries, I want 'em hot."

"They just came out of the fryer," assured Peter.

"I don't want them unless they can burn my mouth." Elijah slid into the booth and began doctoring his coffee.

"What took you so long?"

"I went berry picking with Chrissy Butler. Lost track of time."

"Oh." Peter squeezed out diet-ranch dressing from a packet onto his large container of salad. "I thought maybe you were spending the afternoon with Annie."

Elijah glared at Peter. "No. Don't let your imagination get carried away. I'm not some kid with a teenage crush."

"That's right," Peter said with a sardonic grin. "I forgot. But lately you've had this youthful glow, this radiant effervescence."

"Excuse me," Elijah said abruptly. "I'm gonna say a blessing over this food. You want me to bless yours too?"

"No."

"Well, I'm gonna anyway." Elijah bowed his head for several seconds. "Amen. Whether you like it or not."

Peter was already chomping on lettuce. He swallowed and said, "Are we going to the park after dinner to watch the re-enactment?"

"I guess so. I'll bet you ten bucks Betty escapes the Indians again."

"She must have been a fast chick." Both men shoveled fries into their mouths with machine-like repetition. Peter stopped and spoke again. "So you're not going to ask Annie out on a date?"

"I didn't say that. I said I'm not some loved-crazed teenager. I might ask her out."

"Did you see her today?"

"Saw her at church."

"How'd she look?"

Elijah bobbed his head, tapping himself on the cheek with his hand. "That's the problem."

"What do you mean?"

"She was . . . radiant." Elijah raised his eyebrows.

"Why would that be a problem?"

Elijah quickly chewed a mouthful of fries and swallowed. "She had this pretty blue sun dress on with white, little flowers. All the curves in all the right places. Her hair was clipped up on her head. Some strands fell down across her shoulders. Even in the sunlight she looked like she was about thirty years old."

"What's wrong with you, man?" Peter said, reaching for his sandwich. "That woman likes you, she's beautiful, she's youthful, she's available, and you can't make up your mind about her? Are you crazy?"

"You don't understand. And if I explained it to you, you still wouldn't get it."

"Try me," Peter said.

Elijah stared at the picture above Peter's head; it was a print of an airbrush rendering of a 50's McDonalds with the arches spanning the building and hotrods and roadsters filling the parking lot. The image reminded him of how quickly things change. "Listen to what I'm saying. Her beauty, her youthfulness—all those fleshly attractions—could be my downfall. For the last ten years I've grown spiritually. My relationship with God has come first. When my wife and daughter died, I committed myself—mind, body, soul, spirit—to seeking God. That commitment saved me. Spiritually, I'm stronger than I've ever been in my life. I'm fulfilled. I don't need a woman. I've learned to stand alone with God. Annie, I'm afraid, would be the one person who could knock me off balance again."

"Elijah."

"What?"

"I want to let you in on something."

"What?"

"You're still a human being. You're not some angel. You still live in this world. You need to eat, and sleep, and exist. You are a man with a man's natural desires."

"Yeah, but I choose to deny that part of me until . . ."

"Until when?"

"Until God shows me that she and I are meant to be together according to God's will."

"God never lets you decide anything for yourself?"

"I'm always free to do what I want to do," Elijah said. "But I choose to please God. If I would allow myself to fall in love with that woman, it's possible that I would lose the greatest thing in my life—my first love—the Lord."

"I think you're wrong," Peter said.

"That doesn't surprise me."

"I think you're denying yourself the best thing that could happen to you in your golden years."

Elijah shook his head. "A woman doesn't hold my happiness. And I could never make her truly happy."

"Elijah, Don't get me wrong, but I know you. I've known you a long time. The words you're saying are coming from your head and not your heart. If you were completely honest and listened to your heart, you wouldn't waste any more time fighting your feelings."

"Since when did you become a romance advisor? Are you gonna start a column in *The Times Leader*—Dear Peter?"

"That's not a bad idea. You could be my guinea pig. If you take my advice and ask that lady out, I might start my own column."

"If I ask Annie Ferrier out, your advice will have nothing to do with it. It'll be between me and the good Lord."

"You're a stubborn man. Let's change the subject." Peter stuffed his empty fry box into a white bag and took a long drink from the large paper cup in front of him. "What else do we have to talk about?"

"You'll never guess who came to church today."

Peter took another drink, placed the cup down, and swallowed. "Who?"

"Nathan Kyler."

"You're kidding?"

"I wish I was."

"Maybe you shook him up pretty good. Maybe he saw the light." Peter's sarcastic smirk reappeared.

"He didn't come to repent." Elijah popped open the hamburger box in front of him.

"Why would he come?"

"He's up to something."

"You think he's going to cause some kind of trouble?"

Elijah chewed and swallowed half of the contents in his mouth and spoke somewhat garbled: "He's out to get revenge."

"On you?"

"On me and everyone and everything."

"Could be. He's definitely disturbed."

"That boy has a lot of hate and anger inside. It takes years of abuse and torment to get that mad at the world. Unfortunately, my visit may have been the last straw. He's reached his breaking point."

"I told you about his father beating him during his high school days."

"I guess our experiences tend to shape our lives to some degree. We take what comes our way and turn it into something," Elijah said.

"Now you're starting to sound like some guest on the Oprah show. What do you mean, 'turn it into something'?" Peter popped the last bite of the chicken sandwich into his mouth.

"You know what I mean. We take what happens to us and try to make some sense of it. Without the Lord's guidance most people have a hard time dealing with the bad things that happen. Bitterness creeps in and their souls become cold and hard. They begin to look for some way to get even—some way to make someone pay for what happened to them. Take Kyler for instance. When his father beat him, no one came to his rescue. His mother didn't care. She abandoned him. When the old man slapped, or whacked, or pounded him, no one stood up for him. Now it's his turn to hurt someone."

"So when you man-handled the boy in his own house the other day, you may have pushed him over the edge. In his mind, he connected your intrusion with the abuse he received from his father."

"And the neglect of his mother."

"What do you think he'll do?"

"If he has been fantasizing about some act of violence, he may be ready to act."

"You seem to know a lot about his state of mind."

Elijah took a deep breath and his focus on Peter blurred as he remembered the cold and cracked walls of a jail cell. "I was an angry young man once. I went over the edge."

"What changed you?"

Elijah immediately refocused on Peter's eyes. "The power of the resurrection."

"What do you mean by that?"

"It's the power to die and live again."

Peter shrugged. "I don't believe in heaven or hell, so the resurrection means nothing to me."

"If you're right, and there is no heaven or hell, then we'll never know. If I'm right, then one day we will know, or at least I will." Elijah's smile widened. "Now tell me. Who has more hope, you or me?"

Peter looked beyond Elijah's shoulder. "I'll have to reserve my answer for another session. We've got company." He nodded toward the entrance.

Elijah glanced over his shoulder to see two boys coming his way—the redheaded McGlumphy boy and the Thompson boy. In an instant they shot across the restaurant and slid to a stop at Elijah's table.

"Mr. Mulligan!" Joshua spouted. "Where's Chrissy?"

Elijah looked at the boy, tongue-tied for several seconds. "W-W-Where's Chrissy?
. . . I would guess she . . ."

"Is she with you?" interrupted Joshua. "Did you bring her into town?"

"Why no. Was I supposed to?"

"She never came home from berry picking," Billy said.

"What! I watched her walk almost all the way home. What do you mean she never came home?"

"Pastor Butler called us twenty minutes ago, looking for her. He said he called you, but you weren't home. He picked us up and brought us into town to find her. He thought maybe you brought her into town to watch the Betty Zane pageant."

"Why would I do that without his permission . . . without letting him know?"

Joshua shrugged. "I don't know. But she never came home."

"Where's Pastor Butler now?" Peter asked.

"He's down at the park, looking for her," Billy said. "We told him we'd walk up town and look, and we saw your car in the lot."

"Let's go," Elijah ordered as he slid his large body between the table and seat. Peter jumped up immediately. The two boys stepped to the side as Elijah plowed toward the door. Peter and the boys followed, leaving behind a table scattered with crumpled papers and cups.

The sky brooded, an ugly gray, making the world outside the brightly lit restaurant gloomy. Elijah and the boys jumped into the blue Suburban, and Peter followed in his Lexus. As Elijah sped along the four blocks through town to the park, a few rain droplets spattered on the windshield.

The two vehicles turned into the Citizen's Bank parking lot on top of the hill above the ball field. Finding no parking spaces, Elijah skidded to a stop, not caring if he blocked two cars in.

Peter stopped behind him and emerged from his car. "We're blocking these people in."

Elijah looked into the charcoal sky. "We won't block them in for long. I know she isn't down here. Let's find Byron and get back home."

"How do you know she's not down here?"

"I just know," Elijah said impatiently.

Below them at the ball field, a scratchy voice from a public address system blared out: "We would like to welcome all of you here tonight for the 35th annual Betty Zane Days Re-enactment. Our festival this year has been highly successful and enjoyable thanks to our sponsors . . ."

"Boys!" Elijah called. The two stood on the bank looking down at the ball field. In center field stood the cardboard box painted to look like a powder house. In right field several British soldiers meandered along with a host of red-skinned warriors with feathers, brightly painted faces, a few skinned heads, Mohawks, and some long pigtailed black wigs. The war party shouted, whooped, yelped, and hollered with bows, guns, and feathered staffs jabbing into the sky. The plywood Fort Henry surrounded home plate as three lookouts sat faithfully at their posts atop the ledge of the front wall.

"Boys!" Elijah yelled. They shifted their attention to Elijah. "Where did Pastor Butler say he'd be?"

"Either in the park or around the ball field," Joshua said. "He probably looked in the park first, by the carnival rides."

Looking to his left and across a basketball court, Elijah spied the top of the Ferris Wheel above the walnut and sycamore trees that lined the east side of the park. The ride had stopped. No one sat in the carriages. The few people he could see through the branches and leaves were walking toward the little league ball field to watch the re-enactment. He panned to his right across the ball field at the playground and cement-tiered stands. By the drinking fountain at the corner of the right field fence that separated him from the shouting Indians, the silver-haired preacher stood, scanning the playground for any sign of his daughter.

"There he is," Elijah said. "Let's go."

As the four descended the steep embankment, droplets of rain splattered random spots around them with one or two striking Elijah on the bare skin. The piercing jolts raised goose bumps on his arms. At the bottom of the hill they looked through the fence at the right of home plate to see the band of charging Indians. Screams, shouts, whoops, and gunfire erupted as the warriors assailed the fort like a red wave. The guns of the sentinels on the front wall exploded. Elijah ignored the action as he walked with long strides across the playground, but the boys and Peter lagged behind, caught up in the drama unfolding before them.

Elijah raised his hand when he saw the tall preacher. "Byron!" By now the playground was empty. All the kids were at the fence or in the stands watching the battle erupt.

"Elijah!" Byron waved from the far side.

The barrage of gunfire from the fort and infield sent a hazing of ghostly smoke hovering above the clamoring participants. The red-skinned attackers, according to script, retreated to the right field corner dragging two wounded braves. When Elijah arrived at the fountain, he looked at the horde of wild-eyed warriors heaving and huffing ten feet beyond the chain-linked fence. Peter and the boys trailed about ten yards behind.

"Did you find her?" Elijah asked.

"No. Did she come with you?" The preacher's voice was tinged with anxiety.

"No," Elijah said. "I never brought her into town."

"Well, she never came home."

As Peter, Billy, and Joshua stopped beside the two men, Betty Zane in her white bonnet and long gray dress rushed out of the fort's door. Her white apron flapped in front of her. She sprinted to the powder house. The rain, intermittent droplets until now, fell from the threatening sky, and umbrellas popped up like morning glories across the stands and around the fence border of the ball field.

The water splattered Elijah's bald head and streamed down his face. "I don't understand. I watched her walk almost all the way home. I was sure she'd made it back."

The Indians shouted: "Squaw! Squaw!" Pointing at the running girl, they watched in amazement as she entered the powder house.

"Where did she go?" Byron asked.

Straining to sort out his thoughts, Elijah turned toward the ball field and looked to where the warriors were pointing. Betty reappeared clutching her apron bottom in front of her as it overflowed with grayish-white powder.

"Oh no," Elijah gasped. The Indians began to whoop and yell again. "She forgot her ring at the Healing Place. Her Watchover Ring. I was in a hurry to get into town, and we forgot to stop and pick up her ring."

Betty ran. The savages pursued.

Elijah shook his head. "She went back to the woods by herself to find that ring. She probably made a wrong turn. Those woods go on for miles and miles."

"It's going to be pitch dark soon," Byron said, squinting through spotted wire-rimmed lenses.

"Let's go," Elijah commanded. The four headed back toward the bank parking lot, their fast march turning into a gallop.

The Indians, with raised tomahawks and spears, closed in on Betty.

Chapter Twenty

Elijah flew up Nixon's Run, trying to keep up with Byron Butler. The preacher hit his brakes and turned into the manse's driveway, the Chevy Astro van sliding slightly off the gravel and into the yard. Byron jumped out almost before the car stopped. He hurried to the front porch yelling, "I'll see if she's here! She might've come back while we were gone!" He pushed the door open and jetted into the house. Elijah emerged from his Suburban into the rain, which now fell steadily. Thunder rumbled at a distance like the stirring of a hungry grizzly in spring.

Turning to look for Peter, Elijah faced Joshua and Billy who peered up at him through the jabbing droplets. He noticed strained expressions on their faces as if they were holding back words waiting to burst through their mouths like water from a crumbling dam.

"What's wrong with you boys?" Elijah asked. "Do you want to tell me something?"

"Mr. Mulligan," Joshua said, his voice cracking. He swallowed. "Chrissy sat in the Chair." After Joshua's words streamed out, the boys peered up at Elijah, their eyes large and fearful.

"What!" Elijah had clearly heard but didn't quite understand.

"The Chair," Joshua repeated. "Last night at midnight she sat in the Chair. The curse is on her."

Elijah pointed a large index finger into the boys' faces. "You mean to tell me you kids are the ones who were fiddlin' around up there last night?"

They lowered their eyes to the puddles forming around their feet.

"You kids lit that candle and burned the picture?"

"No." Joshua glanced up immediately. "We were up there, but we didn't light the candle."

"Who did?"

"We're not sure. Chrissy sat in the Chair, but when we saw someone comin', we hid."

"Does your mom and dad know you were up there last night?"

"No," Billy said. "They'd kill us if they found out. We all three snuck out of the house after our parents went to bed."

"What's going on?" Peter asked as he approached the trio.

"Chrissy sat in the Chair," Joshua repeated on the verge of tears.

Peter's eyes questioned Elijah.

"All three of them were up at the church last night. They think Chrissy may be the victim of the curse of the Chair." Elijah shook his head, feeling disgusted.

"No, boys," Peter said. "That chair can't hurt anyone. It's just a dead man's marker. The dead can't hurt you."

"It's the living you have to worry about," Elijah said, an image of Nathan Kyler forming in his mind.

"She's not here!" yelled Byron from the porch. He wore a hooded yellow raincoat and raised a large black flashlight. He clicked on the light, pointed it in their direction, and walked to them. "We'll need good flashlights."

Thunder growled again, much closer this time, and rain pounded the top of Elijah's Suburban. "Did you call the sheriff?" Elijah asked.

"Yes. He said if we can't find her tonight, he'll bring the bloodhounds, and we'll try to get a big search party together in the morning. Sheriff Taylor claims 90 percent of the time a kid will go off with a friend and not tell the parents, then comes back wondering why everyone's upset. But I'm sure Chrissy wouldn't do that. She'd tell us if she was going to a friend's house."

"Did you call all of her friends?" Peter asked.

"Yes. Lila did. No luck. She's calling church members now to help with the hunt. I told her to tell them to meet us at the top of the hill. The sheriff's not going to organize anything until morning. Let's hope we find her before then."

"Let's go. We can't waste time if she's out in the woods wandering around in this thunderstorm," Elijah said. "We'll meet up at the path in ten minutes. I'll drop you boys off at your houses. Get your dads to help us hunt."

The boys scurried around the blue Suburban and jumped into the back seat as Elijah and Byron climbed into the front; the engine roared and the lights flashed on as Mulligan turned and glared out the back window to see Peter slide into the Lexus and throw the car into reverse. Flying backwards and swerving onto the road, Peter almost lost control but then sped up the hill. Elijah followed close behind, his headlights slashing through the pouring rain.

* * *

Fifteen minutes later, eleven people gathered at the top of the hill where the path began. The two boys and their fathers, Harvey Hershaw, Christopher Ross, Colin Dutton, Betty Pritt, Peter, and Byron huddled together, listening to Elijah's instructions.

"She must've made a wrong turn somewhere along the way. She could be anywhere out there. These woods go on for miles. If she headed west, she could be halfway to Cadiz by now. If she went north, she might end up in Yorkville."

"It's almost dark," Byron shouted above the pattering of the rain. "Does everyone have a good flashlight?"

Yeses echoed around the group and beams of light shot forth from their rain coat sleeves cutting through the deluge into the murky twilight. Shifting shafts of yellow crisscrossed from the ground to the bushes and faded beyond into the violet-gray woods.

"We'll walk to where the path is broken up by rocky ground. She may have gotten lost at that point, " Elijah said. "From there we'll break up in different directions. Follow me." He pointed his light into the center of the path and moved forward sloughing through the wet grass and mud. The storm made the ground treacherous; Betty Pritt, Harvey Hershaw, and Peter Nower took turns slipping, falling, and splattering into the mud along the trail.

At the opening where the path disappeared, Elijah counted heads. "Is everybody all right?"

"My flashlight stopped working when I fell. I think I broke it," Betty said.

"You can come with me," Byron said.

"It might be better for everyone to pick a partner," Elijah said. "If you get lost, you can get lost together." The volunteers quickly paired off. "Christopher and Colin, you go east toward the river."

"Gotya," Colin said as they moved out.

Elijah pointed his light to the left of where the two cut through the trees. "Byron and Betty, you head northeast." He shifted the beam again.

"Joshua and John, north. Billy and Big Bill, go northwest. Peter and Harvey—due west."

"How 'bout you 'Lijah? You don't have a partner," Harvey said.

"I know these woods better than I know the 23rd Psalm. I'll be fine."

"Are we gonna meet somewheres or what?" Big Bill McGlumphy said, his freckled youthful mug peering through the green plastic hood—a larger copy of his son's face.

"Hunt until we find her, or until you're too pooped out to hunt. We'll gather back at the road where the path starts at dawn. If you have to go home and get some sleep, that's okay. All we can do is try our best. Don't kill yourself out there. We don't want anyone to get sick or hurt. Just keep looking until you're too tired to go on. If we can't find her, we'll meet again in the morning with the sheriff back by the road where the path starts."

The pairs diverged in their appointed directions, and Elijah stood alone, watching the beams break up through trees and thick growth as the searchers went deeper into the woods. Shouts of "Chrissy!" resounded in the darkness from all over. Elijah cleared his mind. He knew the woods well, even in the dark. He had hunted squirrel, rabbit, and deer through them for many years. *Better follow the path to the Healing Place. I need to see if the ring is still there.*

When he reached the bottom of the knoll, about halfway to the natural sanctuary, lightning ripped down, blanching the entire landscape white-pale. Thunder crashed instantly like a bomb blast belching hot air into his face. Above, the whine of splintering wood screeched into the night, followed by sounds of colliding branches and swishing leaves.

"The elm tree. My tree!" Elijah cried. He rushed up the knoll, the flashlight's ray jerking before him. The light steadied on a huge fallen hickory that sprawled its branches across the path, making him halt. He directed the light along the fallen torso back to the smoking severance ten feet up the trunk. Shreds of woody fiber still clung, holding the fallen portion off the ground slanting toward him. Elijah quickly shifted his light to the elm tree fifteen feet farther up the hill. He could see the carved names, and his heart slowed; his breathing steadied. *Thank God the tree's all right. I've got to get to the clearing. Got to find Chrissy.*

He stepped through the branches of the fallen hickory and almost tripped as his toe caught on a thick one. At the path, he steadied himself and directed the ray to the elm tree. He stepped up to it and fingered his wife's name. Lowering his hand he gently brushed against his daughter's carved letters—A-M-Y. The steady drone of the rain through the woods, limited Elijah's ability to hear any far off sounds. No "Chrissys" had been audible for several minutes as the searchers distanced themselves from each other. He suddenly realized he had not yet yelled her name, not expecting her to be near the path.

"Chrissy! Chrissy!" he yelled. The din of the splattering drops persisted. During the half-mile walk from the top of the knoll to the meadow, the rain eased slightly and the thunder traveled eastward, lessening in volume. Walking up the path through the open field, he gradually escaped the thrumming of the rain. *My voice will carry out here.* "Amy!" he hollered. "Amy!" In the middle of the meadow he paused and shook his head. *What am I thinking?* "Chrissy!" Although he didn't think anyone could hear him, he still felt embarrassed. "Chrissy!" he yelled again. The aching of loss caused by his daughter's death had risen within him again, and the thought of Chrissy in possible danger had turned into a haunting fear. He fought back the image of Kyler's sadistic grin and sounds of grotesque laughter. He didn't want to give that possibility any foothold in his mind. But as he mounted the path to the Healing Place, the chilling vision of the dark-eyed man luridly gazing upon the pretty girl appeared, and one word kept repeating: *sacrifice, sacrifice, sacrifice.*

As he neared the entrance to the natural sanctuary, he prayed, *If he has done anything to that young girl, God, help me. If he has harmed one hair on her head, Lord, I'll be tempted to kill him.* Kyler formed in his imagination, blocking the entrance to the Healing Place. Elijah grabbed him by the collar with his left hand and pounded his face with the full force of his right fist. Blood spurted in all directions splattering Elijah's face and clothing. He stopped. The face bled profusely. Kyler's eyes popped open and his mouth widened into a demonic smile. Demented laughter erupted. Elijah reached back, and with all his power, whacked the head again. Kyler stumbled backwards through the leafy entrance into the sanctuary. Elijah charged through the branches of the opening as laughter reverberated, echoing around the clearing. Kyler sat in the middle on the Robin Stone, eyes wide and glaring. "You can't always keep your eye on me, old man," he hissed.

Elihah's steps slowed as he approached the middle. His inner vision faded; Kyler disappeared and the stone, illuminated by the shaft of light, was empty. He cleared his thoughts. Closing his eyes, he prayed aloud, "Forgive me, Lord. Forgive me for the violence of my thoughts. I'm ashamed. I don't want to return to the acts of the past. Forgive me,

Lord." When he opened his eyes, the darkness unsettled him. Usually he saw the beautiful treetops and shafts of light whenever he prayed there; usually he heard the calls of the jays and chirrups of the robins. Now his vision was limited to the flashlight's glow. He stared at the circle of light on the sandstone. *It's not there.* All was quiet except for the pattering of raindrops in the trees above. *She must have found her way here and took the ring.* He fell to his knees and groped through the mud around the stone but couldn't find the ring.

"Chrissy!" he yelled from the center of the sanctuary. To inspect the outer rim of trees and brush, he lifted the light and turned. The beam scanned over wide trunks and tangled forms that repeated and faded into black beyond the outer rim. "Chrissy!" *If she found her way here, certainly she could have found her way back.* "Where could she be?" He staggered to his feet. "Where would she go?"

Chrissy's words from that afternoon's outing re-entered his mind: *Can we go see it? I love to explore old houses. Sometimes people leave neat stuff behind in old houses.* Elijah wiped his muddy hand off on his t-shirt and headed for the opening toward the meadow.

Maybe she decided to look for that farmhouse. She could get hurt in a place like that. If those old floors are rotten, she could fall right through. As he stood in the open field, he noticed the rain had slowed to a drizzle, but the clouds were still thick and the night had grown dark and heavy. *She's brave enough to explore things by herself. What a strong-willed kid. If she puts her mind to something, she does it. Better head over there and look just in case.*

The violet-black field stretched out before him; his flashlight cut into the night with a long swath of muted yellow that drained into the grim purples thirty feet ahead of him. The top of the weeds waved in the light as minute water particles passed through the glow. The meadow dropped down and rolled up four hundred yards before him. He knew the house was somewhere on the other side of the next hill. Halfway across he stopped and yelled, "Chrissy!" He listened intently. Nothing. Not a sound. Looking up into the violet-black sky he prayed, "Lord, help us. Help us. Please help us find her. Keep her in your care. Hold her in your arms. Whatever has happened to her. . ."

Walking another fifty yards into the valley and up the next hill he forced negative images and possibilities from his mind. ". . . whatever has happened to her, Lord, keep her safe in your arms." At the top of the hill he stared down into the blackness of the next hollow. There, hidden in the deep shadows of the glen, the old farmhouse waited in silence.

Directing his light into the darkness, Elijah peered, straining to detect any form of gable or geometric silhouette, but the house hunkered in the pit of the valley, consumed by shadows. "I know it's down there." He descended.

With every step, anxiety increased. His stomach knotted and his throat tightened as if the house could see him coming—anticipated him. When he closed to within forty feet, it materialized—a hulking, black form, looming against the hillside. Piercing through the misty rain, the shaft of light illuminated the sagging steps. He drew nearer. The two-story structure's porch roof and posts became gray lips, and the porch, a gaping mouth. Elijah shuddered as he directed the beam to the front door; half-opened, it beckoned him, dared him to enter into its hold.

"Chrissy!" he yelled. The two front windows, shattered glass still clinging to the frames, eyed Mulligan as the yellow glow of the flashlight reflected off the surface, exposing jagged black holes. The steps groaned as he mounted. He swallowed the lump in his throat, but it reappeared seconds later. *I've got to go in there and look for her. God forbid Kyler followed her into the woods and stalked her to this house. God forbid.* He breathed deeply and gathered his courage. He directed the light to the half-open door. Crossing the rotting wooden porch, he hesitated at the threshold and then entered.

The house smelled musty and corroded. He sensed the walls and floors were crawling with insects and rodents. Spiders had spun thick webs that drooped and sagged from every corner and doorway of the entrance hall. Elijah panned the room with the light and noticed a staircase rising into a black void. At any minute he expected some creature of the night to dart toward him. Widening his eyes, he swiveled his head back and forth following the yellow circle around the walls. *I might as well start at the top and work my way down.* He approached the staircase.

Thick dust coated everything. The dangling webs caught on his forehead and shoulders as he ascended to the upstairs hallway. Thin strands anchored and pulled down floating heaps of the flimsy networks. It settled onto his bald head and clung to his back, drifting and hovering behind him. Elijah wiped the tickly film away, but slapped instantly against his left temple upon feeling the scurry of delicate prickling. Looking into his hand, he saw a spider's mangled legs and bloody body against his palm. He wiped it onto his shirt.

There were four doors along the hallway, the first one several feet to his right. "Chrissy!" he yelled. *Silence.* He reached, grasped the cold knob, turned, and shoved the door open. An old-fashioned bathtub with four claw-feet stood in the corner. Three pipes shot up from the floor with handles flanking a waterspout. The medicine cabinet had been pulled off the wall leaving a gray rectangle against a pale green expanse above a faucetless sink that sat in a warped, wooden cabinet. In the other corner, the commode was stationed without a cover or seat. One small window, centered on the outside wall opposite the doorway surprisingly had intact glass. Elijah shifted the glowing shaft from the window back into the hallway.

The next room was about ten feet down. The door was completely closed, but he heard trickling noises inside. He pointed the light to the floor and saw dark shiny liquid puddling at his feet as it seeped from under the door. He reached for the knob and turned, but the handle came off in his hand. Banging on the door with his forearm and shoulder wouldn't budge it. He stepped back, raised his right leg, and kicked at the knob hole with incredible force. It crashed open sending broken trim flying into the room. From a large cavity in the ceiling that exposed plaster, lathe, and studs poured a steady stream of water splashing onto the floor and spreading out like a pond across the room and out into the hallway. *That floor has to be completely rotted. No one's in here. No way.* He turned from the room and proceeded down the hall.

The next door was open wide. The air reeked from a moldy mattress that had slid half off a broken down bed. Stepping into the room and turning to his left, Elijah suddenly confronted the wide-eyed face. His heart jumped. He stepped back thrusting his flashlight forward at the terrorized man. At the same time, the stranger flashed his light at Elijah and the beams met perfectly on the plane of a dusty mirror above a wide, oak dresser. "It's . . . it's me," he coughed out with nervous laughter. "I almost gave myself a heart attack." He placed his hand on his chest as he examined his reflection in the mirror. "Come on," he said to his image. "This room's empty too. Don't think we'll find anyone in this house. Follow me."

For a second in the darkness, his reflection seemed not to match his motions, and in the eyes of his image he sensed a disagreement as if the man in the mirror contradicted his thoughts: *Don't be so sure. There is someone here.* Elijah stepped back from the mirror and rushed into the hallway. "Where am I?" he asked aloud. "In the *Twilight Zone?* Come on,

Mulligan. Get your head on straight. Don't lose the few marbles you have rollin' around up there." He turned from the doorway and walked toward the last door. But the impressions from the mirror clung to him like the wispy webs.

Carved across the chest-high wooden panel of the last door, illuminated by the light, were the letters H-O-W-A-R-D-S-R-O-O-M. *This was the boy's room.* A lingering sadness from fifty years before penetrated his consciousness. He turned the knob, and the door whined open. The room was completely empty—no bed, no dresser, no objects. The windows were unbroken and closed. Breathing was difficult—the air was acrid and stale as if it had not circulated since the day the boy's belongings and furniture were removed. The emptiness seemed to swallow hope and life. It ached from decades of sorrow left behind by a couple's mourning for the loss of their only son. Elijah empathized with the spirits long gone. *What if he hadn't gotten killed in the war? He might still be living here today. He would have been an old farmer by now. I might even have known him. He would've probably been a member of the Scotch Ridge Church.*

"Howard," he said aloud. Elijah looked around the room . . . perhaps to see back into time when the boy sat at a desk or stretched across his bed. "Howard, we might have been friends if you were still here." He shook his head. "You probably can't hear me wherever you are, but if you can, I want to thank you. Thank you for paying the highest price for good ol' U.S.A. Somebody told me you were a good Marine. Got killed on Peleliu. I heard you dived on a grenade and saved your buddies—gave your life for your friends. Wish I could have known you."

Elijah turned and shined his light at the header of the doorframe. A large heart had been carved into the wood with the words: HOWARD-LOVES-HELEN-FOREVER. *Could that be Helen Kinloch? Of course. She's one of our board members at church. They must have married right out of high school before he entered the service. And she never remarried. Been a widow for more than fifty years. Now that's what I call undying love.* Realizing he hadn't been able to get Annie Ferrier out of his mind for the last few months, he felt a stab of guilt deep in his soul. He hurried down the hallway, trying to remember his wife's face, but the features were skewed like a blurred photo.

Descending the steps, he could see his up-walking footprints in the thick dust. *I didn't think about footprints.* He traced them back to the entry hall and carefully inspected the floor to see if other prints could be detected. There were none. *No one has been in this house for years and years.*

It's useless for me to even look. But then he remembered his image in the upstairs mirror and the eerie sensation that had come over him. *I better look anyway.*

Quickly, he toured the first floor, moving to the right into the parlor where the broken front windows had reflected his light before entering the house. Three baseball-sized stones lay on the floor covered with dust beside scattered fragments of glass. "Kids or hunters," he concluded. He kicked the closest stone and it rolled across the floor toward the doorway to the dining room. He followed the trail of the stone making a cursory inspection as he went. The dining room was empty, but a three foot center section of the ceiling's plaster had dropped to the floor as the steady drip from the upstairs bedroom splattered against it carving out rivulets that channeled the water to the floor sending the liquid in all directions like a miniature creeping flood. He walked around the puddle and turned left into the kitchen.

There were no tables or chairs, no stove or refrigerator. The cupboard doors hung open, and a few had fallen off. A branch protruded through a broken window above the sink, which had no faucets. He noticed animal prints and empty walnut shells on the floor in front of him. *Probably squirrels.* Turning left, he could see the last room through a short hallway. A closed door filled most of the left side of the passageway. Elijah reasoned the door led to the basement, knowing that the steps to the second floor would be located above the door. Grasping the metal knob, he pushed the door wide open.

Cold air rushed up and out like the chilling exhale of the cellar's long-held breath. Elijah directed the shaft of light down the throat of the basement into the choking dust motes and swirls. He reached into the cold air and yanked the door shut. An indefinable terror welled up within him like a child's fear of the monster in the dark. *There's nothing down there worth seeing. It would be a waste of time. She didn't come into this house anyway. I would've seen her footprints. I'm wasting my time here.*

Shaking off the frightful uneasiness that still clung to him like the webs that had collected across his shoulders, he walked into the final room—the living room—and shifting the light around the walls and floor, seeing nothing, he exited. Walking through the short hallway, he noticed the basement door had reopened. The cold air engulfed him again. He sensed icy hands on his back. With the eerie chill flowing down his spine, he rushed through the parlor and out the still-open front door into the thick night. He crossed the porch and trotted down the steps. Despite the humidity, he felt relieved to be outside.

The rain had slowed to a mist. Crossing through the high grass, he headed for the nearest woods, wanting only to distance himself from the cellar's cold breath. The woods swallowed him. He walked through trees and briars until he found a deer path, and then without a plan he walked aimlessly, as if he had forgotten his purpose. As he trudged along, his thoughts whirled and blurred through his mind . . . *wonder if she is in that cellar . . . no that couldn't be possible there were no footprints . . . no one is in that house, but my image in the mirror—the feeling that someone else was there . . . how would that be possible, it couldn't be . . . there were no footprints, but the cellar the cellar the cellar— it breathed on me like a dead man's last breath—dead but still forcing out air . . . my imagination is running way out of control . . . no one has been in there for years and years and years.*

But what if what if what if he followed her . . .what if she ran . . .what if she ran to the house and he caught her and hurt her no no no what if he dragged her into the house into the basement and beat her and beat her no no no there would have been footprints . . . I would have seen them leading to the basement door I would have seen them I would have seen them, but what if . . .what if he dragged her into the basement from an outside cellar entrance—a back basement door . . . there wouldn't be prints . . . what if he dragged her down the outside entrance steps into that death-breathing cellar and she is there in the cold darkness waiting for me to save her bleeding suffering dying no no no I am wasting time thinking like this . . . she is lost in the woods somewhere, she is out here somewhere wandering lost . . .

"Chrissy!" His voice unleashed into the night. The thick mist hung in the air and the shaft of the flashlight cut through it to the trees and tangled greenery before him. The woods fell silent as if he suddenly became deaf, as if the mist absorbed all sound—the saturated ground, weeds, and trees had deadened any noises that could have been heard.

"Chrissy!". . . *Silence.*

He plowed deeper into the woods and his thoughts reeled again . . . *where could she be why did this happen maybe they found her maybe she is home by now but what if she's out here I can't go back I must keep looking what if she's lost walking in the wrong direction soaked completely by this storm and walking in this blindness of the night or maybe she fell and is unconscious lying in a ditch and she cannot hear our shouts O Lord O Lord where is she I must keep looking I will keep looking but what if he followed her what if he dragged her into that cellar what if she is unconscious in that cellar no no no she is not there she is in the woods . . .*

Elijah wandered through the shadowy maze for several hours, and his thoughts jumbled and knotted like the creepers, vines, and branches before him. He couldn't shake the haunting exhale of the abandoned house's cellar. He couldn't forget his own image in the mirror on the second floor. Somewhere deep in the Appalachian hills he stopped and looked at his watch in the flashlight's glow: 3:15. "Chrissy!" he screamed. The silence overwhelmed him. "I've got to go back and look in that cellar." He began to pray, *O Lord guide me back to that house. Direct my steps. I've run away scared. You want me to go back. Direct my steps, O Lord. Help me get back there quickly.* He turned completely around and directed his light through the misty trees until he sensed the direction in which he thought the house must be and marched forward into the wet-slapping leaves and branches.

An hour and a half later, when he stumbled through the thorny berry bushes and saplings that choked the edge of the woods and into the meadow, he noticed his flashlight was losing power. He turned it off and reoriented himself, trying to guess the direction of the farmhouse. Recognizing the slopes of hills and treetops, he figured he was on the far north side of the field. Through tall grass he plowed forward, up a slight hill, and at the top, looked down into the darkened valley where the house squatted in the pit of shadows.

He didn't turn on the flashlight again until he stood before the front porch. The door hung open bidding him to enter again. He decided to walk around to the back and see if there was a basement entrance. A huge walnut tree extended a lower branch like an arm through the kitchen window. Its other branches reached down before Elijah as if to block him from proceeding any farther like a guard unwilling to allow him to pass. Ducking, he scooted underneath the branches as they poked and scraped his back and neck. Past the tree, his circle of light fell upon the weed-infested steps leading down to the basement door. He descended slowly. He turned the knob and pushed. It wasn't locked, but stubbornly edged forward as if it was sealed by suction.

It popped open and the chill of the air engulfed him. He immediately looked for footprints but the floor was damp. The tension that knotted his stomach tightened even more.

Lifting the light, he squinted through the weak shaft as dust motes floated down and swirled before him. He felt like he was in a crypt. Cautiously he inched forward approaching the center of the basement. There, like a hulking monster, stood the round-bottomed coal furnace.

Two open intake pipes jutted out of the top like bulging eyes, multiple arms of cylindrical ductwork extended from the heating chamber in all directions. An angry mouth—a two-foot-square, grilled feeder door—snarled at him. He moved closer. He knew he had to look in the belly of the creature. The flashlight's weak glow centered on the mouth of the monster as its vertical air slots separated huge steel teeth. A handle was locked into place on the right center of the hatch. He reached for the handle and tugged downward, but it jammed. To get better leverage he stepped closer, placing his right palm on it and shoved with great force. The lever broke free and the door popped open, cold against his belly. He jumped back, dropping his flashlight, and the steel door clanged open as if someone had pushed it from the inside. The light had gone out when it struck the cement floor. Elijah dropped to his knees in the utter blackness and fumbled across the cement until his hand knocked into the cylinder rolling it toward the base of the furnace. Like a blind man he groped for the flashlight. When he clasped onto the plastic cylinder, his thumb fidgeted for the button and clicked it again and again. No beam. He shook it and clicked again. The light flashed weakly for a second. He shook it again and a stronger connection occurred, streaming the light's oval onto the floor. Still kneeling not more than three feet from the furnace, he slowly raised the pale circle up the rounded base toward the mouth. When the feeble glow reached the opening, the skeletal face confronted him through stringy strands of blonde hair.

"Chrissy!"

Chapter Twenty-one

"Chrissy!" Elijah gasped again.

He struggled to his feet and stepped back, his wide eyes focused on the ghastly visage. Slanting diagonally, the head hung forward, eye sockets empty and mouth agape. Long teeth, whose gums had long-since dehydrated, protruded from the jaw. Where the nose should have been, a hole exposed the nasal cavity. Blonde hair dangled across the bony cheeks, and a shriveled hand pressed against the corner of the opening.

"It can't be," he said. "It can't be Chrissy."

Elijah moved closer. A grimy pink blouse sagged over the ribs. Directing his light into the belly of the furnace, he could see dark blue jeans covering thin legs. *This can't be her. This person's been dead for years.* He brought the weak light back to the skull. *Someone murdered this girl years ago. God have mercy on her soul.*

In the cellar tomb of the farmhouse, Elijah felt a strange peace flood over him. Now he knew why he had to return there. "I'm sorry you've been trapped in this God-forsaken basement for who knows long. It's not a proper resting place. Someone took your life and stuffed you in this furnace." He nodded. "I promise I'll make sure you're buried, with dignity. . . whoever you are." As he looked through the stringy blonde hair into the hollow eye sockets he sensed the agony of the woman's death, the sheer horror of her last moments. In Elijah's mind, the frozen grimace of the corpse seemed to plead to him, as if she wanted to reveal a secret—cry out the name of her murderer, but couldn't.

When Elijah emerged from the cellar, his flashlight barely emitted any ray so he clicked it off and stuck it into his back pocket. He pressed the button on his watch and the glow revealed 4:33. He peered into the sky. The misting had stopped. A gentle easterly breeze pressed against his wet shirt eliciting goose bumps across his forearms and chest. *It's almost morning. I wonder if they found her yet. I'm gonna go back to the Healing Place and pray till dawn.* After praying, he could head back to check on things. If they hadn't found her yet, the sheriff would be there with the dogs, getting a search party organized.

The natural sanctuary was about five hundred yards away from the house over one rolling hill and up the next. Although it was hard to see without a flashlight, he sloughed through the high grass stumbling a few times as he climbed toward the top of the hill. The oaks and maples stood tall against the pre-dawn sky.

When he crested the hill, he breathed heavily. *Can't remember the last time I was this pooped.* He separated the leaves and branches where he normally entered. The clearing was dark, but not quite as dark as the farmhouse's cellar. Walking to the center, he dropped to his knees and leaned forward, pressing his hands upon the Robin Stone. He lowered his forehead and rested it on the back of his hands. When he closed his eyes, he noticed very little difference between the darkness outside and the darkness inside. "My Lord, my God," he prayed. "Wherever Chrissy is, may she be alive. Don't allow death to take her away from us. Keep her safe in your presence. I've looked death in the face tonight. Someone snuffed out the life of that woman. Have mercy on her soul. I promise you, Father, she *will* have a Christian burial.

"O Lord, I have sought you sincerely with my whole heart for ten years now. Day by day I come here to be filled by your Spirit. I listen to your voice. I ask you, O Lord, please preserve Chrissy's life. Speak to me, Lord. Give me assurance."

He was motionless, listening intently with spiritual ears. "Let me know, my God, if she is still out here somewhere." His mind blanked again as he tried to discern the whispers of the Spirit. "Show me some kind of sign, O Lord."

His head felt heavy against his hands. In the silence of his mind, as he listened for spiritual stirrings, the inundation of exhaustion overwhelmed him—all thoughts, words, images slowly faded into sleep.

* * *

The chirping above opened his eyes. He pressed his hands against the Robin Stone and lifted his body perpendicular to his lower legs. Squinting into the branches above him, he saw the blue flecks of morning sky. In a four inch opening straight above on a thin limb of an oak, the bright orange breast of a robin glowed. The shafts of the newly rising sun shot down into the natural cathedral from east to west.

"The sign! The sign! Are you showing me a sign Lord? Are you speaking to me Lord? I'm here. I'm listening." The robin chirruped loudly in the bright shaft. It fluttered down from the branch and slanted westward through the beams of light. As it neared the ground, it shot back up, but Elijah noticed a glint of gold under the out-stretched branches of a small pine tree where the beams dappled the ground. The gold sparkled in the light. "The Watchover Ring!" He lifted his knee and stumbled to his feet like a large horse struggling to stand.

Walking toward the golden glint, he noticed a mound of wet leaves piled around and behind where it glistened. Half buried in the wet soil, it had been exposed by the night's rain. Elijah reached down between the scattered ochre leaves and pulled the ring from the dirt—a blackened finger rose up with it. He released instantly, and the finger fell back into the wet earth. Grabbing into the soaked soil and leaves behind the ring, he grasped an arm. He pulled it upwards spilling dirt and leaves as the ring, finger, and hand emerged hanging from the wrist. The arm, suspended by Elijah's grasp, protruded from the large pile of leaves and dirt. Frantically he scattered the leaves in all directions and scooped at the mud and soil flinging it behind him as the body of the girl emerged.

When he removed the dirt from around the face, the muddied features appeared with earth-clumped hair, and he screamed, "Chrissy!" She did not respond. He lowered his ear to her nose but could not feel a breath. "Chrissy!" He noticed, even with the smears of brown camouflaging her face, a large lump over her left forehead and a two-inch gash on her neck where blood had clotted. Dipping his hand into the dirt under her neck and shoulders, and his other arm digging under her upper legs, he pulled her up from the shallow hole and stood, staggering to his feet. Her hair, matted with clods of dirt, dropped over his biceps. Leaves and soil tumbled off her torso spattering on the ground. Like an over-sized marionette, her limp body hung in his arms. Her long bare legs were covered with darkened earth and dangling, almost touching the ground.

"*God, God, my God help me!*" he cried. He had to re-grip her around the back of the shoulders, and her head hung back clearly exposing the cut on her neck. He stumbled forward into the beams of light and squinted into the eastern branches, the bright rays almost blinding him. He lifted the girl chest-high into the luminous shafts. "*My God. Help me!*" His voice trumpeted like a panicked elephant. *"Bring this girl back to life. Resurrect her. Don't let Death take her from us!"* He trembled as the slumped body glowed in the shafts of light. *"Touch her, O Lord. I believe you can return her to us. I believe. I believe."*

Glancing down and to the left, he noticed the tangled body of a large black snake. He stepped back and staggered to the right, his heart thumping. He steadied and looked again. The snake was dead, twisted and writhed in a misshapen ball. He marched forward to the exit, but stopped at the Robin Stone. He looked up, and there in the four inch opening on the thin branch of an oak was the bright orange of the robin's breast. *"I believe O Lord. I believe."* He started again, turned and backed through the branches of the opening and into the meadow. The sun shone brilliantly just above the eastern hill, lighting the cloudless blue sky.

As Elijah paced down the path through the golden grass, the girl's head and legs jounced with every step. He tried to walk as carefully and as quickly as possible without jolting her too much. Energy charged his body—the exhaustion he'd felt as he knelt over the Robin Stone had vanished with the rush of adrenalin into his system. The woods were alive around him: jays and sparrows tweeted and whistled; thousands of shades of green and brown splashed across the scene. He steadily advanced, trampling through the mud and puddles--nearly falling on an incline that crossed a ravine rushing with run-off water.

He mounted the knoll where the Emily tree stood. The large fallen hickory, slanting from the charred and splintered trunk, blocked his path. His arms ached. He looked at the names carved into the elm. E-M-I-L-Y. . . A-M-Y. Looking down at the exposed neck of the girl, he noticed the two-inch cut was straight as if made by a sharpened blade, and about a quarter-inch deep. The slick mud was drying on her face in light brown patches and the large lump on her forehead bulged above her brow. Suddenly her face transformed into his daughter's face, and a terrible scene from a hospital room appeared in his mind. He stood with a state patrolman blankly staring at the battered head of his daughter. He swallowed, his eyes filled with terror, and his head swiveled back and forth. He wailed, "No! No! No!" He looked away from the face and into the fallen tree. To cross over the sprawling limbs, he knew he had to watch every step, remembering his near spill the night before. Looking back to the carved names he said, "Don't let her die, O Lord. Don't let her die."

In the daylight it was easier to see the fallen branches, and he lifted his leg and stepped onto the top of the limbs pressing them securely down before taking the next step. When he had successfully traversed the treacherous ground, he focused on the downhill trail, and moved cautiously sideways, carrying the limp body with all his reserves of strength. He progressed steadily until he reached the second steep ravine. Bubbling and gurgling, the water splashed violently as it rushed down the rain-slick sides. Elijah turned sideways again to edge down to the water. His third step lost traction. His right leg went sliding, and his left foot flew forward. He instinctively turned to land on his backside in an attempt to protect the girl. His fall jolted her loose from his arms and tumbled her rolling into the water. Elijah scrambled to his feet, but fell again unintentionally pushing her one more turn deeper into the rushing current. The body, face up, began sliding toward the middle of the flow, but he managed to roll over and grab her foot. He pulled her halfway onto the bank, the water splashing over her face. He lunged, caught her arm,

and pulled her out onto the rocky edge.

* * *

"Where's Elijah? Does anybody know where Elijah Mulligan is?" Byron Butler shouted.

Two bloodhounds yelped and pulled at the chains yanking a tall, bespectacled deputy's thin arms. The radio from the sheriff's black Crown Victoria blared an undecipherable communication above the voices of the more than twenty volunteers.

"Has anybody seen Elijah?" Byron called again.

"Who's Elijah?" the sheriff asked gruffly. His cigarette hung from the corner of his lips, and the smoke curled like a spirit snake around his black-brimmed hat. His dark green sunglasses reflected the gray swirls. A thick, brown mustache and sharply squared sideburns framed the tanned and sternly etched face.

"He helped us hunt last night," Byron said, blinking, his eyes dry and itchy from lack of sleep. Swiping his hand across his jaw, he felt the sandpaper stubble of his unshaven face. "He might still be out there hunting."

"Hmmph," Sheriff Taylor turned and yelled, "Bring those dogs over here! Now!"

The lanky deputy lurched forward like a man on stilts about to fall as the dogs pulled him through the milling crowd toward the sheriff.

"Give me the t-shirt," he ordered, and Byron fumbled with the Kroger's bag and pulled out a gray shirt with the words *Martins Ferry Jr. High Track* imprinted in purple on the front with a flying foot emblem. The sheriff grabbed it and spun toward the dogs yelping at his feet. "Here boys. Smell this. Smell this." He knelt with the shirt pressed against their black noses.

"Do you want us to start combing the woods, Sheriff?" Colin Dutton asked as he leaned over the lawman.

"I'll tell you in a minute or two," he said abruptly. "We're gonna do things my way. If you people wanna help, then wait till I'm ready to send you out." He turned back to the dogs, and Colin stomped away, shaking his head.

* * *

Annie Ferrier secured her arm around Lila Butler's waist, supporting the pallid woman. "Everything's gonna be all right," Annie said.

They stood next to the path's opening. Lila's face was strained and tear-streaked. "How do you know that?" Lila moaned.

"I just know. God has everything in his hands. The Lord's in control."

"I wish I had your faith," she said as Annie hugged her. She shook beneath Annie's embrace.

"Help!" the voice bellowed, and Annie turned to see Elijah's bald head bobbing above the greenery fifty feet into the woods. "Help! I found her!"

The dogs erupted into anxious howls yanking the gangly deputy toward the path. Sheriff Taylor charged through the crowd and stood next to Annie.

"Oh, my baby!" Lila Butler screamed.

Rushing toward Elijah, Byron asked, "Is she all right?"

The crowd of volunteers closed in on the big man.

"I think she's unconscious or . . .or . . ." Elijah couldn't complete the sentence. "She has a huge lump on her head."

Sheriff Taylor stepped through the crowd, jostling for position to get in front of Elijah. "Give her to me!" he commanded. "If she's still alive, we've got to get her to the hospital. Now!" He cradled her around the shoulders and neck and then hooked his right arm below her upper legs as Elijah released the body into his arms.

"Someone open the back door of my vehicle. Now!" he shouted. The dogs barked at his heels, and the deputy leaned back like a water skier, holding them at bay. Harvey Hershaw and Colin Dutton rushed toward the car, running into each other. Colin grabbed the handle first and yanked it open. "Reverend Butler, you come with me."

"Yes sir!" the preacher shouted.

"We'll get her there in five minutes. You two. Help get her into the back seat." Harvey and Colin took her shoulders and supported her head on each side as the sheriff extended her legs into the back seat. They lifted and passed her through the opening lowering her onto the vinyl interior.

Within seconds, Taylor had jumped into the driver's side, roared the engine, and screamed the siren. When Reverend Butler pulled the passenger's side door shut, the back tires spun sending dirt and mud splattering the onlookers. The car reeled forward and sped away with lights flashing and siren blaring.

Chapter Twenty-two

Peter Nower put his arm around his big friend. He'd never seen Elijah so exhausted. "Are you all right, ol' buddy?"

"I need to sit down." The night in the woods—the rain, the mud, the physical and mental strain— made the fifty-three-year-old man look more like seventy-three. His shirt was splattered with dark spots, and slimy brown clay from sliding down the ravine caked his jeans. Wads of dirt clung to his beard, and splotches of drying mud appeared on his wide forehead.

Peter ushered him to a tree stump. "Excuse the expression, but it looks like you've been through hell."

"I *have* been through hell. Maybe worse." Elijah sat on the stump. "If hell is as bad as last night, then I pity the poor souls who end up there."

"Do you think she's alive?"

"I don't know. I couldn't tell if she was breathing."

"Looked like she got caught in a mud slide," Peter said.

Annie Ferrier and Lila Butler approached the two men, Annie bracing the woman who appeared to be in shock.

"We've got to get to the hospital," Annie said. "Help me get her in the car."

Nower grabbed Lila's other arm, and Elijah jumped up from the stump, hurried to Annie's blue Mercury parked just off the road, and opened the passenger-side front door. Lila climbed into the vehicle and stared blankly out the windshield.

"Can we come with you?" Elijah asked. Then he whispered, "I've got to know if Chrissy's alive."

"Elijah, you look you've been through a hurricane. You need to go home and crawl into bed. You did your part. We'll call as soon as we get any information."

"No," protested Elijah. "I want to go with you. I don't care how bad I look."

She waved her hand toward the car door. "Get in."

The two men climbed into the back seat and Annie started the engine and rumbled onto the road.

"Are you all right, Elijah?" Annie asked.

"I'll be fine. Don't worry 'bout me."

"What happened out there?" Peter asked.

"I spent all night hunting in the woods. I even looked through an old farmhouse, and all the time . . . the whole time she was right there at the Healing Place, buried."

Peter scrunched his brow. "Buried?"

"Yes, buried."

Peter glanced up to see Annie's face in the rearview mirror, her forefinger to her lips and her head tilted toward Lila Butler.

Peter nodded.

Elijah quietly said, "You wouldn't believe what I found in that old deserted farmhouse."

"What farmhouse? The Kinloch place out by the berry bushes?" Peter asked.

"Yeah. Across the meadow from the bushes."

"What did you find?"

"In the basement, down in the cellar."

Peter leaned toward Elijah, his voice pitched low. "What was down there?"

"In the coal furnace . . . inside the belly of the furnace." Elijah glanced up at the two women. "Never mind. I'll tell you later."

Peter bit his lip and stared out the window at the passing hillside. *Tell me later? Now he's got me wondering. What in Hades did he find?* He shifted his eyes to the women and then to Elijah beside him. *Just be patient. Now's not the time. You'll find out soon enough.*

Elijah leaned forward, elbows on his knees, and placed his head into his spread hands, closing his eyes. "This seems like a nightmare."

"We wondered what happened to you," Peter said. "Most of us went home about two A.M. Figured it was useless. We decided to save our strength for the morning when there would be daylight. You just kept hunting all night, huh?"

"All night. Didn't find her 'til daybreak. I returned to the Healing Place and knelt down. Before I knew it, I'd fallen asleep. Not for long, though. When the sun came up, the birds woke me. The strangest thing happened then. It almost seemed miraculous."

Annie glanced into the rearview mirror. "What happened?" she asked.

"The beams of light shot down through the branches and leaves. A bird, a robin, flew down through the beams toward the ground . . . then I saw it. The golden sparkle, the Watchover Ring."

Lila Butler, as if Elijah's words were a hypnotist's clap, turned, glared at him and said, "Watchover Ring. Did you say Watchover Ring?"

"Yes, ma'am," responded Elijah.

"Mother gave Chrissy that ring."

Annie reached across the seat and patted Lila's shoulder. "Everything'll be all right." Lila shifted in her seat and faced the windshield again. As Annie approached the Route 7 intersection, she slowed the car to a stop and checked for southbound traffic. After a dairy truck rumbled by, she hit the accelerator and roared onto the road. "We're almost there. It won't be long."

"What do you think happened?" whispered Peter.

"I haven't had too much time to think," Elijah said, "but with that lump on her head and the cut on her neck . . . obviously someone attacked her."

"Do you think she might have been ra. . ." Peter glanced up at Lila and never completed the sentence.

"Don't think so," Elijah said. "She was fully clothed."

* * *

At Hanover Street the blue Mercury turned up the hill past McDonald's and then north on Fourth Street toward the East Ohio Regional Hospital. As the car pulled into the emergency room parking lot, Elijah noticed the sheriff's cruiser next to a red and white ambulance. Peter Nower flung his door open and jumped out to help Lila Butler get out of the vehicle. He ushered her into the emergency room entrance. Elijah got out and watched them enter. He felt someone gripping his arm and turned to see Annie.

"You going in?" she asked.

"No. I look like I just crawled out of a storm sewer. There's nothing I can do in there anyway. I'll wait right here. Let me know when you find out something."

"You still look good to me." She reached up and gently caressed his cheek.

He smiled for the first time that morning.

As Elijah watched her walk away, he sensed that inner place, that part of his heart he carefully guarded from the warmth of her touch, break open. He breathed deeply as she disappeared through the doors. Leaning against the Mercury, he stretched backwards, extending his neck and arms. The warm sun felt good on his face. He lowered his head, closed his eyes, and began to pray for Chrissy. The memories of that night tried to invade his prayer. As tired as he was, he found it hard to focus on the words he wanted to say, and the dead woman kept appearing—the hollow eye sockets, remnant dehydrated skin, protruding teeth, and stringy blonde hair.

"You Mulligan?" The gruff voice startled him.

He opened his eyes to confront the black-brimmed hat and dark green shades of the lawman. "Yeah, I'm Mulligan. Elijah Mulligan."

"Sheriff Bernard Taylor," he said without offering a handshake.

"How's Chrissy? Is she alive?"

"Don't know. They're working on her."

Elijah lowered his head. "Lord help them."

"They'll need all the help they can get considering the lump on that girl's head."

Elijah nodded. "I know."

"Do you suppose she fell and hit her noggin on a rock? And how'd she get so muddy?"

"Sheriff, she was buried. Someone tried to kill her."

"I know."

"You know? Why'd you ask, then?"

"Just wanted to hear what you had to say. You don't get a lump on your head that big by falling down in the woods, and somebody put some kind of blade to her neck." He pulled a cigarette from a pack in his front pocket and stuck it dangling from the right side of his mouth.

"I found her buried in a shallow grave covered with leaves."

"That's quite amazing." Taylor flicked a gold-cased lighter and lifted the flame to his lips. "Sounds like a one-in-a-million discovery."

"Well, it was miraculous."

"Where'd you find her?"

"About a mile into the woods . . . a place where I always go."

The sheriff's head raised, the cigarette angling upwards. "A place where you always go?"

"That's right," replied Elijah.

"You were looking for disturbed ground? You were looking for places where she might have been buried?"

"No. Whoever buried her covered her with leaves too, and the rain washed away any footprints. I wasn't looking for a grave. I didn't even think about that."

Looking up, the sheriff blew smoke toward the sky and said, "You didn't know she was buried, you weren't looking for a grave, yet you miraculously found her in a place you always go?"

"That's right," Elijah said defensively, beginning to sense the direction of the officer's questioning.

"How did you know, Mr. Mulligan?"

"Well, we were berry picking together all afternoon, and we were near that spot."

"Do you and the girl often go out into the woods together?"

"No. That was the first time. But like I was saying, we were . . ."

"I see," the sheriff interrupted. "It was the first time you two were in the woods together."

"That's right."

"I want to get more details from you later, Mulligan. Right now I have some pressing matters to attend to. I left my deputy and dogs out in the country."

"But Sheriff . . .," Elijah said.

Taylor lifted his chin.

Elijah couldn't see his eyes behind those dark green sunglasses. The smoke curled upwards and faded above him. "I found another body last night that I haven't told you about yet."

"Go on." He brought the cigarette to his lips again setting its end aglow.

"There's a farmhouse about five hundred yards over the hill from where I found Chrissy. I thought maybe she went down there to explore, or if someone did follow her back into the woods, I thought they'd try to take her there. No one has lived there for about thirty years."

"Were you by yourself when you were hunting last night?"

"Yeah."

"Everyone else had a partner, didn't they?"

"That's right. I was the odd man out."

"Uh huh . . . an odd man out. A lonesome man by himself."

"Right . . . anyway, I looked through the first floor and the upstairs. I couldn't find anything. I didn't look in the basement because I didn't see any footprints in the house. Figured no one could have gotten down into the basement. I went back out into the woods and hunted all night, but kept thinking maybe there was an outside entrance to the basement. I went back to the farmhouse just before dawn and looked around back. Sure enough, there was a cellar door. I went in and found the remains of a woman in the coal furnace."

Taylor crossed his arms again, and the cigarette dangled from his fingers sending curling wisps rising. "What made you look in the furnace?"

"I sensed something inside of me—almost like a voice saying to look in it."

"A voice told you to look in it?"

Elijah knotted his brow and swallowed. "Not exactly. You know what I mean."

"So you found the corpse of a woman in the furnace?"

"Yeah. She had a pink blouse on and blue jeans. The blouse had been ripped half off. She looked like a mummy—real bony. I could tell she'd been dead a long time."

"Two bodies in one night. Two bodies out there—probably the only two unaccounted for bodies within a fifteen mile radius of here—and you found them both last night. You hit the jackpot didn't you, Mulligan?"

"I wouldn't call it a jackpot."

"How do I get out to that old farmhouse?"

"There used to be a bridge that crossed the creek about four hundred yards down from the top of the hill where everyone had gathered this morning. The bridge isn't there anymore. It was unsafe. They tore it out about eight years ago. The road leading out to the farmhouse is overgrown, but you should still be able to follow it. It's about a mile to the house."

"We'll find it." He stuck the cigarette back into the corner of his mouth.

"And, Sheriff, there's something else."

Taylor raised his chin and blew smoke.

"There's a man, a young man who lives about fifty yards up from where the old bridge used to cross over. I don't trust him."

"Why not?" the sheriff asked, the cigarette flipping up and down as he spoke.

"He's a strange one. You ought to question him."

"Anything else, Mr. Mulligan?"

"Yes . . . that woman."

"The dead woman? What about her?"

"I promised her that I'd give her a proper burial. I'll pay for it. She can be buried in a plot up at the Scotch Ridge cemetery."

"If we identify the remains, then the family will determine where she'll be buried. Besides . . . the dead can't hear any promises you make."

"I just want to give her a proper Christian burial."

"I'll be talkin' to you again real soon, Mr. Mulligan. You can count on that."

Elijah shrugged and stood straight. "I've got nothing to hide."

"She's alive!" Peter's voice blasted from the emergency entrance door. Both men turned toward him as he and Annie appeared.

"She's in a coma, but she's alive."

"Is she gonna be all right?" Elijah asked.

"They don't know," Peter said.

"She took a pretty good hit to the forehead, and they stitched up the cut on her neck," Annie added.

"Do they think she'll come out of the coma soon?" asked Sheriff Taylor.

"They don't know. They're not sure how serious it is at this point," Annie said.

"She was hit on the forehead." Taylor rubbed his chin. "She probably saw the man who tried to kill her." He looked directly at Elijah and took a deep drag on the cigarette.

"You're right," Elijah said. "She probably did."

Taylor blew out a long stream of gray smoke. "If the would-be killer knows she's still alive, he may try something." He dropped his cigarette and smashed it into the asphalt. "Where you gonna be in the next four to five hours, Mulligan?"

"I'm gonna go home and go to bed."

Taylor nodded and looked at all three of them without speaking, turned and went back into the emergency room entrance.

"He's an irritating man," Annie said.

"I can tell he's suspicious of me," Elijah said.

"If he is, he's crazy," Peter said.

Annie clasped her hands around Elijah's elbow. "Let's go home. You need to get some sleep."

Chapter Twenty-three

The water rushing into Elijah's face never felt so good. Gazing down, he saw the brown streaming off his body, creating a muddy whirlpool around his feet as the drain sucked it away. *Ain't it odd? Yesterday, just being in Kyler's presence made me feel like I needed a shower. Now look at me. I'm washing off the actual crud that covered me because of what that creep did. At least I'm 99 percent sure he did it.* Elijah shook his head and leaned against the shower wall as the water pelted his neck and back in a rhythmic flow. He closed his eyes and realized how tired he was. *I could fall asleep standing up.* Several minutes passed before he stood straight and reached for the soap to lather himself—his entire body with a thick layer of the foamy suds. He wanted to be clean, and then he wanted to climb into bed and sleep.

After showering, he dried off quickly, tossed the towel into an empty clothesbasket, and crawled into his bed, still nude. He was too tired to bother with underwear. His king-sized mattress caressed his body. He sank into an impression formed by years of sleeping in a favorite position—half on his right side, half on his stomach with his left leg stretched across to the edge of the mattress and his left arm stretched not quite as far. It was a comfortable position that triggered a rapid progression of tired consciousness into unthinking, deep sleep.

It had been almost 9:00 A.M. when Elijah had closed his eyes. It seemed like seconds later the knocking began. The pounding grew louder, and the stirrings of conscious thought like cold splashes on warm skin, jabbed into his sleeping mind. The rapping at first melded into a dream sequence—images of the dark woods and his feet stomping through mud. Far away he heard someone yell his name: "Mulligan. Mulligan." It grew louder. "Mulligan! Mulligan!" Opening his eyes, he knew someone was at the door. He glanced at the clock radio—1:05. More than four hours had passed since he'd crawled into bed.

Half of his body had fallen asleep (the half that had sunken into the mattress). As he sat up the rush of blood tingled his right side. His leg, arm, thigh, chest, and face were pin prickly. "I'm coming," he tried to say but the words garbled out like the bark of a tired old dog.

The pounding was thunderous. "Mulligan!" the man's voice exploded.

"I'm coming. I'm getting dressed," he called more clearly.

His gray sweatpants hung on the doorknob. Leaning forward, he snagged them and whipped them off the knob. He sat on the edge of the bed, jammed his legs alternately into the openings, stood, quickly pulled them up, and tied the string.

From the voice and the shape of the form at the front door with the broad brimmed hat, he knew it was Sheriff Taylor. When he reached the door and pulled it open, he saw the tall deputy behind the lawman. "Sorry. I was in a deep sleep," Elijah said.

"Thought maybe you left town," Taylor said.

"Come on in." Elijah tried to be polite although the sheriff's arrogance strained his patience.

Taylor entered, and the tall deputy followed, wearing a black ball cap; his large nose, over-bite, protruding Adam's apple, and slight hunch made him look like a cartoon vulture.

Taylor spread his thumb and forefinger across his mustache then rubbed his chin. "We walked out to the deserted farmhouse you told me about. Found the dead woman in the furnace. Not a pretty sight, eh?"

"No. Not at all. What did you do with her?"

"The coroner hauled her out to the lab to do a more extensive analysis. She's been dead a long time. More than ten years I'd bet. Don't you think so, Rusty?" The sheriff glanced over his shoulder at the deputy.

The thin, hunched man cleared his throat and said, "I'm guessin' that's about right, Sheriff."

"You mind if I smoke?" Taylor asked.

"Well . . . I guess not." Elijah hated the smell of cigarette smoke, especially in his house, but he figured he'd do what he could to stay on Taylor's good side.

The sheriff picked a cigarette from his shirt pocket and tucked it into the corner of his mouth. As he talked it flipped up and down. "Found something interesting in her jeans pocket." He reached up with his golden lighter and flicked twice, producing a yellow-blue flame, and set the end of the cigarette aglow. He dropped the lighter into his front pocket and quickly pulled out a piece of yellowed paper like a magician doing a sleight of hand trick. He drew hard on the cigarette and handed Elijah the paper. "Recognize the writing or the name?"

Elijah read the paper:

Lynny,

I don't care what you did in the past. I still love you. God forgave Mary Magdalene and gave her a new life. Remember
2 Corinthians 5:17. You are forgiven. Your new life has begun. Keep trusting in God and you will become stronger. Things are tough but don't give up. Jesus has brought you back into the fold. My prayers have been answered.

Love always,

Mom

"I recognize the scripture verse—2 Corinthians 5:17," Elijah said.

"What?" The sheriff stuck the cigarette back into his mouth as the smoke accumulated above his head.

"Therefore if anyone is in Christ, he is a new creature, the old things passed away, behold, new things have come."

Taylor held the cigarette about an inch from his mouth. "Oh good. Very good. You get an *A* for Bible recitation today."

Elijah fought back the temptation to say something smart like *you get an I for being an idiot*. The deputy stood against the wall in the shadow, waiting and watching like a well-trained dog.

"It's gonna be tough to identify her," the sheriff continued. "We have a first name—Lynny. That's probably a nickname for Lynn. Our best hope is to match the teeth with dental records of missing persons for the last twenty years. There's no guarantee. She might end up a Jane Doe."

"I hope you succeed," Elijah said. "Like I told you, if she doesn't have any family, I'll take responsibility for burying her."

"You're a nice guy," Taylor said, raising his chin. Elijah saw his own reflection in the green shades. "But your buddy down the road wouldn't agree with that statement."

"Whadaya mean?"

"Nathan Kyler. Remember? You asked me to talk to him."

"Right."

"He said he saw you and the girl walk up the road together. Said he was on his porch all afternoon reading the Sunday paper. Did you see him when you walked up the road?"

"Yeah. He was there."

"Said he never saw you and the girl walk back by the house again."

"He's lying," Elijah said quickly.

Taking a long drag from the cigarette, Taylor picked it from his mouth and blew a stream of smoke over his shoulder. The deputy coughed. Just then, Juniper, the orange cat, limped into the room to where they were standing.

"He says that you're lying. Said he saw you drive down the hill in your blue and white Suburban by yourself. Is that right?"

The cat rubbed against Elijah's ankles and meowed loudly.

"That was later. I walked the girl halfway down the hill past his house. He saw us." The cat crossed over and began rubbing against the sheriff's ankles. Taylor pushed it away with his foot.

"Do you ever break into people's houses?"

"No."

"He said you broke into his house Friday morning. Entered without his permission and was messing with his property. Is that a lie too?"

Juniper circled behind the sheriff and nudged up against the back of his legs. Elijah lowered his eyes. "I did go into his house that morning."

Taylor stepped forward, away from the cat. Holding the cigarette, he rubbed his nose. "He said you charged at him with some kind of pointed object so he fired a warning shot over your head that blew out the kitchen window. When he saw it was you, he didn't fire again, but you pulled the shotgun out of his hands and threw it into the kitchen. It went off. Blew a hole big as a barn door into the ceiling. I saw the damage myself. He said you proceeded to attack him. Knocked him down." Juniper persisted back and forth against the sheriff's ankles as he sniffed and rubbed his nose.

Elijah shook his head. "Parts are true, but not all of it. He knew I wasn't a thief."

Taylor jerked his foot again. "Could you please get this damn cat the hell away from me? I'm allergic to them. Don't allow them near my house." Crossing his arms, he stepped away from the purring animal.

Elijah reached for the cat, opened the screen, and gently placed her on the porch. He closed the door and faced the lawman.

"Tell me," Taylor said. "Why did you break into his house?"

"I was looking for an arrow."

"Why?"

"I think Kyler tried to kill my cat."

"Now why would he want to do that?"

"Don't know."

"Maybe 'cause it wandered onto his property."

Elijah shrugged. "Juniper may have wandered in that direction."

The sheriff shook his head. "You know, Mr. Mulligan, I don't like cats much myself."

"Obviously."

"You and your cat have something in common then, don't you? You both were where you didn't belong."

"That's a matter of opinion."

"No, Mr. Mulligan. It's a matter of law. Mr. Kyler said he didn't want to press charges against you. I told him he should. You just told me you broke into his house and physically attacked him. He should press charges, but he said you're a crazy old man. If he presses charges, he's afraid you might do something even worse. He's frightened of you. Thinks you're unstable. Ain't that right, Rusty?"

The sheriff peered over his shoulder to the hunched deputy, and his ball cap bobbed up and down. "That's right, Sheriff." Rusty pushed his black-rimmed glasses up onto the bridge of his nose.

"That's right," Taylor echoed. "Now, do you have anything to say for yourself, Mulligan?"

With a growing sense of helplessness, Elijah shook his head and stared at the lawman.

"Because you may not be in trouble with Mr. Kyler, but you are in trouble with me." Taylor stuck the cigarette back into his mouth and sucked hard. The end glowed red-orange. As he spoke again the smoke poured out and engulfed Elijah's head. "Would you ever hurt anyone, Mulligan?"

"No. Never."

"You tried to hurt Mr. Kyler. You just told me you did."

"I . . . I . . ."

"Would you ever try to kill someone?"

"No. I'd never try to kill anyone!" Elijah's voice shook with anger.

"Settle down, Mulligan. You've got a bad temper. Don't you?"

Elijah composed himself and looked blankly beyond the sheriff's shoulder.

"You say you'd never try to kill anyone."

"No. Never," He said more calmly.

Taylor held the half-consumed cigarette between his thumb and forefinger watching the smoke rise. "Let me tell you the facts here." He looked through the smoke, and Elijah met his gaze. "You took a young girl into the woods. She never came out. We've got an eyewitness who sat on his porch all day and saw two people coming but only one going. You've got a bad temper. You just confessed to breaking into another man's house and physically attacking him. Somehow, *miraculously*, you found two bodies—a little voice inside your head told you where they were. Mulligan, I believe you tried to make a move on that young girl in the woods. When she resisted, you got angry. You grabbed a rock and knocked her out. Thinking you killed her, you panicked, so you tried to cover up your crime. It wouldn't surprise me if you had something to do with the death of that woman we found out in that farmhouse. Some killers just can't stop at one. Do you know what that little voice inside you is called, Mulligan?"

Elijah stood silently realizing his explanations couldn't break through the lawman's twisted logic.

"They call that little voice a *conscience*. And yours bothered you all night until you decided to dig that girl up and bring her back."

Elijah's voice trembled. "I would never do that. You don't know me, and you don't know Kyler either."

"You mean to tell me you would never try to kill anyone?"

"No. Never."

"That's another lie." The sheriff licked his finger and pressed it into the smoldering tip of the cigarette. The smoke released rising to the ceiling. "I've looked into your criminal record, Mulligan. You've done more than just hurt someone. You've killed a man. Snuffed out his life." Elijah hung his head. "Mr. Mulligan, you're under arrest for attempted murder. Give me the cuffs, Rusty."

Chapter Twenty-Four

From the cell window, Elijah peered through the bars and across the alley to the roof of the county courthouse where crows were landing like an invading army of paratroopers. Their gathering reminded him of a scene from Hitchcock's *The Birds*—their presence signifying something sinister, something ominous. The sky, turning pale gray-blue as the sun dipped nearer the horizon, contrasted with the shadowed side of the three-story structure. The colors of the red brick and tan sandstone had faded in the shadow like an aged magazine cover. Below, the alley's pattern of brown bricks was broken only by the uneven line of overflowing trashcans. The world outside drained away with the dying sun. Inside, Elijah sensed his life slipping away. He felt numb. He was very tired but couldn't sleep.

Although the scene outside did not inspire him, he chose to look there rather than into the cell. The walls were concrete, cracked, and greenish-gray. Reeking of remnant urine, the toilet sat in the corner. The porcelain was no longer white, but a sickly yellow and spotted with gritty black dirt. Next to the commode, the sink stood on two rusted steel legs as a steady stream of water ran from the spigot, and underneath, dripped from the drain trap, and pooled on the rough floor. On the opposite wall hung the bed, chains on the corners of a wooden frame bolted into the wall, a two inch tattered mattress, half-hanging off. A low-wattage light bulb, centered on the ceiling, shone weakly through a protective covering, casting shadows like black scars across the wall. The scene outside could not uplift him, but inside, the dark room waited to devour him.

From behind, the scuffing of footsteps down the hallway grew louder as the sudden clinking of keys and rattling of steel invaded the hopelessness of Elijah's mind. Turning from the window, he sought to identify the dark figures standing on the other side of the bars. The tall deputy swung the door open, and with his swath of brown-gray hair and gaunt features, Peter Nower stepped into view.

"You took your good ol' time," Elijah said.

"Sorry. I was at the mall all afternoon. If I knew you were here, I would've driven the extra mile to see you."

Elijah spoke in a monotone. "Always willing to go the extra mile. You must be the exception to the Agnostic's Rule."

"When I got home about seven o' clock, I hit the button on my machine and heard your message. Couldn't believe you'd been arrested."

"I guess seeing is believing for you." Elijah glanced at his watch. "Did you stop by the hospital?"

"Yes. I figured you'd want to know any new reports on Chrissy."

"How is she?"

Peter shook his head. "Still in a deep coma. They have no idea when or if she'll come out of it."

"God, O God, why? Why?"

Peter crossed the cell and placed his hand on Elijah's shoulder. "Easy, ol' buddy, you did all that you could . . ."

"Please don't touch me," Elijah growled. "I'm in no mood to be comforted."

"Sorry."

Elijah turned back to the window and leaned on the ledge. The crows flitted and jostled on the courthouse roof. A minute of silence passed. "Figured you'd probably know a good lawyer."

"I do. A good friend of mine—B.J. Tertulian. I graduated with him from high school. He's excellent. One of the best around."

Elijah nodded his head slowly.

"I'll call him tonight as soon as I get home. We'll be over tomorrow morning, hopefully early. We'll have the bail money ready and get you out of here."

"They haven't set bond yet."

"They haven't?"

"No . . . but when they do, you can bet it'll be pretty high—attempted murder of a twelve-year-old girl—they're not gonna let me outta here on a discount. I don't care anyway."

"What do you mean, you don't care?"

Elijah turned from the window and walked across the cell. He grasped the bars facing the hallway and hung forward. He didn't want to look into Peter's eyes. Feeling ashamed of the mental state into which he had sunken, he lowered his head and stared at the floor. He could hear Peter's footsteps circling the cell.

"Man, this place is disgusting. Look at this toilet. It's filthy. How can you stand it in here? Don't they have anybody to come in and clean these rooms up? Why do we pay taxes? This is deplorable."

Elijah gripped the bars more tightly. No one spoke for several minutes. The silence grew uncomfortable. Finally, after Peter had stepped up beside him, Elijah said, "I don't understand why I'm here."

"It's just a big mistake," Peter said.

"God doesn't make mistakes."

"But man does, Elijah. Man does."

"But God doesn't. And for some reason there's a girl in a coma, and she might die. While I'm stuck in this jail, there's a lunatic out there somewhere, free to roam."

"Elijah, you're tired." Peter edged closer. "You've spent a night in the woods and a day in this hell hole. You're not thinking straight, ol' buddy." The wiry man put his hand Elijah's shoulder and then quickly pulled it away. Elijah closed his eyes and rested his head against the bars.

"Maybe, if I fall asleep this will all go away. But I've tried. I can't sleep. I feel like everything has drained out of me. I'm empty—nothing left inside. Physically, mentally, and spiritually I feel wiped out. Totally spent. Yet I can't fall asleep."

"You'll feel better in the morning. Believe me. I know you."

"Maybe you don't know me. Maybe I'm not who you think I am. Maybe I'm pretending to be someone I'm not. Maybe I fooled myself and everyone else into thinking I'm some kind of spiritual tower of strength when the fact is I'm a weakling."

"Elijah, listen to me." Peter grabbed him by the arm. "Look at me." He yanked Elijah from the bars.

With great surprise at Peter's physical force, Elijah met his gaze.

"You haven't changed. You're the same man you were yesterday and the day before. The circumstances around you have changed, but you haven't changed, and your faith in God hasn't changed."

"Dammit. Don't talk to me about God. You don't even believe in God. How can you know anything about faith? Anyway, I don't want to talk about God . . . especially with an agnostic." Elijah turned back to the bars. "Deputy!" he yelled. "Let this man out of here."

"Elijah, listen to me," Peter pleaded.

"No. I want you to go. I don't want you to see me like this. I'm sorry, Peter. I'm not myself. I don't want to talk to anyone anymore. Deputy! Get this man out of here!"

"I've never seen you like this," Peter said. "I've had my doubts in the past, but now I'm sure."

Elijah raised up and faced Peter. "Sure 'bout what?"

"Now I'm sure you're just a human being like me—flesh and blood. For a while there I thought you might be an angel like on one of those TV shows—sent down to convert me."

"I'm no angel. That's easy to see." He lowered his head and stared at the ground.

The tall deputy shuffled down the hallway with his clinking keys. He fumbled with the lock, and after several tries, released the mechanism, and the door swung open.

"I'll see you tomorrow morning, ol' buddy," Peter said as he exited the cell and headed down the hall.

Hanging on the bars, Elijah called out, "Peter!"

Peter turned and said, "What do you want?"

"I'm sorry."

"No need to apologize. Just hang in there. I'll be back tomorrow morning."

The deputy slammed the door and locked it. Elijah stood and walked over to the suspended bed. He straightened the mattress and sat down. The chains stiffened, and the bed groaned. The mattress smelled like old soiled clothes. He lifted his legs, reclined on the hard surface, and stared at the ceiling. The light from the window slowly faded. Above, the pattern of pale yellow and black shadow stretched across the ceiling and elongated into blurs of lights and darks, melding into a brownish gray where he lay. As the outside light died, the hopelessness that had started with the gathering of the crows fully saturated him, and the acrid odors seeped into his soul. The bed seemed like a pallet being lowered into the depths of despair.

Peter's words returned to him: *She's still in a deep coma. They have no idea when or if she is going to come out of it.* He looked up. The ceiling resembled a hellish dartboard with yellow-gray and black sections that widened and blurred as it extended to the corners of the room. *This must be how Jonah felt in the belly of the whale.*

He thought about Peter Nower. *He doesn't believe, yet he sets a better example than me. I'm supposed to walk the walk of faith to show him the way, but look at me—I'm all talk. What a hypocrite I am. I'm a fake. He loves me like a brother and takes his time to come out here as soon as he finds out what happened, and what do I do? Told him I didn't want him around me. Told him to get out. He's more of a Christian than me, and he doesn't even believe. I'm a fraud. I'm supposed to be the one who's strong. Supposed to be the one who encourages and supports, but he's the one who always comes through for me. I say the words and preach to him all the time, but when it comes down to it, I'm a phony, an embarrassment to God. I've been living a lie. All those mornings I spent praying and look at me. I'm no spiritual giant. More like a spiritual failure.*

Elijah gazed at the ceiling again. When he closed his eyes, the pattern of light and dark swirled in his mind. From the center of the vortex crows flew and alighted around the jail cell and on top of him. *The crows have come to remind me I have failed the Lord. They've returned—the sins of my past, my failures, my weaknesses, my problems, my mistakes—one by one surrounding me, weighing me down. One by one crowding out the faith the hope the light the joy the love the Spirit the crows have come back one after another and God has left me he is punishing me I didn't learn my lesson when Emily and Amy died I haven't pleased him in my spiritual walk I have let God down and now and now and now he has taken another one away from me . . . he has reminded me of my daughter and then ripped away the one who brought back the memories and she will die like Amy and Emily never to see her smiling face again never to hear her sweet voice never to know her friendship I have failed I have failed where are you God? I am alone.*

He felt the growing darkness of the room and the imagined birds crushing him, pressuring his soul into a dense, cold metal, like a junk car turned into a block of scrap. Suddenly the face of an angry young man appeared—short, butch-cut blond hair and blue-eyes—a face he hadn't envisioned for years.

"Come on, you son of a bitch!" the blond challenged. "Come on if you think you can whip me. I'll knock the crap out of you. I'll hit you so hard you'll wake up in the hospital in Peking. Come on you big, red-neck bastard. You white trash. You and your whore girlfriend. That's right. She's a slut and a whore. We all called the number. Right, boys? She gave us all turns." The bodies of players crowded around them, the numbered jerseys, the sweaty faces . . . *No . . . No . . . I'm not him anymore. That's not me he has died and I'm a different person. You are a killer sitting atop the body with the bloody fists and the players pulling you off . . . you are a killer and a convict in a dark jail cell paying the penalty for your own sins . . . you are a life taker, a murderer of his parent's only son and his mother's tears streamed down as his father's arms embraced her and he screamed,* "You murdered my boy!"

The cell became one of thirty-three years gone by when day after day a twenty-year-old boy-man stared at a gray-yellow ceiling with black-scarred shadows. He closed his eyes, and the minutes slipped by excruciatingly, but he couldn't sleep. He sank into a lead gray haze of numbness—as if a fog had risen up from the dark pit of the past and engulfed him. In the abyss of the cell, he sensed a terrible emptiness as if all he had become over the last thirty years, in one day, had dissolved, melted away, seeping out of him moment by moment, drip by drip, crow by crow, shadow by shadow, bar by bar, until the emptiness began to collapse in upon him like a dying star. And in that moment he knew the cold presence of death, of separation, of isolation, of damnation—it breathed upon him, and he could not battle back. He lay helplessly with his eyes closed, and the cold steel hands compacted him until his soul froze solid. Then he began to shiver. He trembled on the hard, chain-slung wooden slab . . . until . . . from beyond the bars . . . a whispering voice said:

"Elijah."

He opened his eyes thinking he imagined the whisper. But then it came again.

"Elijah."

He sat up and squinted through the bars into the hallway. The glow of the corridor light behind the shape of the figure blurred the edges, making it difficult to identify the form.

"Who's there?" he asked.

"I've come to visit you," the warm, deep, feminine voice said.

"Do I know you?" Elijah stood and stepped forward sensing an unsettling prickling like one feels when putting on a garment full of static electricity.

"I'm a friend of a friend," she said.

He stepped closer and could see it was a black woman; because her face was on the side opposite the hallway light, he could not clearly see her features or guess her age. A purple and white flowered scarf reflected the light behind her, and curls of thick hair sprang out from the border of the scarf. As he drew nearer, he looked more closely at her face. She blinked, and her eyes seemed cloudy but compassionate. Her smile widened, and the expression on her face crinkled and crackled the layer of ice that had been forming on the surface of his soul.

"A friend of a friend?" Elijah asked.

"Yes."

"Are you Annie Ferrier's friend?"

"Yes, Elijah, I know her well."

"Do you live along Treadway Road?"

"No. I'm from St. Clairsville. I live down the street."

"Oh. I thought I'd seen you somewhere before. I'm acquainted with most of Annie's friends, and your face looks familiar."

"My name is Dilsey. Dilsey Phillips."

"I'm Elijah Mulligan."

"I know."

"Peter must have called Annie and told her what happened."

"I've come to encourage you, Elijah. I've got good news." Her voice had a musical quality, almost like the rich chimes that echo through a church sanctuary right before the service starts. The bars between them, tarnished-hardened steel, created a physical boundary, but her tone relaxed him.

"You don't know how much I need good news right now."

"That's why I'm here."

"God must have sent you. I haven't felt this lost and lonely in over thirty years."

"The Lord did send me."

"What's the good news?"

"The girl you found . . ."

"Chrissy?"

"Yes, Chrissy. She is not going to die, as you fear. Tomorrow night she'll come out of that coma like Christ came out of the tomb on Easter morn."

"What? . . . I mean . . . How do you . . . Did the doctors say this?"

"Trust me. I know."

"I can see you are a woman of great faith," he said. "I wish I could believe your words. I wish I could say with confidence that Chrissy would rise up out of that coma. I thought I was a man of great faith, but I'm weak. I'm spiritually weak."

"You're in the midst of a storm." Her eyes seemed to fill with dark clouds.

"I feel like God has left me," he confessed.

"No, Elijah. Just the opposite has happened. The Lord has brought you along with him."

Elijah reached up, held onto the bars, and leaned forward. "What do you mean?"

"Only those who were committed disciples got into the boat with him, and all of them lost faith in the storm."

"'O you of little faith, why are you so afraid?' Then He got up and rebuked the winds and the waves, and it was completely calm . . . Matthew 8:26," Elijah quoted.

"This prison cell is the boat. He hasn't left you. He has considered you worthy to bring along to face the storm. God is here," she said.

Elijah turned and looked around the foul cage. "Here?"

"Yes. In every circumstance and every situation God is here. The Lord knows what you're going through."

"I lost faith in the midst of the storm."

She nodded. "O you of little faith, why are you so afraid?"

"The Lord wants me to learn to trust him until he calms the winds and the waves."

"Trust him, Elijah."

"The Lord brought me here to test me, but I failed Him."

"No. The test isn't over. Have faith. The girl is only sleeping. She will arise tomorrow evening."

Within his spirit her words gained confirmation. He sensed a strange unity with the woman and nodded his head. "I believe you," he said.

"Believe God."

"I do."

"One more thing before I go."

"Yes."

"It's all right for you to love again."

"What?"

"God be with you. Goodbye, Elijah." She walked down the corridor and disappeared into the shadows.

What did she say? It's all right for me to love again? As he turned back to face the cell his heart lifted. *What a wonderful lady. Annie must have told her to come and see me. I'm surprised they let her in here this late.* He looked up at the shadow-bitten ceiling. "Lord, I trust you," he prayed aloud. "There's a reason I'm in this cell. You have the power to raise the dead. The old me died thirty years ago, and you raised me up anew. I refuse to return to the darkness of my past. Strengthen me. Build up my faith. I believe you will raise up Chrissy tomorrow night. Help me battle against my doubts, O Lord."

He walked over to the window. By the glow of a street light from the corner of the alley he could see the connected dark forms of the crows atop the ledge of the courthouse roof. "I'm not who I used to be," he announced as if testifying to an audience. "I'm a new creature. The old things have passed away. New things have come." As he walked back to the slung bed, a melody entered his mind and he began to softly sing the words:

"There is power, pow'r, wonder working pow'r,
In the blood, of the Lamb.
There is pow'r, pow'r, wonder working pow'r,
In the precious blood of the lamb..."

He lay down on the tattered mattress, cupped his hands behind his head, and continued singing until he completed all the verses he could remember. Another hymn entered his mind.
"O Lord My God, when I in awesome wonder,
Consider all the universe displayed . . ."

He sang hymn after hymn until shortly after midnight, halfway through the third verse of "Amazing Grace" he fell asleep.

Chapter Twenty-five

Colors floated—reds, pinks, yellows, blues, violets, golds, whites—and Elijah breathed them deeply. They rose up and entered his nostrils sweetly filling his lungs, permeating his entire being with the aroma of geraniums, pansies, marigolds, sword lilies, and dahlias. With the colors, he floated upwards. Looking down on the petals, he focused on the bronze and yellow shades of marigolds. As he arose, he tilted his head back into a brilliant blue sky. The sense of weightlessness and rising fluttered his stomach like when one reaches the top of a Ferris wheel at the exact moment of descending. When he peered down through the colors and flowers, he saw Annie's smiling face in the glow of the sunshine; and as he exhaled, he descended like a balloon returning to the earth. As he neared her, almost to the ground, she held out her arms; but when he reached for her, the image shattered into a thousand pieces with the clanging of a steel-barred door down the hall. He blinked his eyes and cleared his vision to see the gray ceiling above him. Then steps continued down the hall to the next cell door, and the keys jangled.

What a beautiful dream. He had slept soundly through the night. Rolling onto his side and sitting erect, he noticed the splash of light on the floor from the window. He stood, walked to the window, and looked out into the bright morning at the courthouse's red-tiled roof. The crows were gone, and below, men in overalls and t-shirts dumped overloaded trashcans into the back of a garbage truck. The clinking of keys at his cell's door caused him to turn in time to see the tall deputy holding a tray with a plate of scrambled eggs, sausage, glass of orange juice, and a cup of coffee.

"Breakfast time, Mr. Mulligan," the lanky man said.

"Don't they ever let you go home, Rusty?"

"Don't seem like it. Had to work overtime yesterday. Here I am again already this morning."

"The tips aren't too good either, are they?"

The deputy laughed, a snorting, nasal laugh. "What tips?" He walked to Elijah and handed him the tray.

"I'd give you a tip, but then you'd probably arrest me for bribery." Elijah chuckled.

"Nothin' wrong with a lawman acceptin' a little on the side." He smiled and shook his head. "It's in the Bible."

"Really."

"Don't ya remember what Jesus said? *'Ya won't get out of jail until you've paid the last copper.'*"

Elijah shook his head, smiled widely, and put his hands on his hips. "That must have been a corrupted text."

"Did you sleep good last night?"

"Like a baby."

"You must be an innocent man then. A guilty man could never sleep after doing what was done to that girl."

"God knows I'm an innocent man. And I pray God brings that girl back to us."

"Well . . . If you are the wrong man behind these bars, I'm sure we'll find out sooner or later."

"I'm not worried. The good Lord knows I'm here. In time I'll be free. Anyway, *Stone walls do not a prison make, nor iron bars a cage.* Do you know who said that?"

"No, sir."

"Richard Lovelace."

"I'm guessin' Mr. Lovelace never spent much time in the Belmont County jail."

"Yeah. This place ain't quite the Waldorf-Astoria Hotel."

"More like the Cockroach Motel, but we don't hold prisoners here too long anyway. Maybe a week at the most."

"Hey, Rusty, do you got any cleanser and rags or scrub brushes— anything I can start cleaning this place with?"

"You kiddin'?"

"No. If I'm gonna be here a week, I want to get the place cleaned up."

The deputy straightened up. "Sure. If you want to clean, I can supply you with the supplies."

"And that light up there; it must be only a 40 watt bulb. Do you got a 60 or even a 100 watt I could put in there?"

"I'll look."

"Thanks." Elijah walked back to the suspended bed and sat down with his tray. The ball-capped deputy smiled and tilted his head in bewilderment, then walked out of the cell, turned and locked the door.

By the time Elijah had devoured the breakfast, Rusty returned with an armful of cleaning supplies and a new light bulb. Springing to his feet, Elijah carried his tray to the cell door, slid it onto the floor, reached out, and began taking the supplies through the bars.

"I'm gonna need a chair to stand on to change that light bulb."

"You'll need a screwdriver too to take that cage off. I'll get you one in minute or two. Let me unlock the door and get your tray." He jangled the keys until he found the right one and clunked back the plunger.

"My hands are full or I'd hand it to you," Elijah said.

"That's okay. I got it." Stepping out with the tray, he headed down the corridor without closing the cell door.

"Hey. You forgot to lock me in!"

"I know. You ain't going nowhere. You got too much cleanin' to do. Besides, iron bars don't a prison make," he said over his shoulder.

Elijah carried the supplies—a can of Ajax, a toilet scrubber, a stiff bristled cleaning brush and a couple of old hand towels—to the corner of the room and plopped them down in front of the sink. He dumped a heap of cleanser onto the sink, reached over and shook a spattering all over the commode. He scrubbed with the brush first and then used the hand towel to shine the surface. Within fifteen minutes both the sink and toilet sparkled: white porcelain against the greenish-gray walls.

Rusty entered the cell with a stepladder. Elijah faced him. "Let me see that," He yanked it open, centered it below the light, and climbed the ladder. "Give me your screwdriver, and I'll get the cover off." He worked quickly, removing the protective cage, unscrewing the bulb, and taking the 100 watt bulb from the deputy, he screwed the stronger light into the socket, and the room brightened like when one removes sunglasses in the bright sunshine. "There." Elijah handed Rusty the old bulb. "We're seeing this place in a whole new light."

"Gettin' so bright in here it's hurtin' my eyes," Rusty said, laughing and snorting.

"If I scrub down that old mattress, could you hang it outside to dry for me?"

"Sure. Anything else? Wees aims to please."

"Another bucket of clean water?"

"Okay."

After Elijah stepped down, Rusty collapsed the ladder, reached down to clasp the bucket handle, and exited the cell, dragging the back of the ladder behind him. Elijah closed the cell door. "You gonna lock this door? I don't want to see you get in trouble."

"I'll lock it before Sheriff Taylor gets here," Rusty hollered, his voice echoing in the hallway.

After he finished cleaning the old mattress and scouring the wooden slab and chains, the monotony of scrubbing the floor drifted his mind back to that morning's awakening dream: the colors, the flowers, the sweet aroma that lifted him into the sky, and then slowly downward, toward Annie who stood waiting. Her face became ultra-clear in his mind—the gentle features, the long brunette hair, the youthful smile. *What will she think of me? What if she knows about the man I killed?* He gritted his teeth, his jaw becoming rigid. *I'm a new creature. The old has passed away. I am a different man than I was thirty years ago.* The rhythm of the scrub brush and soapy lather across the floor transported him to times and places when he was near her—smelling the fragrance of her hair, seeing the colors of flowers surrounding her, looking into the translucent blue-green of her eyes, brushing against her and feeling the softness of her touch, holding her hand as they united in prayer.

Suddenly the words of the black woman returned to him: *It's all right for you to love again.* He wondered if he imagined those words. Was God leading him to a deeper relationship with Annie? The visit of Dilsey Phillips seemed like a dream. Her words had lifted him out of a dreadful chasm. *God did send her to help me. She knows about Annie and me. She could sense the confusion in my heart and let me know God has brought me to the place where I can love another woman again. But love is a choice. It takes more than one person deciding to love. Two people must choose to love each other.*

He moved the bucket over and scooted to an unwashed section. Dipping the brush into the soapy water, he began again—swish, swish, swish. *I'm in jail. I've been accused of a horrible crime. A long time ago I killed a man. She may not look at me in the same light that she did yesterday. Maybe she's afraid of me. How could I blame her? I took a young girl into the woods and now that girl's in a coma. Thirty-three years ago I beat a man until he died. If she is afraid of me, if she has changed her feelings toward me, I understand. Why should she want to risk a relationship with me—a convicted killer and a man accused of such a terrible act against a child?* Dropping the brush back into the water, he crawled forward about three feet. Only a small section in front of the bars remained to be cleaned. He dragged the bucket beside him, pulled the brush out and continued scrubbing.

Wouldn't that be ironic. I'm ready to fall in love with her, but now she's no longer ready to love me. He shook his head as he scrubbed, then he stopped. Rising up, he looked over his shoulder toward the rectangle of light from the window behind him. Where the water had dried, the floor was noticeably brighter. With determination, he plunged the brush into the half-full bucket splashing the soapy water onto the floor in front of him; he scoured with greater intensity.

His thoughts started again: *God has cleansed me. He has washed me. If she can't accept me for what I am, then that's her problem, not mine. I would be better off alone. Me and God. We made it these last ten years. We could go another ten or twenty.* He scrubbed even harder driving the suds into the floor. *That's right. If she doesn't trust me, if she thinks I'm a killer, then we don't belong together. Me and the Lord have been strong. I can make it in this life by myself. God is my strength. I can travel the path of God's will alone.*

Elijah gave the floor one last swipe and sat back on his haunches, brush in hand, to survey his handiwork. Where once there had been filth, now the cell reflected the splash of sunlight. Nothing could restore it to any sort of beauty, but it was clean, from the newly scrubbed toilet to the walls and floor, relieved of their patina of grime and graffiti.

Suddenly a shadow crossed over the soaked floor and the fragrance of lilacs halted his thoughts. Standing there in the soft morning light was Annie. Her hair, freed from its usual ponytail, flowed over her shoulders. She held his Bible in her hand.

"Elijah."

"Annie." He looked into her eyes as he approached the bars. Her beauty enraptured him.

"Well, Elijah. You gonna stand there staring or let me in?"

Elijah hastily swung back the cell door. "I . . .I w-wasn't sure you'd come." He stammered.

"Why on earth not? I thought you might need some inspiration," she placed his Bible on the bunk.

"Thank you." He wanted to say something else, something suave or funny, but words wouldn't come. Instead, emotions he had suppressed for months now threatened to overwhelm him.

Annie turned and met his gaze. She must have seen the look of helplessness on his face because she smiled that warm, comforting smile. Elijah opened his mouth to speak but the words tangled like tree branches clogging a creek. Without hesitation she moved into his arms, wrapping her arms around his waist and pressing her face to his chest. Her warmth sent a fire through him.

Taking a deep breath, he filled his being with the fragrance of her hair. It lifted him. He gazed into her eyes, her hands still on his shoulders. As he exhaled he drew her closer placing his hands on the small of her back. She snuggled against his wide chest pulling him closer. Her body felt soft as it pressed against him. Lowering his nose into her hair, he breathed her in again, and as his lungs filled, she seemed to rise with him. He exhaled and loosened his hold. Without thinking, he lowered his head and pressed his lips against hers. For long moments they were lost in the wonder of one another. The wet connection broke slowly, and he raised his head and looked into the teal depth of her eyes.

"Oh, Annie, I love you. I've loved you so long!"

Annie had no problem finding her voice. "Elijah, I thought I'd never hear you say those words! I love you too and for just as long!"

She looked up at him, and he caressed her cheek brushing a tear with his thumb. He kissed her again as she gently stroked his ear and rubbed her thumb against his beard. Both trembled slightly as their lips slowly parted.

Elijah took her hand and pulled her down beside him on the bunk. She fit so perfectly into the curve of his shoulder as he sat with his arm around her, the other hand clasping one of hers. So many emotions were at war in his heart—worry for Chrissy, love for Annie, dread of the sheriff's suspicions, wonder at the sweetness of their confession of love. Suddenly the glow on his face faded.

With her hand, she angled his face toward her. "What's wrong?"

"This happened to me before."

"What do you mean?"

"I was in love with a women thirty-three years ago, and in the middle of it all, I got sent to the penitentiary for two years."

"It's not gonna happen this time. You're an innocent man. I'm gonna do everything I can to prove it."

Elijah leaned back, surprised at her feistiness. "What can you do?" He smiled as he noticed the determination in her eyes.

"Well . . .well . . . I can . . . I can . . . well, you just wait and see. I'll figure out something."

He pulled her close again and absorbed her warmth. "You know, I believe you probably will." He caressed her cheek. Breathing the fragrance of her hair again, he remembered his dream. "I woke up with a vision of you this morning."

"Really."

"Really. I dreamed of flowers and the beautiful aroma lifted me into the sky. As I floated back down, you were there surrounded by all the colors and fragrances. It was so real; the aroma was so strong, I thought I would explode with joy. But when I reached for you, I woke up and you were gone. I never got to hold you."

"You're holding me now," she said, "and this isn't a dream."

"Much better than a dream."

They sat holding hands and talking about the multitude of things that link the minutes of the day into hours. Words flowed back and forth. With the words came laughter, with the laughter, longing looks, with the longing looks, gentle touches.

"Did you stop by the hospital today?" Elijah asked.

"Yes. The doctors aren't very hopeful. They're trying to brace the family for the worst. But I laid my hands on Chrissy and prayed. I don't believe the words of the doctors. I believe in the word of God."

"Amen," Elijah said. "Thank you for bringing my Bible."

"I thought you might want to do some reading today. "

"I forgot it in all the confusion. It's nice to know you were thinking about me."

"I think about you all the time. I love you."

"You don't know how good it feels to hear you say that. For a while last night, I wasn't sure if anyone loved me."

"You silly hillbilly. Everyone I know loves you."

"I can think of two people who don't: Sheriff Taylor and Nathan Kyler. Right now my fate might be in *their* hands."

"Your fate's in God's hands. Trust me. You'll see."

Holding Elijah's hand, she walked him to the cell door. "It's time for me to go. I've got so much to do before I get back to the hospital. But I don't want to leave."

"I understand," Elijah said. "I'm just tryin' to capture these moments in my heart. You've made this one of the best days of my life."

"Our time has just begun." She looked into his eyes, and he melted inside as they engaged again in a lingering kiss.

They slowly separated, lips clinging with wetness. "You better get going." He pulled open the barred door. She stepped into the hall and waved as he pushed the door shut. Almost out of sight, Elijah called to her: "Annie! I forgot to tell you something."

Turning and walking back, she stood, the bars between them.

"What is it, Elijah?"

"Your friend visited me last night. What a wonderful lady. She told me she and you were good friends. Her wisdom was incredible. Somehow she knew exactly what I was going through. I've never met her before. I thought I knew most of your friends."

She placed her hands on his as they gripped the bars. "Who're you talking about?"

"You know, the black lady . . . Dilsey. . . Dilsey Phillips. I was so depressed. She knew exactly what to say to me. Thanks for sending her. She made me realize that the Lord was testing my faith through this storm. My whole attitude changed after talking with her."

"Dilsey! Oh, what a precious woman. Golly, I spent half my childhood at her house playing with her kids. She practically raised me. Took me to the St. Clairsville Baptist Church every Sunday with her family. She used to visit the prisoners here once a week to share the gospel with them, but that was years ago. Elijah, I never told Dilsey you were here."

"You didn't?"

"No. Was she alone?"

"Yes."

"I can't see how that could be possible."

"What do you mean?"

"Dilsey suffers from macular degeneration. She's been blind for five years."

Elijah's mouth dropped open and he shook his head. "Blind?"

"Yes."

Elijah slowly nodded and his eyes widened. "God led her here to tell me something."

"What?"

"The doctors are wrong. Chrissy's coming out of that comma sometime today."

"She said that?"

"Yes, and I believe her. She can see much more than the doctors will ever see."

Chapter Twenty-six

"Come in. The door's open," Elijah said when he looked up from the open Bible. The crimson book rested in his hands as he leaned his elbows upon his knees. Peter Nower swung open the cage door and entered, followed by a short, stocky man with thick, slick-backed black hair, the comb marks still visible; he wore a black, pin-striped suit, thin tie, and carried a black attaché case.

"What a difference a day makes," Peter stood in the middle of the cell and scanned the room nodding his approval. "You must have some connections with the judge to get this place cleaned up so fast."

"I do," Elijah said. "But not the county judge. It took someone with more power than him to get this place clean." Elijah stood up and dropped the Bible onto the bed.

The short man lowered his briefcase to the floor and extended his hand to Elijah "Benjamin Julius Tertulian. B.J. to my friends and clients."

Elijah, almost a foot taller, shook his hand, a firm exchange. Peter continued to circle the room, commenting on the transformation.

Elijah placed his hands on his hips. "The truth is I woke up a new man this morning, and I decided to clean the cell up myself. Figured if I'm gonna be here a while, I want this place to look . . . well . . . halfway decent."

"We're getting you out of here today," Peter said.

"Well then, it will be nice and clean for the next guy."

"How'd you sleep last night?" Peter asked.

"Great. Haven't slept that well in a long time. Like I told you. I woke up a new man."

Peter finally stopped inspecting the cell and stood beside the lawyer. "That's good to hear, ol' buddy. You were in no mood last night for a social call."

"I needed to learn an important lesson. Sorry about my attitude."

"No need to apologize," Peter slapped Elijah on the shoulder. "Did you stop at the hospital today?"

"Yes." Peter lowered his eyes. "Nothing has changed. She's still in a deep coma. They're worried that she may never come out of it."

With his voice pitched low, Elijah said, "Don't be afraid, just believe . . ."

Peter met Elijah's eyes. "What'd you say?"

"Oh . . . just a scripture I was reading when you got here this morning. I don't want to say anything right now, but you may be in for a surprise tonight."

Peter raised his shoulders, eyes questioning. "Okay. If you say so. Anyway, B.J. has come to get you out of here."

The lawyer stepped forward, brown eyes intensifying as he looked at Elijah. "Yes, Mr. Mulligan, I believe we can have you out of here very soon. Have they set your bond yet?"

"No. The sheriff should be getting here soon, though. Don't get your hopes up. I'm a man with a criminal record, convicted of manslaughter, and now accused of attempted murder of a twelve-year-old girl. And that's not all. He thinks I may have had something to do with the remains I found at the farmhouse."

"What remains?" Tertulian asked.

"I found a corpse, mostly bones, in the basement of an abandoned farmhouse when I was hunting for Chrissy. The sheriff had a hard time believing I found two bodies in one night. He thinks I was overcome by guilt and exposed my own foul deeds."

"That *is* pretty amazing," said the lawyer. "Who was the woman in the farmhouse?"

"Don't know. She'd been dead a long time. It was pretty gruesome. She had a note and a cross in her pocket. The note had a name on it— *Lynny.*"

"Lynny?" Peter said. "A missing woman by the name of Lynny." He looked out the window, sliding his hand across his jaw. "That sounds familiar."

"It's all circumstantial," Tertulian said. The short man began pacing the cell. "The sheriff can't hold you here just on suspicion, even if your story seems incredible. You were looking for a lost girl, and you found her. So what if she was buried. You were lucky. Somehow you found a buried girl. How did you find her, anyway?" He stopped pacing and glanced up at Elijah.

"I was praying in my favorite place in the woods just after sunrise, and the beams of light coming down through the trees fell on a pile of leaves and dirt. There was a golden sparkle near the leaves. I remembered the golden ring Chrissy had worn. I walked over to the pile. When I lifted the ring, her finger appeared. Someone had buried her in a shallow grave right there—in my outdoor sanctuary."

Tertulian stared at Mulligan, incredulously. Then slowly he began nodding his head. "Okay. Okay. You found her buried in a place you always go . . . an outdoor sanctuary did you say?"

"That's right. The Healing Place I call it."

"Okay. Okay. The Healing Place. It's possible. It's possible. With the light coming down and the golden ring, you found her; you dug her up. There's no proof whatsoever that you tried to kill her. They can't hold you here even if your story is incredible. Even if you have a criminal record. No way. No way." He stopped pacing and eyed Elijah again. "Tell me about your conviction for manslaughter."

Elijah looked down. "I don't like talking about it. That was a long time ago. I was only 19 years old."

"I need to know if I'm going to represent you."

Elijah took a deep breath. "Well, okay. If you insist. I was a freshman at West Liberty State College in West Virginia. The college offered me a scholarship to play football for the Hilltoppers back in 1963. I was a tight end on offense and a defensive end on defense. West Liberty had a senior star fullback by the name of Jimmy Nickleson. He and I didn't get along. He was the kind of guy who abused the freshmen players, and I was the kind of guy who wouldn't take any abuse. Most of the younger guys were scared of him. He was big and strong—a bully. If he didn't like you, he'd try to pick a fight with you. After a couple of the freshmen got roughed up, they all fell into line except for me.

"In practice I'd tackle him hard as I could. He hated me. He'd get in my face and call me names to try to make me fight. I had a bad temper, but kept hold of it 'til. . ." Elijah eyed the ceiling and waggled his head. Grimacing, he blinked his eyes and raked his beard.

"What happened?" Tertulian asked.

"One day he came into my dorm room. I knew something was up. He never rubbed elbows with the Bricks—the freshmen, so to speak. Said he was just stopping up to see how white trash lived. He walked around my room, looking things over and throwing out insults. Told him I wouldn't put up with his mouth in my own room. Before he left, he warned me to let up on him in practice or else. Fat chance, I said. He promised me that if I kept it up, he was going to beat the you-know-what out of me one day soon. I slammed the door in his face. That evening I noticed my picture of Emily was missing. It had been sitting on my desk. I knew he'd taken it.

"Emily and I were high school sweethearts. We wanted to get married that next summer. After she graduated, she was going to work while I went to school and got my degree. When I got to the locker room the next day, all the guys were crowded around the bulletin board. Jimmy was in the middle of them. When they saw me coming, they parted like the Red Sea. They knew what was gonna happen. Jimmy stood there blocking the bulletin board. He said, 'Did ya see this, Mulligan?' He stepped to the side. Emily's picture was tacked to the middle. It had been glued to a piece of paper. Under her picture were the words: 'Want to get laid? . . . call Emily.' Then her telephone number. I don't know where they found her number. Jimmy said, 'Look here, Mulligan. You ought to call this girl. She really puts out. All of us got a piece. Didn't we boys?' The seniors all laughed.

"I said, 'You son of a bitch.' He called me a fat bastard and pushed me. I exploded. I hit him once on the chin as hard as I could, and he went down. I couldn't control myself. I jumped on top of him and began punching his face. Blood splattered everywhere. I must have hit him five times as hard as I could before the seniors pulled me off. I stood there with blood all over my fists and shirt. I could feel it dripping down my face . . ." Elijah stared into another world, another time. He shook his head again. "He died within the hour. They convicted me of manslaughter and sentenced me to three years. I was paroled after serving two in the state pen near Morgantown.

"Emily's dad wouldn't let her come and see me. They forbid her to write, but she got off a letter now and then without them knowing. Prison life had turned me into an angry young man. After I got out in '65, I was able to get a job at the steel mill in Pittsburgh, but I had problems. I started drinking. Never touched liquor before. I needed something to fill the emptiness and numb the pain. My whole perspective on life had changed. I worked my eight hours at the mill, and then I'd go get drunk. Within six months I was an alcoholic. I had gotten in several bar fights, but luckily had never been arrested—I would have been sent right back to prison. I was a foul-mouthed, violent, young man.

"Then one day Emily showed up at my door. I was living on the south side of Pittsburgh in a rundown apartment. She had turned nineteen, and against her parents' wishes, she came to see me. She said she still loved me. I was afraid to be with her knowing what I had become, but she was much stronger than me. All our lives she was the strong one, spiritually anyway. That's hard to believe seeing how big I am, isn't it?" Elijah glanced from Peter to Tertulian. They listened intently.

"From that day on things began to change. About a year later, after I quit drinking and settled down, we got married and started our lives together. We bought a small house in Pittsburgh. Believe me, I was still a troubled young man, but I was headed in the right direction."

After Elijah finished speaking, Tertulian nodded his head as if thoughts were falling into ordered slots with every bob. When the nods slowed to a stop, he spoke: "Mr. Mulligan. It all comes down to this: Everything the sheriff has against you is circumstantial. Yes, you went into the woods with this girl; yes, she never returned home; yes, you miraculously found her and the remains of another person; yes, you have a criminal record; yes, you even killed a man, but he has absolutely no solid proof: no weapon, no motive, no witness. It is all circumstantial. I will have you out of this jail cell probably within the hour."

The short man crossed his arms and tilted his head back, and a slight smile appeared.

"Just one thing, Mr. Tertulian," Elijah said.

"What's that?"

"There's a witness."

"Who? Wha . . . what do you mean?"

"A man told the sheriff he saw me walk by his house with the girl on our way to the woods, but he said I lied about walking the girl home. Said he was on his front porch all afternoon and never saw the girl again after we passed by the first time. He insisted I drove by his house by myself later that evening, about six o'clock. Swears he never saw the girl again."

"Maybe he went into the house right before you two walked by. Maybe he had to go to the bathroom or something and just missed seeing you."

"No." Elijah shook his head. "I walked the girl by his house, and he was on the porch. We even exchanged some unfriendly words."

Tertulian raised his hand to his chin. "Why in the world would he out-right lie to the sheriff?"

"For one of two reasons," interjected Peter. "He doesn't like Elijah and he wants to see him get into trouble, or he's the one who tried to kill the girl and he's lying to save his own skin."

"There's something else you should know, Mr. Tertulian."

"What now?" The lawyer's eyes had lost their intensity.

"I broke into Kyler's house earlier in the week to look for something. When he showed up we had a scuffle. He tried to kill my cat. I was looking for the weapon. A bow and arrow."

"Does the sheriff know about this?"

"Yes. I admitted it to him . . . because it's true."

The lawyer shook his head and looked at the floor. "This changes things. Maybe it won't be as easy as I thought getting you out of here."

Just then a scurry of footsteps and jangling metal sounded down the hall as the deputy fidgeted with a handful of keys. "Sorry. Got to lock you in. I just saw the sheriff's car pull in. He's back earlier than I expected. I'd get in trouble if he knew I'd left this door unlocked all day." The plunger clanked into place, and Rusty nodded and walked toward the front office.

Tertulian continued: "Like I was saying, this complicates things. Not only are you suspected of attempted murder, but also there's a witness who contradicts your story. Not only that, you've admitted to breaking into his house. You fought with him. Even if he's lying, it's your word against his, and the sheriff seems to be on his side. All of this will increase the validity of the sheriff's grounds for holding you in the judge's eyes."

The soft scuffle of footsteps echoed down the hall and grew in volume. The trio turned and looked through the bars to see the deputy followed by the sheriff and Annie Ferrier. Rusty inserted the key, cranked the lock back, and swung open the door.

Standing without his hat or sunglasses, the sheriff appeared vulnerable, more human, almost humble, and Annie stood beside him with a curious sparkle in her eyes.

"You're free to go," Sheriff Taylor said.

Chapter Twenty-seven

"What?" Elijah asked.

"I said you're free to go." Taylor glanced down for several seconds and then up again.

Annie skirted around the lawman, her smile erupting, and rushed into Elijah's arms. She hugged him, squeezing him so hard his breath heaved out as he embraced her. Stepping back, Peter raised his eyebrows, and Elijah couldn't prevent a wide smile from breaking out. The short lawyer appeared disappointed like a second string basketball player who didn't get a chance to get into the game.

Nodding his head, Rusty pushed his black-framed glasses up onto the bridge of his nose. "You worked all morning cleanin' this place up, and now you don't even get to stay."

"I don't mind," Elijah said. "I just want to know what happened."

Annie pulled back from him and looked up. "Your dream."

"My dream?"

"Remember the dream you had this morning—all the flowers and fragrances?"

"Yes, of course I remember."

"I drove back home after I left you earlier today. It was so warm and beautiful outside. I had my window down as I headed up Nixon's Run, and I saw the beautiful flowers along the border of the front yard of the parsonage. I slowed the car and the aroma filled the air. Then I thought of your dream and had to pull over. I walked across the road and looked at the wonderful splotches of color before me. Then I saw the marigolds and felt strangely drawn to them. As I knelt down and peered through the flowers and leaves, I saw it. Tucked beneath the overgrown plants was the pail of blackberries."

Sheriff Taylor stepped forward. Everyone turned to look at him as he spoke. "Ms. Ferrier did the right thing. She didn't touch the pail. She left it right there and contacted me. I got there as fast as I could. I took the pail to the lab and we dusted it for prints. Sure enough, the only prints on the pail were Chrissy Butler's." The sheriff paused and glanced from face to face. "I knew then Nathan Kyler had lied to me when he told me Chrissy didn't pass by his house on the way home. Mr. Mulligan, I owe you an apology." The sheriff held out his hand, and Elijah, first looking at everyone and then to the sheriff, extended his hand. They shook firmly.

"I'd give you a big hug, Sheriff, but I don't want to get shot."

For the first time by Elijah's recollection, the sheriff smiled. Rusty began to laugh, and the others joined in. When all quieted, Elijah said, "I figured sooner or later the truth would come out. It always does."

"I want to see more than truth prevail," Taylor said. "I want to see justice served."

"Does Kyler know you found the pail?" Elijah asked.

"No. I haven't talked to him since yesterday."

"*Now* do you think he's the one who tried to kill Chrissy Butler?" Elijah asked.

The sheriff met Elijah's gaze. "What do you think?"

Elijah nodded. "I hate to accuse anyone without any real proof, but I'm almost sure he did it."

"We have no substantial evidence."

"But he lied to you," Peter said.

"He lied to me, but I'm guessing that if I confronted him about that, he would suddenly remember that he had to go inside the house for a few minutes—to go to the bathroom or whatever—he'd claim that Mr. Mulligan and the girl must have passed by then."

"What kind of proof do you need to arrest him and hold him until you find more evidence?" Annie asked.

"A lot more than what we've got. We have no weapon, no footprints, no motive, and no witness. If we could substantiate our suspicions, the judge may grant us a warrant to search Kyler's premises. Perhaps we could find the weapon he used to slice her neck and blood evidence. Maybe we could find some small clue on his property."

"We do have a witness," Elijah said.

"Who?" asked the lawyer, wrinkling his forehead.

"Chrissy Butler."

An uncomfortable silence followed. Peter shifted his feet, casting a glance to the floor. No one would make eye contact with Elijah except for Annie. In her eyes he sensed a confidence that contrasted with the doubts the other four must have felt.

"Well . . ." Taylor said. "We can always hope."

The others mumbled and nodded.

Elijah wanted to say something, but he knew they wouldn't understand, so he held his tongue.

The sheriff said, "There are two unsolved crimes I'm dealing with. I have no evidence against Kyler for attempted murder, and I have another victim—the woman you found at the abandoned farmhouse—Lynny. We still haven't identified her. Couldn't find any Lynns in the missing-person files. It'll take some time for forensics to determine when and how she was killed. By the looks of the remains, someone murdered her at least a dozen years ago."

"Do you think that woman could be linked to Kyler too?" Peter asked.

"Anything's possible," Taylor said. "Maybe Chrissy isn't his first victim. He could be a serial killer. There might be other victims. I wish we could put him behind bars until we find some evidence."

"Sheriff," Elijah said, "if Kyler would run . . . if you got behind him in your car and hit the lights and blared the siren, and he tried to escape, would that be enough to arrest him and get a search warrant?"

"Yeah, but why would he run? He knows he has covered his tracks well. He thinks you will be convicted and sentenced for the crime."

"I've got a plan. I think I know what I could say to scare him enough to make him run."

Peter rubbed his chin. "What would that be?"

"Trust me," Elijah said. "Now, what would it take to charge him with attempted murder?"

"I'm afraid it would take more than Kyler just running from the law. We'd have to find something at his house to prove he did it. These kind of perpetrators like to keep souvenirs. We could get lucky. Let's just hope he hasn't destroyed all the evidence."

"Do you think it's worth trying?"

The sheriff looked around the circle of faces. "It's definitely worth trying. Does anybody have a better idea?"

All shook their heads.

"Mr. Mulligan. You're the only man with a plan."

Chapter Twenty-eight

Elijah Mulligan pounded on the flimsy screen door. Peter Nower rocked nervously from his heels to toes, glancing to the right then left, and even looking behind him into the junk-strewn yard and across the wooden bridge to the road and hillside. Twilight had faded the day into neutral shades of brown and gray as if the setting sun had liquefied the colors and sent them draining into the creek that ran down to the Ohio River two and a half miles to the east.

Peering into the darkened house, Elijah saw a figure in the kitchen doorway. "There he is. I hope he doesn't greet us with his shotgun."

"Me too," squeaked Peter. "Do you know what you're going to say to him?"

"I think."

"What do you mean, 'I think'? You told me you knew how to make him run."

"I do. Trust me."

"You're not even sure what you're gonna say?" Peter shook his head and blew out a long breath of air.

"Shhhhhhh. He's coming this way."

Elijah saw Kyler turn right through the front room and walk to the closet on the far wall. He banged on the screen again and heard Kyler's footsteps approaching. The dark haired man materialized, staring at them from the shadows just beyond the light. Kyler's eyes and mouth appeared like dark holes; he clasped the shotgun slanting downward at the ground.

Elijah broke the silence: "You gonna invite us in, Kyler?"

After a half minute of dead silence, Kyler raised the shotgun. Peter stepped back, reaching out and clasping Elijah's arm.

"Why are you trespassing again, old man?" His voice was cold, metallic.

"Surprised to see me, aren't you?"

"Did Mr. Nower here put up your bail?"

"No," Elijah said, and Peter shook his head.

"Some slick lawyer must have got you out on a loophole."

"Wrong again," Elijah said.

"To tell the truth, I really don't give a damn. Now get off my property."

"To tell the truth is something you don't do very good, Mr. Kyler."

"Go to hell."

"They've canceled my reservation in hell. But the devil is patiently holding yours."

"I'm not as patient as the devil. Get off my property."

"Before I go, I came to warn you about a couple of things."

Kyler raised the gun and pointed it straight at Elijah's forehead. "Mr. Nower, if I were you I'd get out of here right now unless you want Mulligan's brains splattered all over your pretty Polo shirt."

"Now h-hold on, Nathan," Peter said. "We d-didn't come here to cause any t-trouble, did we, Elijah?"

"Nope. Just wanted to tell you two things."

"You've got ten seconds."

"The sheriff knows you lied about the girl and me. He's convinced that you're the one who tried to kill her."

"You're lyin'."

"I'm out of jail, ain't I?"

"That don't mean nothin'."

"The sheriff found something that shreds your story to pieces."

"What?"

"The pail."

"What're you talkin' about? What pail?" The gun barrel began to waver, and Kyler shifted his feet, inching backwards.

"Don't you remember? You said you were on your porch all day. You told the sheriff that Chrissy never returned from the woods."

"So what. It's my word against yours."

"Not any more. The sheriff found the pail of blackberries. You forgot she had a pail of blackberries, didn't you?"

Kyler glared through the screen for a few more seconds, but then his features lost their intensity, and he lowered the gun barrel. "What're you talkin' about?"

"When she walked down the road past your house, she carried a pail of blackberries. When she came back up the road past your house again, she didn't have the pail. She hid it in a patch of flowers in her front yard. Sheriff Taylor found the pail. He took it to the lab and could find only her prints on it. That proved to him you were lying."

The gun now pointed at the floor. Kyler's eyes shifted back and forth, up and down, not focusing on anything in particular. Finally, he met Elijah's gaze. "You said what you came to say. Now get out of here."

"One more thing," Elijah said. "I got word from a trustworthy source that Chrissy'll come out of the coma soon, probably tonight sometime."

Peter stopped rocking. With raised eyebrows, he glanced at Elijah.

Elijah continued: "The sheriff is convinced she saw her attacker. Before you knocked her out, she saw you. So, I came to tell you not to go anywhere. Don't leave town. Come to think about it, don't even leave this house. I want my name to be cleared completely, so make sure you stick around. The sheriff'll probably be here soon to take you into custody. Like I told you before, you hurt someone, and I will make sure you pay."

"I've had enough of your bull crap. Get off of my property."

"Take it easy. We're leaving. Come on, Peter." The two men turned toward the steps. Before Elijah descended, he looked over his shoulder and said, "See you in jail."

Peter looked up at Mulligan as they descended the steps. "Shhhhh. I want to get away from here alive," he whispered.

Through the yard they angled around an old transmission and cut between the rusted push mower and a gray-primed fender. After crossing the bridge, they turned up the hill, and Peter said quietly, "Where did you come up with that information?"

"What information?"

"That Chrissy was coming out of her coma. The last report I heard this afternoon wasn't very optimistic at all. In fact, she was no better than she was two days ago. Maybe worse."

"Is that so?"

"That's right. And I've never known you to lie to someone, but maybe this situation requires some moral compromise."

"Nope. I didn't compromise or tell a fib. It's the truth, as far as I know it."

"Did you get some news that I haven't heard yet?"

"Yes I did."

"When?"

"Last night."

"Last night?"

"Right. But the news didn't come from the hospital or a doctor."

"Huh?"

"I'll tell you later. Here's the cruiser."

Peter shook his head. "Tell me later? Why do you always leave me hanging?"

The sheriff's car was parked in a patch of weeds under a large willow tree on the side of the road forty yards up from the bridge. Strands of leaves hung over top of the car, creating a convenient blind. At the wheel sat Sheriff Taylor, smoking.

Chapter Twenty-nine

Elijah climbed into the front seat and quietly shut the car door.

Sheriff Taylor flicked ashes out the side window. "Well, boys, what do you think? Is the rabbit gonna run?"

Peter Nower pulled the back door shut, slid to the middle of the seat, and leaned forward. "We shook the bushes, but I don't know if we scared him."

"He's scared all right," Elijah said. "I'm guessin' ten minutes at the most—enough time to throw a few things together—and he'll be out the door and hitting the highway."

Taylor licked his finger, touched the tip of the cigarette to extinguish it as he blew out the last lungful of smoke through the window, and then flicked the butt into the woods. "I figure if he runs, he'll head down the hill to Route 7 and then south to Interstate 70."

"No doubt," Elijah said. "He'll want to get as far away as fast as possible."

"If we chase him, he may turn down one of these old dirt roads to try to lose us," Taylor said.

"So be it," Elijah said. "That old Escort can't be too fast."

"I'm not takin' any chances with you two in the car. Let's hope that Escort hasn't been super-charged and fine-tuned."

"If he doesn't run, can you still get a warrant to search his premises?" Peter asked.

"I have my doubts. We have nothing on him except that he told a possible lie, and I'm sure he'll lie his way out of that one."

"Eventually your lies catch up to you," Elijah said.

"With the girl still in the coma, no weapon, no footprints, no motive, and no witness, all we can do is squeeze the sonovabitch like a pimple and see if he pops. If he does run, I'll arrest him. It'll be up to the judge to issue a search warrant."

"I'll be surprised if he doesn't run scared," Elijah said. "Kyler's like a cockroach. When the lights come on, he bolts into the darkness."

"After what you told him, he just might," Peter said.

"What exactly did you tell him?" the sheriff asked.

"Elijah told him you knew he was lying and that you were coming after him when the girl comes out of the coma and identifies him," Peter said.

Elijah shifted in his seat. "I didn't exactly say that."

"Something like that."

"That just might work," Taylor said. "If he thinks he's in big trouble when I turn on my lights and hit the siren, he'll put the pedal through the floor."

"You have to understand Kyler," Elijah said. "A person doesn't do what he did by accident or chance. His dad taught him to hate, but rebellion came naturally. If you say, 'Don't do that,' he does it just because you told him not to. If you tell him not to leave, he's out the door."

"Fellows, I hate to interrupt, but look." Peter pointed toward the house. "The rabbit's about to run." Crossing the bridge, the white Escort pulled onto the road without stopping and turned down the hill picking up speed as it descended.

"Do you think he saw us?" Peter asked.

"Don't think so," Taylor said. "Kyler glanced up the road, but we're tucked in the weeds pretty tight."

"What are you waiting for?" Elijah asked.

"I don't want to jump the gun and bear down too quickly. He might catch on to what we're up to. I'll try to catch up about a mile and a half down the road." The sheriff turned the key and the engine started. "This downhill stretch is almost two miles long. I'll be right with him by the time we get to the bottom." He hit the gas and swerved onto the road and within seven seconds the car had climbed to fifty-five miles per hour down the curvy run.

As Elijah braced his elbow on the armrest and placed his hand on the dashboard, he heard Peter fumbling with his seatbelt buckle. *Peter's a little nervous. Don't blame him. We're in for some ride.*

"Whoa!" said Taylor as he touched the brakes. "We caught up with him already."

"He's about four hundred yards ahead," Elijah said. "Just disappeared around the turn."

"Hope he didn't see us," the sheriff said. He slowed the Crown Victoria to forty miles per hour and leaned forward, focusing on the road ahead.

"What if he saw us," Peter said. "What if he took off?"

"I don't think so," Taylor said. "I just got a glimpse of him. I'm going to let him go for about another minute, then I'm going to reel him in."

"He must've been going about fifty. He hasn't panicked yet," Elijah said.

"We'll see how much longer he can keep his cool." Taylor pressed the pedal bringing the vehicle up to fifty-five again.

They approached the next turn, and the car swayed through the curve hugging the yellow line. Elijah could feel Peter gripping the back of his seat. Elijah planted his feet firmly on the floor and stiffened his arm with his hand gripping the dashboard.

"Well boys, are you ready? Here we go," Taylor said.

When the cruiser completed the turn onto a long straightaway, Elijah saw Kyler's Escort about a quarter mile ahead again. Taylor floored the pedal, the LTD thrust quickly to eighty-five miles per hour, and the vehicle lifted and fell with every roll and dip of the road. Elijah inhaled quickly and braced himself as his stomach rose and sank with the car.

"We're catching him," Peter said.

They closed to within three hundred yards before the white car disappeared around the bend.

The sheriff said, "I don't know if he saw us yet or not, but once we get around this turn I'll hit the lights and siren." As they approached the curve, Taylor pressed the brakes, and the speed dropped, causing the passengers to fall forward. With both hands on the dash, Elijah braced and straightened himself.

The car whirled around the turn, sliding into the left lane where an old red Chevy pick-up truck swerved onto the berm as the cruiser drifted back into its own lane. The blast of a horn faded behind them. "Sorry about that, old fella, but we're in hot pursuit," Taylor said, smiling. Coming out of the next turn onto another straight section of road, with Kyler's car now only a couple hundred yards ahead, Taylor engaged the siren and lights. "I just played my ace. Is the boy going to fold or stay in the game?"

Both vehicles were nearing the bottom of the hill when Kyler sped up. Elijah figured he must have heard the siren. At the bottom of the hill, a bridge crossed a twenty-foot-wide, copper-water creek where the road ended abruptly. Turning left led to Route 7; turning right led out farther into the country to Colerain. Kyler barely slowed, spinning around the turn and heading right. A rusty Dodge Omni traveling up the run crossed the lane and skidded off the road on the left. The Omni scudded into the hillside where a fallen tree punched a hole into the radiator, steam spurting out of the front end. An heavy-set woman climbed out of the passenger side and began shouting at Kyler's escaping car, shaking her fist. The sheriff's LTD slid to a stop.

"Are you all right?" yelled the sheriff.

The woman cussed away with her fists in the air, angry eyes still flaming at Kyler's disappearing Escort. Her wrinkled, bald husband crawled out of the door, appearing unharmed, shaking his head.

"A little angry, but I think they're fine," Taylor said. He floored the accelerator. Roaring around the turn, the cruiser headed west onto Glenn's Run Road.

"I believe Kyler decided to stay in the game," Peter said.

"Indeed he did," Elijah added. "Figures he's got a lot to lose—namely freedom."

"Let's hope he doesn't have any wild cards," Taylor said as they surged forward and closed to within two hundred yards before the Escort vanished around the curve.

"These curves up ahead are doosies," Peter said. "It's a large S curve. One-eighties both ways. Be careful."

"I know these roads," the sheriff said. "I've been driving this county for years."

"There's a long straight-a-way after the curves," Elijah said. He shouldn't be more than 175 yards ahead of us. You'll 'bout catch him on that straight stretch."

"I'll see what I can do," Taylor said. "Hold on, boys. Here we go." The sheriff hit the brakes as the car dropped from seventy to thirty miles per hour in the forty yards before the hard right turn. Even at thirty-five miles per hour the curve was incredibly sharp, and the vehicle slid to the left through the turn into the other lane. Jerking the car back onto the right side of the road, he regained control just as the second half of the S curve began. He crossed back into the left lane and careened to the right. The black LTD exploded from the shadows of the sharp turns where the steep hillsides slanted to the road. Onto the sun-brightened, wide open straight stretch they flew.

Elijah leaned forward and squinted down the deserted straightaway. *Where'd he go?*

"What in the world?" Taylor said as he punched the gas pedal.

"Stop!" Elijah cried.

"Why?" Taylor exclaimed.

"Stop! Now!"

"What happened to him?" Peter asked.

The sheriff hit the brakes and the car skidded, slowly turning sideways and stopped about two hundred yards down the straightaway.

"Turn around," Elijah said. "I know where he went."

"Where?" Taylor asked.

"There used to be railroad tracks that ran alongside the road from the Florence Coal Mine down to the river. They had to cut a straight channel right through the hill back there because a train can't take those kinds of curves. It's all grown over with weeds, but a small car could plow right through the channel. I'm guessing he pulled in, shot through the channel and back out onto Glenn's Run headed in the opposite direction to Route 7."

"In other words, he's getting away from us right now."

Taylor stomped the gas pedal and peeled the tires. The vehicle skidded off the road spraying dirt and cinders in all directions. The front wheels bounded back onto the asphalt and headed east toward the *S* curves.

As they slowed to re-enter the turn, Elijah peered out the passenger window to see where the channel cut through the side of the hill. "There it is! The white Escort! Stop!"

The sheriff slammed on the brakes, and the car skidded to a stop. "Did you see him?" Taylor asked.

"Back there. His car must have got stuck trying to cut through the channel."

Throwing the car into reverse, he shot the vehicle backward and brought it to a stop where Kyler's tire tracks entered the weeds.

The three men jumped out. Pulling his gun from his holster, Taylor said, "Follow me." With the pistol aimed at the Escort, twenty-five yards deep into the growth-tangled channel, he cautiously moved forward with high, weed-tramping steps. Elijah followed, and Peter trailed behind. The driver's side door was wide open, and steam rose from the front of the car.

"I don't see him," Taylor said. "He must have hit something halfway through the channel. Holy boulders. Look at that! Look at that!"

Elijah peered over the sheriff's shoulder. Through the weeds he could see the massive shape of a four-foot-tall rock that had slid off the steep hillside into the middle of the channel. The overgrown greenery had camouflaged the obstacle, and Kyler's car had plowed into it. The front windshield above the steering wheel had a radiating shatter pattern where Kyler's head had hit.

"Look there," Taylor said, pointing with his gun to the driver's seat where blood was splattered. "He's injured."

"I think he cut up over the hillside. You can see where the weeds have been trampled down," Peter said, pointing behind them.

"Let's go," Taylor said, holstering his gun. He cut between Peter and Elijah and strode to where Peter had pointed. Looking up through the weeds he said, "No doubt about it. He went this way. We might be able to catch him. Are you guys up to a good manhunt?"

"Count me in," Elijah said.

"Lead the way. I'm right behind you," Peter said.

The sheriff leaned forward and charged up the hillside following the stomped-down-weed path and grasping for saplings and small trees to help secure and advance his climb. Elijah, steady and sure-footed, progressed more slowly, and Peter followed Elijah, pausing every few seconds to glance into the woods and back down to the car. Elijah told him to keep pace and not worry about what was behind them. Obviously the trail would lead to Kyler—somewhere farther up the hillside.

The sheriff advanced quickly to where the weeds thinned out and the trees began. He turned and looked back at Elijah, who was straining steadily up the path. Taylor Inspected the trampled weeds, trying to figure which direction Kyler headed. Breathing hard, he said, "We've lost . . . his . . . trail." He took a deep breath. "Not sure . . . where he went . . . from here."

Elijah caught up. "He either went up through the woods, or possibly turned left here and went along that rocky ridge toward the shale piles and the old mine shaft."

Taylor tilted the brim of his hat, sweat beading on his forehead. "Well, what's your guess?"

Elijah gazed into the woods and then back up the ridge. "When the lights come on, cockroaches scramble for the dark. I betcha he went up to the mine shaft."

"We'll look there first. Let's go." The sheriff took off along the ridge.

Peter shook his head. "How'd I let you talk me into this?"

"Come on," Elijah said. "This'll be something you won't soon forget." Plowing forward, Elijah traced the steps of the lawman, and Peter mumbled incoherently as he followed. "What did you say?" Elijah asked.

"I said I haven't had this much fun since I had my molars removed."

Elijah laughed.

At the coal bank Elijah leaned forward and climbed on all fours, but Peter, beside him, remained erect and managed to ascend standing up. When Elijah reached the sheriff, he said, "Do you see anything?

Taylor breathed heavily now, shaking his head sideways. "That hill . . ." He gulped down air. ". . . 'bout killed me."

Peter pointed farther up and to the left. "The mine entrance is up there on that plateau."

Still gasping, Taylor said to Peter, "Man, you're not . . . even . . . breathing hard. I've got to quit . . . smoking one of these days . . . and get back into shape."

"Look here." Elijah pointed to the leaf of a milkweed. "A drop of blood. Kyler definitely came this way."

The sheriff inhaled deeply. "Let's go." He climbed the next ridge of sandstone and scattered coal shale, but this time he slowed his pace.

When they arrived at the plateau, they noticed the planks that had once covered the mine entrance had all been stripped off. "Kids have been up here over the years," Elijah said. "Teenagers come up here, drink, and then explore the mine. It needs to be permanently sealed up."

Peter pointed to the ground about fifteen feet in front of the entrance. "There's another blood droplet."

"And there's another one," Taylor said. "Five feet ahead."

"If he's in the mine, it won't be easy finding him," Elijah said.

"He can't stay in there forever," Taylor said.

"You got a flashlight?" Peter asked.

"Yeah. There's one down in the vehicle." Taylor glanced down the steep hillside. "You're in good shape, Mr. Nower. How 'bout going back down and getting it?"

Peter looked from Taylor to Elijah. "Oh . . . all right. I'll be the gopher." He turned and skidded, almost skiing, down the steep, coal-chipped incline.

Taylor and Elijah stood before the mouth of the mine. They could see about twenty feet into the tunnel; the black beyond the fading light brought forth the cold breath from the depths. The temperature change sent a chill through Elijah's chest and down the back of his legs.

"It's at least fifteen degrees cooler at the mouth of this cave," Elijah said.

"It'll be colder still down there," Taylor said.

"I kinda get the feeling we're chasing a demon into hell."

"Maybe we are." Removing his sunglasses, Taylor glanced at Elijah. "Have you ever been to hell, Mr. Mulligan?"

"Yes, I have. And I really don't want to go back."

Taylor nodded. "I've seen hell many times." Looking into the mine, the middle-aged lawman continued: "I've seen hell in the bloody face of a teenager who got drunk and plowed his car into a tree, leaving the scattered body parts of his buddies all over the ground. I see hell 'bout every day—in the eyes of a cocaine addict who slit a young father's throat just to get a few bucks to buy crack. Yessir, this job keeps me knocking on the Devil's door. Last week I went into the home of an old lady who was beaten to death by three teenagers. They weren't satisfied with just killing her. They each took turns standing on her dresser and jumping on top of her again and again. When we arrested them, they had no remorse, no guilt, no shame . . . only hate. They said they did it for the fun of killing."

Elijah eyed the Sheriff and then glanced at the ground. "No doubt about it. You don't have an easy job. Why do you keep doing it?"

"Someone's got to do it, Mr. Mulligan."

"Someone's got to chase the devil."

"That's right. It's my job to keep hell at bay."

"I appreciate your efforts."

"Thanks."

The two men stood in the chilled air of the mouth of the mine in silence until the sheriff raised his head.

"Did you hear that?"

"I didn't hear anything," Elijah said.

"I did."

"My hearing's not what it used to be."

"There it is again. Someone just yelled for help."

"Maybe it was Peter."

"No. It came from down in the mine."

Scrambling up the steep coal bank, Peter raised the long chrome flashlight into the air. "I found it, boys."

"Get up here. Now!" the sheriff ordered. "I just heard Kyler yell for help. He's definitely down there."

Peter approached the two men, tilting his head toward the mine entrance. "I heard him. Sounds like he's in pain."

"Maybe something happened to him," Taylor said.

"There're probably a lot of sink holes along the shaft. With so many tunnels and shafts through this hillside, portions will cave in and create sink holes in the tunnels above," Elijah said.

"Maybe he fell into one and broke an ankle," Peter said.

"This is what we're going to do," Taylor said. "Two of us will go in, but one of us will stay here just in case."

"Just in case what?" Elijah asked.

"Just in case something happens. He may be hiding down there somewhere waiting for us to go by. Then he can escape while we're looking for him. We could spend three days searching this mine while he's on his way to Canada."

"Or else . . ." Peter said.

"Or else what?" Elijah asked.

"Or else we might fall into a sink hole and need someone to go for help."

"Mulligan, you stay here and wait. Me and Nower will go looking for him."

"But . . ."

"You're bigger than both of us. If Kyler comes bolting out of the cave, you tackle him."

Elijah nodded. "You're the boss."

From deep in the mine came a tortured scream.

"Even *I* could hear that one," Elijah said.

"Give me the flashlight," Taylor said. "Let's go."

* * *

Peter Nower followed Sheriff Taylor into the mineshaft, the beam cutting a swath of light through the blackness. Thirty feet into the mine the temperature dropped into the mid-fifties. They noticed the mine cart tracks had been removed. Following the oval of light, they inched forward inspecting the terrain. Nearly fifty feet into the mine they came upon a large hole. The sheriff pointed the beam into the depths.

"Careful. That looks like a bottomless pit. Kyler! You down there?" No answer.

After a half-minute wait, a cry for help echoed from farther down the mineshaft.

"He made it past this hole but must have fallen in another," Peter said.

"Watch your step," Taylor said. "There's a two-foot wide ledge we can cross over on. If you fall into that hole, you might end up in China." Taylor shifted the light back and forth as he and Peter sidestepped for about eight feet until they were safely beyond the pit.

"Kyler must have known about that pit or else he would've fallen into it," Taylor said.

"Maybe that was plan A. Maybe we were supposed to fall into it."

"Maybe."

They continued down the coal-walled corridor until they reached what seemed to be a small room where the tunnel separated into three directions.

"Where to now?" Peter asked.

"Kyler! Where are you?" shouted Taylor.

"I'm down here!" came the painful cry. "I think I broke my ankle! Help me!"

"This way," Taylor motioned to the left tunnel. The two walked steadily forward until they came to a three-foot pile of coal that had dropped from the ceiling. Taylor handed Peter the flashlight and went first. He had to straddle the coal pile and duck his head to get through the opening. Peter handed him the flashlight and crawled over the pile. From that side of the fallen ceiling they could hear Kyler whimpering.

"Hurry up!" he screamed. "It hurts! It hurts!"

"We're coming!" Sheriff Taylor called.

"He sounds like he's in a lot of pain," Peter said. "Maybe we better call an ambulance."

"We'll check him out first."

As they progressed along the tunnel, they heard Kyler breathing, loud choppy breaths interspersed with short excruciating gasps.

"Please! Hurry!" he cried.

"Hang in there, boy," Taylor said. "We're right here."

Suddenly they came upon another sinkhole—a wide one with no ledges to cross to the other side, and at the bottom, about six feet down, sat Nathan Kyler, staring at his ankle.

"Can you stand up?" asked Taylor.

When Kyler looked into the glare of the flashlight, Peter was overcome with momentary fright. The face of the young man was covered with blood from the seeping gash across his forehead. His expression contorted in agony as he squinted into the beam. He breathed with short anguished bursts, twitching and jerking as if pain shot through him causing involuntary spasms. When his eyes opened against the light, black orbs looked blindly upward to where the two men hovered above him.

"I don't know," he whined. "I'll try." He braced himself by placing his hand on the wall of the pit and stood slowly on one foot. "It's my right ankle. I think it's broken."

"Give us your hands," ordered Taylor. "We'll pull you out of the hole. Keep your right leg bent so it doesn't brush against the side."

Grimacing, Kyler reached both hands toward the men. Holding the light in his left hand, Taylor grasped Kyler's right forearm as Peter grasped his left.

"All right," said Taylor. "Slow and easy."

As the two men pulled, Kyler's breathing quickened with short grunting heaves. He squeezed his eyes shut and gritted his teeth. Taylor and Peter edged backward and slowly pulled him up and across the edge of the pit onto his belly. Kyler moaned with every breath. When they released his arms, he began to cry: "My ankle. My ankle. It hurts. It's killing me." He rolled slowly onto his back and lifted his right leg.

"Take it easy now, boy," Taylor said. "Let me see that ankle." The sheriff directed the light to Kyler's foot and leaned over top the young man to get a closer look. When Kyler ripped the flashlight from the sheriff's hand, for a moment Taylor seemed confused, still focused on the man's ankle. Then the beam jumped uncontrollably in several directions. Below the sheriff in the darkness, Kyler scrambled onto all fours. Like a sprinter exploding out of the blocks, he shot forward with flashlight in hand, beam darting up, down, and sideways off the walls of the mine. The sheriff dove, clasping at the churning legs but missed, and Peter, frozen by surprise, watched the unclear figure running with light in hand down the dark tunnel hurdling over the coal pile. Within moments the two men were enveloped in absolute darkness.

"That must have been plan B," Peter said.

* * *

When Elijah heard the footsteps, and, looking deep into the black hole, saw the light appear, he thought they were coming. But when the light bounced in several directions, and the footsteps came running toward the opening, he knew something had gone wrong. Spreading his feet and hands like a line backer, he focused on the beam that jerked up and down like a kid's sparkler on a 4th of July night. Ten feet from the mouth of the mine, Kyler's bloody face appeared wide-eyed.

Elijah readied himself. Kyler did not slow down. At the opening he faked to the right, but then darted left. Elijah wasn't fooled. He lunged with the full force of his large legs and clamped his arms around Kyler's waist, bringing him down instantly. The flashlight banged loose from Kyler's hand and rolled down the hill. He tried to pry away Elijah's grasp, but within seconds the big man had crawled atop him and pinned his arms to the ground. Elijah's large hands held the wiry young man securely.

"Get off! Get off! You're hurting my ribs!" Kyler screamed.

"I don't think so," Elijah said.

"I can't breathe. Get the hell off me. I can't breathe!"

"I don't believe you."

"Old man, if you don't get off of me, I'm gonna kill you. I swear I'm gonna kill you!"

"If I'm such an old man, why am I on top, and you're on the bottom?"

From behind him Elijah heard footsteps in the tunnel. He twisted his head to see the flicker of a small flame in the black hole. Peter and Sheriff Taylor appeared at the mouth, and Taylor flipped the lid of the golden lighter over top of the flame.

"Did you boys lose someone?" Elijah asked.

Chapter Thirty

Elijah had one question on his mind when the Sheriff's car pulled into the emergency room parking lot: How was Chrissy Butler doing? Dilsey Phillip's words kept echoing in his memory—*She'll come out of that coma like Christ came out of the tomb on Easter morn.* The cruiser slowed to a stop. Elijah popped the door open and stepped out, waiting to see if Sheriff Taylor needed help with Kyler.

Taylor got out of the car, ambled to the passenger's door, and jerked it open. "Watch your head." Taylor placed his hand on Kyler's noggin to make sure he didn't bang it against the car doorframe. Kyler scooted forward and leaned, thrusting to rise up and out of the back seat of the Crown Victoria. A square of white gauze stuck to his forehead above his left eye, and blood had soaked through to the middle of the pad. Although most of the blood had been wiped away, a few remnant streaks had dried along the grooves of his face. In contrast to his black hair and dark eyes, the pallor of his complexion gave him a cadaverous appearance. Grabbing him by the elbow, the sheriff led him into the emergency room entrance as Elijah and Peter followed.

Elijah peeked at his watch. "It's almost seven o' clock."

"*Tempus fugit,*" Peter said, his sarcastic grin breaking across his face.

"What?"

"Time flies."

"Yes it does. Times flies when you're catchin' bad guys," Elijah said.

"It was sort of a rush, wasn't it?"

"We were like a couple of T.V. crime fighters. Do I look more like Starsky or Hutch?"

Peter eyed Elijah up and down. "You look more like Detective Frank Cannon."

Elijah knotted his brow. "Frank Cannon? Okay, smart guy, in that case you remind me of Barney Fife."

Peter laughed. "You sure showed some of your old Purple Rider form today when you brought down Kyler."

"Felt like I was back in the Bellaire game and had to make the saving tackle. He thought he could out-maneuver this old lineman."

"He sure out-maneuvered me and Sheriff Taylor. If the sheriff hadn't had his lighter, we'd probably still be back in that mine shaft."

"I guess you can thank Joe Camel for that one."

The sheriff had stopped at the registration desk. Elijah and Peter waited patiently beside them. "You boys can go. I can handle it from here," Taylor said. "I'll get him stitched up and take him out to the jail."

Kyler, with his shoulders slumped and hands shackled behind him, glared at the receptionist.

"I'm gonna go up and see how Chrissy is doing. I'll be on the third floor if you need me," Elijah said.

"Me too," Peter said.

"Thanks, boys. I'll talk to you later."

As the two men turned and walked down the hall to the elevator, Peter said, "Do you think he'll confess?"

"No. He's gonna keep his mouth shut. He's not that anxious to make the state pen his home address."

"They probably won't be able to hold him for very long."

"I know. He'll say he ran because he thought he was being framed. Lying is his specialty. Hopefully, Sheriff Taylor will be able to obtain a search warrant and find evidence at his house."

"Kyler's pretty smart. He might have covered his tracks."

"Not much we can do about it but wait and see."

"No. We've done about all we can do." When they arrived at the elevator Peter reached out and pressed the button.

"Now it's up to the Lord," Elijah said.

The metal doors separated, and a stocky, dark-curly-haired nurse pushing an empty wheel chair charged forward. Peter and Elijah divided, allowing her to pass. They entered the elevator and faced the closing doors.

Elijah pushed the third floor button and then stared straight ahead. "Do not fear. Only believe."

"What?"

"I keep thinking about a passage of scripture I was reading this morning when you arrived with your lawyer friend. Jesus said the words to a man named Jairus."

"What was the occasion?"

The elevator doors separated. "The man's daughter was in a coma—possibly dead." The two stepped into the hall in time to see the tall preacher, Byron Butler, running toward them with an amazed expression on his face. As soon as he saw them, his hands began to flail as if he were trying to speak, but couldn't. He charged up to them and skidded to a stop, almost knocking Peter into a gurney behind them. His words exploded: "She's conscious!"

Elijah's heart accelerated into overdrive. "Out of the coma?"

Peter's eyes widened.

"Ten minutes ago! She's wide-awake. Annie and the two boys stopped to visit. Joshua said we ought to surround her, put our hands on her, and pray like all of you did for Buster. So that's what we did. My wife, the two boys, Annie, and I got on all sides and laid hands on Chrissy. Annie began to pray. The power of the Lord came down upon us. I could feel his presence charging through me. While Annie poured her heart out in prayer, Chrissy woke up. We all jumped back like we'd just seen a ghost. She looked at us and said, 'Where am I?'"

"That's incredible," Elijah said.

Peter's jaw dropped.

"I've got some phone calls to make," Byron said. "There've been a lot of people praying for Chrissy. God brought her back to us." He cut between them and rushed down the hall toward the lounge.

"How did you know?" Peter asked.

"How did I know what?"

"You told Kyler that Chrissy was coming out of the coma tonight. Then you told me you truly believed it would happen. How did you know?"

"An angel told me."

"What? When did that happen?"

"Last night. After you left my jail cell."

"What kind of angel? Was he dressed in white? Did he have wings? Come on now."

"Actually, she was a blind, black woman wearing a purple and white scarf."

Peter shook his head. "Quit yanking my chain, Elijah. Tell me the truth."

Elijah shook his head and smiled. "Come on. Let's go see Chrissy."

When the two men entered the hospital room, Chrissy was sitting up, smiling; her mother and Annie stood on each side of the bed, and the boys stood next to the women.

"Mr. Mulligan . . . I mean Elijah!" Chrissy shouted.

Captured by her wide smile, Elijah approached the bed tentatively. Her forehead badly swollen, left eye purplish, and neck bandaged, she smiled and spread her arms as he neared. He bent over and wrapped his arms around her as she hugged his neck. Within the big man erupted an overflow of love and gratitude; blinking back tears of joy, he said, "Hey, kiddo, you are a miracle from heaven."

"I feel like I've been to heaven, but I finally made it back here to be with all of you again," she said, still holding Elijah tightly.

"I'm glad you came back," he said as they released their embrace. Elijah held onto her shoulders and examined her face. "Wow. You've got quite a knot on your forehead."

"Someone hit me."

"Do you remember anything?"

"I remember picking up my ring, my Watchover Ring. Look. I still have it on." She held her hand for all to see. "Then I heard something behind me. I turned around and saw a person, but then everything went black. It all happened so fast."

"Do you remember the person's face? Could you identify him?" Elijah asked.

"I don't know. Maybe if I could see the person again, I'd remember."

Byron Butler entered the room. "I got a hold of Ella Ross. She's calling everyone else on the prayer chain. Praise the Lord." He came to the bedside and hugged his daughter and kissed her on the cheek. "God answers prayer."

"Amen. God does indeed," Elijah said. "Byron, can I talk to you a second out in the hall?"

"Of course."

Elijah led Byron out the door and Peter followed. When they had walked about ten feet down the hall, Elijah stopped and faced the two men.

"What's on your mind, Elijah?" Byron asked.

"Chrissy told me she remembers being hit."

"She does? Does she remember who hit her?"

"She says she's not sure."

Peter said, "If she were able to see the person's face again, maybe she'd remember."

"I'm sure she'd do her best," Byron said. "Too bad we don't have a suspect."

"But we do," Elijah said.

"We do?"

"The sheriff has Nathan Kyler in custody."

Byron nodded. "I had a funny feeling about that guy. Maybe the sheriff could bring him over to the hospital and let Chrissy take a look at him."

"The sheriff and Kyler are in the emergency room downstairs as we speak," Elijah said.

"Unfortunately," Peter said, "the sheriff doesn't have enough evidence to hold him for very long on attempted murder charges."

Byron put his thumb and finger to his chin. "Maybe if Chrissy is up to it, she can take a look at him. You may be right. Seeing his face could trigger the memory."

"I was hoping you'd say that," Elijah said. "I want to see this guy locked up for a long time so he doesn't hurt anyone else. If he goes free, Chrissy won't be safe."

"Let me talk to her," Byron said. "I'll leave the decision up to her."

Elijah bobbed his head. "Good idea. Better make sure she's feeling up to it."

"Let's go." The preacher turned and walked toward the hospital room.

When Elijah entered the room, he saw a nurse and a doctor at Chrissy's beside. The doctor, clad in blue scrubs, pressed a stethoscope to Chrissy's chest while the nurse stood with a clipboard shaking her head and smiling. Propping herself up by extending her hands behind her, Chrissy glowed before them.

"I'm hungry," Chrissy said.

"I'm amazed," said the doctor. "Here. Put this in your mouth." The nurse handed him a thermometer, and the doctor stuck it under Chrissy's tongue. "Check her blood pressure, Nurse Simmons, and order a good meal for her. How's chicken and mashed potatoes and green beans sound to you?"

"And ice cream," added Chrissy pulling out the thermometer long enough to speak.

"Now you put that back in your mouth," the doctor said.

"Sorry." She popped it back in.

"Dr. Recowitz, how's my daughter doing?" asked Byron.

"I'm wonderstruck," he said. "Sometimes unexplained phenomena happen around here. This is definitely one of those occasions. She's bright, clear minded, chipper—except for the bump on her head, she's seemingly the picture of health."

"Must've been the Lord," Butler said.

"I can't disagree," the doctor said. "I have some duties to attend to, but I'll be back in about an hour. If she's still doing well, and gets a good meal in her, we might talk about sending her home in a day or two"

"All right!" spouted Chrissy with the thermometer bobbing up and down from her lips.

"Let me see that thermometer before you drop it or swallow it," the nurse said.

"Sorry," Chrissy said.

"Nurse, you can remove the IV's. I'll be back in a little while," the doctor said.

Elijah and Peter separated as the doctor cut between them and exited the room. The nurse un-velcroed the blood pressure wrap from Chrissy's arm and began removing the I.V. needle from her wrist.

Butler walked to the other side of the bed. Lila reached out for his hand, and he grasped it, then took his daughter's hand. Elijah moved to where Annie was standing on the other side and placed his hand on the small of Annie's back. She gazed up at him, smiled, and leaned her head against his chest. The two boys quietly watched from the foot of the bed.

Joshua finally spoke up. "Golly, Chrissy, we thought you were a goner!"

"Someone tried to kill me," she said.

"You should've never sat in the Chair," Billy said. Immediately he slapped his hand to his mouth.

"What did you say?" Byron asked, looking at the two boys and then at Chrissy.

"Nothing, Dad," Chrissy said. "Josh and Billy are just superstitious."

Byron let go of his wife's and daughter's hands and crossed his arms. "You sat in The Chair? At midnight?"

"Yes, but Elijah told me there is no curse. He said that people create their own darkness when they believe things like that."

Byron's expression sobered. "We'll talk about that later." He reached and patted Chrissy's shoulder. "We've got something more important to deal with now."

"Way to go, Billy," Chrissy said.

"Chrissy," her father said firmly. "If you saw the person who tried to kill you, do you think you could identify him?"

"I don't know, but I would like to try. That person needs to be put in jail before he tries to kill someone else."

After a few moments of silence, Butler continued, "Do you feel well enough . . . strong enough right now to face the person who may have done this to you?"

"I'm not afraid," Chrissy said.

"Okay, Elijah. Tell the sheriff to bring him up."

Elijah nodded and left the room.

* * *

Chrissy felt a tremor of fear travel up through her insides. She remembered hearing the footsteps behind her at the Healing Place and the flash of orange before everything went black. She took a deep breath, let it out slowly, and swallowed. *Maybe I'm not so brave. But I've got to do this. The least I can do is look at the guy and try to remember.*

"I don't know if this is such a good idea," her mother said, concern etching her face.

"If this man is the one, then they need more evidence to hold him in jail," her father said. "Right now they don't have much against him. He'll be out in a couple of days and on the streets again."

"I don't want my little girl in any danger," her mother said.

Seeing the worry in her mother's eyes, Chrissy said, "Mom, I'm not a little girl anymore. I can handle it."

"Now listen, Chrissy," her father said. "You must try to remember whatever you can. This man they are bringing here may or may not be the one. They don't have any solid evidence."

"I'll do my best, Daddy."

The room grew silent. The two boys looked at one another and then moved to the side of the bed opposite the door. Joshua said to Billy, "I betcha I know who it is."

Billy nodded, eyes growing wide. "Me too."

Chrissy knew who they were talking about—Nathan Kyler. She glanced around the room. Annie walked to the bed and placed her arm around her mother's waist, pulling her close. Chrissy was glad Annie was there to give her mom support. Her father held Chrissy's hand. Standing by the window, Mr. Nower rocked back and forth from his heels to toes. Joshua's and Billy's faces looked pale. *Everyone must feel as nervous as me.* She squeezed her father's hand and he squeezed back.

Several minutes passed before the wide form of Elijah Mulligan appeared in the doorway. Two steps behind, Nathan Kyler entered with head lowered and hands behind his back, his forehead patched with a white gauze square. Wearing a black-brimmed hat and dark-green sunglasses, a lawman followed with his hand on Nathan Kyler's elbow. When they stopped at the foot of the bed, Kyler raised his head and peered at Chrissy through the narrow slits of his eyelids. Eliah stood next to Kyler, arms crossed, keeping his eyes on the young man. Removing his hat and sunglasses, the lawman nodded toward her and her father.

"Chrissy, this is Sheriff Taylor," Elijah said.

"Good to meet ya, Sheriff," Chrissy said.

"Pleasure's mine," the Sheriff said. "Sorry to interrupt this family celebration, but I know you realize the importance of the work that has to be done to protect the public. I want you to look at this young man, Chrissy. Look at him very closely, and tell me if he's the one who hit you."

Kyler scowled at her, narrowing his eyes and clenching his teeth.

Chrissy squinted. She focused upon his face for many seconds before her head swiveled. "I. . .I . . .can't remember. I really can't."

A slight sneer rose at the corners of Kyler's mouth.

"Do you remember anything about what happened?" Sheriff Taylor asked.

"Yes. Let me think." She looked down at her lap and then up again. "I remember picking up my Watchover Ring and putting it on. Then I heard a noise behind me. I turned and saw a flash of bright orange. Then everything went black. In the darkness I could tell there was a struggle above me."

"A struggle?" the sheriff asked.

"Yes. Like two angels were fighting. I couldn't see with my eyes, but a scene appeared inside my mind—like on a movie screen. The evil one must have been some kind of demon. He wanted the man to kill me. He kept saying, 'Do it! Do it! Do it!' I could feel something on my neck. The other tried to protect me, like a guardian angel. She yelled at the man, 'Don't kill the girl! Don't kill her. Turn around! Turn around and look behind you.' She wanted him to face the demon—to destroy it instead. When he turned around, the demon called him names and accused him of being a coward, but the angel kept fighting for me."

Chrissy glanced around at the faces in the room. Everyone listened intently. Kyler's sneer had faded and now his eyes widened.

Chrissy continued, "Their voices slowly faded, and I found myself walking in a large, green pasture. It was so beautiful. I felt someone's hand on my shoulder and looked up. It was the Lord. He didn't have to tell me who he was. I just knew. We walked and talked about so many things. It was awesome. I began to understand all of those words Daddy uses in his sermons—words like redemption and grace. Then we came to a bridge. It crossed over a deep canyon. He told me I had to go to the other side. 'Listen,' he said. 'Do you hear them praying?' Far away I could hear the voices of people praying for me. 'Many people love you,' he said. 'Their faith is strong.'

"I knew it wasn't time for me to die, but before I crossed the bridge, I had to ask a question—'Why did that man want to kill me?' The Lord's eyes were so kind. He said, 'I want you to meet someone.'

"I looked up and saw a person crossing the bridge. It was the angel— the one who tried to save me. The Lord introduced us, and she gave me a hug. Her eyes glowed with joy and hope. She said she had just seen someone she loved very much. The Lord told her I had to cross back over the bridge.

"She nodded and said, 'Please take this message with you.' I wondered what kind of message she would give me. She put her hands on my cheeks and said, 'Close your eyes. Do not be afraid. This is only a memory.'

"I closed my eyes and suddenly I entered a dark room—a bedroom. A large man appeared in the doorway. He had long hair and a beard. He came closer and I could see his face—it was covered with scars and his eyes looked strange. He reached out and began to choke me. But it wasn't me he was choking. It was the angel who defended me. I wanted to scream, but I couldn't. Then she pulled her hands away and I opened my eyes. Suddenly I knew. Someone had murdered her."

"She said, 'Remember this: I did not abandon my son. I loved him very much.'"

Chrissy looked directly at Nathan Kyler. He blinked, and his lower lip trembled. His hands began to shake, and the sheriff re-gripped his elbow. The coldness in Kyler's face had faded. He closed his eyes.

Sheriff Taylor said, "Chrissy, is that all you can remember?"

"I'm sorry," she said. "I can't remember who hit me."

Kyler's eyes popped open. He burst forward, breaking the sheriff's grasp. With his hands still behind him he banged into the foot of the bed thrusting toward the girl. Sheriff Taylor and Elijah reacted instantly. Each grabbed one of his arms and pulled him back. Kyler's voice erupted almost as if his throat had been jammed, but now exploded like lava from a volcano: "What was her name? What was her name? The angel! What was the woman's name?" His eyes were wide, black irises against white orbs.

"Her name. . .her name. . ." Chrissy took a deep breath as she watched Elijah and the sheriff hold the man back. "Her name was Marilynn, but she said her friends called her Lynny."

Closing his eyes, Kyler stood straight; his head began to wobble like a top losing momentum. He slumped over as Sheriff Taylor and Elijah struggled to hold him up by his arms.

"Help me get him out into the hall," the sheriff said. "I think he passed out."

The two men dragged Kyler toward the door, and when Taylor saw a nurse, he yelled, "Nurse! Nurse! Help us. This man has fainted."

Chapter Thirty-one

The tall grass shimmered as Elijah emerged from the shadows of the woods and peered to the top of the hill. The oaks and maples stood majestically against the blue sky, and the morning sun dappled the world with vibrant color. Sensing its warm rays on his face, he breathed deeply. *Great day to be alive and walking amidst the beauty of God's creation.* The breeze pressed and released the grass as he mounted the hill.

Elijah envisioned the images of the last three days like a collage pasted together memory by memory: the faces of Chrissy, Annie, Peter, Byron, Sheriff Taylor, and Nathan Kyler; each face, each scene brought back vivid recollections. At the top, before the entrance to the outdoor sanctuary, he turned and looked into the valley and across the next hill to where the abandoned farmhouse hid in the glen. *The storm has passed. It's bright and sunny today. Tomorrow it may rain. Won't be long before the chill of fall arrives and the leaves turn.* He smiled and shook his head. *And then the cold and snow.* Looking into the sky, he said, "I'm a slow learner, Lord. But I'm still here. Still taking one step at a time. Sometimes it's hard to get through this thick skull of mine, but one thing you can count on: I will endure." He listened. The songs of jays, swallows, and robins whistled and chortled through the air.

He pushed aside a low hanging branch and entered the shadows of the Healing Place. Near the center the beams spotted the ground with a ghostly pattern over the Robin Stone. As Elijah approached, the writhed form of a large black snake caught his eye and startled him. He stopped and remembered seeing the snake the morning he had found Chrissy. Stepping closer, he nudged it with his foot. The smell of decomposition entered his nostrils. He crouched and latched onto the tail with his thumb and forefinger. When he stood and lifted it, the tangle uncoiled and hung limp. The snake was about six feet long, but as Elijah examined it, he noticed the head was missing—it had been chopped off. Inspecting the ground around his feet, he couldn't find it.

"That's odd," he said. "It's gone."

Like a horse shoe competitor aiming at the peg, he gripped the snake in the middle of its body, swung his arm back, and let the long carcass fly high into the woods between two large maples. It twirled above jumbled vines and landed deep in the shadows. Elijah turned, wiped his hands on his overalls, and walked toward the center.

When he entered the rays, they striped his body with strokes of light. Squinting into the sun through the framework of branches, he said, "Good morning, Lord! I'm alive and still kickin'. It's a brand new day." He knelt, and looked up again. "I know what I'm asking can't be easy with a hard head like mine, but please, open these eyes and help me to see what really matters. You're the potter. I'm an old chunk of clay. Been around awhile. I know I mess up all the time. Every day I still make dumb mistakes. But I'm here. Ready for you to slap me back on the potter's wheel."

As he prayed, faces entered his mind. Intently concentrating, he prayed for Chrissy and asked that God would heal her completely. He prayed for Joshua and Billy. He thanked God for his best friend, Peter Nower, and asked the Lord to open a door in Peter's life. Then he envisioned Annie. He raised his head and looked at the beams shining through the branched ceiling. A flood of warmth rushed through his body. A robin appeared on a limb that extended into the sunshine. Elijah said, "I need more courage, Lord, if I'm gonna ask her that question. What if she says no?" He looked at the ground and shook his head. "I'd rather get tossed out of the ring by Andre the Giant than have Annie toss my heart out the door." He paused and looked skyward. "Guess I'll never find out unless I'm willing to step in the ring and pop the question." Then he prayed for Kyler, asking God, "Is it possible for a guy like that to change?"

The answer came quickly when he sensed the Lord saying, *I changed you, didn't I?*

His prayers continued for many minutes. After singing "Amazing Grace," he stood and said, "That's all I have for you today, God. Thanks for the new start. I'll try to make a positive difference wherever you lead me. If I get off track, I know you'll whack me upside the head.

Sometimes that's what it takes to get my attention. Anyway, I'm ready to face the day."

On the way down the path, Elijah saw Peter Nower appear in the shadows at the edge of the woods. Peter ran up the hill waving his hand. "Elijah!" he yelled. "I was hoping I'd find you here."

"What's going on?"

He met up with Elijah near the middle of the meadow. "I just had a long talk with Sheriff Taylor. You won't believe it."

"Try me."

"Kyler confessed."

Elijah bobbed his head and smiled.

"That's not all," Peter said. "Kyler wants to talk to you about the Big Man upstairs."

Elijah chuckled, looked skyward and said, "The Big Man upstairs, huh?"

"I think Chrissy's story did the trick," Peter said.

"Her vision was something special. Did Sheriff Taylor check it out?"

"Yes. The dental records matched. Lynny was Marilyn Kyler, Nathan Kyler's mother. Nathan had believed his mother had abandoned him. That's what his father had always told him. When he was about ten, she got religion—one of those born-again experiences. She gave up everything—smoking, drinking, dope."

"Sounds like a real turn around."

"Must have been," Peter said. "But his father didn't like it. She refused to turn tricks to supply him with drug money. For several weeks she kept preaching the gospel to her husband and the boy. That turned the old man hostile. Started slapping both of them around. Kyler said he wanted to believe his mother and find God like she did, but then she up and disappeared. When the police investigated, the old man told them an ex-john showed up late one night, and she left with him."

"Had his story all set up, didn't he? Used her former life against her."

Peter nodded. "Because she'd been arrested several times for solicitation of prostitution, they believed his story. After several weeks, Nathan believed it too. He hated his mother for leaving him alone with his father."

"Can't blame him, I guess."

"Not at all. After that, the old man took everything out on the boy. His grandmother was the only one left who would show him any kind of love, but they put her in the rest home a year or two after his mother disappeared. According to the sheriff, that's when Kyler started killing animals. In some perverse way, it gave him satisfaction—a feeling of justice."

Elijah thought about his encounter with Kyler a few days ago. "He told me he was a religious man. The violent acts became symbolic—some kind of ritual. Killing and torturing animals must have given him a sense of control—the ability to determine life and death."

"Guess he got to the point where snuffing out the life of a dog or cat didn't satisfy him," Peter said.

"You're right. With all the mental pain he suffered, animals didn't quite do the trick any more. He wanted to offer the ultimate sacrifice—another human being. He chose Chrissy, a young, innocent girl. Through her death he could inflict a lot of pain on a lot of people. It was his way of evening the score."

"But what stopped him from following through?"

"I'm not sure, but I think it had something to do with Chrissy's vision."

Peter nodded. "She experienced something very strange while in that coma. Do you think Kyler's mother actually spoke to him from beyond the grave?"

"Something stopped him from . . . you know . . ." Elijah slid his finger across his throat.

Peter nodded. "When he realized his mother loved him, just like Chrissy had said, he confessed to Sheriff Taylor. He figured his father must have strangled her and stuffed her body in the coal furnace of that abandoned house sixteen years ago. Kyler told Taylor his father would have strange dreams about his mother. One night about six years ago the old man woke up yelling and screaming with chest pains. He died on the way to the hospital of a massive heart attack triggered by a nightmare."

"Your bad deeds eventually catch up with you," Elijah said.

Peter looked at the ground and shifted his feet. When he met Elijah's gaze he said, "You'll never guess what Sheriff Taylor discovered when Kyler emptied his pockets at the jail."

"Something weird?"

"Very weird."

"You don't believe I can guess?"

"Not in a million years."

"If I could, would you do me a favor?"

"What's the favor?"

"I'll tell you if I get it right."

"Just one guess?"

"That's all I need."

"Well . . . considering the odds. Okay."

Elijah looked into the sky as if he was seeing into another dimension. He closed his eyes and said, "Yes. Yes. I'm beginning to see something. I've got it. I've got it."

"Enough of the dramatics," Peter said. "What's your guess?"

"The head of a black snake."

Peter's eyes widened and his jaw dropped. "How did you know?"

Elijah smiled and walked down the hill.

Peter tagged behind. "Come on, tell me how you knew that?"

"You owe me a favor," Elijah said.

"I know. I know." Peter smiled. "You're not going to tell me how you found out about the snake head are you?"

"I will after you do that favor for me."

"What's the favor?"

"What are you doing two weeks from Saturday?"

Chapter Thirty-two

On a warm September morning, Elijah Mulligan stood with Peter Nower in the middle of the Healing Place. Rocking back and forth from toes to heels, Peter nervously glanced around the circle of people who had gathered around the perimeter. Elijah smiled and gazed heavenward as the beams from above splashed over him.

Peter nudged Elijah's elbow. "They should've been here by now. What's taking them so long?"

"Relax. It won't be much longer. Do you have the ring?"

Peter patted his breast pocket, and then, half-panicking, slapped his pants pockets. He let out a long sigh. "Yes. Yes. Here it is. It's in my pocket."

"Don't lose it," Elijah said.

Stationed at the entrance to the outdoor cathedral, Colin Dutton turned and announced: "They're at the bottom of the hill. I can see them."

Reverend Byron Butler strummed an introductory chord on his guitar. "All right everybody. Look at your programs. We're going to sing 'Fairest Lord Jesus,' and then, before the bride enters, 'Sweet, Sweet Spirit.'"

When he strummed again, all joined in as their voices lifted with the songs of robins and jays. Elijah sang robustly as he panned the circle of friends. Suddenly he sensed an awesome oneness with the people, nature, and God. The sensation increased with each verse of the song. When they finished, an intimate silence followed, and Elijah, through openings in the leaves and branches, could see the form of Annie Ferrier bathed in sunlight. Byron strummed the opening chord to "Sweet, Sweet Spirit," and the two bridesmaids entered—Chrissy Butler first, and then Lila

Butler. They walked to the center and stood next to Peter Nower. When the last verse began, Annie entered through the beams of light.

She wore a light blue, almost white dress that seemed to glow in the shades of the oaks and maples. For the first time that day Elijah's heart pounded. With every step she made toward him, the thumping in his chest increased. He could not take his eyes off her. Elijah reached out and took her hand. He lost himself in the teal depth of her eyes. The voices of those who encircled them seemed angelic. When the song ended, Elijah and Annie turned and faced Byron.

The preacher cleared his throat and said: "Friends, we are gathered here today to witness the union of two wonderful people. Together they are going to begin a new life. Both Annie and Elijah love the Lord. They have experienced his resurrection power. How appropriate it is for us to gather here in this outdoor cathedral. The presence of God is here. May all of us sense the wonder of this place. May all of us know his resurrection power."

The preacher talked about commitment and love. He read scripture. Annie and Elijah squeezed each other's hand. Byron then announced that the two had memorized their vows.

They faced each other. Annie began:

"As we face the path of our future,
I promise to stand with you.
I promise to share your hopes, ideals, and goals.
I will be there for you always.
Through times of triumph and trial I will walk with you.
If you stumble, I will catch you.
If you hurt, I will comfort you.
If you smile, I will share your joy.
Everything I am and everything I own is yours,
From this day forth and forever.
May God bless us and unite us."

A tear trickled down Elijah's cheek. He lowered his eyes and then looked into Annie's and said:

"I offer you not the springtime of my life,
but the fall, old but colorful.

I promise to love you day by day through the winter of our lives.
I pledge you commitment in good times and bad,
My strength in sickness and in health.
I will be tender and warm when the cold wind blows.
We will value the memories of our pasts;
And create new pages as we face this world together.
Above all, we will put God first. May the Lord bless us and make us one."

"Could I please have the rings," the preacher said. Peter Nower again slapped his hand against his pant's pocket, inserted his fingers and pulled out the golden ring. Lila Butler presented Annie's ring for Elijah. Reverend Butler took them and held them up into the beams, the smaller inside the larger. They glistened as one ray shot through them.

Byron said, "The wedding ring is the outward and visible sign of an inward and spiritual bond which unites two loyal hearts in endless love. It is a seal of the vows Elijah and Annie have made to one another. Bless, O God, these rings that Annie and Elijah, who give them, and who wear them, may ever abide in thy peace. Living together in unity, love, and happiness for the rest of their lives."

Each took the rings from the preacher's hand. Elijah gently slid it onto Annie's finger. She gazed at it and then into his eyes. She pushed the large ring onto his finger as he clasped his hand around her hand.

Byron Butler stepped back and announced: "In as much as you have each pledged to the other your lifelong commitment, love, and devotion, I now pronounce you husband and wife, in the name of the Father, the Son, and the Holy Spirit. Those whom God has joined together let no one put asunder. Elijah, you may kiss your bride!"

They placed their arms around each other, and their lips gently touched. When their faces separated, Elijah felt a tingling through his entire being. They kissed again. The people encircling them whispered and giggled. Their lips broke apart again with wide smiles. Applause erupted.

"Ladies and gentlemen, I present to you Elijah and Annie Mulligan," Byron said.

* * *

Within fifteen minutes everyone had descended the path through the meadow on the journey back to the church for the reception—except for Chrissy. She managed to lag behind without anyone noticing. She stood just inches from the Robin Stone and raised her face to the beams of light. The woods murmured and whispered. Oaks and maples moaned softly in the gentle breeze. Poplars and locusts joined in as mottled shadows and specks of light floated across the ground like a ballroom in need of dancers. The spots drifted back and forth over the stone where the bird was buried. But then a robin chirped and fluttered through the maze of cascading light and flew upward through an opening in the outdoor cathedral's ceiling. She watched it until it disappeared into the deep blue of the sky. Feeling very alive, she walked back to the church.

LaVergne, TN USA
23 July 2010
190631LV00003B/44/A